By John Craig
Published by CraigArts Entertainment

CARNAGE OF THE DEVILS: EPISODE I A NEW THREAT©

Carnage of the Devils

EPISODE I
A NEW THREAT

WRITTEN BY
JOHN CRAIG

CraigArts Entertainment

Published by CraigArts Entertainment

ISBN: 978-0-992168704
PUBLISHED BY CRAIGARTS ENTERTAINMENT
Toronto
Printed in the United States of America

To my family, and extended family
Satan, & Carolyn,
Greg, Sheldon, Liam, Marie, Kobie &
Sylvia the cunt
Also special thanks to my supportive Weston Road
friends, and other friends
I've grown up with or met
online who've been just as supportive.
Also special thanks to my fans!

The text "In the beginning, God..." is synonymous with truth for many of the mortals on Earth; however, we know it is just a fairy tale. As a matter of fact there was never a beginning, nor will there be an ending. There is only evolution and adaptation throughout the universe. For life has always existed throughout the universe, this is particularly true for single cell organisms, to bipedal, quadrupedal, and other limbed species that roam freely on planets across the universe.

When Earth formed, life slowly began to evolve just like it did on planets similar to Earth, and the species that were on Earth, adapted to their surroundings just like on other planets. As for us, we were stranded upon this desolate planet because we were betrayed by our kind. They wanted to rid the universe of us and left us here to die. For years we stayed upon this planet. We watched these earthlings and we endured all the natural disasters that shaped this planet alongside these creatures throughout the centuries. Billions of years later, a species evolved from these creatures; they are known as humans. At first we hid from them, because we did not wish to deal with their primitive kind, or as some of us would call them 'monkeys with skin suits'.

There were two different forms of life on Earth: predators and prey, and as years passed by, an unexpected twist of fate changed everything. The human species learned new ways to stop attacks on their kind. They created weapons from the Earth and were able to kill off the other animals that were more powerful and vicious.

These evolved animals, the Humans, were superior in almost every aspect to the other hominid species that existed, and the humans battled, and slaughtered them off the face of existence, or some were not able to cope with the ever changing elements and evolution did not favour them. Eventually the humans herded together to kill off anything, whether it was food or not, to prevent being prey, and to show their dominance while scaring off predators. The humans left animal heads on stakes, and pikes hoisted high in the air to scare off animals.

Humans began to be one of the most relentless predators this planet had spewed out of it, and as time passed by they began killing off their own kind; however, our species is the original reason for that.

We were the other animals that lived amongst them. We had the power to not reveal ourselves to other beings. We watched the humans grow in populace and dominance, and we decided to test our superiority against the humans using their primitive weapons, seeing the weapons we had from a time and galaxy far away, had eroded them. Some of our kind would rape these humans, others would torture the humans, and some would kill the humans for sport to satisfy their blood lust.

Some of us did not care for these pathetic games that our counterparts were playing as they used cheap parlour tricks, and pretended to come to the humans' aid as saviours or gods and goddesses. Some of our kind became drunk with our powers that we possess, as we are far superior to these human creatures.

This happened a very long time ago, when our galaxy was at war. Unfortunately, it started to take place on this forsaken green rock. Of course this sparked a civil war amongst our kind. The civil war between our people came to an end, and the winners of this war put the losers on remote parts on the Earth. We guarded them and made sure that they would not poison these humans with their lies.

However, when the humans populated more of the Earth, including areas where the losers' prisons were, this began another conflict on the Earth. They began telling the humans that they were gods and told the humans about us, and said that we were Demons and Devils and could not be trusted, and if they followed us, we would spend forever after they died in another life torturing them.

Because of the gods' lies which was their new warfare tactic, we were now seen as evil beings, devils that would make the humans crazy and would give them pleasure on Earth and spend forever after they died torturing them, so we began to separate ourselves from the Humans due to the immense confusion and sorrow.

We abandoned the prison sites and freed the gods from their prisons, seeing the humans were populating everywhere on the Earth, and were being influenced by the gods anyway. We did not have it in our hearts at the time to commit mass murders and kill these gods for their lies.

As time bore onwards, the gods gained control over the humans, and manipulated the humans into killing off each other in the names of each of the gods. And like before, the humans learned how to overcome their predators. The intelligent and powerful humans began to take control over other humans, and called themselves Kings and Queens, Pharaohs, Emperors, Tribal Elders, Witch Doctors, and Priests. They invented religions, and forced the weaker kinds of humans to worship their creations. Thus, the real gods were beaten by the humans, and so they tried to start a final war of all wars, and we retaliated and destroyed every god right down to the last one.

After the war of the gods, some of us tried reaching out to the humans, but the humans were slaves to their own religions, and that was that. The gods had ended the relations between us and Humanity, so we no longer cared; it did not really matter to us anymore. Soon the intelligent humans would learn theories on their existence.

After years of separation, a few of us old friends found each other and reunited with one another. We had been on the same side fighting wars on distant planets before. We walked amongst the humans, dined amongst the humans, and began to have feelings and desires towards the humans.

One of our friends, Belial, hypnotically seduced a lady named Sharon whom he thought he had impregnated. Eventually she gave birth to a child named Joshua. Leviathan had a child with someone as well, however he had been with so many humans that he did not know and would not have cared.

As for Joshua he grew and he was trained to use our powers, and he kept journals of all the wisdom that he acquired through our training. We taught him how to use the forces of his brain and nature to accomplish whatever he wanted. He was already an accomplished warrior by the time we approached him. This is when we informed him about his origins.

Eventually Joshua met a girl Elizabeth (who ironically was Leviathan's daughter which was unknown to him), and she was having a child. Before the child was born, Joshua was already obsessed with learning these powers from us. He did not express concern for Elizabeth, so she left him before the child was born. After she gave birth she abandoned her baby boy.

As the short years passed by, tensions grew and our friendships dissolved. Eventually we fought each other, and there were only three of us that had survived that battle: Joshua, his son and I. How his son ended up in that battle is a story for another time itself.

Time went on and the humans served the religions they created with great enthusiasm. While pretending their religions created them, they made excuses for killing off other humans that belonged to different religions in order to make their own religions more dominant.

And so it was the Christians, Catholics, Jews, Muslims, and Pagans became the most dominant religions and it did not matter how much in common the inventors had made these religions, they hated each other. But most of all, they hated Devil worshipers or any religions that seemed to not be of a godly faith, and so a witch hunt began. Witches and warlocks were killed off. Some of them went into hiding, then the religionists began killing off anyone for nearly any reason with the guise that they were Devil worshippers or heathens.

ERA 1
Abandoned

1

As rain beats down against the ground and lightning streaks across the sky as the thunder crackles, shaking the ground, Elizabeth hurries her way through the forest, nestling her infant child in her bosom. Fatigue sets in from her journey, so she rests in the cover of a tree, as the cold rain spits at her. Letting out a sigh, she brings her son closer to her chest to keep him warm from the rugged weather.

Elizabeth does not want to sink into her depression. She continues to walk through the thick of the forest. She knows that if she continues to walk some more despite how weak she feels at the moment she will feel better mentally, as she can keep her mind on other things; however, she cannot keep her mind off Joshua.

She clenches her teeth tight, and swallows hard, while trying to block the memories she shared with the man she intended on marrying, who is the father of their son Ethelwulf. Her newborn son's calmness helps her from the overwhelming memories, and from thoughts of despair. Elizabeth holds her son close and feels a strange aura emanating from him; this is the same strange aura that she felt in the presence of her fiancée and his friends.

They are the whole reason that her sweet man had changed. If it wasn't for his new friends, she is positive that she would still be embraced by her lover's arms and together they would be as one with their newborn child.

Elizabeth does her best to recant what took place; however, no matter what she thinks, or however she re-lives the moments in her mind, it is not changing the present. Her thoughts shift towards finding a loving home for their child, her thoughts consumed by giving their child to a couple that could provide their child with a practical and emotional love and care, and provide their son with a better life.

Noticing that the sky is clearing up, Elizabeth senses that the rain will dissipate soon, *thankfully*, Elizabeth thinks as she smiles down at her beautiful son.

Sensing danger, Elizabeth stops and surveys her surroundings. From time to time, she can sense and feel events that are about to take place, although she cannot explain how, or why she can feel such things, it happens. This is a similarity that she shared with her beloved Joshua; yet, for some strange reason, her abilities were always clouded around Joshua's friends. She is not in leagues with Lucifer and dares not tell anyone of such things lest she becomes subject of persecution, or worse from the ever growing Christian populace which took place after Emperor Constantine's rule.

Her senses serve her well. She notices the head of a rather skinny wolf peeking out from the thick of the bushes nearby, baring its teeth, followed by a couple more hungry wolves, and they start to position themselves around her for the attack.

Holding onto her son for dear life, Elizabeth backs up a few paces. She senses the wolves have not eaten a decent meal for a long while, and that her time is close at hand. The wellbeing of her son is all that is on her mind; yet, that thought is fading quickly as the wolves circle around her. Tears stream down either down either side of her cheeks, mixing in with the rain pouring from the heavens down upon her.

The first wolf makes a break for her, and rushes towards her through the thick of the bush and into the clearing. Impulsively, Elizabeth kicks the beast. She feels the ribs of the wolf crush with the might of her powerful kick. The wolf flies through the air and smacks against a nearby tree and its spine breaks. The wolf lets out a yelp as it falls to the ground, twitching, while trying to roll over onto its paws, yet quickly dies from its internal damage.

Without thinking of what just took place Elizabeth stretches her free hand out, and grabs the next wolf by the throat that is leaping towards her, and then crushes its oesophagus with her bare hand. Luck is not on her side as the last wolf slips behind her, biting her on the back of the neck. She does not let go of her baby, and falls to the ground. As the wolf continues to maul the back of her neck, while growling as it bites down harder, the wolf inserts several pounds of pressure on her neck, and Elizabeth starts to go unconscious.

Elizabeth goes in and out of consciousness as she holds on for dear life to her son. The wolf tears a chunk of flesh from the back of her neck and slips backwards in the mud. Elizabeth turns around and notices that the wolf is rushing back to attack her again. She swings the back of her hand at the beast and punches it in the head. The wolf lets out a yelp and staggers backwards, slipping into the mud again. The wolf tries to stand back on its paws again, and staggers around the grass, and then places its paw upon its head to wipe away the pain from the blow to the head as it yelps from the pain. The wolf shakes its head as it continuously yelps, and then flees for safety from its prey.

"O blessed be, the gods are watching over us, my son," Elizabeth says to her son who is unfazed by the events that just took place.

Elizabeth stumbles to the ground, not having the strength to get up to her feet again, and she feels an overwhelming dizziness. She reaches behind her neck and softly touches her wounds, and screams out in dire pain. As she looks at her hand, she notices that it is covered in blood. The rain falls on to her palm and dilutes the sticky, thick coat of blood, and then she wipes the rest of her blood on to her garments.

Collecting her thoughts, she determines the best thing to do at this moment is get her son to safety. Tapping deep into her inner strength, Elizabeth does her best to get up to her feet, despite the raging pain. The rain slowly comes to an end, however, the sky is still overcast and it is still miserably cold. Walking out of the forest, and into a clearing, Elizabeth notices a small building. She also notices a consecrated burial ground behind the timber built building. Judging by the symbolism, this area was more than likely the holy grounds of worship for the new god, the god of the Christians.

This is the first time that Elizabeth has laid eyes on a place of Christian worship, and she is intrigued with the beauty of the building of worship and the idols of crosses in the field. After her moment of intrigue she decides to take her son to this place, which appears to be a good place of safety. She decides to do this quickly as her wounds are starting to get the better of her. She can no longer fight off the fatigue, nor the pain, let alone stand long enough to marvel at the beautiful landscape, and architecture. Stumbling to the door, Elizabeth bangs limply upon it.

A rather small man, about her height, opens the door. His stern features take her breath away yet his voice is soothing and he seems charismatic, and he welcomes her inside the church gleefully. "Cometh into our home... O heavens, no! Ye are wounded!"

"Aye, my Lord, I was attacked by the beasts of the field, whilst I searched for safe keeping for mine offspring."

"Aye woman, thou hast nothing to fear within the house of the Lord... Gilda! Tend to this woman's cynn!" The man hastily shouts to his wife, who quickly rushes to aid the stranger.

Knowing that she is in good hands, Elizabeth relaxes and slips into unconsciousness. Hearing her son's faint cry, Elizabeth springs up into a sitting position, doing her best to free herself from her sleeping spell. Still feeling weak and a bit dizzy, she slumps back into the comfort of her bed. Her mouth dry and her throat parched, she still needed to be assured that her sweet baby boy is in good hands. "Ethelwulf!"

"Continue to lie down woman; thou hast been asleep for three nights, my dear. We were worried about thee. We thought perhaps a plague had warmed over thee."

Looking around the room Elizabeth cannot see her son, but notices that a cradle has been built. Elthelwulf is resting snug, safe and sound in the cradle. "Aye woman, thy baby rests in the cradle. Thy baby hath been quite content, a little too content for a lad his wee age. This is the first peep we have heard from him since he hath been here."

Elizabeth, distraught and fathoming the worst, is comforted by the safety of this new haven and she smiles at Gilda. She does not notice the underlying hint of concern within Gilda's tone in regards to her son.

As evening arrives, Elizabeth is feeling well enough to tend the dinner table. Her strength has rapidly improved throughout the course of the day Elizabeth rarely got sick. As a matter of fact, these last few days have been the longest stretch of time that she has been ill.

"Gilda tells me that thy health hast been restored. It must be a part of God's blessing unto thee."

"My Lord, ye believeth in one God?"

"Aye woman, God is the King of Kings, and he is the Lord of Lords, the one true God of all Gods, the only God that man should worship. All other gods are an abomination unto him.

It is our duty to preach the word of the Lord our God, through his son Jesus the Christ's message."

Elizabeth nods her head, finding the Lord of the house's speech intriguing. She eats another mouthful of lamb, and listens more intently to what Gilda's husband, Jacob has to say.

"Thou appeareth to be healed. Wilt thou return to thy husband on the morrow with the child?"

Joshua... Elizabeth looks down at her tray of food taking in a deep breath of air. Clearing her mind, she finds deliberate words to describe the vague intent to her new marital status. "Umm, no my Lord. My husband fights the Germans at the moment. Our home has been ravaged by pillagers. What flock and cattle they could not take, they have slaughtered. I was in search of a new home where I may work for shelter and food rations, until the battle is over with the Germans and my husband returneth home unto me."

Leaning back in his chair, Jacob believes deep within his heart that this is not just their home; he believes that this is the house of the Lord his God. Although he enjoys the solitude with his wife whom he shares responsibilities of the
the church with, he takes in a deep breath and agrees to let her stay.

"Aye woman, thou shalt stay with us, along with thy lad. Thou canst start with cleaning the stables on the morrow and milking the cattle. If thou art unsure of how to perform such tasks Gilda will show thee."

"I thank thee, my Lord."

Throughout the evening, Elizabeth contemplates moving on. She knows that Ethelwulf will be safe with these strangers. She only hopes that her son does not bare one of her curses. Since the time of her birth, she remembers everything never knew her father. She is a bastard child, and her mother never spoke about her father. Thus, her mother was consistently persecuted for being a whore. Elizabeth did not want the same fate to befall Ethelwulf.

Quietly walking over to the cradle that Ethelwulf is lying down in, she picks her son up for the last time and kisses him gently on his lips, and then lowers him back in the woven covers that Gilda prepared for her child.

Fighting back her tears, Elizabeth quietly hopes once again that her son will not remember this moment, the moment she left him in hopes that he would have a better life without her. Turning around, she walks over to the battered door, glancing back at her son, and makes her exit into the starry night.

She cannot help letting out her emotions as she continues to head to the forest; she had left Joshua, now she had abandoned her only child.

Her grief is cut short. Unlike the meeting she had with the wolves, she was unable to sense new danger within the forest. A kick to her back startles her as she lands face first on the ground, banging into a tree. Spinning around to see who is attacking her, with expectations of Jacob behind her, a chill sends shivers up and down her spine, as she is now staring at a man dressed in a pitch black dark cloak with a hood concealing his face. The shadows of darkness hide all but this man's stern and angry features. Trying to figure out who her attacker is, Elizabeth's head lurches backwards as the man viciously kicks her in the face and she is nearly sent into a state of unconsciousness.

The attacker is quick and sudden with his movements. Each moment is as deliberately frightening as the next. He pulls a sword without haste from within the flaps of his cloak, and rushes towards Elizabeth. This menacing domineer of a man leaves Elizabeth in a state of shock, and her muscles tighten, causing her to curl her limbs into a foetal position.

Shaking in fear trying to fight off the agonizing pain and the despair of the moment, she notices this nightmarish man a few paces in front of her, his sword at the ready. "Please do not harm me, I have naoght of interest, nor am I of purity. I have born offspring, and have committed my soul to the gods as I have bound myself to mine husband in sacred matrimony."

The man does not look away from Elizabeth as he menacingly lets his eyes burn into hers. After what appears to be an eternity, he grips onto his hood and then lowers it, letting it fall to his back, revealing his face to her.

"Joshua?"

"No! But as a matter of fact where can I find him?!" The man's voice bellows to her.

After a terrifying few minutes exchange of questions and answers, Elizabeth's direct aggression is let out against the menacing individual that attacked her, "What is it that thou wishes from me?"

A venomous hatred spews forth from his mouth as he gazes into her eyes, "Your life!"

The roosters cry out. This would normally have woken Gilda from sleep, had she have been sleeping. However, she woke up a short time ago and is looking around the premises for Elizabeth, and then she walks to the barn to see if Elizabeth is tending to the cattle. She is not there, or any other place she looked.

In the distance Gilda's eyes notice a section in the field where the morning frost did not settle, and a body lying next to the thicket of trees. Screaming loud enough to wake her husband Jacob, he urgently runs toward his screaming wife, to see a body in the field, next to the feet of his wife. Armed with an axe, Jacob inquisitively prods the body with the handle. His assumptions are that the headless body belongs to their guest Elizabeth, as these are the clothes they last noticed her in. Turning his head away from the body, something catches his attention: a severed head, face first in the ground, pushing the thick blades of grass parallel to the ground.

2

After Elizabeth's death, Jacob builds a community near their church and he recruits people from neighbouring villages over the course of a few years. He provides shelter to soldiers returning from battles that are taking place around just on the outskirts of Britannia. He also works on creating a thriving community to ensure his wife is well protected, and to a lesser extent, the child that they were left to raise.

He regrets taking the stranger Elizabeth into his home, the house of the Lord, and he has also grown strong feelings against the child. His discontent for Ethelwulf is fastening deep within the fibre of his being, and the older his adopted child gets, the less he refrains from beating his son. He feels the child is an abomination to God, and suspects Ethelwulf is releasing sorcery when his emotions spring to life. Feeling that Ethelwulf is no mere mortal child, he considers him to be from the loins of Lucifer the Devil.

Together, Jacob and Gilda do their best to conceal the child's dark side. They hide their son from church events, services, and force him tend to the chores in the stable when company is present. They also keep Ethelwulf away from other children in the village so they do not discover Ethelwulf's unChristian-like behaviour.

Hiding Ethelwulf is no small feat as the soldiers and their families are fully aware of Ethelwulf, and consider their adopted son friendly, adorable, and like any other child. Some are open to letting him play with their children. However, Jacob finds many excuses to keep him from playing with the other children.

Ethelwulf grows up lonely. The only knowledge he has of his real parents are that they were killed in a war, a lie that his foster parents keep telling him; yet, Ethelwulf remembers the very night his mother kissed him goodbye and abandoned him, and he knows that they are lying to him. He also recalls the following morning after his mother's death, and remembers the burial of his mother.

Ethelwulf loathes his parents' treatment of him, and despises them when they beat the word of God into him. The anger festers deep inside of him. He wonders how a creator who supposedly loves all his children could allow such horrible things to happen to them, including him. He is terrified to death of God, and the stories about him.

Ethelwulf hates the beatings, and at times when his parents beat him, material objects float around the house, and he is aware that it is his responsibility; yet, he denies having any part of it to them when they beat him. He recalls the first time he showed his parents his magical abilities and playfully performed his feats, and that being the first time, Jacob severely beating him with the handle of one of his swords, and he was scared of Jacob from that day forward.

As an intellectual child, he analyzes various methods on how he can do these magical feats, and how he can do them without having his emotions charging them. He discovers that he is able to discern people's thoughts, and learns how to become stronger at reading their minds, their innermost deep dark secrets, and how to turn on this ability, and shut it off. He is aware of what they will say before they say it, or if they've changed their minds about saying what is on their minds, and knows when people are lying to him, or others.

He reads people's thoughts flawlessly. Sadly, he is able to read the thoughts of his father Jacob, and sees images associated with the thoughts in his father's mind. They are usually about his father killing him therefore, he pre-emptively does what will make his parents happy, while fawning over them to gain their approval. When he reads negative thoughts against him from his father, he quickly leaves to play by himself in the barn or with the animals in the barn, and sometimes with his friend Annex who at times is able to go outside and sneak into the barn.

Tonight is one of those nights. Feeling glee, Annex leaves her parents' home and runs over to Jacob and Gilda's barn to play with Ethelwulf. Ethelwulf is her best friend in the world, and she thoroughly enjoys being in his company since her parents' arrival to the small village. Although Ethelwulf does not get along with the majority of the other children in the village, she is happy that he gets along with her. She enjoys his innocent charming allure which gives her warm, cosy, cuddly feelings each time she sees him, not to mention the overwhelming crush she has on him.

She grabs hold of a broken piece of plywood on the barn, pushes it aside, and sneaks inside the barn, and notices Ethelwulf is nowhere to be seen. Usually he is placing barrels of hay on top of one another so that he can be strong like the adult soldiers, or he would be doing some of his parents' chores, or something to pass his time. Walking past some of the stables in the barn, she wonders if he is hiding in in them, and looks in each of them. As she circles around inside the barn, looking for her cute curly-haired friend, she looks up towards the attic, and hears a faint whimpering, and muffled cries.

Wondering what is happening she firmly takes hold of the shaky ladder, and climbs up, and she sees a body covered inside of blankets, the source of the small cries. A shiver goes up her spine as she senses a tense presence coming from the body wrapped in the blanket. Walking over to the shivering blanket she grabs a hold of the cloth and gently tries to tug it away from the body; however, Ethelwulf holds on to the blanket tight. He does want Annex to see him.

"Leave me be, Annex!"

Taking a step back, she places her hand on her chest with feelings of despair. She is crushed as all day she was looking forward to spending some time with her best friend. *What is going on* she wonders, stepping away from Ethelwulf. He has never dismissed her like this before. Straightening up, she looks at her covered friend cowering in his blanket, and places her tiny hands on her hips, snapping at him to get in line. "I wish to know why ye are cowering and crying? Come hither!"

Fidgeting with her hands and feet, Annex's patience runs thin as any delighted young girl's feelings would get while in the presence of a cute young boy that is yet to even acknowledge her presence. She takes her hands off her hips, and tries to yank the blanket from Ethelwulf. He senses what she is about to do, and holds the blanket tighter.

"I do not know why ye cower like a little boy; I shalt have no part in this charade. Fetch me when ye cease snivelling!"

Flicking her hair back, while turning around and marching down the ladder, Annex leaves the barn, slamming the wooden doors behind her, and then sneaks to where she initially entered the barn in order to spy on her friend.

As she sits quietly on the ground, she listens intently to see if Ethelwulf will leave his hiding spot, and start playing in the barn without her. Patiently waiting, and despite her assumptions, she gradually hears footsteps in the attic above her; his breathing is heavy. The atmosphere intensifies within the barn with each of Ethelwulf's breaths. The breaths get heavier, and objects within the barn start to rattle and shake. Ethelwulf screams and it echoes throughout the barn. A rake lying on the ground next to her begins to rattle, shake and then levitates with unseen hands next to her. The rake flies into the barn door.

Annex screams. She clutches on to her chest and is terrified. Suddenly the tense feeling within the barn stops.

"Annex?" The inquisitive boyish voice of Ethelwulf somewhat soothes her.

"Aye, a ghost is amongst us. Come hither at once. Protect me from the evil spirits, Ethel my dearest."

Disappointed that Annex would say such things, he understands that she does not know that he is the cause of what took place. Had he have known that she was in the barn, he would not have released his repressed angry feelings for his parents. Making sure she does not see him in his state, he reaches for his blanket and picks it back up, securing it around him and climbs down the ladder.

Looking up, she quickly sees that he is still wearing that ridiculous blanket. She is fed up with his strange behaviour, and greets him as he gets to the bottom of the ladder, and yanks the blanket off him. The sight is unbearable, Annex gasps, staggers backward and breaks down in tears. Her beautiful friend's face is beaten beyond recognition.

"My dearest Ethelwulf, what has happened unto thee? Did the ghost harm thee?"

Disappointed yet again, he firmly reclaims his blanket and wraps it around himself to conceal his wounds. There was a reason he was wearing it to begin with. *Why did she not trust my judgment? Why did she have to take it off? Why could she not just leave him alone for a few more days? And why did she have to come now?* Ethelwulf wonders.

"Nay. As I... the horse I tended is a fret and frail beast, and it jumped upon me. Yes, that is right. It kicked me, and jumped upon me, ye must believe this to be true, and that can happen, as yes, this is the truth of the matter."

The material of his blanket quickly vanishes from her fingers, as he yanks it from her, while she watches her friend, horrified. As she continuously inspects him, she notices his face has bruises, is swollen, one of his eyelids is split open and bruised so badly that knuckle marks are still visible on the clear patches of his tanned complexion. Inspecting further, she notices the bruising looks like finger marks around his throat.

"It was thy father that did this unto thee again!"

What is the point in hiding anything from her? She knows him too well at this point in his life to hide anything from her. His emotions begin to get the better of him and he starts to sniffle once again; however, the aching pain that courses throughout his body is too overwhelming, and he clutches his ribs while kneeling to the ground in pain.

Feeling horrible for what she said earlier, she hugs her poor, dear friend. He jerks free from her embrace, and moans from the pressure of her hug. The pain is too much for him, despite how gentle she is.

"What hast taken place, my dearest?"

"Promise me thou shalt not speak mine words unto anyone." Ethelwulf whispers.

"Aye."

"My father thinks I am in leagues with Lucifer. He saith unto me, 'I am the offspring of the serpent the Devil'. He speaketh unto me and saith he 'wilt beat the Devil out of me and send it back from whence it came, even if it means my death'."

"How horrible. How mean. It is too much!" Tears well in Annex's eyes and she quickly conceals her emotions, bringing her tiny hands up covering her eyes so Ethelwulf will not see her weep.

"Why does he do such heinous acts unto thee. Is he not a man of the cloth? Surely he can pray that the Devil leave thy soul be?"

"Aye my dearest Annex; however, I knowest there is no Devil that liveth within my soul. These things that taketh place are because I think them to happen and it cometh so. I will things to happen, and they shall come to pass. Moments ago, thou spokest unto me saying that a ghost is amongst us. I say no, for look upon me with thine own eyes and command me to do something and it shall be so."

"Ethelwulf my dear, thou art no Devil and ye could not possibly do anything the likes of that of a wizard or witch. These people have grey hair and death is nearly upon them, thou art no witch."

The pain still seething throughout his body impacts his endurance to kneel any longer, and he closes his eyes, slumping to ground. Dust and hay scatter softly into the air, from the impact of his weight.

"I will take thee unto my mother. She will tend unto thy wounds and treat thee with the herbs of the field until thine health is restored."

Looking toward Annex, feeling fatigued, the only thing Ethelwulf is able to do is shake his head, yes in approval. However, he is not permitted to leave the barn under any circumstances. He has to remain inside the barn until he heals, which would only be a day or two. He heals miraculously fast, and his father Jacob knows this. This is why his father beat him with all of his might, feeling the Devil inside of him will heal his wounds quickly. This validates his belief that Ethelwulf is possessed by the Devil, demon, or demons.

"My wounds will heal by the next sunrise or the next, my dear. I am grateful to have thee in my life Annex. Thou always thinkest of what is best for me. No others have, and if they do it is because of thee."

Sympathizing for her dear friend, she decides to sit down next to him, and she rests her head upon his shoulder, and feels his warmth, and the fibre of his being. There is no denying her feelings and affections. She is in love with Ethelwulf, and she feels within her heart that he feels the same feelings for her as well. It has to be true, as he will not even look at the other village girls. When she is there or not, she is the only girl around and he makes her feel special. It is true the only thing in her heart for Ethelwulf is compassionate love.

"Dost thou think of the future, Ethelwulf?"

After a long hesitation to her question and wondering if something happened to his hearing, she repeats herself.

"There is no need to repeat thyself, Annex."

Annex removes her head from Ethelwulf's shoulder, wondering how he was able to read her thoughts like that. There was no way he could, he is no wizard; he is just a boy. Smiling and wondering at the same time if he is playing a game, she thinks of a number that he can try to guess if he thinks he is some sort of wizard, *umm seven, because that is how old I am...*

Ethelwulf does not respond, leading to her disappointment, confirming that he is not a wizard.

"I knew it was not true, thou art no wizard. Oh Ethelwulf, thou hast deceiveth me with thy crafty tongue," Annex giggles.

Elthelwulf tries to smile regardless of the pain he feels coursing throughout his body. He also does not want Annex to see his missing teeth that were knocked out in the fight.

"Annex, I am in too much pain to play with thee. I am thinking of what will befall me the next time my father strikes me down. I am scared of him but if thou wisheth to play a game, and if thou wisheth me to tell thee what number thou hast concealed within thy mind, seven it is!"

A dead silence creeps over the room. How could he possibly know the number?

"I cannot explain how I know thy thoughts. I have the ability to do many things. That is why my father striketh me. He saith unto me that I am an abomination unto the Christ and like with thee, I have read his thoughts and he wishes death upon me."

She sees her dear friend in dire pain doing his best to look at her through one of his swollen shut eyes. She also notices that his spirits are down. Not just the pain of his beatings are keeping him in pain, he is emotionally distraught. Annex rests her head in Ethelwulf's lap keeping close to him and decides to rest closing her eyes. She repeats the question.

"Dost thou think of the future Ethelwulf, when we are of age, wilt thou take my hand in marriage?"

Trying his best to conceal his emotions, Ethelwulf blushes, nervously leaning down. The palms of his hands start to sweat. His heart begins to race. Yet, despite his anxiety, he continues to lean down until his full lips press on her warm, rosy cheek.

Looking up into Ethelwulf's eyes, she is not taken aback by his bruising, and smiles, "Dost this now mean that thou art to be my boyfriend?"

Forcing a smile on his face, supressing the pain, he does not care if she sees his missing teeth, Ethelwulf gleefully responds, "Aye."

Together they sleep in each other's arms, nestling together on the floor of the barn.

9 years later
Over the years, the population of the village grows, and the villagers build shops, and offer services such as blacksmiths, merchants, trades, fur shops etc. Jacob and Gilda have the citizens construct a bigger temple that will fit the growing congregation inside of their church for services in their ever-growing Christian community. The word of the Christ spreads throughout the village and beyond, and Jacob is more than thrilled to be God's voice.

Although the man of God is highly revered amongst the townsfolk, some of the villagers talk behind his back about his son Ethelwulf. The townsfolk discuss Ethelwulf's strange abilities, the things that he does when provoked to anger, eyewitness accounts and everything from actual events to a vivid stretch of imagination. Ethelwulf is the focal point of persecution within the village.

Some note Ethelwulf cannot be the son of Jacob, and jump to conclusions and allege that Gilda is a harlot, and slept with a man who is not Caucasian. Ethelwulf's real father is a mixed race individual, which explains Ethelwulf's tanned complexion, coarse hair and full lips. Despite having taken Ethelwulf in as their son, they continued to withhold information that they'd adopted him and lied to the villagers saying that he is theirs to prevent others from harming him. This is also the best strategy to conceal Ethelwulf's not-so-secret abilities.

Both Annex's parents, Bancroft and Palmyra, grow distant to Ethelwulf the older he gets, and the more they know him. Bancroft taught Ethelwulf mêlée combat should he ever be drafted into battle, and Palmyra cared for him like a mother who would her own child, nurturing him, always tending to him when he was beaten by his father, and giving him a shoulder to cry on.

Those feelings vanished over the years as he trusted her parents more than he should have. He grew too comfortable with them. When training with Bancroft who is the most gifted swordsman in the village, who fought alongside notable war heroes against the German Saxons, he would use his magical powers and might to overthrow Bancroft while training with him. Bancroft, sceptical of Ethelwulf's unnatural strength, learning capabilities, and other mysterious occurrences, came to the conclusion that all of his feats were too unnatural for any boy his age, to match an experienced swordsman such as himself.

When Palmyra would tend to Ethelwulf's wounds, she would listen intently to his explanations of why his father beat him. She'd help nurture him back to health as if he were her own child, and Ethelwulf trusted her as if she was his own mother, in fact better than his own mother. He recalls memories of the day his mother left him, abandoning him at Jacob and Gilda's home. Although she was murdered, he remembers feeling that something was wrong the moment she bent down to kiss his lips, as if it would be the final time he would see her. If he had the means to, he would have killed her himself for abandoning him to these foster parents, these Christians.

When sharing such strange and bizarre stories with Palmyra, his emotions happened to get the better of him. At times objects in the room shattered and broke with his uncontrollable psychokinetic anger, or would fly across the room and smash against walls. After realizing Ethelwulf was the cause of such strange events taking place in her home, Palmyra never welcomed him back again, and forbade Annex to see him.

As for Annex over the years she fell into a state of depression in lieu of such horrible things the townsfolk would say about her beloved Ethelwulf. Some even mentioned that if it wasn't for the fact that he was a man of God's son, they would have killed him long ago. However, her love for Ethelwulf grew stronger with each passing year.

Forbidden to see him, she'd sneak out and make her way to seem him in private in order to be together, to have and to hold one another, sometimes if even if it were only for a few minutes, if only to say I love you. They cherished these moments more than some couples who spend a lifetime together.

Waiting underneath the starry sky for his beloved, visions race through his mind, the thoughts and plots of villagers worry him. Clenching his fists as the cool air surrounds him, he is not able to bear such frightening sensations creeping over him.

The snapping sounds of small twigs on the ground, and the rustle of branches and leaves swaying, gain Ethelwulf's attention. Within a split second all of his worries vanish. Smiling, he embraces the woman of his dreams and holds her in his arms.

They walk together hand in hand in the forest, Annex's eyes not completely adjusted to the dark. However, that does not matter as she feels safe being close to Ethelwulf guiding her along the way. They reach a clearing, and near a body of water where the villagers bathe or get water at, and they hold one another staring at the ripples of water moving towards the shore.

They say nothing as they hold each other's hands, savouring the moment. Ethelwulf's palm sweats in the hold of Annex's hand as his heart and mind race again. His heart beats fast as he grips her hand tight, barely able to contain his emotions.

Freeing her hand from his grip, she wipes his sweat on her garments, and then looks at Ethelwulf inquisitively, "What troubles thee, my dear?"

The very question makes it harder for Ethelwulf to breathe the more his nerves escalate, and the very thought of answering her question makes him sweat more. Standing still like a marble statue while gazing at the water, he swallows hard, despite his throat feeling like it is closing in on him.

"Ethelwulf, speak unto me!"

Turning around and grabbing her hands Ethelwulf's eyes look down towards her feet. He knows if he makes eye contact with her, there would be no way he could ever get the words out of his mouth. *Great!!!* He thinks as her hand gently cups his chin so she can look him in the eyes. She softly raises his chin so their eyes meet one another's.

"I love thee Annex. I always have. I always shall. I will even love thee when twilight is upon us, and I gaze into thy wrinkled face with thy withered grey hair and see that thou art the woman that the angels have sent down from the heavens for me. I love thee Annex. Be my wife."

"O my dearest Ethelwulf. That was so beautiful! Of course I will be thy wife, and I shall beget many children unto thee, as many as the Lord can bestow upon us."

Half-heartedly smiling after hearing the word God, he bites his tongue and minds his place. He's learned from previous beatings to not speak out of turn towards his parents' god. It was clear that he was an abomination to god and it was also clear his parents did not love him.

"My dear, ye are troubled?" Annex breaks the racing thoughts in Ethelwulf's mind. "Speak unto me, what is troubling thee?"

"Aye my love, thou art the only one who hath accepted me for who I am. I know I was abandoned from when I was a child. Whilst I cannot prove that the man who has taken me in for all these years hath murdered my mother, I know within my heart that he hath hatred in his heart towards me. I know my days are numbered within our village. I must kill him. I must kill the entire village."

"Ethelwulf, what speakest thou? It is one thing if thy parents hate thee. It is another to break God's commandments and commit murder! What of my parents? Wilt thou kill my parents?"

As painful as it is confronting the man of her dreams, this is the first time she's heard him speak in such a manner. It frightens her very being hearing such things from her husband-to-be.

Trying to contain his rage, Ethelwulf focuses on the dark waters, watching the ripples of the water sliding to the shoreline, while staring at the fragmented reflection of the stars on the dark water.

Knowing that he can be stubborn at times, she fears that he may try and kill a few people. What if his visions can be altered? What if they have their family elsewhere? This way no one has to be killed, and her husband-to-be will not be murdered in the process.

"We could leave the village and start a life elsewhere, my love?"

"Aye that is possible, but dost thou think that they shall let thee flee with me and not fetch thee once we have left the village. They will send the dogs to fetch us and they will not stop tracking us until they have captured us. They will lash thee, and surely kill me. I have foreseen this."

Why now? Why after the proposal? Oh the sadness and pain. She fights her tears. The madness of the villagers is too overwhelming for her to contend with any longer.

"I know now why it is that thou hates the Christian God. Promise something unto me, my love?"

Trying not to read his love's mind, he focuses on listening and blocking her thoughts out. Knowing everything before it happens, cheapens his enjoyment of people and life. Letting out a sigh he nods his head.

"Promise unto me that thou shalt not slay my parents unless they try to slay thee?"

He grimaces. It is inevitable Bancroft will attack him, as he has foreseen it in his vision. How can he tell his love that her father will fight him, and he will kill him? Choosing not to upset her, he nods his head and tries to think of a way to avoid this confrontation.

Months pass by, and in that time no one bothers Ethelwulf for his differences. They avoid him completely, and trying to read the villagers thoughts seem impossible, leaving him feeling anxious, worried, and at times scared.

To add to his perpetual state of depression, Annex has not seen him since he divulged his vision to her. However, she was not leaving her abode, leading him to wonder if her parents were behind her disappearance.

Ethelwulf's very being, every fibre in his body yearns to knock on their door to find out how she is doing, and to make everything alright in case her parents are troubling her because of him.

Sadness fills his mind, what if she no longer wanted to be his wife? It has been over two full moons since they last saw one another. She could have easily changed her mind? Or perhaps this had something to do with a few years ago when she was forbidden to see him. Perhaps her parents had clued in to her sneaking out of the house late at night to see him?

Regardless if she did sneak out at night, perhaps she was fearful of what he conveyed to her, especially about killing the villagers and her parents. After all, telling your fiancée that you want to kill everyone including her parents is not the best way to charm the heart of a woman you love, or a great proposal idea.

It is hard to focus and even harder to think. A cloud of anger fills his mind. A cloud of rage takes over the anger. Rage bottles inside of his very being, and he cannot let any of the villagers see him getting angry. Growling angrily, he storms into his parents' barn, the barn he is usually sent to for punishments as if he is an animal.

As he storms into the barn, he carelessly wills the doors open with his powers, and slams them shut with a slight of hand gesture once inside. The animals grow restless as he storms around inside the barn. He steadies himself in the centre of the barn. All loose inanimate objects begin to rattle and shake, in lieu of his uncontrollable rage, and mystical powers.

As the initial phase of his rage begins, the barn doors slam open. His father Jacob marches inside of the barn. He is furious. This is not unusual. Furious that his son is using his demonic, sorcerous powers again in front of the whole community to see, he knows he must beat the demons out of him.

Jacob slams the doors shut, and grips tighter on to his club. Ethelwulf turns around to face his father and reads his father's thoughts as if he were actually speaking. His thoughts are veering between murdering him and severely hurting him.

If Jacob did not punish him, he would be dishonouring God, and he will lose the respect of the villagers. Jacob tightens his grip on the club and takes a few paces toward his son. Ethelwulf keeps his posture as his father walks toward him. He can feel the hate illuminating from his father as he takes each step closer toward him.

Ethelwulf reaches out with his mind's eye. He can see where each object within the barn is, and he can see the rakes, the axes, everything in the barn, in his mind. He sees everything that he needs to use just in case his father carries out his thoughts and feelings.

Jacob hears scuffling sounds in the attic, and looks up to see if anyone is there. An axe flies towards him and lands mere inches in front of his feet. The blade deeply penetrates the ground, as if to warn Jacob not to come any closer. Jacob does not care. He has to teach this offspring of Satan not tempt the lord his God. He takes another step and a rake flies directly in front of his other foot.

A smirk crawls across his face, and he gloats as the powers of God are no match for the Devil. He cannot be harmed as he is a man of God, with the protection of the almighty Christ on his side.

"Ethelwulf the reason that no harm hath befallen me is because I have the lord upon my side. In the name of Jesus, I rebuke thee oh Satan."

Ethelwulf lets out an inner laugh that makes his chest heave, while he looks down at his father. His height and weight trump his father's, yet Jacob is none the least bothered by his son's physical stature. Furthermore, Ethelwulf has never previously raised so much as a finger toward him in any of the beatings he has dished out to him.

Jacob rushes toward Ethelwulf and swings his club at his face. To his shock, he cannot believe that Ethelwulf would defend himself and grab his club in mid-swing. His son tosses him over his back, and he crashes down on the ground. The club is snatched from his hand due to the brute strength of his son. He tries to shake off the pain as he lies on the floor, catching his breath.

Standing above his father who is now at his mercy, he looks at the man that took care of him throughout the years; yet, he is the same man who has beat him relentlessly, and without mercy all these years. He hates him so much; there is no one he hates as much as he does him. Impulsively tightening his grip on his father's club, he raises the club in the air, and swings it up and into the attic, and then walks away from his defeated father. Although he hates his father, he cannot hurt him, nor does he have it in his heart to kill his father.

As Ethelwulf turns to leave, his father gets up from the ground, brushes the debris from his garments, and rushes after his son. How could Ethelwulf disrespect him like this? This is outrageous! He is to obey him as that is the commandment of God. The other is having false gods and Ethelwulf is in clear violation of this commandment, serving the Devil.

Ethelwulf senses his father's rage and anger, and spins around raising his hand toward his father to stop. As he raises his hand and focuses on letting his father know that he wants him to stop, an energy force pushes through his arm, and leaves his body. The only other times he felt anything similar is when he would use his strange magical powers to direct objects in the air. However, this never came out with such force until now. He watches his father fly backwards and skid across the ground, hitting a bale of hay.

While wondering about the extent of his magical powers, and fighting off the depression caused by his father who continuously finds every reason to harm him, Ethelwulf turns his back again on his father and starts to leave, sensing his father will not try and attack him again.

"I have tried to protect thee all these years, and now thou hast displayed thy demonic powers unto the community. They will desire to smite thee. Thou knowest this to be true! The might of the Lord will prevail against thy demonic forces and thou shalt surely perish before the men of the Lord."

Turning his head slightly to look at his father lying on the ground, he can feel the urge to rush over and strangle the life out of Jacob, yet he still is not able to find it in his heart to do so.

"Now what shall I do? Everyone knoweth that I am a man of God, and now thou hast shown people that thou hast the devil with thee."

Shaking his head, he only pities his father, and leaves the barn. As he opens the door he is alarmed to see a few villagers eavesdropping on their altercation. They were hoping Jacob would kill him, and for the first time in a while, Ethelwulf feels the emotions of the villagers, a feeling of disappointment, as he leaves the barn unscathed.

Nonetheless, Ethelwulf continues to walk toward the wretched church, his home. He turns his head slightly. The villagers are following him. He notices some of them have weapons in their hands. Turning back around and stretching his hand out so that they can see, he wills the door of the church open. He is the one in control, and he wants people to see that he is not possessed by any evil beings. He wants people to see that he controls everything, and he wants them to know that he does not fear them or whatever they think of him, regardless if he fears for his life, and Annex's.

Ethelwulf walks into his room and wraps his belt around his waist, and puts on his sword and sheath. Taking all that he needs from his home, he heads to the waters that will further remind him of the times he used to share with his beloved Annex, who has not seen him in quite some time. If he is not able to physically be with her at least he can be with her in memory.

The rock only skips four times across the water this time as Ethelwulf looks for anther rock to toss across the water. He cannot find any more good rocks. They are all pebble sized, and too big. Sitting down, Ethelwulf stares at geese swimming. There are also a few ducks on the other side of the pond and the geese are at peace which brings his mind to peace as well.

Startled by rustling noises in the bushes, he turns around and notices a person getting off a horse, and walking toward him, "Annex?"

Ethelwulf jumps to his feet and rushes to his beloved and wraps his arms around her tight, and then quickly jerks himself free from her embrace as something in his excitement startles him. As he looks down he senses and feels life within her.

"Thou art pregnant?" Ethelwulf gasps as he backs away slightly.

"Aye my love, my father has kept it a secret from the villagers because of thee. If they are to find out that this child is from thy loins, they will surely persecute me as they do thee."

Ethelwulf watches tears run down the sides of his beloved's cheeks, and brings a finger to wipe them away and caress her tender, beautiful face. There is also something else that he is picking up from his beloved, yet he keeps promising himself that he will do his best to not read her thoughts, and trust her to tell him what he needs to know. Cupping her face with his hands and gently wiping away her tears, she grabs his hands and breaks into hysterical sobs.

"Is there more?"

"Aye my love, everyone including my father gathers in the house of the Lord as I speak to thee now. They plot to smite thee if thou returns to the village."

Letting go of Annex's face, he clenches his fist. Ethelwulf marches toward Annex's horse and hops on, letting his rage dictate his actions. Annex rushes quickly behind him, expecting to come along.

"My love, wait for me here. I shall destroy each and every one of them, whether or not I am from the loins of the Devil or his agents, I am a person. I am no monster. I have done no wrongs. This ends today! This ends now! They will bring no harm to our child!"

Annex grabs Ethelwulf's leg, and holds onto it for dear life. Her fears bring cramps to her stomach as the village is filled with soldiers and they are all experienced warriors. She fears greatly for his safety and knows they will kill him if he goes back. Furthermore, despite his great stature, he is only a young man. He is only sixteen and they will definitely kill him if they get their hands on him.

She knows that it is possible that he may kill a few of them, if that, and despite the fact that he trained with her father, he was surely taking it easy on the boy, and even if he was not, they were not fighting for real. If her father was to fight him for real, he would cut him up into so many pieces that not even wild dogs would find him a meal of interest.

"Wait for me here, woman. I shall return."

"No! Do not go. Please, I beg of thee my beloved, they will surely destroy thee. Stay! Together we can leave and make a place elsewhere that we may call our own. Who will father our child once thou art dead?!"

At that moment, nothing could persuade him to think otherwise. Grimacing and letting his rage flow through him, he kicks the sides of his horse and speeds off through the forest. If they hate him with this intensity, with enough urge and desire to kill him, there was no telling what they would do when they found out Annex is pregnant. He needed to put an end to their lives. He would not let Annex or his child be killed, because of himself.

Rushing through the forest and into the blazing afternoon sun, Ethelwulf draws his sword from his sheath and hops off his horse as he nears the village. He looks around as he walks closer, he does not see anyone. Letting his powers take him over, he feels them, nearly everyone inside of the church. He rushes toward oil and kerosene barrels and grabs a few of them, and then he rushes toward the church. In his rage he douses the sides, front and back of the church with the kerosene and oil.

He hears his father Jacob yelling to the congregation, telling them his lies, saying that his son is an agent of Satan, and that he needs to be killed. He hears roars of excitement and applause inside of the church. As he is pouring the contents all over the church, his father carries on, telling everyone in the congregation that he took Ethelwulf in as a baby, and that he is not his. He was only trying to save Ethelwulf as he is the child of the great whore of Babylon.

Tears stream down Ethelwulf's face and anger wells deep inside of him as he continues to douse the sides of the church with kerosene. He is barely able to focus on what he is doing, as his father's words are too much to bear. Everything is a blur as he fights the emotional pain, and he fails keeping quiet and cries out loud.

"Hey, demon child!"

Ethelwulf turns around to see a villager, with a sword in his hand. Ethelwulf pulls out his sword and charges the man. As Ethelwulf ducks to one side, his enemy swings his sword down at him, missing him completely. Ethelwulf bobs to his other side, and jumps in the air and shoves his blade right into the man's neck.

Gagging while spurting out blood, the man tries to stop the pain and holds onto his neck. He drops his sword and watches helplessly as Ethelwulf marches toward him as he feels dizzy and crunches to a knee on the ground.

Fuelled and controlled by rage and his dark emotions, Ethelwulf spins around and chops the man's head clean off. Ethelwulf senses that more people are alerted to his presence due to the fight and they rush out to see the altercation, only to find Ethelwulf hovering over a body, sword in hand.

As Ethelwulf turns around the corner of the church building, there are a few men waiting for him, one with an axe, the others have swords.

The first of the trio to attack is the one with the axe. He spins his axe from side to side, trying to intimidate Ethelwulf, and then when he is in range, he tries to kill him with a death blow. Each swipe narrowly misses the muscular kid. He relies on his speed as he believes the rumours about Ethelwulf's demonic strength, so he does his best to kill the kid as quickly as possible. His speed serves him well, as he drives the blade deep into Ethelwulf's shoulder.

Ethelwulf screams in dire pain and spins around falling to the ground, and drops his sword. He clutches onto his wound with his free hand.

Gloating at the easy victory, the attacker raises his axe over his head, while triumphantly smiling because of his victory against the demon child, savouring this moment as he flexes his muscles, readying himself in preparation for a death blow to Ethelwulf.

As the man hovers in front of him, fear grips Ethelwulf. Despite this fact, Ethelwulf resorts to his magical powers on instinct and feels his sword within his mind lying on the ground a few feet away from them. He notices how anxious the man is as he is savouring the moment, and about to kill him. With the fear of this man wanting to end his life and with the will of wanting to preserve own, he wills the sword from the ground to fly into the skull of his attacker. The sword sinks into the man's skull with one sharp crack, bringing the man down to his knees, and then on the ground dead.

Ethelwulf uses his powers to slam the church doors shut, and then rises to his feet. He can feel the anxiety of the villagers as they frantically try and escape, desperately trying to smash their way free from the church. Pulling his sword out of the enemy's skull, Ethelwulf walks towards the church.

The other two attackers charge Ethelwulf together. The exchange of metal sings as their swords meet, and

Ethelwulf does his best to parry blow after blow, while the attackers greet him with an offensive strike. Neither of his opponents are as good as the last man he fought however, there are two of them and Ethelwulf only has one good arm. They have the upper hand.

As Ethelwulf continues to pace backward, on the defensive, he notices his enemy's axe, and levitates it in the air, hurling into the back of one of his opponents, which crushes deep into the man's back. The crunching of bones causes the man to exhale, and drop to the ground. His partner looks toward him for a few brief seconds.

In that few brief seconds, Ethelwulf takes advantage of the moment, and the man is no longer able to turn his head around anymore. While he looks at his partner, he watches streams of blood shooting out of his own throat. He tries to look down to figure out what is happening, and his head falls from his shoulders.

Ethelwulf looks down at the dead and dying opponents, and then continues to walk toward the church. Thinking of what to do next, he notices a plank on the ground. He bends over to pick it up and then continues on to the church. He thrusts the plank into the ground and backs away from the door, releasing his magical hold on the door. The door to the church opens a few centimetres. The villagers inside the church try their hardest to get out of the church so that they can kill him. Remembering his plan, Ethelwulf looks around the village for a source of fire and then notices the blacksmith's shop which is close to the church.

Hot coals are burning underneath a sword that the blacksmith had left unattended. As Ethelwulf smiles in regards to his new fortune, he wills the coals out of the oven, and using his willpower, hurls them at the church. The first coal that hits the side of the building, crushed against the wood in a puff of smoke, and red ash from the coal falls to the ground. Not impressed with of the first coals results, he wills another into the wall and the kerosene ignites and fire begins to spread along the wall, then another coal hits the wall and falls into a mixture of kerosene and oil, followed by another. The church is now in a raging blaze.

Ethelwulf backs away from the church, and shields his eyes from the intense fire and heat. Frantic screams trail throughout the village. The door to the church shakes vigorously as the people inside try to escape.

A few wives tending to their children rush out of their homes, in order to try and save the villagers. One by one, Ethelwulf chops them down with his sword until there is hardly anyone left.

Ethelwulf looks at the wound on his shoulder. It had stopped bleeding, and was beginning to close up. Originally the wound was several inches deep and the white of his bone could be seen. *Am I truly from the loins of the Devil?* Ethelwulf thinks to himself as he walks into each home to find survivors. There are only the babies in some of the homes, and some toddlers.

A nauseous feeling creeps throughout his stomach, as he wonders if he should keep these children alive. If he does then he would be letting them face the elements alone and they will certainly face starvation, or get eaten alive by the wild beasts of the field. If none of these things happened, and some people by chance came to the village and took them in as their own, and by some sort of miracle they figured out he was responsible for the deaths of everyone in the village including their parents, then they would surely come for him and brutally murder him to avenge the deaths of their parents. Thus, if he killed them now he would not have any of that on his conscience.

Ethelwulf walks over to the church and lights a torch with the flames, remembering the first house he broke into with a baby in it. Before lighting the house on fire, someone yells to him. It is Bancroft.

"Thou hast murdered everyone within this village!!!"

"Aye, Bancroft! It is no secret that they were going to murder me!"

"Thou wouldst have been better off if they had! Thou hast poisoned the womb of my daughter. Thou hast slain everyone that I know in the most cowardly act, and I shall hack thy limbs off one by one and feed thy body to the vultures!"

Tossing his torch aside, Ethelwulf reaches for his sword and pulls it slowly from his sheath, "I want no quarrel with thee, Bancroft!"

Bancroft jumps from the hill to the path that Ethelwulf is on, "Thou should have thought that through before thou poisoned my daughter's womb with thy seed and murdered this innocent village!"

Ethelwulf looks at his wounded arm. It was nearly healed. He grips the handle of his sword with both hands as Bancroft is no rookie, and even though he beat him in a few sparring matches, this is no training match. This is real. This is a matter of life and death.

They study each intensely while pacing around in a circle waiting for the other to make the first move. "I do not wish to harm thee. I have promised thy daughter that I would not harm thee."

Smiling Bancroft answers Ethelwulf in a snide tone, "Than this shall be easy for me, as thou hast chosen thy destiny!"

Bancroft's sword howls through the air, and sings as it chimes off Ethelwulf's sword. Again and again, Bancroft chops and slices at Ethelwulf. His opponent immediately uses defensive strategies. His speed outmatches the overgrown young man, while his swift movements gracefully help him stride across the path. His deliberate moves are in tune with perfection, and Ethelwulf's clumsy steps and off centre balance is but a mere joke to him.

Ethelwulf is furious, and uses his rage to dictate the swing of blade, trying to give a devastating chop at Bancroft.

Using speed and precision Bancroft dances around the clumsy young man's emotionally filled strike, and he opens up the side of Ethelwulf's stomach, and then rushes behind him shoving his sword deep into Ethelwulf's kidney, bringing the giant kid down to his knees in agony.

Bancroft rolls his eyes; the fight was way too easy. In desperation, Bancroft eats his thoughts quickly as he frantically parries the blow of the child who seems to have cheated any source of pain. Bancroft falls to his back and rolls free from Ethelwulf's swing that tears a chunk of soil from the ground. Jumping back to his feet, Bancroft rushes to the top of the hill to come to his senses.

Ethelwulf knows he cannot allow him to regroup, or give him a moment's thought to conjure up a strategy. Ethelwulf's steps become more graceful. Each swing of his sword becomes more powerful than the last, and although they are just as clumsy, it does not matter. Skilled or not, each swing against Bancroft is sending him back several paces. He will no longer play skill for skill, remembering that he is the more powerful of the two. He knows Bancroft will not risk being hit by him. And despite all of the knowledge he has on the battlefield, he knows that it is unwise playing into Bancroft's game of skill for skill. This is why he is using his own method against him, using the method he remembers from their sparring matches.

This is outrageous! How can Ethelwulf turn the tides of battle? This is even more unfathomable as he was just penetrated with the edge of my blade, he thinks to himself, and then has an epiphany, and reaches to the side of his utility belt and pulls out a dagger and throws it directly at Ethelwulf. To his dismay Ethelwulf parries it away as if this was all part of an easy game. Feeling like this was his first time in battle, Bancroft knew that he was in the match of his life.

The only chance he stands is finding a way to outsmart the kid in order to win. Still perplexed at how this kid is still able to keep fighting after being severely wounded, he really contemplates if Jacob was telling the truth, if Ethelwulf is a child of Satan. He did not believe in Jacob's God or his Satan before today as he has his own gods. He prays to the new Christian god for strength against the Devil's child. He thinks of running away from the fight to figure it out after saying a small prayer, but quickly reconsiders as the thought of running away makes him consider Ethelwulf throwing a sword into his back. He thinks of pretending to be at the mercy of Ethelwulf and killing him that way.

Bancroft changes his defensive pattern and rushes towards Ethelwulf who continues to stand his ground. Bancroft tries to use his speed to his advantage, yet gets nowhere, Ethelwulf is parrying each quick and precise blow as if he could see five moves in advance. Unbeknownst to Bancroft, Ethelwulf is using his foresight to see each move before it happens. Ethelwulf is taking full advantage of his magical powers.

Bancroft leaps in the air to take a chop at Ethelwulf and he parries his sword as if it is second nature to him. However, he knew Ethelwulf would not expect him to do a cheap shot and thrust his sword into his foot. Ethelwulf growls in pain and Bancroft smiles. It was a cheap shot but he was not going to let this kid win, no matter what. Bancroft quickly pulls the sword out of Ethelwulf's foot and cuts open Ethelwulf's throat, blood squirts out of the kid's neck in streams.

Ethelwulf falls to the ground clutching his throat, and tries to take in a deep breath only to partially drown in his own blood. He tries to apply pressure on his wound, Bancroft continues to smile and nods his head towards Ethelwulf, and then walks up to the young man and drives his sword through his heart. Letting go of his throat, Ethelwulf tries to scream but gurgles on his blood. All he is able to do is feel pain as the edge of the sword continuously penetrates his chest, breaking his bones while sliding through him.

Ethelwulf uses every last bit of energy to grab onto the gloating victor's arms and looks deep into his victor's eyes. Ethelwulf reaches down onto the ground and picks up his sword and slams it into Bancroft. The look of victory vanishes from Bancroft's eyes as he noticed Ethelwulf's sword deep inside him. Ethelwulf closes his eyes then falls to the ground.

The sounds of someone crying, wakes Ethelwulf. At first he thought it was Annex who was crying and then realises it is not. Pain courses throughout Ethelwulf's chest and affects the rest of his body. Doing his best to remain conscious, he tries yanking the sword free from his chest. With each tug, he slices his fingers and his palms as he tries gripping onto the swords blade, pulling it out. Finally after a few tugs the sword is free from his chest and he tosses it to the ground. Rising to his feet, Ethelwulf notices the person crying is Palmyra, Annex's mother.

"Thou hast murdered my husband. Take my life there is nothing left for me, demon."

Bending over, Ethelwulf puts his hand on Palmyra's shoulder. He will not take her life. She could be a mother to the children in the village that had lost their parents, and he would uphold his promise to Annex. Staggering off, he walks inside his parents' barn and gets his horse and then limply climbs astride to leave.

Palmyra greets him at the barn with a sword in her hand. She continues to walk inside the barn and raises it at Ethelwulf, "Thou hast murdered my husband and taken him from my life. I will be damned if someone comes to kill thee whilst thou is with my daughter. Take this sword and protect her from whomever may wish to strike thee down."

Reaching out the sword, Palmyra gently gives the blade to Ethelwulf, and then she begins to cry.

Do not fret I shall be a good husband unto her, Ethelwulf calls out to her from his mind, as he is unable to vocalise what he needs to say as his vocal cords are severed, making it impossible to speak. Frightened,
Palmyra takes a few steps back from Ethelwulf.

Do not fear me, I shall bring thee no harm, and I shalt bring thy daughter happiness all the days of my life.

"Aye, I have no doubt that thou shalt be a good husband and father, whether or not thou art the offspring of the Devil, thou hast proven thyself worthy of my daughter. I only wish things were different," Palmyra replies, although she is still angry and upset over everything this abomination of God's nature has committed. She does not want it to strike her down, so she tries her best to play coy with the young man she feels is a demon.

Ethelwulf nods and gently strokes the side of Palmyra's cheek, and then he rides away from the village hoping to never return again.

Racing through the forest and into the clearing, Ethelwulf sees his fiancée lying down on the beach. She is asleep and waiting for him. He is not able to call her however, she wakes up hearing the sound of the horse approaching.

Getting to her feet she notices Ethelwulf is severely injured and blood is all over his garments. She gasps and rushes to help him off the horse. Her fiancée's wounds take her breath away as she is horrified at what she is seeing. By no accounts can anyone survive what he has gone through yet, her fiancée lives. She tries to hold him steady but he collapses, and she is not able to maintain his weight. He falls to the ground. She quickly lowers herself and hugs him dearly "My love, I saw a fire in the distance what happened?"

They are dead, my parents, the villagers, almost everyone.

Annex is not surprised to hear Ethelwulf speaking to her from his mind. He has done so several times in the past when he needed to tell her things in secret. Unfortunately, there is no other alternative. "What of my parents?!"

Thy mother liveth.

"And my father?"

We fought, I told him that I have no quarrel with him. It did not matter to him. I swear by the gods he killed me, yet I still live. He placed his sword through my heart. I grabbed him by the arm and then...

"Enough my Lord, I cannot bear to hear any more."

Waking up, Ethelwulf notices his clothes are changed. The wound on his throat is only a small scar, likewise the wound on his chest. Wondering where Annex is, he notices that she is at the pond with her arms folded, gazing at the geese and ducks.

Getting to his feet, Ethelwulf gracefully walks over to his fiancée and wraps his arms around her, and extends his palms over her stomach so that he can feel his unborn child kicking within her womb. He does this as he tenderly rests his chin on her shoulder.

"How am I to be with thee, Ethelwulf? Whilst thou hast slept for five nights, I have done some thinking. Are we to live in solitude? If not, are we to live amongst other people? And if so, how wilt thou conceal what hath taken place? And if thou dost not speak of such things, how wilt thou conceal thy emotions? I have seen thine anger when people have caused thine emotions to come to wrath. Thou shalt bring harm upon me, and our child."

Testing his luck he clears his throat, and tries to speak. It is hard and a little painful but he is able to get some audible words out despite how rasping it sounds, "Then we shall live in solitude and not worry what anyone is to think of us."

Annex turns around and reciprocates Ethelwulf's love, "Aye, alright. That seems to be a good idea, my love."

3

"My Lord, you have summoned me?" Leviathan asks, knee pressed to the ground, as he respectfully bows before General Satan.

"There is a new threat, I am unable to track this being down. He lives in secrecy, and he lives in the future. He also lives in this time zone. I allowed for the construction of more time machines so that it will be easier for us to find this being. I sense that he is the son of Joshua; this means he is powerful. I must find him and get him to be under our control."

Leviathan's faith in Satan's ability to command was shaken the moment they were deceived and deserted on this primitive planet. He stands up and inquisitively looks at his master.

Satan brings his white sleeves on his silk shirt, up to his elbows, and turns his back to Leviathan. Together they walk towards the patio. The clean crisp air of Earth's atmosphere is refreshing in comparison to Ares, which is a concrete war torn planet, devastated by the war that they initiated in order to seize control, and not only dominantly rule their own planet; others were included in their tyranny.

"We have Joshua, and we are training him to be like us. He is the most powerful half mortal we have come across, so why do we need his son?"

Satan stretches out his hands and a crystal ball forms in his palms, transferring potential images of the future. He shows Leviathan the new threat he is speaking about. *"Joshua?"*

"No! But as a matter of fact where can I find him?!" The man's voice bellows to her.

Leviathan watches this being dressed in his ceremonial dark black robes confronting Joshua's wife Elizabeth. His eyebrow raises a few notches as the encounter between the couple is intriguing, yet,

perplexing at the same time. *"What is it that thou wants of me?"*
 "Your life!"

Leviathan watches this being cut Elizabeth's head off, and then goes into a state of shock and awe as transference of power leaves Elizabeth and flows into the being, "He knows the secret now, but how can this be? Elizabeth?"

"Yes, search your feelings on this matter Leviathan. What did you notice about her?"

Within a split second it comes to him, although the timing of realisation on this matter is a split second for mortals, for them it is a very long time. "She was my daughter! It does not make sense; why kill her?"

Thinking this through carefully, and seeing everything that surrounds his epiphany, Satan conjures words to make a compelling revelation to Leviathan, while withholding pertinent information that only he needs to know.

"Simple; he is looking for Joshua, he goes to Joshua's wife Elizabeth. What would motivate someone from the future to return to the past to look for Joshua? How would they know where to find her as there are no records of her in the future? This being has personal ties to both of them. I sense he is their son, your Grandson."

"Joshua is tainted by Belial and Lucifer. They are plotting against me, and soon they will approach you to side with them. I have the tools to find your grandson and together we destroy the others. Without me, he will find and destroy everyone. We cannot allow this to take place. From this moment forward they are the enemy. We will hunt them down and destroy them."

Leviathan respectfully bows before Satan, and silently confirms his allegiance to his master, and accepts the declaration of war against the Devils.

A decade passes by. In that time, Annex gives birth to a beautiful son. They live in seclusion, a comfortable distance away from communities of any sort; however, they occasionally see soldiers riding along the trails where they built their home.

Their son Cynric is a young boy and shares many of the same characteristics that his father has. This includes his abnormal strength and his magical powers. The good thing far from people is Cynric is not subject to persecution. They live in harmony. However, he is under constant reminders from his parents to not apply any of his magic in the midst of company, because they will not understand, and they will try to kill him. Additionally they take liberty in sharing with him what had happened to the village that they were from, so that he knows what consequences await his differences, should he disobey.

"Papa, soldiers are coming our way again." Cynric notes to his father.

Ethelwulf leaves his hut and watches the soldiers approaching their home, figuring they were just passing through the area, Ethelwulf thinks nothing of it, and places his hands on his son's shoulders while watching the soldiers approaching.

Usually the soldiers would pass by. Some would ask for refreshments, and Annex shows her courtesy and support by serving them water, and tending to some of the wounded if needs be; yet, this time is different. A distinguished looking gentleman dismounts his horse and approaches Ethelwulf.

"Top of the morning to thee, sire."

"Aye, top of the morning to thee sire." Ethelwulf greets in response.

"We need more soldiers. The Saxons have pillaged more land in the southern parts and seeing Rome no longer cares for our land, we must protect our fellow brothers on the southern shores of Britannia. I select thee to come with us so that we may crush these pillagers and take back what is rightfully ours!"

"With all due respect sire, I am a family man. We have built a home here in these lands and I provide and protect my family at all costs. I am sorry sire, I cannot come with thee and thy men."

The soldier motions a few of his men to come to his aid. "I understand this however, I am not asking thee. I am telling thee to side with us. It would be a shame if anything were to happen unto thy family..."

Cynric turns and hugs his father. Cynric reads the thoughts of the man and is terrified by what may happen if his father continues to defy this person. *Father, I do not wish anything to happen unto mother, we can fight but they wilt smite us, I do not wish to see mother fall at their hands.* Cynric reaches out to his father with his thoughts. His father nods at him, acknowledging his words.

"I understand, I shall fight by thy side."

"Good. Gather thy belongings, if thou hast weaponry gather what thou canst. It will serve thee well in battle."

"Aye."

"Gather thy livestock and family. Thy family will seek refuge in a town close by to where we are heading. This way they will be close unto thee, if thou manageth to survive."

They arrive in the next town and Ethelwulf shares his goodbyes with his family, and heads to battle with the soldiers and the other recruits they find along the way. They coercively recruit others in the same fashion. Unfortunately, the ones who refuse are murdered after their wives are raped and murdered before their eyes. Ethelwulf feels relief knowing he did the right thing joining the Britannia army.

The men walk in droves, as the afternoon sun sets. The scorching sun's setting, gives relief to most of the soldiers as the cool evening air envelops them. As the night sky rolls in, the men break for camp. Ethelwulf is not fond of lying on the dirt ground.

It depresses him remembering the days that he was treated like an animal by Jacob, each time he was sent to the barn when he was a kid; however, he does not have a choice. As Ethelwulf looks around figuring out what he will use as a head rest, someone tosses something towards him. Sensing this he turns around, and catches a soft comfortable roundish thing. He looks up and stares at the soldier that tossed it.

"My woman made me a couple of these things; it should keep thine head comfortable as ye sleep."

Ethelwulf feels it, and pushes his palms into it, inspecting it ever inquisitively. It is very comforting and surprisingly cushiony, and he smiles as he continues to inspect it.

"It is made of bird feathers; it took her a while to create this."

"I thank thee. I am Ethelwulf."

"I am Drake. My father always wanted a youth that would be the likes of a dragon, and well, here I am a soldier that fights the Saxons like a ferocious dragon."

Ethelwulf nods and lies down. As he does, he watches his new friend Drake setting up for the night, "Is thy father amongst us?"

Drake does not respond immediately. Carefully reading Ethelwulf, he feels Ethelwulf is genuine, and then decides to respond as he sits down, "Nay, he was slain in battle years ago. And now I fought for the ones that have slain him." Drake sighs as he buries the back of his head in the pillow.

"Whence comest thou?" Ethelwulf asks.

"From the Northern shore of Britannia. I am from one of the Gutan tribes."

Ethelwulf nods his head. It is finally nice to meet someone other than his immediate family. "Hmm Dragon Drake the Goth. I shalt remember thy name for as long as I live."

Laughing, Drake turns over to his side, "That is great lad; as for now I must rest. We shall talk more on the morrow."

Visions haunt Ethelwulf as he sleeps. He sees the Saxons slaughtering many fellow soldiers, and a halo of arrows penetrates their advances from both sides. Tossing and turning, he lets out a growl. Nearby objects begin to shake, due to his uncontrollable strange power.

Drake opens his eyes slightly, because of the racket and noises his new friend is making. He tosses a stone at Ethelwulf's head before anyone notices what is taking place. Ethelwulf snatches the stone in mid-air before it smacks his head. This frightens Drake. He stares in disbelief. Trying to control his thoughts, he gasps out loud. He cannot believe what he saw. Is his new friend a sorcerer? "Thou art a witch!" Drake whispers aloud.

"No, I am a Christian! Thou shalt hold thy tongue before thou makest such accusations against me again!" Ethelwulf whispers in a hostile tone, and in stealth, reaches for his sword, wondering if he has made an enemy of his new friend.

"Oh sorry. I shall hold my tongue!" Drake whispers back, and turns back over to sleep.

Scouts successfully penetrate the Saxon's camp and are now returning to give their reports. Sensing this, Ethelwulf wakes up. He saw this in his vision and he knows the rest of his vision will unfold itself accordingly. His dreams have never failed him before. As he collects himself, he knows it is best to warn the General, because if he does not act responsibly, the majority of soldiers will die. He needs to stop his dream from fulfilling itself. He will not allow it to come true. In his vision he sees his death, and as a freak of nature he will rise from the dead again to the horror of his fellow soldiers, and they will turn on him and kill his family for being aligned to him. He feels compelled more than ever to ever to alter his dream as his family's lives are in jeopardy.

He rushes through the camp, and over to the tents in the back of the massive camp, sensing which tent the person in charge is in, he walks inside. "General, sire?"

"What!" The General angrily shouts at the peasant. Coming to his senses the General thinks he recognizes the peasant "Joshua?"

"Nay, I am Ethelwulf, Sire."

After a second glance, the General wonders why he is being disturbed "What is it?"

"I have a way to smite the enemy in one swift stroke. We can save many men in upcoming battles."

The General angrily gets to his feet, grabs his sword, and rushes over to Ethelwulf, screaming at the top of his lungs, "I am the General and Commander of this army. Who art thou to speak unto me saying that thou hast a better way of winning our battles?"

Ethelwulf channels the pain away as the edge of the General's sword tears through the bottom of his chin, as he is in his clutches. He ignores the staring eyes that are on them. He focuses on his task at hand, "God hath spake unto me in my dream. He spake unto me saying that we can set up camp at dusk on the morrow and hide within the bush. When the enemy hath reached us, we can smite them. To prove this, two of thy scouts will approach us shortly and speak unto thee saying that the Saxons approach us."

"Place him in chains," the General yells to the nearest eavesdroppers.

They comply with the General's wish.

Just as Ethelwulf said, not more than ten minutes pass and a couple of scouts on horseback arrive, and immediately head to the General's tent. This startles the General.

"My Lord, the Saxons are on their way. They are three day's journey away."

Word spreads around the camp fast. There is amazement circling around the camp about having a man that can speak directly to God, and just as he prophesised, the Saxons are on the way. Regardless of the growing excitement in the camp, Ethelwulf is sick to his stomach. This whole charade is only a ploy. He will not have his visions unfold and is altering the future to save his family. Despite the excitement, he senses his friend Drake, and his disposition towards having a prophet of god in the midst of the soldiers. Regardless of Drake laughing and sharing jokes with other soldiers, he senses Drake is not like the others and that he is against them. Perhaps this has something to do with his father being killed by them years ago, he ponders. Then he puts pieces of his Christian statements into the equation, and entertains for a brief second again, that perhaps his father is like him and was killed for it?

"What is thy name peasant?!" the General asks.

"Ethelwulf, my Lord."

"Unbind this man," the General asks a guard, this time with a soothing tone. "It has come to my attention that thou mayest in fact be a man of God. Whether or not thou may be, thy presence has given the soldiers something to be hopeful about. I have consulted with some of the others. We shall let thee command this army, if thou art indeed a man of God, thou shalt prevail over the Saxons. If thou art not as thou sayest, I shall remove thy head with a swing of my sword and carry out the battle myself!"

"My Lord, if I may?"

"Speak!"

"I have seen in my vision, a valley about a day's travel away. The Lord hath spoken unto me saying that we are to set up camp there and wait for the enemy which will arrive in the night. At that moment they will charge our camp but we shall be in the bush and send a halo of arrows in the night sky to smite them. The remainder of our men will flank their forces their forces and smite them before they rush off into retreat, giving us a total victory over the Saxons."

The General nods his head, "Pray thy vision comest true. It will be thy worst fate if not!"

It is the night of Ethelwulf's prediction. The cool night's air is soothing, and the men eagerly await the Saxons while hiding in bushes close to the valley. The buzzing sounds of crickets hum in unison as the gentle breeze blows in and around the trees.

Drake is aloof to Ethelwulf as they sit quietly side by side. Sensing this, Ethelwulf feels it is time to probe Drake's mind and thoughts. He sees images of Christians murdering his family, his mother, his father and his older brothers. He feels Drake's hate for him. After his false statements of being Christian, all of Drake's friendly domineer is a pretence to him.

"Drake my friend, I have committed something that I must share with thee. I need thy advice."

More thoughts and images flow into Ethelwulf's mind from Drake's. He senses Drake will do anything he can to kill him. Sensing this, Ethelwulf finds words to turn his friend's hatred around, so that they can be friends again.

Drake looks around. He is caught off guard and did not expect Ethelwulf to confide in him. He can use whatever Ethelwulf shares to him and turn it on him so that he can be the new hero of the army. He has to be coy, and he has to manipulate this man of god. "Aye my friend, thou mayest share the thoughts of thy mind with me," Drake whispers, unaware Ethelwulf is reading his true thoughts and feelings.

"Aye, I knew that I could count on thee Drake Dragon the Goth. I am scared of these Christians my friend."

Does he jest? This is rather confusing. Is he not a Christian?

Drake thinks. "They hold thee in high esteem my friend. Thou shalt lead them into victory just as the Lord God hath shown thee," Drake says, playing his cards close.

"Nay, my friend. Mayest I speak unto thee in the strictest of confidence, my friend?"

Without hesitation Drake nods his head.

"My mother abandoned me when I was but a few days from her womb. She was murdered that same night she left me. Twas a good thing it was not when I was older or I would have tracked her down and

removed her head myself! I have never known my father, and the people that raised me in their place, assumed me to be from the loins of the Devil. They plotted my death, Drake," Ethelwulf continues and shares what took place all those years ago.

Remembering the fear that circulated his village years ago, Drake remembers a folk legend about the Devil's offspring. A chill rushes up and down his spine as he assumes where this conversation is going to head.

"Drake, I burned them alive. I smote them all. However, I battled a fierce warrior. Bancroft was his name and he struck me down with his blade. I died and was resurrected from the dead that same night. I pulled the blade from my chest. I have lived in solitude since that day until now, Drake."

Trembling, Drake takes a few moments to recollect his thoughts. This news changes everything that he feels about Ethelwulf. His family was slaughtered by Christians because of their pagan beliefs. Out of fear, he kept his beliefs to himself since the day his family was murdered. They were murdered because of the story about Ethelwulf, which was only believed to be an excuse to murder pagans in the name of God.

"My... my family was killed because of thee."

"Aye, now ready thy bow and arrows. The enemy approaches."

"How dost thou knowest these things that come to pass?"

"I must find my father to know such things. I feel he holds the key to all my questions."

The soldiers can hear metal on metal from the Saxon army in the distance as they approach, confirming what

Ethelwulf said. The low rumble of footsteps sounds towards the camp. The enemy swarms the camp, taking down tents, chopping through the tents with their weapons, and they come out of the tent areas shocked that there is not anyone around. They now realise it is an ambush.

Ethelwulf gives the army a signal, and several archers light their arrows and shoot them up in the air and into the camp. The camp is soaked in kerosene, and as the arrows land, they kill several Saxons. Others suffer severe injuries and then are lit up in a sea of fire which spreads throughout the camp.

The survivors begin to retreat yet, they find no comfort in escape as Britannia soldiers on horseback flank them, and kill them all, one swift strike after the other.

As other survivors leave the lake of fire, one of the Britannia soldiers holds his sword up high to rush out and kill them however, Ethelwulf raises his hand and gives a final order to the army, "Let them burn. Britannia is ours!"

Buzzards cry out loud for others to come to feast on the dead as morning breaks. The Britannians rummage through remains of the Saxons to look for anything of worth. The stench of the burnt corpses is unbearable for some of the soldiers. Ethelwulf does his best to block the stench seeping into his nostrils as he looks for a better sword, and if he can spot one, a shield as well, in case they encounter more Saxons.

"Come hither, peasant."

Ethelwulf turns around, and snatches a sword that is tossed to him in mid-air. He stares at the sword, admiring the craftsmanship. It feels sturdy, a lot better than his other sword. His other sword is flimsy at the handle, despite his attempts to forge it. "I thank thee, my Lord."

"Tell me peasant, doth the maker have any messages for thee and our next battle?"

Hesitating to speak, Ethelwulf clears his throat yet, is unable to get the words out as he is reading the General's thoughts. He now knows the General does not believe that he has the power to speak to the Lord, which is true. He has never felt the presence of any such being. He is aware that it is all him and he tries to read more into the General's thoughts to make sure he is not aware of this as well, "Nay, my Lord."

"Of course not, and because thou hast managed to bear falsehoods amongst the people and be a hero amongst them, do not expect us nobles to fall into thy trap. Thou art no General and thy battle strategies were but a stroke of luck. Honestly, I look forward to having thee take my place. Each time 'the lord speaketh unto thee' it shall bring me that much closer to removing thy head!"

Ethelwulf watches as the General rides his horse off with his companions and heads to the camp, while Drake who was eavesdropping walks over to him after the others leave, "He surely takes a liking unto thee."

Ethelwulf laughs as he holds his sword, admiring the fact he had been granted a sword by a noblemen, "Aye he surely wants my head. Dost thou think he will keep it as a souvenir?"

Annex feels relief as she puts the last of her son Cynric's garments on a line to dry. Annex kisses him on his head and then leaves to the market for meat to prepare for dinner in the evening. Bringing back groceries from the market is a tedious task, more so without Ethelwulf to help out with family duties. She did not want the help of the villagers today. She is feeling low and needs time by herself, she needs to get out and clear her mind. Disturbing thoughts of what may happen to her husband while he is battling, are getting the better of her and she feels some alone time will help alleviate how she is feeling.

Although Annex feels her husband will be safe, especially after what took place over a decade ago, she still feels what happened back then was luck, surviving the fight with her father. Despite what happened she is not able to explain her husband's strange abilities, the strange powers he possesses. At times she feels he is a sorcerer, which is why he survived the fight against the village.

Oftentimes she thinks of her mother. She remembers how upset she was when she was pregnant with Ethelwulf's child, and that her mother had often told her prior to becoming pregnant that she can find someone better than him. However, this conversation only happened after she became aware of her husband-to-be's strange powers.

She closes her eyes as she walks to the market, trying to remember what her parents looked like, as she misses them and tries to conjure memories to see them once again. Oftentimes she feels upset with Ethelwulf for killing her father, and sometimes regrets being with him, yet no one was ever as kind-hearted and nice to her as he is, and she loves him dearly. She loves her Ethelwulf more with each passing day and is thankful to any given god for bestowing a beautiful child on them.

Yet, she still wonders how her mother is doing. Perhaps if the war drags on further, or if she is in desperate need of help, she can turn to her mother, regardless of Ethelwulf's pleas to see her. He made it specifically clear that grave danger would await her, should she return to the village. She feels that he is forcing her not to see her own mother, and secretly feels that he may have killed her also. However, she also feels that he says such things because he cares. If her mother was still alive she would be so delighted to see her grandson, and to see what a bright young boy he is.

Still wondering if it is a good idea to see her mother, and reflecting on other thoughts, she notices a wild rose bush. Smiling, she walks over to the roses and giggles, remembering the when her dear Ethel brought her a wild rose. His poor arm was severely cut by the thorns and broken parts of the thorns were sticking out of his arm, and his hand was caked with blood by the time he had come to her with the broken-petaled rose. Laughing at the dear memory, she breaks off a rose and smells it, remembering the tears at the sides of his cheeks as he was trying to block out the pain to impress her with the dilapidated rose. Sighing, she takes in another scent of the rose, keeping in the fragrance as long as she can to bring life to her memories.

She is startled as she sees a soldier a few paces behind the rose bush. Jumping back, she places her hand on her chest, collecting herself. She comes to not understanding how deep in memory's lane she went, to have and to hold onto a memory of her dear Ethel. She takes notice of the soldier. His armour is shiny, and his clothes are well kept. He is more than likely a well-to-do soldier and is a commander of some sort, as he does not dress like other soldiers. *Odd that he is in a place like this.* She notices that he is rubbing his garments where his penis is, while looking at her in a repulsive way. Her heart beats faster as she knows it is time to run to safety.

Collecting her thoughts, Annex pretends that she does not see the soldier, and looks around for the fastest way to the market so she can blend in with the crowd and lose sight of this person who is about to harm her. A few more soldiers walk around mounds of dirt patches that are along the dirt road side and block passage to the road.

Annex's muscles begin to tighten. Her heart races faster. Her skin colour goes flush. She can barely breathe as she feels as if her throat is closing in on her, and her mind is racing. She knows these other soldiers will not help her. She can see the grins on their faces, as they block her path.

"Top of the morning to you, ma'am," the man from the other side of the rose bush says, as he walks closer towards Annex. She frantically looks around for somewhere to run.

Annex notices an open field and runs into the thick of the open green grass. As she runs, she thinks of the last moment spent with Cynric and her beloved Ethelwulf.

"This ought to slow the wench down," the man laughs as he picks up a large palm size stone. It bears some weight to it. It is heavy, just enough to do the trick and demobilise her. As he grips onto it, watching Annex rush into the open field, he aims and launches the stone into the air. The stone crashes against her back, and she skids through the thick blades of grass.

In extreme agony, she tries to call out as she slides across the green grass, yet she is hurt so bad she feels no pain. She gasps for air, yet is unable to breathe. She is in shock, and she grabs a hold the thick grass to try and make good her escape by pulling herself along the field, grabbing locks of grass along her way, while writhing in pain. As she tries to pull herself up, she feels her bones cracking out of place, and drops to the ground again. Gasping aloud to Ethelwulf for a last source of comfort, she closes her eyes and thinks of Cynric. *Who will watch over him should they kill me while Ethelwulf is at war?*

"Mother?" Cynric cries out, as a disturbing vision suddenly haunts him.

"Annex? Annex!" Ethelwulf cries out, falling to his knees, holding on to his head while trying to block out what he sees from his lover's eyes.

Rushing out of his house Cynric grabs an axe, and rushes as fast as he can to look for his mother, using his powers to find her along the way.

"Rick, stay here lad. Thy mother will return within a short while!" one of the villagers shouts at him. Cynric does not pay her any mind and continues to run off faster than any child she can remember running before.

"Drop that axe! I will tell thy mother on thee, drop that axe before thou hurtest thyself!" She yells again to no avail, then sits down, knowing that she will set him straight when his mother returns, thinking of what a strange little boy he is.

Cynric does his best to feel where his mother is, and as runs along the path with his axe in hand to find her, he feels her presence all along the trail as he looks all along the dirt road for her. He finally notices a few soldiers in the thick of the field. As he is about to call for help, he sees their pants are down. He is embarrassed to see grown men with their private parts hanging out however, he senses extreme pain, and realizes these men are not using the washroom. He feels the extreme agony of his mother, and they are raping her.

He rushes through the thick grass, using his cloaking powers to remain undetected. The soldiers are masturbating over his mother, while one of the soldiers is raping her. Cynric's raises his axe above his head, screaming in full rage as he charges for the soldiers.

As one of the soldiers turns around to see what all the commotion is about, he sees a little boy swinging an axe at him. Fortunately, the little boy misses. Or so he thinks. His knees buckle, and he looks down, there is a stump where his penis used to be, and he hears and sees blood hissing out of half of his penis, and looks over to see the other half of his penis in the thick of the grass. The sight of not having his manhood is almost as unbearable as looking at it in the ground.

Cynric thrusts his axe into the back of the man that is on top of his mother, swaying his hips up and down on her. Cynric presses his foot down on the soldier's back to take the axe out. Before he is able to get the axe out of the man's back, the remaining soldier punches him in the face, sending him flying a few metres into the grass.

In a daze Cynric tries to come to his senses. The soldier kicks him in the bottom of his jaw and he falls backward. The man jumps on top off him and begins severely punching him over and over again. The punching stops. Cynric looks up and notices part of a sword sticking through the front of the soldier's throat, and his mother holding onto the other half. The soldier gags on the cold steel from the blade. He is wiggling his hands trying to take the sword out of his neck, slicing the palms of his hands to pieces as he tried vigorously to take the sword out.

Cynric wiggles his way from underneath the half-naked man on top of him and runs to embrace his mother who has collapsed from the beating and rape she just endured. Unlike his father, Cynric does not have enough of the unknown power they both have to help and give her the energy that she needs to get to her feet, so he uses what strength he has to place his mother's dead weight around his shoulders and begin to carry her to safety.

"We cannot go back to the village. They will come for us," his mother says.

"Mother?" Cynric has no clue on where they can go, and holding the weight of his mother on his shoulder is already proving to be too much for him.

"I shall guide thee to the village whence I came."

4

As the soldiers arrive back to their village, Ethelwulf notices a heavy occupation of soldiers. Some are scattered in the open plains of a field, and others are with dogs walking around the field. Something happened, and he knows this has something to do with what he felt not too long ago in regards to his love Annex.

Drake did not say much to Ethelwulf after he watched his friend have his nervous breakdown. He knows something is troubling him. He also notices how upset Ethelwulf is, as they are taking notice of all of the soldiers that are in the nearby field and surrounding areas.

Soldiers start to pull a few bodies from the field and Ethelwulf drops to his knee, as his emotions are getting the better of him, and he thinks the worst case scenario about his wife. He loses his breath as he looks in the field, trying to catch a glimpse of the bodies. His friend Drake grabs him by his under pit, and yanks him to his feet.

"Thou art drawing unnecessary attention to thyself. Compose thyself lad; get to thy feet," Drake whispers to Ethelwulf, hoping everything is alright with his friend at the same time.

He still has reservations about mentioning his past history to Drake, although they are getting to know one another. However, Ethelwulf sees how his friend composes himself around him, and he reads no ill intent in his mind. Ethelwulf is able to read certain thoughts and he knows that Drake wonders what else he has committed.

Although Drake is wondering what else his friend has done, he knows that this is not the time for pondering over such things now, as his friend needs him. He composes himself, and keeps a watchful eye over him. He feels compelled to remain at Ethelwulf's side.

The soldiers begin to leave for their homes, while some of the nobles leave the field to see what has taken place in their absence. Quickly learning what transpired, they hear an attack took place on one of the Dux Bellorum's soldiers. The initial soldiers had determined that a sexual relation was taking place, and a vigilante murdered the Dux's men in return.

"Man of God, tell us what hath transpired here?" the General asks Ethelwulf.

Drake stands in between the two and addresses the General. "My Lord, he is not well."

"Hold thy tongue. I asked 'the man of God'."

Clearing his throat, Ethelwulf looks at the General, and then walks in front of Drake. "I only knoweth what mine eyes see. The Lord hath granted me foresight of that battle but not of this incident."

Chuckling under his breath the General walks away without furthering the meaningless conversation. He knows that Ethelwulf will not take his bait for the sake of keeping his head on his shoulders. He climbs on his horse to further the investigation.

A couple of soldiers that are from the Dux's battalion, rush up the dirt path. They meet with fellow soldiers and then within a few seconds of meeting one another, they all take off, rushing through the field. They have information leading to the whereabouts of the vigilante.

"Drake, I know that this has something to do with mine family. Art thou with me?"

"How can ye be sure of this?"

"My vision?" Ethelwulf says with uncertainty.

"Aye. I am with thee."

Together they rush to the camp and retrieve a pair of horses. Upon returning, a few of the locals point towards them. This catches the eyes of some of the soldiers. Looking around, Ethelwulf is not able to see his wife and son amongst the villagers that are being interrogated by the Dux's soldiers. Using his powers,

Ethelwulf is not able to feel them in the village's midst either.

Together, the pair speed away from the village. Ethelwulf uses his powers to help him find his wife. He taps into her mind. He is able to feel that she is in trouble. He senses that she returned to the village where they lived as children.

When he taps into his son's mind, he feels extreme, intense pain and agony, so painful that he has to refrain from tapping in. Fuelled by his rage, Ethelwulf wishes that his horse could run faster. As they near the village where he had slaughtered everyone years ago, Ethelwulf and Drake notice smoke rising through the thick of the trees.

Entering the village, they hear people chanting and yelling. The chants appear to be coming from where the fire and smoke are rising.

"Ethelwulf, let us find out what is going on before we engage anyone."

"Aye," Ethelwulf says as he jumps from his horse and pulls his sword out of his sheath.

A crowd is circling around the fire in the distance. As they walk closer to the chanting crowd, Ethelwulf notices a couple of bodies tied to stakes burning in the fire. He notices that it is an adult body and a child in flames. The adult is dead and the other body on fire is the child thrashing on the pole he is chained to.

"Cynric? "Noooo!" Ethelwulf cries.

"Ethelwulf! No, not yet!"

Drake tries to snatch his friend by the arm, but it is too late. Ethelwulf swings his sword at the crowd, as he rushes towards them.

"He's a witch," people yell. "Burn him too!"

Ethelwulf recognizes the voice. It is Palmyra, Annex's mother. Ethelwulf sees in his mind, images of her condemning her daughter and grandchild, his son, to death.

She has waited years to kill Ethelwulf, since he poisoned her daughter's womb, and she lived in misery since the day her husband lost his life in the fight against Ethelwulf, the Devil's child.

She shared stories about Ethelwulf to the children, and she told them she took them in as her own children, and did not hide the fact that Ethelwulf slaughtered their parents, and that the Lord softened his hard heart and spared her from the atrocities that she was committing that day.

She never forgave her daughter for carrying the Devil's son's child, and she disowned her after she did not return when her father was killed. She did not feel any remorse or conscious in regards to informing the soldiers that came to the village looking for anyone of suspicion, about her very own daughter Annex and grandchild.

Now that Ethelwulf was here, her day was now complete. She had seen the death of her daughter, and if that was not enough to give her pleasure, she was enjoying the show watching her grandson writhe in pain on the stake that witches burn on, and now God had delivered Ethelwulf right to her hands.

She raises her hand and points her finger at him. "Burn him!"

"Well if it isn't the man of God. I will deal with him," the General mockingly says to his commanding officer, the Dux Bellorum, showing off before the greatly revered warrior in response to Palmyra's shouting.

As Ethelwulf rushes closer to the crowd, the General rushes towards Ethelwulf on his horse, drawing his sword in anticipation of the fight.

Ethelwulf stretches his hand out, and wills the horse to fall down. The horse falls on the ground face first, and the General topples over. The General quickly gathers himself together, grabbing his sword and shield and rushes towards Ethelwulf.

Ethelwulf pulls out his other sword. Now he has one in each hand. He reaches the General, and swings his sword downwards. The General blocks it with his shield, and tries to slice Ethelwulf's mid-section. Ethelwulf parries and smashes his sword at the General's left side, and tries to kill him once again with his other sword in hand. The General falls backwards.

The General is no match for Ethelwulf's power. As he does his best to recollect himself, in the process he lets go of his shield that Ethelwulf's blade had cracked right down the middle with his incredible strength. With merciless swipes, Ethelwulf chops repeatedly at the General, sending him staggering back, as if he is an inexperienced warrior that has never seen the light of day in battle.

The General sees an opportunity and lunges forward to jab his blade into Ethelwulf's stomach, but Ethelwulf has set him up. With a quick jab, Ethelwulf quickly places his sword through the General's leg armour and the sword slices through the other side of his leg. He lets out a short scream which ends when Ethelwulf spins around, severing the General's head, and in mid swing Ethelwulf retrieves the other blade from the General's leg.

Ethelwulf growls as he stares at the numerous amounts of soldiers rushing his way and begins to charge towards them. Drake catches up to him, ready to fight by his friend's side.

They rush towards the soldiers. Archers begin firing arrows at them in order to end this fight quickly; additionally, they do not want to lose more men than necessary against this rather skilled man heading their way.

Ethelwulf sees the archers firing at him. He uses his powers to guide his sword and foresee where the where the arrows will end up. He takes the broad side of his sword and parries off the first arrow with ease, and then the other arrows that follow the first. Now he stands before another soldier who dares to fight him.

He positions himself in a crouching position as he nears the soldier. The soldier lowers his shield to block a potential blow to his legs; however, Ethelwulf in mid stride leaps up in the air and thrusts his sword through the soldier's neck. The soldier drops his sword and shield and grabs his neck, gagging as blood spurts out. Ethelwulf does not finish him. There is no need. That soldier would die quickly without being anymore of a threat. Lastly, he enjoys knowing that the soldier will die an agonising death.

Drake could not believe his eyes. Who was this person that he was fighting alongside? All his life he wanted revenge against the very Christians that killed his family, and he never did anything about it until now. Drake rushes ahead of Ethelwulf and begins chopping down the archers that are running for safety.

Smiling, Drake looks at the man who is responsible for his family's deaths all those years ago, the Dux himself, and then runs to kill him. Anger fills Drake's heart as he rushes towards the Dux, his hands trembling as he runs faster to kill the man that haunts his dreams every night since his family was slaughtered.

Drake feels a sharp pain and topples over, and he drops his sword. A remaining archer shot Drake in the knee, and before Drake could pull the arrow out, a spear penetrates his shoulder and he falls backwards. The spear still has enough force behind the throw to dig its way into the ground as Drake falls backwards.

Ethelwulf rushes to the fire. He watches his son writhing in pain. Ethelwulf ignores the pain of the searing heat as he tries to get near his son who is still somewhat moving around from the pain. "Stop it!" He commands the fire, and the flames die out.

By all accounts, Cynric should be dead. An normal child his age would have died after a few minutes of excruciating pain after being lit on fire. Cynric's hair has been burnt completely off. His lips are melted away. Ethelwulf notices his son's mouth and sees his son's charred teeth. As he holds his only son, he looks at his face in horror. Remains of cartilage where Cynric's nose should be still remain orange, and green puss oozes from his eye sockets. Ethelwulf only sees his beautiful boy that he loves and cherishes as he tries to hold his hot smoldering body close to him, nestling him in his arms. "I must get thee down!" Ethelwulf cries out.

A crowd circles a comfortable distance away from Ethelwulf, as he frantically tries to get his boy off of the pole that he is chained and burned to. Cynric's body parts are so hot and charred that flames burst from them as Ethelwulf grabs hold of him. Charcoaled ash breaks from him, and some of his limbs break off and fall to the ground like logs breaking apart in a fire; yet, Cynric still lives on. He is unable to move. His body is more ash than anything else yet, what remains, is his mind and he calls out to his father, begging his father repeatedly from every fibre of his being, *I love thee father, Kill me! I love thee father Kill me! Please!*

Ethelwulf takes a step back, tears stream down the sides of his face. Ethelwulf cries out loud, how can he do it? He feels the crowd's eyes upon him. These damned Christians! Ethelwulf's mind races frantically.

Father please, I can feel thy turmoil, but my pain exceeds that of thine. Let me go!

While Ethelwulf holds his son who is burned beyond recognition, a few of the other children in the distance begin to cry as they watch Ethelwulf stroking his son's charred head and kiss his son's severely charred cheek frantically.

"Do not fret children. If it were not for my husband, the monster would have burned ye all in the same manner!" a woman shouted.

Father, please!

"No! I can save thee. I can use this power that I have to save thee. I will save thee. I will figure out a way!"

With a roar Ethelwulf puts his son on the ground
and stumbles to his feet. There is no way that he can
allow his son to live like this, and he knows within his
heart that he does not have the powers to save his son.
He grips his sword and begins to cry frantically,
stumbling around and throws up at the very thought of
ending his beautiful boy's life.

Ethelwulf swipes his sword through the air and
takes his son's head off with a clean strike, charcoaled
hot red ash flares everywhere as his son's head topples to
the ground. Thunder clouds begin to roll in. Lightning
strikes at Ethelwulf several times as winds begin to howl,
sweeping in and around him.

Picking up his son's head and nestling it in his
arms, stroking the scarred remains of Cynric's head,
Ethelwulf walks over to his wife's corpse. Before getting
closer, he notices a cloth on the ground. He touches it
and senses that it was part of his blanket that he had
from when he was a child. Opening it with his free hand,
he sees the first rose that he had given his beloved Annex
all those years ago. Ethelwulf can barely focus on the
withered rose as it falls apart in the wind. He looks up to
see his beloved Annex's limp remains upon the stake
where she had been burned, ash still falling from her
body. "Noooo!"

"Kill him, he's a witch!" cries out the old lady
Palmyra who has no concern over what just took place.

Before Ethelwulf has a chance to gently place his
son's head on the ground, the soldiers rush towards him.
He drops his son's head in order to kill the soldiers
rushing his way until he notices the Dux Bellorum with a
sword to his friend's neck, the only friend that he has
ever made in his life save his wife and son.

Drake is unconscious and the blade that is slightly
penetrating his neck does not wake him at all, "Drop thy

sword if thou dost not wish to see me bring harm upon thy friend!" Dux Bellorum says.

Opening his fingers, Ethelwulf feels the handle of his sword trickle free from his fingers, and then feels the pressure of his sword slightly shake the ground next to his feet. What few soldiers remain, chain Ethelwulf up and bring him before the Dux, who says nothing to him. He instructs his soldiers to take Ethelwulf to the edge of the cliff nearby along with his friend Drake.

Drake wakes up as he is being dragged along the ground. He looks up to see his friend chained and knows that his hero had been defeated as well. At least Drake was honoured to fight alongside someone that killed more of the Christians than they had of his family, and with that, a slight smile creeps across his face as they are dragged to the edge of the cliff nearby.

Both Ethelwulf and Drake are standing up straight by the soldiers, as the Dux Bellorum heads their way to say a few last words to them both. "Any confessions ye need to make unto the Lord before ye die? If so, confess unto the Lord now."

"Aye," Drake says, staring directly into the Dux's eyes, "When I get before the Lord God, I will take him by the throat and tear it out and I shalt smite his angels alongside Ethelwulf and wait for thee to enter the gates of heaven by the fate which awaits thee and sever thee limb by limb and defecate into thy skull and hold it aloft for all to see!"

The Dux rolls his eyes, and points towards the cliff giving his men the cue to toss both men over.

Ethelwulf does not say a word and Drake does not have anything left to say as they are both hurled off the cliff to their deaths below.

Palmyra rushes over to the Dux Bellorum and grabs a hold of his leg, shouting frantically, "Ethelwulf is in leagues with Lucifer. He will rise from the dead once again to be in the service of the enemies of the Lord."

The Dux kicks her free from his leg, knocking her to the ground.

"Lucifer shall resurrect him!" she cries.

"She is crazed men. Let us go."

5

As Leviathan meditates in his chamber, sitting cross legged on the floor, he foresees a being with immense powers. This being is the Emperor of the world Earth and this being is not general Satan, nor any of the remaining devils. This is in contrast to the plan of Satan ruling the world Earth incognito as Taras Ivanov.

Satan must have been overthrown, he contemplates, as he foresees a weakness in Satan's leadership abilities in the future. There is no room for serving a failure, he thinks to himself, and wonders who this other being may be, as there is a cloud surrounding his visions on this being.

"There was transference of power. I want you to go and spy on Belial, Lucifer and Joshua, see which one of them is dead," Satan says.

Startled, Leviathan looks towards Satan who is staring at him matter-of-factly. He can potentially lose a strike against Satan, and does not entertain the thought of striking him down yet. "Yes Master."

"Master, our future is clouded. I see another being ruling this planet in future."

"Don't be absurd Leviathan. Do you think any being can overthrow us?"

"We are on this very planet because we were overthrown. Your judgements are getting weaker"

"I have just returned from the future and last I checked, I still rule this planet. The cabins are in place to capture our grandchild. He will side with us, and then we will return to Ares and re-take what is ours. Now remember who you serve and do my bidding."

"Your Highness we've received an archaic message from someone who claims to be Leviathan from the Milky Way galaxy. What is interesting about the delivery of this message is he states that they are on a planet called earth."

Searching her feelings Queen Mika uses her powers to assess the truth in the matter. As she opens her eyes she looks on the computer monitor in front of her. Contemplating Altarium's revelation she dismisses the information as a ploy to set her off course. "No. As it stands these are General Ombassi's last known coordinates. Our fleet shall continue to scour the nearby planets for signs of life, and apprehend Satan, and the rest of the Ares tribe members. That is all."

"Your Highness with all due respect I do not mean to speak out of term, he says our former King Lucifer is among them. He asks to be permitted to stay on what he claims is a primitive planet, and seeks asylum there, provided we apprehend General Satan, Belial and former King Lucifer. He also claims they had a civil war on the planet and only four of them remain. We can leave a partial amount of the fleet to scour the Andromeda system while we discover the truth of the matter. Our searches here have turned up nothing so far. What does it actually hurt to follow up with this lead seeing we are so far away from home? If the lead is wrong, or it is an ambush we will deal with it. We will at least be one step closer."

A small glimpse of the future floods Queen Mika's mind, and what she sees is conflict surrounding her fugitive Satan. However, Satan has manipulated her people once before. He full well knows how to use their powers against them. She considers Altarium's words for a moment, and senses that this is the best approach.

"Set course for the Milky-Way system, and coordinates for the planet Earth. We shall discover the truth of the matter and bring the former King Lucifer to justice and place General Satan, Belial and Leviathan of Ares on trial for crimes against our people. Inform the Unified Galactic Republic that we are following a lead, and that we may need their full support."

"Yes your Highness." Altarium says as he bows before Queen Mika, and then rushes to cubicle on the bridge of the ship to follow through with the Queen's orders.

The bright lights of the stars, and distant planets flicker on the computer monitor as the ship turns around and they head towards the primitive planet Earth.

Altarium sends word to Leviathan, and like the other times before only a telegraphed message through primitive laser technology is sent back his way "No! I assure you that this is not a trap. I wish to remain on this planet with the indigenous beings here, many of which are insects, quadrupedals, and some primitive like beings called humans which are at an early phase of what we were once like billions of years ago."

"Your Highness."

Rising from the Captain's chair the Queen approaches Altarium, and reads the transcription sent to Altarium. Assessing the situation once more she senses that millions of years of search are at an end.

"Are you pleased my Lady?"

"Not entirely. Be mindful King Lucifer betrayed us all, and General Satan is the master of war. We must treat this situation with care. Records show Leviathan is Satan's right hand in the dictatorship of the Ares elite. Our way has never been war, it has been brought on us, and we must do what we can to avoid danger. I sense something awry. I sense Satan and I sense our confrontation. Perhaps this is not a good idea. I must meditate on this it will become clear."

"Your majesty if I may?"

"No you may not, I am the woman in command, you are a mere male, and under my command, and will only listen to what I have to say."

Realising she is speaking out of term from the angst she has endured for millenniums she allows him to speak "Be quick about it. Speak your mind candidly."

"I was just going to say, your sister has shown us that war has been beneficial since the atrocities we've endured. I don't mean to speak out of term, but we can no longer live in the days before General Satan enslaved our people, and inflicted genocide on us. We must live in the now, perhaps she is right?"

Darting a look of utter contempt to Altarium, Queen Mika folds her hands behind her back and walks toward the full screen monitor and watches the dark of space and the occasional stars dart past the ship in peripheral view along the way.

As she stands before the screen she does her best to envision what will take place; however, only sees a new threat amongst the Ares tribe, and can vaguely read his mind. His powers grow strong. She understands that her confrontation will not be without incident, and wishes that she had brought her war Lady Sister along for the confrontation which will take place soon.

"I've intercepted a transmission from an ancient one Alterium, who has left the Andromeda system with Queen Mika of Insuranious in pursuit of the folklore legend General Satan from our planet. The transmission describes that they're in literal contact with one of his lieutenants 'Leviathan'. He claims they're in the 'Milky Way' galaxy, and on a planet called 'Earth'. And they're checking the source of this claim now. I don't understand why an Insuranian well beyond our mental capabilities would endeavour researching a folklore, nor do I understand why I am being blocked from accessing information on either of them?"

"Great follow me in here we can speak more candidly." Zthorox says placing his hand on the back of Ereh to guide him into an empty conference room.

"It's so strange Zthorox. Literally all information on the Insuranian Mika is classified. I know at one point we used their planet as a base of operations, historians state there was some malpractice with our soldiers and they faced the death penalty for it. But I am not able to find out any information about her, Satan, Leviathan, or others in that time era. I should have clearance to access that information, so why don't I?"

"Come inside this board room. No one is in here just keep your voice down. Who else have you told about this?"

"I haven't told any except for you.

"I see. You do realise how strange this sounds pursuing a folklore 'Satan', and 'Leviathan'. Can you tell me about this transmission you received again in full detail."

Ereh chuckles. He understands how silly it sounds. He sits on a chair in the boardroom offered by Zthorox and proceeds to repeat the story.

Zthorox snaps Eher's neck, and then jabs a knife into his skull while holding his head tight, waiting for Ereh to finish convulsing before letting go. There is no transference of power. While Zthorox was looking forward to the rush of power surging through his body, he is thankful that the transference did not happen so that he can wipe down the blade, and door handles, and look for any evidence that he was there and remove it from the crime scene before anyone notices Ereh's body.

He reaches into his pocket after wiping down the room and pulls out his communication device "Swar it is Zthorox. I have confirmation that General Satan is alive. Gather the others, it is time to commence Operation Overlord."

Covering his face, Ethelwulf crashes on the rocks below. His bones break and snap like twigs all at once from the impact. Pain sears throughout his body, and the shock of the impact on the rocks sends him in and out of consciousness. His friend Drake dies immediately.

Each time Ethelwulf wakes, he wonders if he will soon meet the same fate as Drake, wondering if his battle with Bancroft was a stroke of luck, seeing that he had survived that battle.

Yet, as he lays motionless for several hours, and as night passes and turns into day, and day turns into night, he feels his bones reconnecting and his body rejuvenating in the same manner they would when his father beat him and would break his bones.

The next night he is feeling completely regenerated. He grips onto a rock and helps himself up. He wonders how he healed so quickly, moreover, he wonders how he survived another fatality. He wonders who or what he is. Perhaps everyone is right about him. Perhaps he is in leagues with the Devil. Ethelwulf sits down upon the stone, and begins to contemplate everything that has been taking place.

He is absolutely fine, as if nothing took place, yet the body of his friend sprawled out on the rock beside him gives Ethelwulf that unfriendly reminder that everything that he remembers took place a few nights ago. Ethelwulf stares at the corpse of his friend. Drake's eyes are open yet, they are staring back at him as lifeless as the rock Ethelwulf is sitting on.

Rising to his feet, Ethelwulf walks towards Drake's body and swats the flies circling around Drake's body. This is the only person that was friendly towards him aside from his wife and son. Ethelwulf closes Drake's eyes and grabs his body.

After a few hours, Ethelwulf buries Drake's body under a mound of rocks pebbles and anything else that he can get a hold of to place on top of his friend's body. "My friend, I will fight these Christians until I have destroyed each and every last one of them. Each time I strike at them I shall honour our kinship and take on thy name 'Dragon the Goth'. They will see the fierce anger of the Dragon within me as I lash out at them. I shall leave thee now but thou shalt always be remembered by me in my fight against these savages! Wherever thou art, my friend, I hope thou shalt find peace, and if ye are in heaven..." Ethelwulf looks up to the dark night's sky as if he was looking towards Drake in the heaven's. "Take heaven over. Impale God's head and leave it on a stake for all the cherubim and angels to see!"

A few of the village teens are hanging out together, talking about the current events that happened over the course of the last few days. Some do not believe it was morally right to burn the little boy Cynric, to death, however they did not feel anything for the mother and father who were killed. Of course, they had their reasons against Ethelwulf, as Palmyra is the one who is responsible for raising him from infancy and as young children, she told them about the horrors of Ethelwulf rising from the dead and being taken away by Lucifer.

Some children did not believe her stories. Yet, when they saw Ethelwulf first hand they all cringed in fear, all the more so when he killed off some of the Britannian soldiers. As the teens continue speaking with each other, one of them notices a stranger walking towards their village, which was kind of strange to see, as hardly anyone traveled to their village at night. As the man nears, they realise the stories about Ethelwulf, which used to frighten them all as children are true. Ethelwulf has risen from the dead.

Some of the teens run away to the old burned down church that has been abandoned for years. Some of the teens flee to their homes screaming, and others flee to the forest so that they can keep their eyes on whatever it is that the ghost of Ethelwulf or Ethelwulf himself is about to do. The remaining teens watch Ethelwulf walk to the stakes where witches burned. Ethelwulf takes his time to bury his wife and child's remains.

Palmyra rushes out of her home armed with a crucifix in one hand and her late husband's sword in her other hand. "Thou hast killed my husband; thou hast murdered my daughter. Now I shall smite thee."

Ethelwulf turns around snarling at the frail old woman, as he was in the midst of burying his family. The anger and rage that wells within him is the fiercest anger he has ever felt in his life, a thousand fold what he ever felt for Jacob.

"I rebuke thee in the name of Christ! May the power of Christ repel thee!"

Ethelwulf imagines that silly little crucifix of hers in flames. *The fused pieces of wood wrapped together by fine ropes burning on fire.* He wills it as strong as the times he would will his pains to go away when he was younger. With his uncontrollable rage mixing in with his dark, strange, magical power, the wooden crucifix in his mother-in-law's hand erupts in flames.

Palmyra screams in pain as the scorching heat from the crucifix causes her to drop the crucifix. She stares at Ethelwulf, the man she feels is responsible for the deaths of her husband and daughter. She lifts her late husband's sword and takes a step to her unarmed son-in-law. She feels no love for him, and does not care if he was in the midst of burying her own daughter; she takes another step towards him, "I shall save thee from the Devil Ethelwulf. I will bring thee to the graces of God, may he have mercy on thy soul!"

Ethelwulf slightly turns his head to the side as he watches the cautious old woman approaching him, the same woman that used to tend to his wounds as he was a child. Ethelwulf stretches his hand out and telekinetically wills the sword free of her hand and into his. Palmyra stares with fright and disbelief as she watches Ethelwulf holding her sword now.

Ethelwulf stares at the sword for a second, and remembers what his wife asked him years ago, and the promise that he made to her. Facing the trembling old lady, he speaks calmly to her as he continues to semi-glance at the sword in his hand. "Years ago I had promised thy daughter that I would not strike thee down. I promised Annex that I would not strike down thy husband either. She said I could kill either of ye only if it was in self-defence. I did not break my vow unto her. Bancroft attacked me and I killed him, yet as I stand before thee I am still reminded of the promise I had made unto her, not to strike thee down."

Palmyra let out a sigh of relief as Ethelwulf calmly speaks to her more. Although she hates him, she will do her best to remain calm and sweet talk him like that night in the barn when she last saw him. If he spares her again, she will do her best to try and kill him in future.

Ethelwulf takes a few steps closer, "Yet as I stand here before thee and I am committed to my vow that I made unto her all those years ago, I feel I was a different person then. I was Ethelwulf, a man that did not know who I was, scared of the likes of ye Christians, beaten down by the likes of ye Christians and still I, Ethelwulf remained loyal unto this vow, this vow that was Ethelwulf's, and now I see no reasons why I should obey this promise. Ethelwulf died that night he watched his wife die and beheaded his son to save him from the agony of the flames. On that night that Ethelwulf died, a new man was born, a man that now understands his destiny, a man who is not Ethelwulf."

Ethelwulf's voice begins to change. He growls as he speaks to Palmyra. She begins to shake with fear as he speaks, "My fierce anger towards ye Christians is like that of the wrath of the Dragons. Ethelwulf is dead. I am Dragon the... I am Dragon... Dagoth. Aye, I am Dragon Dagoth! I am the Devil, for there is no man the likes of me. I cannot die and I am no man of God. I ask where is thy God? Yea, I say unto thee I am thy God. Aye, I am both thy Devil and thy God; either way I am not bound by that promise!"

Growling Dragon Dagoth swings his sword back and around his head and brings it down penetrating and slicing through Palmyra's skull. Her blood splashes out of her head as the sword sliced right down the middle of her face.

Dragon Dagoth savours each bloody moment he holds the sword, watching Palmyra violently twitch and shake at the end of his sword as she dies. Dragon Dagoth growls and screams out loud as he blocks the memories of everything that has taken place in his life, even that of his family, then he lets go of the sword.

Palmyra's lifeless body thumps to the ground and Dragon Dagoth turns to leave the village, hopefully to never return again for as long as he lives.

The children walk over to Palmyra's lifeless body sprawled out on the ground. They hug and kiss her while mourning her loss. A cry is snuffed out and there is a bit of commotion heard behind some of the children. A large man, dressed in a dark black cloak stands before them with his fingers wrapped around a seven year old child's throat, holding him aloft for all the other children and teens to see.

He had just finished informing the soldiers at one of Satan's cabins that if any being comes around to kill him, his plan is to destroy this potential threat from taking the world over and then to get his transference of power from the others, and then destroy Satan, and rule Earth by himself until he is able to return to Ares and rule.

"There is a man who doeth magic that came here. Whither art this man?"

"We knoweth not whither he sped, only that he hath come here, sire," a teen answered.

In fierce anger, Leviathan crushes the little child's neck and tosses him to the ground, "I will slaughter all of ye until I know whither he has gone."

"Leviathan!" Belial screams out, "Is it us that ye searcheth for, harm not the innocent,"

Snapping his fingers, another child ignites in flames and falls to the floor curling in a foetus position screaming in agony as the flames engulf her.

"He was tossed off a cliff, sire. He is dead; please leave us alone!" cries out another child.

Belial uses his magic to extinguish the flames on the poor innocent child and then looks to Leviathan. Lucifer and Joshua materialise from thin air and stand next to Belial. So far his plan is unfolding, and he will take their powers from them all.

Together all three of them use their powers against Leviathan and they all appear in a remote location far away from anyone else, as they read his thoughts and know that they are about to do battle. So in order to protect the children, they materialise in a wooded forest. This is where the Devils plan to battle.

Several centuries have passed since the murder of his family. During this time, Ethelwulf has travelled around Britannia, in search of the source of his mysterious power. He feels that there is more to know than the bits and pieces that he has already figured out for himself. Ethelwulf assumes that the source of his power came from his parents. And seeing that his mother was killed centuries ago, he had been searching for years for his father, knowing that if he has this bizarre blessing or curse of eternal life, then surely his father would have his unique abilities as well, or maybe be like him and not know the source whence they came.

He initially began his quest, searching nearby cities, towns and villages for his father close to where he grew up. Some people spoke of a man named Joshua that had strange powers. The tales were scanty and all he heard was that Jacob left to serve the Romans before the Roman occupation ended in Britannia.

Perhaps his father lived in the shadows just as he once did with his family. Perhaps his father did not wish to have his powers discovered, just as Ethelwulf once did not. When asked what his name was, Dragon Dagoth felt it was best to use an alternate name when he was not lashing out against the Christians and decided that he would choose different names throughout the ages. For now he uses the name 'Abandoned', and feels this suits him best. For that is what he was, abandoned by his Father, and abandoned by his Mother for whatever her reasons were, and still even until this day, several centuries later he still hates her for what she put him through by abandoning him.

Abandoned has brief visits with each town or village that he passes through while he searches for clues to who his father is, or for any knowledge as to who or what he is. Some towns he visits he stays for a year, others for a few years, one or two cities he stayed in for over a decade and then left realising that others were questioning why he was not aging or never getting ill. He did not wish to have questions brought up in regards to his mysterious powers, and cause any trouble with the ever growing Christian population that was taking the world over. After years of searching and feeling unfulfilled in his quest, Abandoned takes to living in the forests, building homes for himself out of the public's sight.

Abandoned is a lonely old man, yet his complexion is that of a twenty year old man. He is still fit, strong and powerful, and he still has the agility of a young lad, even in the water's reflection he still has the appearance of a youth. He is depressed that he cannot find his father. There is so much he could learn from him. Perhaps he could even become more powerful than he is now, and if he becomes more powerful than he is now, he could avenge the deaths of his beloved wife and son. It is a long shot. There is no way that he can possibly kill each and every Christian for what they have done to his beloved family.

From time to time, Abandoned travels through the woods, discovering new places and trying to make new friends. The friends he usually makes are the beasts of the field. Strangely enough, they all seem to take a liking to him, and will silently acquaint themselves with him. Abandoned has become so familiar with the animals he can feel what they feel and can sense what they sense. It appears as if he was one with the animals, no matter how vicious any of them could get, and no matter how frail and frightened some of the others can be, he is still able to commune with them as if he is a part of their kind.

It is a shame that he feels the best type of company is spending time with the beasts of the field, as they are the only beings that take kindly to him, whereas nobody save his family and Drake the Goth ever paid him any mind unless it was or is to harm him. What an unbearable life, how could anyone live like this? Let alone live like this and not be able to die, and never grow old, eternal life seems more like a curse than a blessing. Eternal life is a curse.

Travelling through the forest, Abandoned senses some people in the distance. He senses an unusual amount of boredom from them. As he gets closer, not being able to see where they are, he senses that they know that he is coming. A great deal of panic began to surface in the forest. Still, Abandoned is unsure as to why these people have gone from an unusual amount of boredom to a terrible state of frenzied emotions.

A sound of thunder echoes throughout the forest, startling the birds and other animals and a howling sound of wind hisses by Abandoned's head. That was no wind, Abandoned thinks to himself and then the same noise of thunder echoes throughout the forest once again. This time, Abandoned stumbles backwards.

The wind seems to be sucked right out of him. He is in a daze and short of breath, and feels like a solid iron club struck him. Abandoned slowly rises to his feet. The same noise of thunder rumbles across the forest once again, and Abandoned drops to the ground again. This time he does not get up.

Abandoned hears a couple of people rushing through the forest speaking in Russian. He is not familiar with their dialect. Limply using what strength he has, Abandoned grabs his chest and feels where the pain is coming from. Blood is all over his hand as he lifts it back up. *What just happened? What was going on?* Several more thoughts flood Abandoned's mind as he continues to lie on the ground in agony. He closes his eyes, and then opens them. He notices the most strange-clothed men he has ever seen in his life.

One of the men pulls out a weapon that is unfamiliar to him. It is a handgun and he opens fire, point blank at Abandoned's chest. The Russian is satisfied with making sure his assassination is complete, and he digs a hole and tosses Abandoned's lifeless body in the grave, and covers it back up.

"He's General, okay. He says President Ivanov wants us to kill everyone who comes around here, we kill everyone who comes around here, okay?" Sasha says.

"No, it's not okay. General or no, he not President, okay," Vladimir counters Sasha after taking another shot of vodka. Wiping the burn away from his lips and swallowing hard, he continues, "The President came to us, we follow his orders. Now we disobey, how will this look?"

"I don't care, job is done. We get paid, we go home."

As the evening settles in, Abandoned coughs up some of the dirt that he inhaled. Sitting up in the mounds of dirt that were piled on him, he notices a bright light in the distance. The lights were inside of the cabin in the distance. The cabin appears to be well constructed. He doesn't know whether or not his eyes were playing tricks on him but one thing is for certain, the people inside of the cabin tried to kill him. He needs to know who they are and why they tried to kill him.

Keeping low, Abandoned rushes over towards the cabin with his sword drawn. The closer he gets, he can hear quite a few people inside the cabin. Peering in through the corner of one of the windows, it isn't the strangely dressed men that catch his attention. It isn't their strange dialect of Russian either, nor the strange weapon that he was shot with. It is several different pieces of equipment that are inside the cabin. There is nothing inside of the cabin that he can properly identify.

Sitting down on the grass against the wall of the cabin, Abandoned begins to wonder where he is. He begins to question his reality. Is this what he has been searching for all this time? Are these people inside the cabin the answers to what he is looking for? There is only one way to find out.

Rushing around the corner of the cabin to the door, Abandoned opens the door using his telekinetic power, startling all the men inside as he rushes in. They reach for their weapons as he rushes in. Using his will power Abandoned flings all of the weapons to the floor by the sheer thought of wanting it to happen and slices the first person he reaches across the throat with his sword. Jumping on the table, he shoves his blade through the chest of another person, killing him in an instant.

One of the last two Russians jumps out of his chair and grabs his gun on the floor. When he tries picking it up, he notices the other half of his arm on the ground, blood hissing out of his veins. Abandoned takes his sword and shoves it through the man's face. There is only one Russian left inside the cabin.

The last of the Russians opens fire on Abandoned, shooting him repeatedly, dropping the massive warrior who breached their cabin. Perhaps if they were not drunk they would have caught the oversized warrior on one of the camera feeds. Sobering up rather quickly, the remaining Russian rushes over to Abandoned's body. It was then that he realises he shot this man with his sniper rifle earlier in the afternoon.

He is still uncertain, still wondering if his mind is playing tricks on him, or if he is beyond drunk at the moment. However, the bodies of his comrades all sprawled across the floor of the cabin, dead, gives him a grave reminder that his mind is not playing tricks on him. Staggering backwards, he could have sworn that he saw the person on the floor earlier during the daytime. This is just a testament to himself that he needed to stop drinking.

In the blink of an eye, Abandoned jumps to his feet and kicks the gun out of his hand and grabs him by the throat, raising him high in the air. He is gagging by the might of this warrior's strength as the fingers close like vice grips around his throat. Eventually he passes out.

The sunlight rays beam through the trees of the forest and into the cabin, and like usual, Sasha grabs his pillow and puts it over his eyes to block out the sun and turns over to sleep his hangover off.

Unaccustomed to the silence in the cabin and not having one of his partners kick him to wake up and get ready for his shift, Sasha calls out to his partner, "Why are you so quiet this morning, huh?"

"I have slain thy friends. Dost thou speak my language?"

Sitting up in a frantic daze, Sasha looks around the room to see his friends dead on the floor, and on a chair less than a few feet away, is the man he swore he had killed the other day. Quickly glancing around the room, Sasha cannot not see any weapons.

"Ah, thou lookest for thy weapon? I have it. Such an impressive tool, truly magnificent. What is it?"

This has never ever happened to any of the teams sent back to the past before. Each team that was sent back to the past is the best of the best, the most elite fighting soldiers trained in all of Russia, and to be defeated by such an oaf, such a pre-historic member of the human race was beyond all comprehension.

"Dost thou speak in my tongue?"

"A little," Sasha replies in English gazing at the man as he holds onto one of the hand-held guns, staring at it as if it was the greatest thing in the world.

Abandoned nods his head then looks at the strangely dressed man, but then again everything save the wood of the cabin is strange to Abandoned. The only thing that he can make any sense of within the room is the weapon in his hand. He understands this is the greatest weapon in the world. "My Lord... what is all this?"

Sasha wonders how he is going to explain this to his superiors. They were the most elite soldiers and to have three of the most elite members killed, his superiors will definitely suspect foul play. But fortunately there is the surveillance footage. Sighing while trying to figure out how he is going to kill this stranger, he responds to the man, "It is an experiment."

Abandoned senses the man is lying, and then reads his thoughts to confirm this, yet he nods as if he was impressed with what he had to say. He also senses the man is plotting a way to kill. He can feel this man is an experienced assassin. "Aye, indeed. What kind of experiment?"

Careful conjuring up a story, the Russian chooses his words carefully so as not to be careless and give the stranger too much information, "We are at war, yes. This is to help the war, uh huh. For your sake I suggest... that you leave before the others come, with better weapons than what you are holding... of course."

Although Abandoned can understand the Russian, his dialect of English is strange as well. Abandoned reads thoughts and sees images inside of the man's mind. He can see the man's loved ones inside a strange house. He can see a strange surrounding and a city that not even his imagination could conjure up. Freeing himself from the Russian's mind, Abandoned quietly tries to comprehend everything. Standing up from his chair he walks over to some of the machines and continues to look around.

"What is this that I hold?"

"That is a gun."

"And this? Over here, this strange thing that keeps the food in here cold?"

"A refrigerator."

"Ah... and this?" Abandoned points to something on the counter in the kitchen.

As Abandoned turns around to point to the item on the counter in the kitchen, Sasha grabs a dagger he normally keeps at the head of his bed post and tucks it up his sleeve, "A microwave."

Nodding without caring what a microwave is, Abandoned looks over the strange complexity of the cabin again, and then walks over to a rather intricate looking piece of machinery that seems to be the centre of attention inside the cabin. Everything in the room revolves around this device. He opens its door, "And this?"

Sasha thinks of a quick way to kill this stranger. If this stranger survives knowing what he does now, it will have a profound effect on the future, not to mention that if an inspection team from the future suspects anything happening, they will come back and kill them both, "Ah yes that, well... "

Abandoned points the gun towards Sasha's head as Sasha starts to walk towards him, "Drop thy dagger!"

Sasha stops dead in his tracks. There is no way this stranger saw him place the dagger up his sleeve, nonetheless, he smiles and obeys. "Sorry old habit, I apologize."

Taking another step while trying to think of what to do next, Sasha begins to answer Abandoned's question, "It is a time machine..."

Abandoned stretches out with his mind while aiming the gun at Sasha's head. As he stretches out with his mind he feels in control, and one with Sasha and drops the man to his knees by mere thought and will power.

Mouth wide open, Sasha falls to the ground trying to shake off the invisible control that Abandoned has over him, frightened to death of what is going on. Sasha blames everything that is happening on his hangover.

"Thou shalt speak unto me, divulging all thy knowledge that thou hast on this time machine!"

Looking up, Sasha slowly begins to realise by the look in Abandoned's eyes that he has some magical control over him, and there is nothing that he can do to stop it. Sasha agrees to tell Abandoned everything about the time machine, figuring it will not matter if this person knows, as when he travels to the future others at the base will kill him.

Sasha tells Abandoned everything from the beginning about time travel, telling him about the scientific theories on time travel, and then from the theories to possibilities, and then on to the secret experiments, all of which is heavily promoted by the Russian President Taras Ivanov.

Sasha explains that he does not know why anyone is being sent to isolated parts of the past, however, he informs Abandoned that they are waiting for further orders which will come directly from their president. His cabin has not received any orders yet. Sasha even shows Abandoned a list of the countries where other time machines are. It does not matter if he shows the stranger anything because if he travels to any of these places he will be killed.

It is a lot of information to take in at first. Although Abandoned can understand everything that Sasha is saying, what he says seems way too unreal. It is as if Sasha is imagining everything, however, the evidence is rather compelling as he has the technology from the future right there in the same room. "I am going to have to smite thee if I am to journey unto the future?"

"Even if you do, in a couple of years people will be sent back in time to take over our shifts, realize that we are all dead and call it in, but that won't even matter... no. By the time you get to the future there will be a new shift here and they will shoot you down, yes? Your best bet is to stay here and live long until you die. No one will know who you are and you live peacefully, yes? Why get killed?"

Abandoned nods his head then looks deep into Sasha's eyes, and growls his next words out slowly and clearly, "I am the Devil Dragon Dagoth. I cannot die!"

Sasha snorts out an inward chuckle and shakes his head, feeling that his captor surely needs help. Dragon Dagoth pulls the trigger and executes Sasha. Without feeling an ounce of care about what he did. Dragon Dagoth stares at the gun with fascination. *Unbelievable how such a tiny tool has such a devastating impact. This has the power of a club, the effect of an arrow and the speed of lightning. This gun can kill the greatest of warriors in combat*, he thinks to himself as he stares at a fine mist of smoke coming from the barrel of the gun. "Ha ha," Dragon Dagoth chuckles, smiling at his new toy.

He is convinced now even more than before that he has to go to the future to see what it holds in store for him. Taking off his garments, Dragon Dagoth changes into one of the large soldier's clothing and puts his clothing on the dead soldier. He needs to dress like the people of the future if he is to go there so he can remain undetected. Grabbing one of the assault rifles Dragon Dagoth walks over to the time machine and programs it fifty years before the technology came out, setting the date for 1983. After entering all the information, there is a slight blackout inside the machine. A cloud of dust billows around the machine making Dragon Dagoth cough. He can hear some rustling noises outside of the door but he thinks nothing of it, thinking it may have been just squirrels. Opening the door, Dragon Dagoth is startled to see four more individuals waiting with their guns drawn towards him.

"Get down on the fucking ground. Drop your weapon!" one of the soldiers yells at him in Russian.

Looking at all the men aiming their weapons at him, Dragon Dagoth raises his. Before he opens fire he sees sparks of ammunition coming from their guns as they open fire at him. There is no pain. He just feels like he is being struck with a boulder repeatedly as they continue to shoot him. In haste, Dragon Dagoth returns fire, shooting each of the men before him, and then collapses to one knee gasping for air.

Unbelievable, Dragon Dagoth thinks to himself as he looks at his wounds. He did not go through the experience of dying like all the other times, and he should have died like the other times. He then starts to feel the pain searing through his body as if it is a thousand hot coals burning his insides up. Yet he is still conscious.

Growling out in pain, Dragon Dagoth lets go of his gun and does his best to block the pain. The lights in the cabin begin to flicker at the immense power emanating from Dragon Dagoth as he growls, metal pans hit the floor and the noises echo in the cabin. Dragon Dagoth feels a weird sensation coming over his body. His pain is disappearing.

Looking at his body he watches the bullet holes close up. *Travelling to the future intensified my powers,* he thinks as he looks at his body and can no longer feel the pain of the bullets nor can he see any of the wounds.

Dragon Dagoth reaches for one of the assault rifles on the floor, and then leaves the cabin. He is filled with disappointment initially on leaving the cabin. Nothing has changed at all. Everything is the same as before he stepped inside the 'time machine'. Taking a few steps out of the cabin, Dragon Dagoth looks around. There are no fancy buildings that Sasha mentioned. There is no horseless carriages he boasted about. Nothing at all!

"He hath borne false witness unto me, liar!" he yells to himself, and then leaves for home in a fit of rage. After walking a few miles, Dragon Dagoth is not able to find the paths to his home. He must have lost his way. Each turn he makes through the forest is a step in the wrong direction.

Dragon Dagoth hears a thunderous growling noise approaching him, and attempts to use his senses to spot the danger, but he is not able to. The ground is starting to shake because of the beast's growling noises.

Dragon Dagoth holds his gun steady and looks in every direction possible for the beast, and then he sees the beast and drops his gun in awe. The beast is in the air. Running for cover Dragon Dagoth hides inside a bush so that he will not be detected by the enormous beast that flew across the sky. The beast soars gracefully across the sky and does not flap its wings, while growling all the way. He notices a trail of smoke behind the beast and assumes it to be a real dragon, and then just like that, it flies to one of the corners of the earth.

His heart slows its frantic pacing. Once he feels that he is safe, he picks up his gun and continues his journey, contemplating how he has never seen a real live dragon until now. His thoughts are quickly interrupted as he leaves the forest and now is in a clearing. Everything is different. There are no more dirt roads. The dirt roads are asphalt. No one is riding horses; they are driving cars. Dragon Dagoth notices a building across the street that matches Sasha's depictions of the future, which is now the present. The only thing that Dragon Dagoth recognises is the trees in the forest behind him. Even the people walking to and fro look different as well as their clothing.

After having a split second vision, Dragon Dagoth realizes carrying his weapon around with him will get him into trouble. Tossing the gun aside, he walks down the street and alongside the road.

There are several buildings around him. He shrugs his shoulders and laughs out of frustration. He has no idea where he is, but guesses that the building is some sort of marketplace.

Someone blasts their car horn at him as he carelessly walks through the parking lot. He jumps back several feet alarmed at the noise of the vehicle, "Crikey mate, are you going to move?!"

He is startled out of his wits, and decides to move aside and watches the car speed away from the mall's driveway. Shrugging his shoulders, Abandoned decides to investigate the inside of the building. Once inside his eyes have a hard time adjusting to the unnatural lights inside the mall, and he shields his eyes. He watches people scurry through the mall, as he walks by some shops, nearly choking at the scent of perfumes coming from some of the stores.

Clothing, shoes and junk... this is what future holds unto me.

"Excuse me, sir."

Dragon Dagoth turns around and notices a few people greeting him with smiles, and holding some books. He nods his head in response to them.

"Are you lost?"

"Aye, as I matter of fact I know not where I am."

Their smiles are heart-warming and pleasant to look at, yet, something feels off about them as he continues to glare at them.

"A lot of us are lost, my friend; but did you know our father can help you. Through his wisdom you can become a part of our great family in his kingdom."

Taking a step back, he understands why they are all smiles and looking at him strangely. "I lust after women not unto the likes of men. Take thy desires elsewhere."

A couple of the men adjust their ties because of Dragon Dagoth's assumptions about them, trying not to get too agitated at what the tall muscular stranger is insinuating they are. The spokesman speaks again, "Umm no brother, we like women as well. Homosexuals are evil, and lust is not healthy. In fact it is a sin. Our father does not like it when we lust after anything."

These people are definitely strange. He also loathes these riddles the men are giving him as it reminds him of his father Jacob.

"How would you like a chance at living eternally, forever?"

"Ye knowest of such things?!" This must be it; everything he ever dreamed of was happening this very minute. They must know his father, they must really be brothers. Dragon Dagoth's heart begins to race frantically.

He has waited for this very moment for centuries.

"O why yes of course. It sounds as if you already know what I am talking about. You speak as if you read and live the bible."

Dragon Dagoth shakes his head. He does not have the slightest clue how to read, but if it means learning about his roots, then perhaps he will have these fine gentlemen help him read, or have one of his brother's bring him to his father if he is still alive. "Nay, I do not know of how to read. Ye hath knowledge on eternal life? Ye art my 'brothers'?"

"Well, have you heard of our Lord and saviour Jesus Christ, through him all... aaargh"

This was not something he expected at all, nor had something like this ever happened in all his days of spreading the word of God. He had never been attacked at all before, and here he is, dangling a few feet from the ground doing his best to pry free the vice grip of Dragon Dagoth's fingers from his throat.

His friends rush to his aid but Dragon Dagoth knocks them away as if he were swatting flies. They are no match for his brutal strength.

"Let go of him! You are going to kill him," someone shouts in the mall as a crowd starts to gather around Dragon Dagoth who is letting his rage out on the frail man, squeezing the man's neck, feeling the man's last breaths coming to an end, and his bones starting to pop as he squeezes harder.

"Thou hast murdered my family. Thou hast murdered my child, now I shalt taketh thy life!"

"I –I never... I never killed... your... aah."

He tosses the Christian on the ground, his chest heaving in and out. He grits his teeth, while staring at the defenseless man who is gasping for air and writhing on the floor in agony.

His friends grab him and tend to his needs as they drag him off to safety.

"Someone call the police. This man is crazy! Someone go into a store and call the police," a person shouts in the midst of the crowd that is gathering around the commotion.

Dragon Dagoth runs out of the mall, through the parking lot and continues to run until he feels he will not be found.

It is late at night and the cool of the night's air is a little too much for Dragon Dagoth. He tosses and turns on the small park bench that he found earlier that night, trying his best to sleep. He feels a jab at his side that is as annoying as it is persistent.

Opening his eyes, he notices a couple of people dressed in uniform. He already knows what futuristic soldiers look like, so he has no clue who these two strangers are, yet he senses that they have authority. It is a man, eight or so inches shorter than he is, and a woman about a couple of feet shorter than he is.

"You're not allowed to be sleeping here, vagrant. Do you have your papers?"

Tired and groggy, Dragon Dagoth rubs his eyes, trying to focus. He does not understand why he is not able to sleep, and is not happy about these strangers waking him up. "I am tired."

"You're not allowed to be sleeping here, do you have any papers on you?!" the man said using a firmer tone of voice.

"I doth not have 'papers'."

The man reaches for his arm and tries to yank him off of the bench. Still half asleep, Dragon Dagoth pushes the man back a few paces. In retaliation the man rushes towards Dragon Dagoth, armed with his baton and strikes him with it.

Dragon Dagoth is more experienced at melee than the police officer. He leaps off the bench and grabs the man's arm in mid swing, and punches the man in his face, knocking him unconscious, and then punches him a few more times in his face for good measure.

Dragon Dagoth turns around, startled by the sound of clicking noises from the other police officer who cocks her gun and aims it at him. "I have no quarrel with either of ye!"

"Raise your hands and get on the ground now!"

There is no way that he could get to the officer and disarm her before she shoots him. He glares at her while she yells at him to obey her orders. He notices that she has a striking resemblance to his deceased wife, Annex. Dragon Dagoth lowers his head and his knotted hair falls down to his chest as he falls into a mild depression.

"Thou hast the graces of my wife Annex," Abandoned says, barely above a whisper.

Tears begin to fill his eyes as he tries to remember some of the good times that he had with his wife and child before he was drafted off to battle. However, the only memories that are surfacing is when he was burying her charred remains along with their son Cynric, whom he had to behead to save him from the eternal pain that he would have endured had he let him stay alive.

The lady cautiously approaches Dragon Dagoth, continuing to bark orders at him.

There is no way that he can bring himself to strike down the lady as she continues to inch her way closer, and no matter how much he can feel that she is a threat to him, he remains well mannered, "I will not strike thee down."

"Listen, asshole. I am the one with the gun, now get down on the fucking ground, mate."

Dragon Dagoth closes his eyes. He feels himself becoming one with the police officer. He reads her thoughts. He feels what she feels. He is becoming one with her. Using his will power, he forces her to her knees and then wills the gun out of her hands and into his.

The officer screams in sheer terror, loud enough to wake the other officer. Dragon Dagoth approaches the lady officer, and aims his new gun at the other officer. Without looking, he uses his power to focus in on the other officer and shoots him in the head.

"Please, I am a married woman. I have children. Please don't hurt me!"

He has no intention of hurting the woman. He is beginning to mistake her for his wife. No matter how many centuries have come and gone, he will never get over the death of his beloved Annex.

"Aye, I shall not harm thee."

"You know you just killed an officer of the law. If you turn yourself in, I can ask for lenience from the courts."

The lady is petrified, she is not able to move and in the midst of her fright she tries her best to understand how her gun flew out of her hand and into his. The invisible hands release their hold on her.

Jumping to her feet, she takes a few paces back from the man who has her gun and who slowly approaches her.

"Please let me go if you're not going to turn yourself in. Please don't hurt me."

"I need thee. I shall not harm thee. I need food and shelter. Take me to thy dwelling.'

"Why are you talking like that?"

"I knoweth not thy tongue, nor am I from thy time; now let us journey unto thine home for I am famished."

"I don't think so!" The lady responds in a stern voice, gaining back some of her self-confidence and nearly forgetting he killed her partner a few moments ago.

"Do not thou forget that 'I' am the one 'with the gun'."

Swallowing hard, she turns around and nods, and then leads the way to her police car. As they drive down the street, she debates whether she should take him to the police station and risk getting killed or take the stranger to her home and call for backup.

"What is thy name?"

"Gavrilovich, Gav for short."

As they continue to drive down the streets, she asks him a question that has been bugging her since they unfortunately met, "So how in the world did you get my gun from me? I wasn't daydreaming. I am no criminal. I don't do drugs. I hardly drink. I just can't help but continue to wonder how you got my gun and then you killed my partner. What the hell, mate. Crikey! Wasn't it good enough that you knocked him out? No damnit, you had to kill my partner and good friend... Fuck you okay. Just... just fuck you alright! What now?! Are you going to take me to my place and fucking rape and kill me? I don't have a husband and kids alright! There, I fucking lied to you okay. You're going to find out anyways. You know what, I don't fucking care, why - why should I? Fuck, just tell me what you want?!"

Dragon Dagoth squirms in the seat, noticing foul use of words to a man. No women speak like this. This is not something he is accustomed to, but that does not matter. The main thing is she is terrified of him. He has no intentions of harming her. It had been days on end since he had- had anything to eat and this is his only intention, to eat.

"I mean thee no harm, indeed."

"Fuck, just stop it, you fucking twit. Fucking speak normally, for fuck's sake. You sound like some primitive out of a medieval novel and it is pissing me off, for fuck sakes! God, you smell like you haven't bathed in years. You speak like a retard and you killed my partner, fuck. Just fuck... fuck... fuck... fuck!" Gav beats her hand on the steering wheel so hard it becomes numb. "What the fuck do you want with me, really?"

Still squirming in the seat, and feeling very uncomfortable with how upset Gavrilovich is, he tosses the gun out of the window "I mean thee no harm woman! Thine..."

"Fuck! Just fucking stop it, will you?!"

"Stop what?"

"Speaking like a retard, for fuck sakes. What is wrong with you?!"

"I knoweth not the words of thy tongue, nor do I speakest thine words, yet, I understand what thou sayest unto me. I know not what 'fuck' or 'fucking' means or half the other words that roll off thy tongue. Ye people should know of our words a little better seeing it has be thine people that hath travelled through time."

"Oh. Fucking great, Jules Vern!"

Gavrilovich slams her foot on the brakes as she drives in front of her house. "We're here!" Gavrilovich mutters as she opens her car door, slamming it shut as she storms off to her house.

Dragon Dagoth follows behind her to the house. Once inside, Dragon Dagoth is mesmerized by the beauty of her place. Everything in this new time zone is foreign to him. Everything seems so intriguing, as he looks around the house.

Gavrilovich watches her captor looking around the house. She feels uneasy about the murderer looking around. "You know I can get you help if you want? Do you take medication?"

Dragon Dagoth ignores her as he continues to inspect every inch of her place, taking in this new world as if he is born again. He opens the refrigerator and says, "I need a morsel to eat."

"Goddamn," Gav mutters as she grabs at various packets in the fridge and tosses various foods from them onto a plate, along with several bread slices. He tucks in fast.

"Okay, can you please level with me? After all, you at least owe me that much. What do you want with me?"

Dragon Dagoth turns around and faces Gav. He offers her a chance to sit down and chat with him. During the course of a few hours, he shares his life's story with her and the events that mattered most to him throughout the centuries.

At the initial part of the conversation, Gav feels the stranger is a lunatic, yet during the course of the conversation she cannot help but shake her head, as his story is rather convincing and seems so life like, as if the things he speaks of actually have taken place 'in the past'.

"So if you are really from the past and everything that you say is true, then you should have no problem taking me to this 'time machine' right?"

Dragon Dagoth shrugs his shoulders, "Aye, let us go."

This is not the answer Gav expected. Nonetheless, she can still use this moment to her advantage, "Alright, give me a few moments to get ready and we'll go alright."

"Aye."

As Dragon Dagoth sits at the table with a strange ale he found in the fridge, waiting for Gav, he senses danger is heading his way. He also feels Gav is responsible for the danger he feels from this vision.

"We must go now!" he yells for Gav up the stairs. There is no answer "We must depart woman! Dost thou not hear me?!"

"Yes, yes, yes. I am coming."

Dragon Dagoth senses Gav's mood has changed. He merges his mind with hers and uses his powers to find out where her sense of relief is coming from and why he is having visions of danger. He sees that she has summoned others to come to her rescue. In a fit of rage, he grabs Gav's arm and drags her to her car.

"Why are you in such a rush; you don't think that the 'time machine' will be there when we get there or something?"

Glaring hard at Gavrilovich, he refrains from smashing her head against the dashboard of the car. "Let us go!"

It didn't take that long for the couple to reach the area where he remembers the clearing in the woods that he left. Together, they walk through the woods and to the area that he remembers where the cabin is.

Gavrilovich follows closely behind her captor. As they walk inside of the cabin, she gags from the foul stench of cadavers in the cabin.

"You killed more people?!" Gavrilovich states as she takes a few steps back, looking at the dead bodies on the ground.

"I told thee of the most recent events leading up to our meet!"

Covering her nose, trying not to look down at the bodies, Gav walks over to Dragon Dagoth.

"As I stepped forth out of this machine, these men tried to slay me."

Gav looks at the bodies. A few of the men are still gripping on to their guns. She turns her head and looks at Abandoned, and then the machine that appears to have been shot in the gun fight.

"Hey, well since this is a time machine, let's go back to your time?"

This is the only way for her to see if Dragon Dagoth is telling the truth. *I can't believe I am here, let alone believing that*

there is a small chance this is a device that actually makes
people travel through time. Ha! Gav thinks to herself.

Remembering how Sasha had shown him how to
work the machine, he boots it up however, some of the
computer lights are not registering on the machine, and
parts of the machine begin to spark and smoke fills the
room.

"Prithee, help?" Dragon Dagoth asks Gav,
shrugging his shoulders.

Gavrilovich walks over to the machine and takes a
quick look at it, doing her best to figure out the switches
and everything else on it. "Well whatever it was, it's
broken now."

"Wilt thou be able to repair this machine?"

Gavrilovich laughs. She has no clue what this
machine is nor will she be able to fix it. "Umm no." After
a few minutes of debating on what she should do at this
point, she caves in and tells him, "I called for backup
while I was at home. They know everything, the fact that
you killed my partner and that you kidnapped me as
well. If we go back to my house together they will arrest
you on sight."

Dragon Dagoth slumps down to the ground. He is
dismayed, not that she called the authorities, but that the
time machine is broken. "I beg of thee woman to help
me; I have travelled through time in this contraption
which I did not believe to work as thine own self did not
believe either. Now I am burdened to live amongst ye
people in a time and place that is foreign unto me. Ye
must help me return! I shall use this machine to go back
in time further and even go to the time that my family
was slain that I may save them!"

A similar strange feeling creeps through Gav, and
begins to take control of her. It is the same type of feeling
she felt when she was controlled by her captor when he
kept her from moving with his sorcerer's ways. Her eyes

grow dark as if she is sleeping; yet, she is not sleeping. She starts to see a crowd chanting, sees a sword in her hand; she sees a child writhing in pain on a stake and a dead lady burned next to the child.

Objects in the cabin begin to shake, and she snaps free from the horrifying visions. She looks at Dragon Dagoth, his long matted hair dangling on the floor, his fists clenched on the floor, as he cries out.

Gav feels a bit of compassion for him. She walks over to him and he grasps her and cries more, while repeatedly uttering his son and wife's name through his sobs, "Annex! Cynric! Cynric! Annex!"

She wraps her arms around his massive muscular body as he weeps, "Alright mate, listen. I am sure we can find a way to get this thing to work. You have to remain here though, because if you come back with me now, you will be arrested. I will be back tomorrow. I will rent a truck as well and we can bring this machine back to my garage and I will look for someone who can help you."

Abandoned nods his head as he continues to grip onto Gavrilovich's leg and continues to mourn the loss of his beloved family.

6

"I did not think that ye would return, "Dragon Dagoth says as he walks away from the time machine to greet Gav.

She is relieved to notice the dead bodies are gone; yet, she feels ill to her stomach as she looks at the half eaten coyote on the floor. "What are you doing?"

"I want to go home. I must fix this... this 'thing'."

"I brought a truck. You can bring that with you and I will take you to my place, and then we can try and find someone to fix it."

After they return to her house, Dragon Dagoth stores the machine inside of Gavrilovich's garage. The following day, she gets him to clean himself up and brings him to a library so that her friend can teach him 'proper English'. She explains to Dragon Dagoth that he needs to keep his identity and his own life story, a secret.

She tells her friend that "Christopher" is an ex-boyfriend of hers, and he is suffering from amnesia after he was involved in an accident. She also explains that he only remembers dialect from when he used to perform in dramatic arts. She returns to work, leaving Dragon Dagoth with her friend at the library.

"I wish to know everything that has happened from fifteen hundred and those days of yore until now, and may'st thou pass on to me, thy knowledge with reading and writing."

"Do you want to learn anything in particular from the past? And yes of course I can help you with your reading and writing."

"Aye, everything. And I thank... 'you'."

The lady walks along the lengthy rows in the library, and reaches an assortment of old books. She takes a few books on England's history, and then walks over to the children's section and selects a few easy-to-read books. She returns to Dragon Dagoth who stares at the books in front of him. Only nobles know how to read. People like him are not able to read; in fact, he didn't know anyone save Jacob that knew how to read. He was glad that Gav has introduced him to Lisa so that she could teach him how to do so.

Throughout the weeks that follow, Lisa teaches Dragon Dagoth how to read, starting off with children's books and then teaches him how to do other things such as mathematics and science. His learning abilities are quite amazing and he soaks up each bit of information flawlessly.

Abandoned learns that the Roman Empire's commonwealth otherwise known as Britannia is now England, and England flourished as an Empire for centuries. It was a lot to take in but so is everything else in the present time period. He also learns how during the English rule, they killed countless numbers of people in the name of Christ.

During the few weeks, Gavrilovich helps Dragon Dagoth try and find parts for his machine. She does her best to figure out what the parts are, and researches how to find them with her friend Lisa, only to realize that these parts do not exist. Gav is realising that perhaps Dragon Dagoth is sincerely telling the truth. Or perhaps there are no books that have information on the components needed.

In his spare time at the library, Dragon Dagoth studies warlords and dictators, and learns about the ones that lived throughout the centuries. He takes a particular interest in some more than others: Washington, Stalin, Hitler, Taras Ivanov, the current leader of the Russian Empire, to name a few. He is amazed at how Britannia had become an Empire and became more powerful than Rome. England wiped out entire civilizations in the unknown Western world which is known as North America today.

He learns about Washington rising up against the British Empire and claiming independence from British control.

He learns about Canada and how they have remained loyal to England, and how the Warlord General Washington, proclaims himself the first President of the United States of America. Looking at the future from a past view is very mystifying. *How were such things possible?* Abandoned often wondered.

He also learns in this time the Christians gained a tremendous amount of power. They tortured and killed off anyone that was of a different faith or even of their faith; yet, believed in different tenets or killed others that were not of any particular faiths. He had even read some stories about himself that were considered to be the reasons why Christians became so frightened of Pagans and those who were thought to be in leagues with Lucifer. Yet, although it was later to be believed that he was just some sort folk legend, a boogeyman invented to scare children. He was one of the initial reasons why the Christians killed as many people as they did in a mass frenzy.

"Gavrilovich, read this story," he says.

She starts to read some of the story. It does not prove he was from the past, yet seems to match the vision that she had a few weeks ago, when she initially felt compassion for Dragon Dagoth, now known as Christopher. She is still not convinced that he is from the past and believes that he is conning her. She suspects that he is just using her so that he does not go to jail, because of the murders that she knows about. However, he fascinates her. Everything that he shares about his magical powers intrigues her very much, and he does prove his powers by demonstrating some of them to her which leads her to believe that he may in fact be telling the truth about his time travel, but still it still seems like a stretch of the imagination.

"Yeah, it seems similar to what you told me before. Is that what happened?"

"No, these stories are not accurate. Bancroft cut my throat. I was weak and fell to the ground. He thought he took me for near dead and figured I could not do anything. When he came over to finish me off, I placed my sword through his heart." Christopher pointed towards his neck showing her a slight scar. "I wasn't burned at the stake that day and Palmyra never lived to teach the children the values of Christianity until she had died. I killed her too."

Gav shakes her head. Killing seemed so natural for Christopher to talk about.

"I'm worried about something, Christopher."

"What's that?"

"If I ever got you upset or did something wrong to you, you would kill me without thinking twice about it, wouldn't you?"

Quite taken aback by what Gav just said, he moves closer to her and hugs her gently, "You have taught me so much within the last few months. Because of you, I have even learned to come to terms with the fateful afternoon my family died. Every day I see you I..." Taking his chance, Christopher leans forward and gently kisses Gav on her lips. Her lips are soft and gentle. He runs his fingers through her hair, and then before the passionate moment escalates, he pulls away, trying his best not to let his emotions get the better of him. "I wouldn't do anything to harm you."

"Thanks hun, you know I can tell when you're blocking your powers, but it doesn't hide the fact that I know you still miss your wife. Please don't get me caught up in your mixed emotions. That will not be good for either of us."

Christopher nods his head, acknowledging Gav's wishes while placing a frustrated smile across his face. Although he is starting to have feelings for Gav, he misses his wife and son, regardless of how many centuries have passed. Although they were dead and the chance of seeing them again is looking slimmer with each passing day, he still loves his family and thinks about nothing other than returning to them once his time machine is repaired, and he regrets not travelling to the past when he first had the opportunity to travel through time.

Rage and anger consumes Christopher with each passing day. His disposition to Christianity consumes him for what they have done to his family and he wonders how he will exact his revenge on the Christians. They have accumulated such power over the centuries he wonders how it will be possible to rid the world of them. Perhaps once this time machine is fixed he will be able to prepare a war against them. It is a long shot but still worth the thought. He considers George Washington, and how he fought the British, and claimed independence and slaughtered countless natives of that new land in order to establish America, and feels that perhaps with the proper amount of planning perhaps he too can use similar strategies to exterminate the Christians for what they did to his family.

As the weeks continue to pass, Christopher is fed up reading the countless stories of atrocities Christians have done. He sits at the desk in the library and veers off in deep thought. The table begins to shake and the lights above begin to swing back and forth. It is no earthquake. Christopher is fuelling his rage, and his dark-sided powers cause the bookshelves to rattle. Books begin to fall off some of the shelves.

Running around the library trying to get everyone to safety, Lisa's attention is diverted to Christopher who is not worrying about the earthquake happening. She sees that he is rather angry about something he is reading as she runs over to get him to safety. As she runs over to him, she feels a very dark and intense feeling surrounding her. Strangely, she feels this dark source is coming from Christopher; yet, it is only for a brief second that she thinks this and greets him and wraps her arms around him gently, saying, "Come on. We have to get to safety".

Christopher snaps out of his angry thoughts and shakes his head. He loosens his grip on the book, and the commotion stops, and everything stops shaking in the library.

Lisa is baffled. She thinks of that eerie feeling she had just moments ago, and associates everything with Christopher once again. Her mind starts to race. She does not recall Gavrilovich mentioning anything about an ex-boyfriend named Christopher. She also finds it strange that after Gav was kidnapped, this man appeared in her life. A chilling thought creeps through her mind; she has a hunch that Christopher is somehow linked to Gav's kidnapper.

Christopher snaps his head backwards and glares at her. Lisa puts her hand on her chest and wonders if she said that out loud. Too many strange things are happening around Christopher, she does not like what she thinks of him at all. "I don't feel that you have anything left to learn from me. If you want to continue learning, I would suggest going to school."

Feeling lightheaded, she does not feel comfortable being near Christopher, and leaves him to go to her office and sinks into a chair. Snapping back up in the chair, she grabs the phone and calls Gav at work. "Hey Gav, how are you today mate?"

"Not bad. Yourself?"

"Umm, alright. Listen, about your 'ex'. I want to talk to you about him."

"Yeah? What about him?"

"He's not your ex is he? If I could put my money on it, you're protecting the man who kidnapped you, aren't you?"

"Crikey Lisa, that is complete rubbish and I can't believe you would be so insensitive as to call me at work and bring something like that up to me. How dare you!"

There is a moment of silence over the phone. Lisa speaks more calmly and tries to not upset her hurt friend already more than she has done so. "He opened up about the incident and corrected himself in the middle of talking to me. I think you are in danger," she lies to see if her friend will give her information about Christopher.

There is another moment of silence. "Lisa, I am at work. I have a lot to do, I don't know what games you are playing but you must have misheard what Christopher was saying. Try asking him again."

"You can talk to me, Gav."

"I am at work; we will speak about this when I get off work. I will see you later, goodbye."

The ride home from the library is quiet, too quiet in fact. Normally Gav chats about her day's events, or speaks about anything in general.

"Why are you so quiet?" Christopher asks her.

"I think you know the answer to that."

"I was being polite and not trying to read your mind."

"That is not what I meant!"

"Spare me this woman crap of speaking and get on with it. Just tell why you are upset or I will read your mind."

"How could you, Christopher? What are we going to do if the police come looking for you?!"

"I don't understand what you are talking about."

"I think you do. How could you fuck up and tell Lisa about kidnapping me?"

"Oh, that."

"Yeah that!"

"I never mentioned anything to her, in fact I read her thoughts this afternoon, and she assumes that I have something to do with it. Should I kill her?"

Gavrilovich slams her hand against the steering wheel "No! She is my friend. God! And she even helped you out. Now you want to repay her by killing her?!"

Christopher leans back in his seat and the rest of the trip home, they do not say anything to each other.

After dinner, Gav breaks the uncomfortable silence. She does not bother looking at Christopher as she speaks to him as she is still upset. "I think whatever you came here in, was from the future. That is why I have not been able to locate the parts for the machine. Good news is I think I can find some people that may be able to help you fix that machine."

Christopher nods and reaches for the information that she has in her hand, "Toronto, Ontario? Isn't that in Canada?"

"Yes."

"Great. How am I going to get there?" Christopher asks while clasping his face with his hands, feeling distraught; yet, as he is thinking of ways to get across the Atlantic Ocean, Gav pipes up again.

"I want to be with you Christopher. Over the last few months I have fallen in love with you. To show how serious I am, I am going to sell my house, and pay for this machine to be transported to Canada as well. We can't take any chances with you being caught for those murders, and I absolutely do not want you killing any more people here. I don't know what I would do without you. What do you say?"

Here he is, trapped in another time warp with a desirably beautiful young woman that loves him and wants to be with him, and is willing to make sacrifices for him. No one has ever paid him any mind since the murder of his wife, son and friend Drake. And he knows that when he fixes the time machine that he will return for them, and he will leave Gav. He is still committed to his wife, regardless if he watched her burn at the stake and the probability of returning is impossible. Is it time to move on, and to be with Gav? Have children and establish a family with her? Christopher feels a terrible pain in his stomach with the stressing thoughts. The stress is insurmountable. His heart is filled with pain and conflict as he is falling in love with Gav as well.

"Hun?" she says.

Clearing his throat, Christopher replies to her, "I am sorry, I don't know what to say other than thank you. Thank

you for everything, and yes I'd love to be with you."
His voice is shaky. He hides how he truly feels. He feels
shame and guilt, and pities her for having feelings for
him while his heart is with his deceased wife.

Gav smiles as she looked at her Christopher,
"Could you say that again, but this time say it like you
would have if you had just come to the future, our
present time?"

Smiling, Christopher complies with her wishes,
"Aye my love, whilt thou be mine?"

"Gladly," Gav says smiling as she rushes over to
Christopher and hugs him.

After a moment's embrace Christopher slowly
pulls away from Gav, "Isn't Canada backward? How are
we going to find people there that will help us with the
time machine. Aren't they the same as America and
under Russian occupation?"

"Yeah, they are under the Empire's rule but
President Ivanov has more sanctions on America than
Canada. America went to war with Russia; however,
Canada was a commonwealth of Britain, so they just
surrendered when Britain did. America is heavily
sanctioned. That is why we are going to Canada."

"I am very interested in the Russian President.
From the books I have read of him, he is either a very old
man, or someone like me."

"He stopped making public appearances in the
seventies, and has other politians acting on his orders.
Maybe they are just using his name for other Presidents,
like the Caesars? Either way I don't know, but one thing
is for sure we can get the help you need to fix that
machine in Canada."

Now why has Gav's smile suddenly disappeared?
"Why the long face?"

"Do we need to bring the time machine?"

"Yes of course; you know that I want to go back to my wife and ... Oh, right"

"It doesn't matter; I know your heart still belongs to them. I just wanted to hear that. I am sorry I even bothered opening up my feelings to you!" At first she glares at Christopher then rushes up the stairs of her house to her room and slams the door behind her.

Rushing behind her Christopher takes a few steps at a time up the stairs and then pauses. He feels how upset she is. He does not need to use his powers. It is quite obvious to him she is upset. He runs his fingers through his hair and bites down hard on his lower lip feeling a bit angry that she is making an already difficult situation worse.

What if things don't work out? Christopher thinks to himself in this moment of aggravating frustration. He will be travelling to a country that didn't even exist when he was born, to be with a woman that he is just getting to know. He would always be wondering had he fixed his time machine, would there have been a chance that he could have gone back in time to be with his wife and son, perhaps even save them. Christopher storms back down the steps and sits on the couch. After half an hour in deep thought, Christopher passes out.

"Where is it?" Satan says out loud, angrily pacing around the cabin.

Satan storms back and forth inside the cabin where one of the last time machines is supposed to be, without seeing a single trace of any soldier around. Satan leaves the cabin and materializes at their base; the soldiers must be punished for their failure.

He materialises at one of the bases and Satan pushes his fingers inside of one of his commander's eyes. The commander screams in pain as the other soldiers in close proximity raise their guns and try and aim it at Satan.

With his incredible strength Satan pushes his fingers deep inside of the man's eye sockets, and then pulls his head up and dislocates the man's neck and rips his head from his shoulders. There are a few gasps and people notice that Satan is Taras Ivanov. With the speed of light, Satan chops people in half with his swords and severs their heads.

Satan walks over to one of the Generals. The General pulls out his hand gun.

"Be still" Satan says. The man is now unable to move. Satan reads the man's thoughts and sees the images in his mind. Leviathan is betraying him. Satan raises his arm and then snaps his finger. The general's kevlar heaves out and then sinks back in.

"Over the next few minutes, your body will experience the most excruciating pain any one of your human species ever has encountered. What has just happened is your insides are under my spell, they are liquefying slowly. I will leave you now to your fate."

The general watches as Satan disappear into thin air, the same way he infiltrated the base. He does not understand why President Taras Ivanov attacked the base, and is scared out of his wits with what he just witnessed. A few moments later, he feels the agonizing pain that the President mentioned. The cramps get worse, they turn into dire pains; yet, still under the spell, he is unable to break free and hold his stomach.

The more time that goes by he feels the urgency of screaming out loud, but cannot. He still holds his hand gun in position as he stares off where Satan put the spell on him. He begins to flatulate, and then his insides begin to run down his legs. He begins to tear up blood while his insides run down the sides of his legs and make a pool of blood at his shoes. As he dies, the spell is released and he splashes on the ground in his own intestines.

The flight to Canada is exhilarating for Christopher. He remembers the first time he ever saw an aeroplane and now he is inside one. Not only did he have the chance to ride in horseless carriages, he is now flying across the Ocean.

Together the pair arrive safe and sound to their new home in a new country, Canada. Gav gives Christopher the task of finding ways to approach people that are on her list, to see about parts for the time machine. She prepares a profile for him to study. It gives the illusion that he is a wealthy business man. This will help him stand a better chance of receiving help.

Although Gav does not like the idea of Christopher killing people, and hopes that he will refrain from doing so in the future, he will need to kill everyone that helps him fix the time machine so that there is no unwanted attention on them. If they are caught with the machine, the Russians will be looking for them, and will try and kill them.

Gavrilovich has plans of her own. She realises that Christopher will leave her for his family, and she will use him to make a fortune. With his inability to die, they can return to the past, create bases, do heists and store a mass amount of wealth away. With the gold and diamonds they will acquire, she can be one of the wealthiest women in the world and that will compensate for Christopher leaving her.

Christopher agrees to obtain the wealth of the past, unaware of her real plans. The plan seems good to Christopher as he will be able to try and get into politics with the money that they will get, and then he can try and get his revenge on the Christians, and avenge the deaths of his family and friend Drake.

She keeps her feelings to herself; a plan of wealth and he would still leave to find his wife and son. She smiles and does not say anything to Christopher, just smiles and knows that she will have this money to herself. In fact she thought this all along; yet, plan in motion is giving her more incentive to put it into fruition. She is not disappointed. She is hurt Christopher still has feelings for his previous wife. She is hurt that she is going through all of this trouble and he is still going to avenge his wife's death. *What would stop him from killing her when he returns to his wife?* She thinks.

"So you're using me?"

"I do not understand?"

"I get it, you have used your magic on me and when we return to the past you will just get rid of me so you can be with her! I don't think so; that is not happening!"

"Hun, that wasn't on my mind at all but if you keep this up, I will definitely consider it!"

She takes her cup of coffee and throws it at Christopher.

He does not parry the cup as it breaks across his forehead. Blood trickles down the side of his head, and then the small wound heals. He gets angry at her volatile state and growls at her.

"Growl at me all you want but I love you. I will leave you right now if I think you are using me!"

"Hun, get it through your head, I am not using you. I want to be with you. I love you. Do not worry. I will not go back for them, that I promise you. We shall work on our plans together."

"You love me? I don't know about that Christopher. You shouldn't say things that aren't true, and if what you say is true I still know that your heart will always be with them."

How can she believe him? All he ever does is speak about avenging their deaths; she knows that she will have to do her best in order to keep him from seeing them when they travel back in time. She loves him and feels she will be empty and dead inside without him. Every day that passes she falls more in love with him, and it is so frustrating to be around him knowing that he is torn between her and a few-hundred-year-old dead wife.

She feels she is wasting her time with her thoughts of wanting to be with Christopher, and rightly so. How can she win him over if he is to travel to the past and see his wife again? She turns around and storms out of the room. She cannot stand being in the same area as Christopher. She needs to clear her thoughts, and at the same time not have him read hers.

Christopher does not know what to expect as he meets several experienced scientists and computer technicians. And they do not have any idea what to expect from him as well; however, the meeting goes well. Christopher explains to everyone he is someone who has immense wealth and he will handsomely reward everyone who participates for their time as they work on his machine. He explains that for those who decide to stay he will explain what the machine is, and for those who leave, he will not.

The people that agree to stay, Christopher gives them instructions to carefully take apart the machine and recreate the components, and make as many parts as they could recreate.

It takes a few weeks before the technicians figure out how to recreate the damaged components and put them together in working order. Christopher informs everyone that they are working on a time machine.

"You mean to tell us you are going to pay us all this money for creating a 'time machine'?" one of the scientists in the room scoffs.

"Excuse me sir, I know you mean well and I do appreciate the money that you are going to pay us but, seriously a time machine? Come on, no such thing can be created and if you are claiming that we just fixed one, I would like to see the results of this, if you don't mind."

Christopher walks around the room, and he surveys the machine. He motions for one of the scientists to bring the specimens for his experiment. "I want you to place the insects inside of this machine that way if anything is to happen to them at least it is on insects and not the animals. Just roll the time back for a few second to see if this thing is operational."

"Yes, Christopher." One of the scientist's says playing along with the charade.

As the scientist opens the door to the time machine he notices the same jars of insects that he is holding inside the machine. "Sir, it appears that someone already put insects in here"

"It's okay, just add the new ones in there," Christopher assumes that what is taking place now already took place and they were already sent back from the future.

Carefully putting the jars of insects into the machine, the scientist wastes no time setting up the instructions and transports the insects a few seconds back in time. He enters the conformation numbers and the insects are transferred through time.

Everyone watches expecting the incident to look like something out of a b side horror film. A little whining noise sounds from the machine, and that was it. The scientist opens the door to the time machine and looks inside; the jars of insects are gone.

"Try the monkeys now."

Frustrated and rather angry, the scientist complies with Christopher's wishes and puts the monkeys inside of the pod and sets up the time machine.

"Wait I want the monkeys to be placed inside of a news station so that we can watch this on the news. Set it for the future, tonight's news cast."

The scientist sets the co-ordinates and presses enter. The machine makes its whining noises and the monkeys are sent to the future. Everyone in the room waits for the six o'clock news, when the news comes on they watch as the monkeys bounce around the news station on live television. The time machine works, and everyone cheers. There is no doubt in their minds that whoever Christopher is, he has just created the first time machine, and they are now a part of history.

"I want to thank everyone here for your hard work and efforts; however, I cannot let any of you leave alive."

Before anyone could say anything to Christopher, he opens fire, shooting them all down with his hand gun.

As Gav returns home she feels something is happening. She understands Christopher more when he shared that he is able to feel things, as she is starting to feel him, perhaps through some sort of link between the two. She opens her car door and steps out of the vehicle; she can feel that something has got 'wrong' written all over it. She isn't sure what is going on, but she knows she will soon find out. As she walks inside her home, she cannot help but notice the time machine is fixed and in the living room, the furniture re-arranged to accommodate the time machine.

As she walks around the house she is not able to find Christopher, until she hears him walking up the steps from the basement. When the door opens, she screams and takes several steps back. There is no doubt in her mind that he is the Devil. He is dressed in a dark black cloak that resembles death, and though he is not carrying a harvest sickle he is armed with a sword. This is it then, Gav thinks to herself as she looks at Christopher while trying to collect her thoughts.

"I am not going to kill you, relax!" Dragon Dagoth growls then hands her a piece of paper.

Gav takes the paper and walks away so she can read it while keeping an eye on Christopher. It reads: Elizabeth born in Londinium, Britannia.

"That is my mother, who left me when I was born. I still remember her kissing me and walking out of the door to leave me with those Christians, cursed to live in that village for all those years. I am returning to find out why she did this to me!"

Gav drops the paper and walks over to Christopher. He looks ever so frightening in his black cloak with the hood that hugs his head; all she can see is a partial part of his eyes and the lower part of his face.

"I guess you are planning on going alone?"

"I must find my roots. The future has no answers for my powers. I must find out who, or what I am. I will see my mother. I must face her alone. I will return to you, my love."

Placing her hand on her Christopher's chest, she cuddles into his chest, not knowing whether or not she will ever see him again. "I love you. Remember I have given up everything for you." She reaches up and removes the hood from his head and gently kisses him. The strange feeling that engulfs the couple disappears as Christopher reciprocates the kiss, becoming more passionate as their tongues slide around one another's, their breathing becoming more heavy until Christopher pulls away.

"I love you too."

7

Opening up the time machine's door, Dragon Dagoth immediately feels right at home as he steps out of the machine. The air is purer than in the future, no deafening sounds from aeroplanes, no busy streets with cars and the nauseating fumes that come with them. He is home, yet, he does not care. He no longer feels like he belongs here. He is accustomed to living in the future. Travelling back to the past meant only a few things: one of which is finding his mother; and the other, to see if the machine will be able to allow him to travel to the future successfully.

As he walks through the forest, he notices how basic and simple life is in the future, in contrast to this point in time. No wells to draw water, no need for farms and killing your own cattle to get something to eat. However, this only makes people in the future lazy and weak.

Dragon Dagoth's thoughts are cut short when he recognises the church he was dumped off at all those years ago. The village is not constructed yet, and the only place of residence is the church. Strange to see things the way they were before he was a child.

A lady in a grey garment rushes from the church property and down the field. Dragon Dagoth growls. *Fucking Bitch not only left me but ran. Ran away from me!* Following in kind, Dragon Dagoth rushes into the forest after his mother and kicks her in the back. She skids along the grass and then she crashes face first on the ground, banging into a tree. As she gets up to see who is behind her, Dragon Dagoth kicks her in the face, nearly knocking her unconscious. Dragon Dagoth is quite surprised that he did not knock her out with his incredible strength.

In a fit of rage Dragon Dagoth moves in to strike her again.

"Please do not harm me. I have naught of interest, nor am I of purity. I have born offspring, and have committed my soul to the gods as I have bound myself to mine husband in sacred matrimony."

Not sure of what to do, Dragon Dagoth's anger subsides for a few seconds, and he holds back. He does not feel compelled to bash her face in again for some reason. Removing the hood from his face, Dragon Dagoth wants his mother to see the face that she just kissed goodbye a few minutes ago.

"Joshua?"

"No! But as a matter of fact where can I find him?!" his deep, dark voice echoes throughout the immediate area where the two are, while he continues to stare down at his mother, who is in a daze from the beating.

"Who art thou?"

"Where is Joshua? If Joshua has placed you in this situation, why do you continue to stick up for him? Tell me where he is now!"

His mother takes in a deep breath. She does not want to say; yet, does not feel her life is worth protecting Joshua's, "Londinium, my husband liveth in Londinium. Thou shalt not be able to slay him for he is a great warrior and practices with the Devil himself in the fine arts of witchcraft!"

"I am a Devil as well. It does not matter what he can do to me, I cannot die! So why is it you felt the need to leave the house that you were running away from?!"

Looking up at her attacker she does not understand him, or why he is asking such questions. "What is it that thou wants of me?"

As she continues to stare at this man she does not understand why he looks so much like her husband. Perhaps it is new forms of magic he is learning and practising and he tracked her to this house? Perhaps it is his brother? Then a realisation slowly creeps over her, but by the gods how can something like this be possible? How could this be her son? It is impossible.

Dragon Dagoth pulls out his sword as he listens to his mother's thoughts racing within her mind. He is angry that she does not even have the courtesy to apologise for abandoning him. He grips his sword tight and growls in fierce anger, "Your life!" He yells aloud as he chops her head off with a single stroke from his blade.

Wind howls through the thick of the trees, storm clouds rapidly gather and lightning strikes down, and repeatedly strikes Dragon Dagoth. Energies flow from her body to his, as the wind howls around them. As he looks down at his mother's lifeless body he realises that he is levitating, and suddenly everything stops. He crashes to the ground.

A strange feeling creeps over him. He feels more powerful, darker; he sees every image and every experience his mother once did. He never felt this experience killing anyone before. Is it because she is like him? He feels stronger, more alive; he wonders if beheading her allowed him to gain her powers?

He picks up his mother's body and head, and leaves the forest. He drops her body on the ground and tosses her head aside while debating if he should slaughter his adoptive parents. He figures it will probably be for the best if he does not, as he is scared of changing his future.

"It's okay, hun. I don't care if you go. I trust you will come back to me. Don't worry, you can go."

Dragon Dagoth laughs at Gavrilovich, but after reading her thoughts he realises she is sincere. "I was gone for almost a full day."

"That is impossible. You just stepped inside of that machine." Gav said looking at Christopher with a peculiar look on her face, as if he was scared to go or lying to her for some strange reason.

Walking out of the machine, Dragon Dagoth takes his hood off of his head, and then puts his sword against the wall.

He sits down on the couch and tries to figure out what took place when he decapitated his mother.

"Are you serious? You were really gone. I guess it does make sense if you had left for the past and returned, it wouldn't seem as if you had left because everything was in the past and you're returning to the now."

"Yeah" Christopher replies half-heartedly, still reminiscing over what took place.

"You know I remember seeing my mother dead when I was a baby As Gilda held me in her arms, I could see my mother's headless body sprawled out in the field, and all this time I thought that Jacob killed her. But, I remember when I was growing up I wanted to kill her for abandoning me. Remembering that image I had from the time I was a baby, I now realise that I was the one who killed her."

Gav keeps her thoughts to herself. It is shocking to hear what he says sometimes let alone know what he does at other times. At times she is scared to death knowing that she is with such a cold-hearted killer. Not a day goes by where she is not haunted by the memory of him killing her partner. She still remembers the soldiers in the cabin he killed before they met. She knows that the heists they are planning will result in people getting killed and she accepts this; however, killing his own flesh and blood, the very woman who gave birth to him sends shivers up and down her spine. Despite the fear that grips her, she is excited that she is with someone that is so dark sided, and is her complete opposite, despite her duty to uphold the law as a police officer.

"What did it feel like killing your own mother?"

Christopher looks up and over to Gav. He gives her a brief look and wonders if she is getting off on this. It doesn't matter; he had no attachments to his mother whatsoever. "I don't know. I was angry. I hated her all those years. I always wanted to know why she abandoned me, yet when I had the chance to ask her, I didn't. I asked where my dad was. After I found out, she just angered me and I couldn't help it. I ended her life."

Gav rests her head on Christopher's shoulder. She still can't believe that she is with such a person but he will make her rich with the time machine and this is all that matters to her.

The fruits of Christopher and Gav's tedious hard work have finally come to fruition after many months of hard work and planning. They have created blueprints for bases that they will hire workers from across the city, to build.

"This is unbelievable! Who would ever have thought that one could travel back to the past?" Gav says.

"I know. Who would have ever thought," murmurs Christopher, as images of Annex and Cynric flash before his mind's eye.

"No roads, no cars, no aeroplanes; this is so weird."

Christopher laughs at his girlfriend. He still could not get over his first memory of an aeroplane, and then when he heard about men landing on the moon, that was a whole other issue that he had to come to terms with. "You know, you think that is weird? How about when I came to your time? I see these things that not even the imagination could have dreamt up and you think it is weird not to see such things. I mean, you guys have astronauts. Go ahead and find someone right now and explain to anyone what an astronaut is. They will laugh at you."

She chuckles. "I think it is time we bring the rest of the construction equipment over to England and then start on having the people get to work."

"Alright, sounds good to me."

They travel back to the future and then bring the equipment back to the past. Gav calls the candidates for the job; soon they had a few hundred people in droves coming to work for the couple. Once everyone is secretly transported back to the past, that is when Christopher informs them of what he is doing. There is a bit of an outcry, as the workers feel they have been tricked and betrayed, while others are furious; yet, there is nothing that anyone can do until they complete their jobs.

A motivating factor; the threat lingering on of something, anything happening to their families motivates the construction workers to complete the task. In less than a year the projects are completed. Yet, to Gav and Christopher it was only a few weeks in their time of making sure that everything went according to plan.

Stepping out of the time machine and walking through the field, Dragon Dagoth sees the bases are near completion. His conscience is deeply troubling him. All he wanted to do is get his revenge on the Christians for what they did to his family; yet, in order to do such a feat there is a price to pay to see such things happen. He wonders if he is turning into what he hates so passionately.

He watches as the construction workers complete the remnants of his task, placing soil on top of the base and building a wooden barn on top of the entrance for the base. He watches them from the shadows and then readies his gun, once they are near done walking out to greet them.

"That man must be from the future. He has a gun." One of the construction worker's points out.

"Are you here to save us? Are our families okay? Has anything happened to them?"

Several people rush over to him and start asking questions at the same time and some of them begin to approach in their despair without care that he is holding Pecheneg light machine gun.

How can he do this? One way of looking at it is they would all be born again in the future and live their lives all over again as if nothing had happened, but then he would still have to kill them to make that true. Either way he will be a monster! His finger pulls the trigger shooting down a few people at first, and as he watches everyone scatter, and then he open fire killing as many of them as possible. His previous thoughts are a distant memory as the intent of his mission is all that is on his mind now. They all need to die. If any of them were to tell people of this time about this base it will be affect the results of his plans in the future.

He uses his powers and tracks down the ones who rush off and hide in buses, in soil, amongst the dead, and kills them all without mercy, and then makes a funeral pyre of all their bodies, and rids the land of as much evidence as possible in case the natives of the area are to come across anything.

He walks through the empty corridors inside of the base. His footsteps echo throughout the empty halls as the echoes and screams and cries from the construction workers do likewise through his haunting memories. Taking a final glance for now although his base is empty, it will soon be full of riches.

He walks through the time machine and up the stairs from the home in his basement, takes off his dark garments and assumes the role of Christopher Robertson. Mentally drained, he sits on a chair in the kitchen as he does his best to block the screams and cries of the workers begging for their lives, grovelling before him, crying about their children that need them. It was a lot to take in. All his life he was treated as a monster and now he is one. He isn't a monster. He has to stop this. Killing innocent people is just not right; it is immoral, and he always believed otherwise. His beloved wife Annex would not have wanted any of this. *Annex...* another haunting memory, he cups his face in his hands, and feels dead inside.

"Hun you look disturbed. You haven't said a word since you've come home; what is it that is troubling you like this?"

Shaking his head, Christopher did not want to talk about what he had done, about what he is becoming.

"Don't shut me out, hun. I am your girlfriend. You can talk to me, what is wrong?"

"I killed them all. They all begged me for their lives and I just shot them down like they were cattle. What have I done?!"

Her fingers trail her partner's chest as she leaves him in the kitchen to grab some papers. They are papers the workers signed when they agreed to work for them. She returns to her partner who is on the verge of tears and hands him the papers. While he looks through the papers, Gav wraps her arms around him, but he shrugs her arms off.

Christopher leaps from his chair, towering over Gav. She is taken aback as this is the angriest she has ever seen him. Appliances in the kitchen begin to rattle and shake, the cups on the counter begin to shatter and break while Christopher's breathing gets intensified and heavier. "Why have you shown me this, woman?! Does it bring you pleasure to see me so miserable?!"Christopher growls out.

Gav remains calm and frozen in place where she stands her ground. Although she is frightened and does not know what he will do, she does not let her fear become visible. "Look at the paper, look at the first person's religious affiliation!"

Taking a second to calm down, Christopher snaps the paper back in front of his face and looks at it again "Dino Mancini: religious affiliation: Catholic." Christopher looks at the next application "Vincent De Luca: religious affiliation: Roman Catholic." Each application form that Christopher looks through, he notices a common pattern. Christopher growls in anger, "You mean to tell me these people were Christians. These Catholics built our bases?!"

Gav smiles without showing her teeth. She is surprised that she is able to control him quite so easily through his temper, and keeps in mind that she can taunt his emotions in future to invoke his rages to perhaps do her biddings. "Yes, in fact they were all Catholic or Christian, but see, you have become so angry that they worked on our bases that you are not even the least bit upset at murdering any of them, are you?"

Christopher is at a loss for words. He wonders why she would be manipulating him, and what purpose it would serve her to do this to him, and then a lingering thought of suspicion is conjured. Does she intend on testing him with her manipulations to serve a future inward plan or goal she is formulating? He keeps the thoughts to himself. "Why didn't you say anything to me?"

"Well, what if one of them was not a Christian or Catholic? What then? Would you still have been upset? Now that you know you just slaughtered a few hundred religionists you don't care about the few who may not have been. I am helping you fight your war, and you have been successful. This is just a start; one day you will kill plenty more Christians."

Although she makes sense, he was still deceived by her and he does not like being tricked like this. Dropping the conversation he no longer feels like a monster. In fact, he feels liberated from prior thoughts and a sense of relief fills his mind knowing that he killed all of them, each and every one of them! Their agonising screams for mercy once made him feel nauseous. Now that he knows that the majority of the people he killed were religious, their screams replaying in his mind sounds like music to his ears.

Months more pass by and Christopher keeps himself engaged with studying politics, and learning Canadian politics as he has no interest in returning to England. If he returns it will only be for the sake of visiting his base, or finding his father.

In order to wage war against the Christians he needs an army, an army that will obey his each and every command. He studies human cloning, and ponders about an army of his own being, an army of his clones; this would be a powerful army. But would it be successful? And if he was to do such a thing he would need a vast amount of money.

Studies and research will only take him so far. It is futile to continuously bury his mind inside books while they could be acquiring mass amounts of wealth. Together they devise strategies that will give them immense wealth. Unlike the last idea about creating the base, this idea only needed a few days to perfect; they plan robberies they will do in points of history.

Together they travel to the past and rob soldiers delivering gold to Fort Knox and return the gold to their bases. In future they will trade the gold for cash, and secretly he will have enough money to finance the creation of clones.

The couple travel back to the past. This time with the last remnants of Gav's money they purchase land mines as well as a sniper rifle. They position the land minds in strategic areas they know their victims will be nearing. Gav waits at a comfortable distance looking through the scope of her trusty L96 bolt action sniper rifle that proved efficient with in her tactical police training. Dragon Dagoth equips himself with an AK-74M assault rifle, and has it slung to his side.

A small band of soldiers approach him as he blocks the path they are on, they are still a distance away.

"Love, the soldiers with the gold are on their way." Mentally prepping himself he lets out a breath of air "Acknowledged".

Gravel crunches beneath his shoes as he walks, his gun lowers and he raises his hand, motioning the soldiers ahead to stop.

They do, mainly because no one has been on this route before, and they were a little curious as to what this man was supposed to be dressed as. He was no Indian. He did not appear to be a runaway slave, and he did not appear to be a part of the Confederates or Yankees, so they were quite curious as to who he was and what he was doing there. Some of them take notice of the odd looking gun he is carrying.

"Top of the morning to you," a soldier says.

There is no need to converse with these soldiers. Dragon Dagoth lowers his hand and Gav fires off a round from her sniper rifle, and she misses all of the soldiers. Keeping his frustrations with his girlfriend at bay, Dragon Dagoth opens fire on the soldiers. The soldiers who are not shot down, run and hide behind the carriages and return fire at him.

Another thunderous boom sounds from Gavrilovich's sniper rifle, taking out one of the mines on the ground. The massive explosion leaves a mushroom cloud of smoke, rock and debris which scatters across the dirt road, and leaves a crater where the mine once was.

Dragon Dagoth rushes a little closer to the soldiers as they fire their guns. As they reload and powder their rifles, although their weapons are futuristic comparing them to swords and shields, they are no match for the weapons that he has. Dragon Dagoth takes the pins out his hand grenades and tosses them in the centre of where the soldiers are hiding, killing the majority of them.

Wasting no time, Dragon Dagoth walks over to the dead horses and men, the surviving few dazed and confused, not knowing what is happening. He senses they are baffled by his weaponry and they feel bested by the situation. Turning around, Dragon Dagoth motions for Gav to meet him and then uses his power to have his vehicle, the Hummer, roll towards him.

They fill the Hummer with the bricks of gold and then travel back to their base, completing their first successful robbery.

After returning to the future, Gav does not hesitate spending her share of the mass fortune. She purchases a new home that far well exceeds regular living accommodations. She also acquires a new taste of friends with her new money, spending her time with the social elite, the upper class, dining at fine restaurants, seeing fine art exhibits, all the while distancing herself from Christopher, on top of setting herself above him with elitist mentality.

Gav's actions do not impress Christopher, nonetheless he does not let her recent course of actions take over his emotions and works on completing the work he initially sought to do. After months of research, he finds scientists that are able to work on cloning him. Until now, there have been only a few successful cloning experiences and this has been practised on animals, never on humans. The reasons for this are because of the high mortality rates that come with cloning. There is also a low success rate with cloning the animal species. Christopher pays the scientists to work on cloning him handsomely enough to cover their moral high ground position, and to not worry about how many of these beings will die.

As expected, the first few batches are a failure, however, money is of no concern for Christopher, who tenaciously encourages the scientists to learn from their mistakes and continue on with their work.

"Christopher, excellent news! The procedure has finally worked," one of the head scientists, Patrick, say, as he guides Christopher to the laboratory. "There they are, all in their pods. We will be monitoring their development, and looking for signs of weakness in their growth."

"Excellent," Christopher says, as he extends a comforting hand and rests it on the scientist's shoulder. "There is another matter that needs the utmost attention. Max Diamond of the New Order Enterprises Incorporated is asking me to have you and your fellow associates develop cloned tissue, blood and skin for a top secret project."

"Max Diamond? Isn't he a Politician?"

Not wanting to dance around and answer questions, Christopher cuts the conversation short, "It appears he has several interests, this being one of them. The New Order Enterprises Incorporated is a fortune one hundred company that will fully finance and support everything you need, including accommodations here, which of course includes your families."

Before he could give it any thought, Christopher broke his thoughts, "The New Order Enterprises Incorporated has developed an entire underground mega-city equipped with everything and more you will ever need. What is more is this underground city boasts the best education system the world is yet to offer. All the money you earn you keep. All food, shelter, clothing, education anything you would have to pay for we pay for. Mind you, there will be a fair usage policy, and added stipulations such as no mind-altering substances This place is the perfect utopia. You'd be a fool to turn down the offer.

It all sounds way too good to be true. Patrick laughs and lowers his head, "To good to be true, what is the catch?"

"Sometimes my friend, there are no catches, and this is one of those times. All you and your associates have to agree to, is work here for the New Order Enterprises Incorporated and you will have everything at your disposal."

A shadow walks amongst the civilians in the dark of night through the city streets of Kabul. The shadow, tattered hijab and other attire are relatively noticeable. He does not seem to fit in with the other citizens. However, he makes his way through the hordes of people scurrying around about their business as he in turn finds his business eavesdropping on conversations patrons at local well-to-do shops are having. He overhears a conversation amongst a few individuals. They are discussing the Soviet led invasion a few years back and how they are planning to counter the occupation, and he slowly makes his way to their table.

"Good day folks. I could not help but overhear your conversation. I know of a person who has such funds; he can help you in your struggle."

The couple look over their shoulders and then pay him no interest, carrying on with their conversation.

"I know this man on a personal level. We are good friends. He is looking to recruit people, and he has the funds but lacks the people. In fact, that is quite opposite of what I heard you speaking not just two minutes ago, correct?"

Turning around in his chair, Jahangir Wahidi snarls at the stranger who is interrupting their conversation, "Mind your business. This does not concern you."

Reaching into his garments, Dragon Dagoth opens up a parcel from inside his coat, slightly unwrapping some paper and shows them a bar of gold. He walks over to Jahangir Wahidi's table and puts the half open parcel down on the table along with instructions on where to meet his contact, nods and then he walks off back into the shadows of the night.

Jahangir Wahidi takes a look at the bar of gold on the table and then laughs, "He thinks he is to fool me by leaving a bar of gold on the table." He swats the bar of gold to knock it free from the table but is taken aback at the weight of the bar of gold. He picks the bar of gold up and examines it.

"I think it is really Niyoosha. Hey, mister?" Jahangir yells out, standing up and looking through the crowd for the man who was at the table behind him. He is nowhere to be seen. Opening the parcel, Jahangir takes out the instructions and reads them over.

Dragon Dagoth knows that the man will accept his rather generous gift and will indeed wish to meet him at his secret location in Tykrit. His gift of foresight has grown stronger over the years, more so after he decapitated his mother. It is almost inevitable that the Islamic extremists will show.

After a day of waiting, Dragon Dagoth notices Jahangir Wahidi and about nineteen other men accompanying him and heading his way.

"You have more gold for us?" Jahangir Wahidi shouts to the man clad in a black cloak

Refusing to respond in Arabic, Dragon Dagoth answers, "Yes."

"Is any of that with you here?"

Dragon Dagoth extends his arm and points his finger towards a few crates of gold, "Does that answer your question?"

One of Jahangir Wahidi's men decides to take full advantage of the situation. There doesn't appear to be anyone else there other than Dragon Dagoth. Raising his gun, Houshmand shoots the cloaked stranger standing a few paces between him and the gold.

Before Houshmand can rush up to grab some of the gold for himself, Jahangir Wahidi and a few others begin yelling and screaming at him for his actions, while a few others condone his actions, seeing the cloaked man was stupid enough to come alone.

The bullet wounds heal instantly. The pressure of the bullets was the cause of Dragon Dagoth falling onto his back. Rising to his feet, he reaches out his hand and wills one of Jahangir Wahidi's men's guns to telepathically fly into his hand. When the gun slaps into his palm, he shoots down a few of the men, emptying out the magazine. Quickly tossing the gun away he pulls out his sword. Some of Jahangir Wahidi's men respond by shooting him in return, as he approaches them the bullets fly in and out of him.

Dragon Dagoth rushes over to one of the closest rivals and chops his head clean off, and then swings around to face the others shooting him. Hoisting up one of the men telepathically, he wills the man's rib cage to break and his bones to penetrate his vital organs, and then lets the man fall to an agonizing painful death.

The remaining few refuse to fight the man they are now convinced is the Jinn Ibliss Shaitan and submit to him.

"That is wise of the rest of you. That gold would have been yours, and now that some of you were so foolishly greedy, and futilely attempted to kill me, I will take it back until you deem yourselves worthy of serving me!"

Everyone is too frightened to speak out against Dragon Dagoth, especially after his raw display of power, killing more than half of their friends and even more remarkable standing and talking after being shot repeatedly. No one is brazen enough to speak out against the man who uses Devil magic on them. None of them would dare even look at him.

Disappointed, Dragon Dagoth turns around expecting someone to say something.

"Sir, I am Rashidi Akim."

Jahangir Wahidi's best friend, long-time associate, and more importantly his cousin with whom he does business, decides to take action as this is the first time he has ever seen his cousin speechless. He needed to take control so that the others will not look down on Jahangir, if they made it out of this mess alive. He rushes over to greet Dragon Dagoth.

Stretching out his hand Dragon Dagoth makes Rashidi fall to the ground using his dark magical powers.

"And so you are. What is your point?!" Dragon Dagoth growls out trying his best to humiliate the humble man before him.

"Please forgive the others but my cousin Jahangir has come here with good intentions. We have done business before with others and this is the first that this has happened. Please forgive my cousin; he is a man of Allah. He will serve you well."

"Perhaps this is true. You are the only one who has had the courage to say anything or apologise, not him! Does Jahangir not have a mouth or tongue that works, or did it suddenly break after he asked for the gold and I was shot?!" Not wishing anything to happen to his cousin, and hoping that his cousin would not be granted control, Jahangir rushes over to Dragon Dagoth and says, "I am sorry for the actions of my friends. That was very foolish of them. I wish to serve you and will do whatever it is you want."

Dragon Dagoth releases his dark hold on Rashidi and then turns to face Jahangir and says, "Good, next time you come to meet me, you will only bring your cousin along with you. If anyone else comes along, I will kill you all and seek out another who may be interested in this money. I will find you when I need you. Now be gone!"

Era 2
The Birth of an Empire
8

18 years later/ 2001

"Mistress, why are you crying?"

Gavrilovich glances at Dragon Dagoth's clone, model Number Sixteen, and then back to the eggshell white tiles on the floor. All the money in the world is not curing the pain of loneliness she feels. And despite her intentions of using Christopher to make her rich, she clenches her fist as she cries, ever more consumed by her jealousy, and his ever increasing solitary moments. Christopher convinced her all these years that the clones are their children. *Our children? Not once has he made love to me, and yet he passes off scientific experiments as our children?* She reminisces over all the years wasted raising these clones, essentially convincing herself that Christopher's lies are truths, and they are like her children, until it dawns on her and she has an epiphany realising Christopher has the upper hand and is using her.

"Mistress, are you okay?" Number Sixteen asks.

Snapping out of her depressive trance she looks at the clone, and sighs. Concealing her tears with a wipe of her sleeve, she stands up and slightly holds the clone's fingers in an affectionate way.

"I am fine. Sorry it is just that I have something on my mind. I am alright though. I will get over it."

"Master Dagoth waits for you at the time portal."

She pushes herself up against the clone and holds him tight. Her breasts rub against his arm, and then to his chest. She slowly wraps one of her arms around his back, and softly places one of her hands on his chest, along with the side of her head, "Promise me you will be careful when you do your mission?"

Her body feels so soft, so gentle to the touch, and so comforting. He hesitantly wraps his arms around Gav to return the hug in a formal way, his body tense with anxiety as he fights off an erection. So many mixed feelings circle in his mind. What if she isn't coming on to him and she is just wishing him well? Yet, his desires for her want more. She is all woman and not like the girls his age that he has only seen on television. She is older, looks more mature, looks like a lady. He shakes his thoughts from mind, and responds formally. "Yes Mistress, I will. I have been trained well."

Gavrilovich slowly retracts herself from his embrace, and warmly gazes into his eyes, until he diverts his gaze elsewhere. She knows how he feels, and she could also feel the bulge in his pants growing. Now is not the time to pursue her desires. They reach the room together, and Gav parts from the clone's side, and elusively shows her lack of affection to Dragon Dagoth as he walks inside of the time portal. She starts up the machine and sends the clones and Dragon Dagoth back in time.

The clones strategically walk behind Dragon Dagoth in box formation after travelling through the depths of time, glancing around and soaking in all the beautiful elements of nature along the way. Being locked inside of a base for most of their lives and seeing virtual nature environments is just not the same as being out in the real world.

Dragon Dagoth does not share their enthusiasm as he is beginning to hate the past. It is so much more different than the future, and everything is easier to do in the future. Fortunately, they do not have a far walk ahead of them and his father's alleged estate is within viewing distance.

As they walk towards the massive house, a man wearing the same type of dark black cloak Dragon Dagoth is wearing, comes to greet them. Dragon Dagoth senses a great deal of power emanating from the man.

"I have been expecting you, Ethelwulf."

This has to be my father, Dragon Dagoth thinks to himself.

"No, I am not your father, but we are related." The man pauses and steps forward, and stares behind Dragon Dagoth at all of the identical soldiers behind him, "Impressive."

"Have you heard of someone named Joshua. I am looking for him. I believe I am his son."

A crooked smile creeps across the man's face underneath the cowl, "Indeed you are his son; you seek him for the knowledge you feel he possesses. What if I told you that I possess the knowledge that you seek, and I can give you all the knowledge you want, and I can train you with the powers that you have."

"I don't know you and I do not have any reasons to trust you."

"Of course son of Joshua, I must contest that you do not know your father either. May I ask what rationale you have for giving him this unwarranted trust?" He pauses for a moment's time and taps into space and time, and sees everything that has taken place leading to this moment, and then a familiar crooked smile creeps across his face, "A trust you give this man after what he did to your... mother, who of course you killed. All she was doing was... protecting you."

Growling in anger, Dragon Dagoth raises his hand, and his clones raise and aim their guns at the man, "You lie!"

"You did sever your mother's head from her shoulders. You received a transference of her powers. If I lie… then explain why you see a lady running away from a man that bears your resemblance, both in your dreams and while you are awake? Could there be a shred of truth to what I am saying?"

The clones grip their guns tight, and do not waiver from their target. The man does not move. He does not fear them and continues to stand his ground, staring at Dragon Dagoth.

"There is something you need to know, son of Joshua. Other beings like us are about to kill your father."

Dragon Dagoth takes a few seconds to consider this and then orders his men to lower their guns.

"Who are you?"

"I am one of your relatives, Ethelwulf." the man says while approaching Dragon Dagoth. "I bet it must be plaguing you, wondering why your father abandoned you?! You see we all have this gift that you possess, and I can read your thoughts. You think these powers are dark arts, sorcery and magic? They're not, you see they are a natural ability. It is just these humans that believe their own fairy tales about us and they hate us for it, which is why we conceal ourselves from them."

Dragon Dagoth tries to conceal his thoughts as the man continues speaking, just staring at him blankly soaking in everything he is saying. Now he knows how his beloved Annex and Gavrilovich feel each time he reads their minds. It is a rather uncomfortable feeling.

"We are from other worlds. Your father was born here; yet, like us you are born with our powers. The humans call us devils, and humans think you are one as well. It is rather unfortunate that your father is too obsessed with his powers. He used to beat your mother senseless. He is out of control, and his lust for power has turned all of us against one another." The man hung his head while trying to study Dragon Dagoth. "Now I understand what has happened. I believe your mother was protecting you from your father. He would have probably killed you both."

Dragon Dagoth knew this to be true from the transference of power that he received from his mother. He saw her images flood his mind but he did not understand them until now. Perhaps his father was going to kill them both. Dragon Dagoth understands this as he easily gets angry. He knows that he is turning into someone that he is not. He has already killed countless amounts of innocent people just to achieve his goal of wiping the Christians off the face of the planet. He would need to see his father more now than ever to find out for certain.

The man starts to walk away from Dragon Dagoth, waving his hand motioning the others to follow him, "We can discuss these things later. The Carnage of the Devils is beginning and we must save your father from death. There is no time to lose."

"Who are you?!" Dragon Dagoth asks once.

"My name is ... Taras Ivanov. Now let's go. There is no time to waste. It would be a shame for any of these other beings to receive your father's powers when you can have it all."

"You're the Russian President?!"

"There is no time for that now. I will explain more perhaps later. For now your father needs our help."

"Take me to him."

"As you wish."

As they head to the destination, dark grey clouds form in the distance. Lightning, rain and hail strike down to an extent Dragon Dagoth has never seen before; yet, he knows this is not natural. As he continues to walk alongside Taras, his clones trail behind him to get to his father. He knows whatever is out there, and whoever he is going to see is in complete command of the elements of nature. He could feel the dark power getting stronger, as if it were wrapping around him like a blanket.

Streaks of lightning tear at the ground and visible heaps of smoke rise in the distance through the thick of the trees in the forest that they make their way through. The dark grey clouds begin to turn into a tropical cyclone. Trees begin to uproot, and fly towards Dragon Dagoth and his clones. Covering his head, he turns to where Taras was by his side and notices he is gone.

Thinking nothing of it, Dragon Dagoth motions for his clones to flank the area up ahead. This will not be a battle he can win using his sword or dark powers. He pulls out his assault rifle and rushes into the tropical cyclone, rushing into the eye of the storm through the howling wind. Dragon Dagoth hears growling noises, and then notices a few individuals fighting back and forth.

Leviathan is on the offensive. He smashes into one of the trees and splinters it from its trunk, and the tree busts into several pieces. Grabbing hold of part of the tree before it falls, he looks towards Lucifer, Belial and Joshua who have the upper hand and momentum are bringing the fight to him. He rushes towards the three in a flash of a second, smashing all three with the tree branch, knocking them all off of their feet, batting them several metres into the distance.

Not as young as his counterparts, yet more powerful, Lucifer gets to his feet within a split second and commands several bolts of lightning to strike his adversaries. The lightning misses Leviathan as he disappears, before the bolts tear through his body. Leviathan reappears and smashes Lucifer with the tree again, batting him several metres away once more.

Had it come to this? Would this be his undoing? He shared all his knowledge with these beings from Ares years ago by sharing the Insuranians secrets of immortality and how to gain their powers. To lose to them years later after watching the people of his home world get brutally murdered, no, this will not happen. He trained each and everyone one of them. He would win. It would be impossible to lose to these mere Arian beings!

Lucifer pulls out his sword, and uses his unseen form. Leviathan reappears and bats Belial with the tree as he is getting up. Sensing danger, Leviathan dodges a deathblow from Joshua. The wind from Joshua's sword howls above his head. Had he been a second too late, Joshua would have severed his head clean off his shoulders.

Dropping the tree, Leviathan looks down at the mere earthling, the demi-devil and growls. In retaliation, he moves to strike at Joshua. Sensing danger once again, he whips out his sword and dodges at the same time. He could feel a gust of air blowing past him and as he looks up, he watches Lucifer flying through the air nearly taking his head off with the swipe of his sword. Leviathan retaliates and slices his sword at Lucifer's back, sending the Insuranian down to the ground screaming in pain. The tropical cyclone stops immediately after Lucifer feels the pain of Leviathan's sword cutting through his back and severing his spinal cord. Twirling his sword around, Leviathan rushes towards Joshua and Belial rushes towards him and they greet one another with steel on steel.

"Open fire."

Belial and Joshua stop in mid stride as they watch Leviathan get shot down. Joshua stares at the men charging towards them. They are oddly dressed and carrying dangerous weapons that he has never seen before in his life. Belial has seen weaponry of the like but this is his first time seeing such weaponry on this planet.

Leviathan gasps for air and drops his sword as bullets penetrate and exit his body. He turns around to see apes in skin suits, more pathetic earthlings. They continuously shoot him until the shock and pain is too unbearable and Leviathan succumbs to his injuries. Smoke rises from his wounds, as blood pours out of them.

Lucifer does his best to heal his wounds, while trying to command the elements of Earth once again. He is too late as Dragon Dagoth and his clones shoot him down.

Straggling behind the rest of the clones, Number Sixteen walks past the dead, while Dragon Dagoth stares at an odd, old looking man whose skin colour is pale with a reddish tint to it, just like Taras Ivanov's. Number Sixteen thinks of his Mistress in the future. He thinks of her warm touches, and finds her compassion and empathy for him exhilarating. He also enjoys the freedom of being outside and seeing trees, leaves on the trees, green grass, flowers, and the smell of fresh air. As he walks towards Leviathan's lifeless body, he recalls Taras Ivanov's.

He wonders if his brother clones are 'Devils' as well, and wonders if he cuts the head off the lifeless being, would he gain these powers, and be as powerful as his Master Dagoth? The very touch of his Mistress' body against his, gave birth to so many questions, and he dreams of a life beyond servitude. He looks at the sword in Leviathan's lifeless body, and presses his contemplation of decapitating the body.

"Brother no, this is our Master's business. We must obey Dragon Dagoth as our Lord and Master. Extinguish any thoughts of individualism from your mind," Number Seven reasons with Number Sixteen while gripping his arm. "Now come before he notices you and reads your thoughts."

With distain, Number Sixteen snatches his arm free of Number Seven's warm grip, reluctantly complying, all the while giving more thought to what Taras said earlier, and looking at Leviathan's sword in hand, and looking at Leviathan's neck.

Dragon Dagoth keeps his eyes fixed on the younger man beside the old man. This man has a normal light skin complexion, than that of a mixed race person. At that moment he realizes this person beside the older looking man, is his father Joshua.

Grabbing Joshua's arm, Belial turns around to flee, "Come hither Joshua, for we are no match for this being!"

Joshua does not hesitate and runs alongside Belial to get to safety. The sage-like old man and Joshua rush out of the woods, while Dragon Dagoth and his clones trail quickly behind them. Strangely they are not shooting them, however, Belial and Joshua sense a great danger from this man.

Leviathan starts to regain consciousness. His fingers start to twitch and his muscles spasm. He gasps for air and comes to. As he gets to his knees, he channels his dark powers, and begins to close the bullet holes in his body, while trying to shake off the pain. Satan materialises from thin air before him. Startled, Leviathan respectfully acknowledges Satan's presence, and slightly bows before him, "My Lord, Belial and his son have escaped; I believe it was a god that tried to kill me. I am not sure?"

Satan does not say anything; he takes his sword from his sheath.

"My Lord?!"

Satan looks at Lucifer who is coming to, and then back down at Leviathan who is trying to understand what his General that he has served millions of years with, is about to do.

"I know you sought to betray me. You are no longer of use to me." Satan slices off Leviathan's head clean off and then rushes over to Lucifer and takes his head clean off before he can fully recuperate. Gusts of wind hurl around Satan and storm clouds gather while Satan receives a transference of power from both beings.

While racing after his father and Belial, Dragon Dagoth contemplates what he should do. He then realises if he shoots his father down, his father will not die unless his head is removed, or a bullet hits him in the head. As he pauses and raises his gun, he notices the pair has reached a cliff. They are trapped, and there is no escape for either of them!

"We must jump before he reaches us. His mind is unstable. Dost thou not feel it?"

"Go father. I shall protect thee!" Joshua charges towards Dragon Dagoth and his clones. Dragon Dagoth opens fire. Joshua creates an impenetrable force around him, and as the bullets near him, they melt into a liquid-like substance, and evaporate before striking him. Joshua punches the ground causing a massive earthquake, toppling the clones adjacent Dragon Dagoth, and bringing Dragon Dagoth to his knees.

Joshua concentrates all of his energy on Dragon Dagoth and the clones. Temperatures drop around them, and frost begins to form on them. Some of the weaker minded clones begin to freeze and ice particles begin to form on them. Dragon Dagoth repels Joshua's magic and he does his best to use counter magic to keep himself and his clones alive.

"Stop at once!"

Joshua turns and notices someone holding onto Belial with a gun stuck against his head. Belial does not move, and Joshua understands that this weapon can end Belial's life. Dragon Dagoth undoes Joshua's magic, while a few of the clones succumb to their injuries and die. They raise their guns and make their way to Joshua.

Number Sixteen pulls the trigger. He knows which of the two his master wants alive, and then aims his gun at Joshua.

"Father, noooo!" In horror Joshua watches as a mist of blood shoots out the other side of Belial's head. Blood begins to pour out of his mouth and nostrils, and from the trauma to the head. Blood begins to seep out of his ears, as his father's lifeless body crashes to the ground with his eyes still open, staring at him. He turns to see the man in the dark black cloak approaching him with the others, cautiously approaching him and aiming their foreign weapons at him.

A few seconds later, Belial's body levitates from the ground, and storm clouds appear directly above Number

Sixteen and streaks of lighting strike at him. Dragon Dagoth and the others watch in amazement as the transference of power takes place. In the few seconds Dragon Dagoth diverts his attention to the transference of power, Joshua takes advantage of the situation and runs for the cliff and jumps off into the waters below.

After the transference of power takes place, Dragon Dagoth and the others rush to the edge of the cliff and stare into the waters below. Joshua is gone.

Number Sixteen scrambles to get to his feet. Billions of years of information are flooding his mind, he feels mad, dazed and confused, and stumbles back down to the ground. He can feel raw power flowing through his veins. He can see images of war. He can see images of beings begging for their lives and other instances of transferences of power. He sees Taras Ivanov for who he really is, Satan. He sees him as the ruler of the planet Ares, a ruthless and cunning warlord. He looks over towards Dragon Dagoth. He sees his master, his creator, a person that he once looked up to as a genius and master mind, someone who he once saw as all powerful, and he now sees him as his inferior.

He watches his master as he stares into the waters below, and now he finds the strength to get to his feet. His master looks towards him, "Are you alright, clone?"

"Yes, 'Master'."

"Joshua used his magic on us as well; some of your fellow clones are dead."

Looking into the distance Number Sixteen sees his fallen comrades, and then lowers his head. Then it dawns on him that his master believes that Joshua used his magic on him to make good his escape, and he is not aware of what really happened. He fights the urge to share what really took place, and conceals his thoughts. "To the fallen!"

Dragon Dagoth nods his head. Together they make their way back to the base, a failed mission, bitter and defeated, and returning to the base with more information about the circumstances of the past. They walk through the empty corridors of the base to the time machine portal. Dragon Dagoth rules out travelling to the past again to pursue his father and considers other measures of tracking his father. This point of time is lost, and his father is too powerful. He has another method that will surely be able to track down and detain his father, and hopefully will be a lot easier.

Dragon Dagoth lets out a sigh, and shakes his head. He does not say anything to his clones as he programs the time machine portal to return to the future.

"We will proceed with our other mission tomorrow," Dragon Dagoth informs his clones and he marches off.

"Yes, Master."

Satan stands before Belial's lifeless body. He considers Belial's weakness; his empathy for the Insuranians is his undoing. He considers this as a key reason he died at the hands of these mortals. Then through the darkness, something grips his mind, for a second's pause in thought. Joshua was under his direct and indirect control. Dragon Dagoth is not. Dragon Dagoth is evolving with his powers and can pose a threat to him. "The time machines, he will bring my empire down through them. Leviathan you were right. Dagoth must be destroyed!"

He stares at the lifeless body for a few brief seconds more and then journeys off to his estate to travel through the depths of time to prepare for battle, as the last of his kind on this planet.

9

"I don't understand what these things are. I keep having them after I killed that person. I have read about dreams in books before. I have read about clairvoyance as well. Do any of you get these?"

"Only humans dream, Number Sixteen. We don't get them; perhaps you are a perfect replica of our creator."

Perhaps, Number Sixteen thinks to himself as he gets out of bed, *or perhaps this has something to do with me killing that being.*

"I dreamt the same dream over and over again last night, and I am not sure what to make of it? After we catch Joshua and bring him before our master, he will kill us. All I have been doing ... sorry, all we have been doing is simulation after simulation; killing random people since the time other kids would be learning how to ride bikes. I have never smelled a flower, or even made love to a woman. I have read about it in books and I read how wonderful such things are, and I want to do these things. I don't want to die!"

The other clones are concerned about Number Sixteen's defiance, and his recent openness questioning their master. He has always been defiant, and they never understood why. If their Master sees fit to see them to their deaths then that will be so. They are not to question their Master's motives. They exist to follow their master Lord Dragon Dagoth's will, and if Number Sixteen continues his defiance towards their Master he will have just cause to kill them all.

"Dreams are meaningless Number Sixteen. You are giving it way too much thought," says Number Seven.

What if they come true? Number Sixteen ponders as he walks into the bathroom to brush his teeth.

After some deep thought, Number Sixteen walks out of the bathroom and addresses his brother clones, "Listen men, I want you to envision what it will be like to be led into a room, and then shot to death. Picture what it will be like after, you know? Absolutely nothing after that. Can you picture this? Can you see this?"

Some of the clones entertain this, close their eyes and they try and imagine their lives without life. They begin to see what Number Sixteen is saying. A few of them become visibly upset and angry. They have trained to be in Dragon Dagoth's services, and if he could kill his own mother, and attempt to kill his own father, what would be in store for them?

"This is what your future will be like, absolutely nothing. I want those of you who did think about it to tell me without thinking anything else other than the question at hand, would you not prefer, or feel it is better to live and live freely, than to live a life of subservience to Dragon Dagoth, or to die by his hand? I believe through my dreams and foresight that I can help save us from certain death."

Number Seven whips his gun out of his holster, and aims it at Number Sixteen's head, "Stand down before I am forced to take you down. You are in complete defiance of Dragon Dagoth! I order you to become silent on the matter!"

Slowly raising his hands, Number Sixteen feels his fellow clones around him; he feels their confusion as they slowly start to indirectly aim their guns at him. These are things he was never able to feel before he shot that man. He feels each of them, and can read their minds. He senses Number Fifteen beside him who wants more power and more wisdom, Number Nineteen who also wants the same. He merges his thoughts with their minds, and they aim their guns at Number Seven. The other clones follow suit.

"See Number Seven, they want to live as do I. After we have completed our mission we are not going to die by anyone's hand. Now put the safety on your gun and drop it."

Number Seven is shocked that the other clones have committed this act of treason against their creator. What compels them to give their allegiance to a rogue clone, over a dream?

"You know you are all defying Dragon Dagoth?" Number Seven says, complying with Number Sixteen's wish as he keeps his hand up visibly in the air and puts the gun on the ground. "If you think that these dreams of yours are going to come true, I can tell you you're right. You are self-fulfilling this dream of yours and you're..."

"Kill him," Number Sixteen growls out.

Number Seven's eyes enlarge with astonishment, and so do the other clones that are merely witnessing these events unfold. At this moment he has an epiphany, and realises what Number Sixteen's dream is about, "Listen, I am sorry. We have a mission to do. Let's do our mission and put this behind us. I will not tell our master. Please, I don't want to die."

Number Sixteen looks at his brother clone. His eyes cringe and slant like his creator Dragon Dagoth's, in anger, "You are weak. You could have killed me and you presented me with mercy and placed your life in my hands. I must kill you lest you rise up against me again in future! Now execute him!"

A gunshot echoes throughout the room and Number Seven buckles and drops to the floor, a mist of blood painting the wall. Number Fifteen shudders with amazement, not just at the fact that he just murdered the closest person to a brother they had, but at the fact that he had been chosen by Number Sixteen, his new master, to execute Number Seven. After executing Number Seven, a strange feeling enters his body. A mere tiny transference of power surges through Number Fifteen.

Rushing down the hall, Gav is greeted by Number Sixteen.

"My Mistress," he says, anxious and excited. He reaches for her hand and brings her close to him. He looks deep into her eyes, and utilising his new found powers he tries to reach inside of her mortal mind, becoming one with her, and taking control of her, "Can I trust you my Mistress?"

"Yes? What is going on?"

"One of my brother clones has done something that could cost all of our lives."

"What?"

"I know you feel something for me. I know you like me in a certain way that goes beyond a love for a son. I see you crying because you are lonely. I can help fill that void. I want..."

"Mind your place, young man. You came to me because you need my help. Please don't waste my time. What did your brother do?"

There must be more to it. Perhaps he is not as strong as he believes. He tries again, and tries to use his power stronger than before.

"Promise me that you will protect us," he appeals to her with his eyes locked onto hers.

She blankly stares at him and agrees.

"I want to give you a life of happiness. I can bring you more happiness than our Master. I love you."

"I love you too, Number Sixteen," Gav blankly responds, deep within his spell.

"I need your help protecting Number Fifteen. He killed one of our brothers. Grant him freedom, not only so he will not die by our Master, but so that he can dispose of Number Seven's body, or we will all pay the price for his actions. Will you do this for our love?"

"Yes, I shall," Gav murmured.

Still under Number Sixteen's spell, she releases Number Fifteen, and Number Sixteen and some of the other clones help dispose of Number Seven's body.

"Thank you for helping me Number Sixteen. I owe you my life, and my freedom," says Number Fifteen.

Number Sixteen motions for his girlfriend and the clones to give them a few minutes alone and they return to the base, giving Number Sixteen and Number Fifteen privacy. "No longer call me by my slave name. From this moment forward I shall be known as Gefallener Klon. From this moment forward, I shall name you Schatten. We are not slaves to be controlled and commanded. We are real people with real feelings. For now, I want you to seek refuge where you are able to, and do not draw any attention to yourself. I will send word for you when it is time to overthrow our former Master. I have the power to do so, and I got it from the man that was next to Joshua, but I do not know how to use it yet. Once I become more powerful, we will rise against our former Master and take control."

Schatten shakes his head, staring off into the starry night sky, observing the beauty of a world beyond four walls, taking in the scent of the crisp cool night's air, "Now that I can speak freely without worry or concern of what will happen to me, Dragon Dagoth has no reason to display the true intent of his powers to us. How will you know when you are more powerful?"

"I will never truly know Schatten, but I will think of something and when the time is right I will send word for you. Go before suspicions arise, and enjoy your freedom, my brother!"

Dragon Dagoth calls his clones to the time portal to depart on their mission to attack the Federal Bank Reserve of New York. "Men, we will be arriving or should I say materialising, on an American freeway. From there we will be making our way towards the Federal Bank Reserve of New York. Once we are there, I want Number Thirty Nine and Number Sixteen to rush inside the bank and take out all of the security men and policemen inside of the bank, while Number Forty Nine takes out the power and phone lines to the bank. Number Forty Four, you and Number Forty Six will accompany me inside of the bank while we use these forklifts to bring the time machine portals inside the three story bank vault so that we can bring the gold inside the vault to this base afterwards. I want everyone to prime and ready explosives inside the bank and the transport trucks, and blow the building and the trucks up on my command. Then we shall return to the future with all the gold, understood?"

In unison all the clones reply, "Sir, yes sir!"

Gav walks over to the controls. All the clones and Dragon Dagoth rev up the engines to take them back to the past. Gav sets the coordinates and presses 'enter' on the keyboard and sends them to the past.

Materialising on the American freeway, a few cars drive away from the monstrous transport trucks, the likes of which no one has ever seen before. The vehicles drive towards the city and down the streets until they reach the Federal Reserve Bank. Right away, the clones take to their orders while many citizens look at the oddly dressed soldiers rushing around the bank.

Number Forty Nine rushes around to the sides of the bank, placing small C4 explosives on the power lines of the bank and on the phone lines of the bank and sets off the charges. Brick and debris fly across the sides of the back street.

Number Thirty Nine and Number Sixteen rush inside the bank with their assault rifles and hand grenades. Number thirty Nine tosses his grenade inside of the bank and after the blast, they both rush inside. Number Sixteen shoots down the surviving bank guards.

"Where are the other banks security officers?!!" Number Sixteen demands to know from the tellers.

One of the female tellers points to a couple of them lying on the ground, severely wounded. Number Thirty Nine walks over to them and blasts each of them in the head and walks around the lower level of the bank, looking for more security men adjacent Number Sixteen.

Dragon Dagoth and Number Forty Four smash through the shattered front doors with their forklifts which are carrying the time machine portals, and head towards the lift inside the bank. As they take the time machine portals down to the lower levels of the bank, Number Forty Nine rushes inside the bank, armed with his assault rifle and explosives.

Number Thirty Nine and Number Sixteen rush outside the bank, head to the transport trucks and grab some more explosives, when they notice a few police cars heading their way, "Don't worry, these police officers carry primitive weapons. Hand me an RPG; this will be fun."

Number Thirty Nine hands Number Sixteen a rocket propelled grenade launcher and grabs more explosives before heading back inside the bank.

Number Sixteen opens fire. The hiss and whine of the rocket frightens everyone that is watching the robbery take place. When the rocket detonates on the first of the police cars heading their way, the car explodes and kills a few onlookers watching the whole ordeal.

A couple of surviving officers smash out their car door windows and climb out of the side of the vehicle, only to hear a halo of bullets smashing against the bottom of the car. "Jesus Christ, they have an army there or something. How are we supposed to take them out with these pistols?"

"I don't know, Vinnie. Let's just get out before we get killed!"

Number Sixteen patiently waits as one of the officers hops out of his car and then watches as the other survivor hops out of the police car, then opens fire shooting down that officer, and looks for the other officer who jumped in behind another car.

He shoves another rocket inside the tube. Number Sixteen fires again, taking out the remaining officer.

Number Sixteen drops the RPG, and then picks up some explosives and joins the others in the bank.

Together they all prime and ready the explosives on the lower level of the bank, while some of the surviving clients and tellers of the bank huddle on the ground, hoping and praying that nothing will happen to them. Some are rather curious as to why they are not being told that they will be killed if they do not sit on the ground, and they decide to run for dear life, out of the bank. The others follow suit and no one else inside the bank is killed.

The time machine portals are set up downstairs surrounding all of the gold that will be stolen and sent to the future. The time is near. All of the clones monitor the entrances of the lift inside the vault to make sure that no unexpected police would show up to complicate the heist.

They blow up the upper levels of the bank as well as the transport trucks and return to the future, billions of dollars in gold richer.

After the sunset, the cool night air seeps through the downtown district. Finishing up his tea, Jahangir Wahidi gets up from his chair at one of the local restaurants. He is tired and is calling it a night; he decides to head for home with his cousin Rashidi. All the while walking home, he can feel aches and pains from the arthritis that he has developed over the years as well as the uneasy feeling that someone is watching them.

Jahangir is not able to shake the discomforting feeling. It is as intense as having sun's warmth blanket around him; even Rashidi kept looks over his shoulder from time to time.

"Why are you looking behind you?" asks Jahangir.

"I don't know it's like I feel someone is there but I only see the locals." Rashidi responds to his cousin.

"I know. I've had that feeling since we left the restaurant."

They continue to walk, and the feeling grows more intense, so much so that Jahangir pulls out his hand gun, and takes the safety off, while placing the gun in between the sleeves of his garment as they continue to walk down the side streets. Rashidi does not say anything as he keeps a close eye on what his cousin is doing. Hopefully their gut feelings about someone following them are not true, but who knows. They have been ambushed once before during the Russian occupation, fortunately survived; but, something about this situation is different, unlike the last time where they didn't feel or sense the ambush.

Ahead of them are some rundown buildings. They turn the corner, hoping to lose the person following them. To their surprise, a dark figure is before them and their uneasiness grows. They both freeze when they recognise who the figure is, Dragon Dagoth. He is standing in the middle of the street, clad in his black cloak, awaiting their arrival. Jahangir puts his gun back inside his pocket. He will not do anything to anger his boss, or get killed by him, and he looks towards his cousin as reassurance, and then slowly makes his way towards the man he believes is the Jinn Ibliss.

"What is it that you want from us, Ibliss?"

"The time has come for you to launch your attacks on my targets," Dragon Dagoth says.

Jahangir Wahidi fidgets with his hands in his pocket. He is extremely nervous about following through with Dragon Dagoth's request, although he has been paid a mass fortune by Dragon Dagoth already. He is not sure whether his men are ready to become martyrs for Allah just yet, or what will be the outcome afterwards. Once they launched their attacks, there would be no telling what the enemy would do to them or their people in general. To date, all they had done is small attacks on American embassies. This attack would surely be the greatest of all the attacks, yet the outcome would be far worse than any of the other attacks if and when there was retaliation.

"I don't think the men are ready. I don't think we can pull off something like this. I am sorry, you will have to give us a new mission. Besides, if we murder just one innocent person, it will be as if we have murdered all mankind."

Rashidi Akim's eyes grow wide and his mouth drops. Memories of their first encounter with the Jinn Ibliss flood his mind. How could his cousin be so brazen as to defy the Ibliss?!

"What?! How dare you guys question my orders, especially after I have paid you so handsomely throughout the years? Have I wasted the last twenty years on you guys for nothing?!"

Rashidi speaks up before the conversation gets further out of hand, "No my Lord, we can do it. We can do it as soon as you want. Please do not listen to my cousin. He has had too much to drink today."

"I am a Muslim and I do not drink. I do not need you to lie for me, Rashidi. To kill all these innocent people is not what I had in mind when I agreed to helping you. Our people will not be subjected to disobeying Allah, the most beneficent, no matter what!"

Rashidi counters his cousin. "Brother, please watch what you say, for the love of Allah the most beneficent. We will be doing his work." Rashidi brings his voice down and whispers. "Besides, there is a time and place for everything and arguing with the Ibliss now is not in our best interests, if you follow what I am saying?!"

"No, no, no! I do not care. I will do anything he wants of us, but I cannot be responsible for the deaths of thousands of people. This is not doing Allah's work and Dragon Dagoth said that he would not have us go against Allah's spoken word and he also said that he would not manipulate the Holy Quran to satisfy his plans."

"I no longer have a use for you Jahangir Wahidi. Rashidi Akim, prove your continued loyalty to me and kill him. I will pay you more than I have paid this worthless slime. If you don't, I will kill you both!"

Rashidi's heart stops right then and there or so it feels. It seems as if time has slowed down to a halt. His cousin is like his brother, and he loves his cousin dearly. His cousin has looked out for him since he was a little boy. Feeling weak at the knees, Rashidi keeps his composure and turns around and faces his cousin, his brother, the only family aside from his own that has been there day in and day out for him.

Jahangir's confidence wanes as he notes the look of confusion, anxiety and what appears to be his cousin contemplating the idea. "Rashidi, are you considering his offer?! Do not give into the Ibliss' lies. He is the deceiver of all mankind. He wants to kill thousands of innocent people and for what, his amusement? Please Rashidi, think about what he is asking us to do."

Rashidi does not respond. Without giving a second thought to this, Jahangir pulls out his gun and aims it at Dragon Dagoth, saying, "Are you a stupid man? Do you think my cousin will actually join you over me? I am in control. I am the one holding the gun. I will kill you. I will put a bullet right through your fucking head!"

"Rashidi, I know you are looking for a life beyond servitude to your cousin. I can read your thoughts. Do as I ask and I will give you a life of riches beyond what you could ever imagine. If you don't, I will kill you both right here and now, then I will go and kill your wife who carries your unborn son."

How does he know my wife is pregnant? No one knows. They were keeping this a secret until at least after the first trimester in case she miscarried. He couldn't have anything happen to his beloved wife, or his son, a son? The thought of having a son nearly puts a smile on his face until he remembers where he is. As far as he is concerned, Jahangir made his choice defying the Ibliss, and he must obey the Jinn Ibliss so no harm befalls his wife and unborn son until he can find a way to gain leverage over him, and turn the situation around.

"Rashidi! Kill him. Now!"

Without thinking twice about the situation, he pulls his gun free from his pocket, and mutters forgiveness for himself. His cousin turns around and realises that he has been betrayed and he raises his gun to Rashidi. Before Jahangir pulls his trigger, Rashidi pulls his, ending his cousin's life in cold blood.

The sound of the gunshot echoes throughout the cold dark street, followed by the thumping fall of Jahangir's lifeless body on the ground. Rashidi drops his gun and lowers himself next to his dead cousin's body, fighting back tears and allowing memories of their childhood to flood his mind. "I am so sorry, what have I done?! Allah! Please bring him back to me!"

Rashidi looks up and notices Dragon Dagoth is walking away, while he is mourning over his dead cousin. He cries out, "What the fuck? Fuck you Devil-man. I kill my own flesh and blood for you, and you say nothing! You do nothing. This is what I get for loyalty towards you? Fuck you, okay!"

These fucking maggots are just as bad as the Christians and this maggot thinks he can talk to me like this? "You have your orders, you know what needs to be done. Do you think I need to waste my precious breath on you further?!"

Humbling himself before Dragon Dagoth's contemptuous glare, Rashidi stays by the side of his cousin's lifeless body, while silently cursing himself for what he has done.

"Sit down 'love'," Christopher says emphatically.

"What for? I thought you brought me back to our first house so we can connect, and at least try to be intimate. But no, just another boring weekend alone with you."

Christopher waves his hand to a chair and adamantly conveys with a non-verbal expression, the need for her to sit down. "I know the years have been tough not only on you but on us. I understand the isolation that you feel, cooped up inside of the base. But starting today, all of that will change."

"That's an understatement if I've ever heard one before. Just get to the point. I'm bored and you don't fuck me, so get this over with so I can go watch TV or something."

"I want to thank you for helping me all those years ago; however, you are no longer of use to me. I have a repaired time machine. The clones have grown up, and now you are having an affair with one of them... Number Sixteen."

Gav froze in her chair. No weapons around her and no way of being able to kill him even if she had a gun. No way to lie to a mind reader to convince him otherwise. This was her moment of despair. "Are you going to kill me?"

"Unfortunately, I gave you my word long ago that I would not."

"Then what is to become of Number Sixteen?"

"He will continue to serve me as he always has until he is no longer of use to me."

"So what are you going to do to me?"

"Oh, I am not going to do anything to you. The police found it interesting that you left England all those years ago without a trace after your partner's murder. They will be here any moment to apprehend you."

"I cleared myself of interest years ago and if you are going to fuck me over with the police, I will take you down and let everyone know about the time machines."

"I know, we've gone through this in a few alternate time frames. It was my way of practising the real situation with you, and this time there is nothing you can do."

The doorbell rings and echoes throughout the house. Gav uses this as her chance to run to the door. She answers the door and the police are there just as Christopher said they would be. She quickly opens the door and greets the police officers hysterically. "He is a cold bloodied murderer. Christopher is the one who killed my partner, and now he is trying to frame..."

"Ma'am calm down," one of the officers says as she grabs Gav's arms and turns her around, placing handcuffs around her tiny wrists. "Who is 'Christopher', ma'am?"

"My partner, he is the one who called you guys and is framing me!"

"We got a call from this place of residence and the telephone is not registered to anyone named Christopher."

"Christopher is my partner. Ask for his identification or something. It will at least prove what I am saying."

The female officer restraining Gav nods to the male police officer.

"Alright sir, can I see some identification?"

Dragon Dagoth looks at the police officers and then at Gav. He reaches into his back pocket and then pulls out his passport, and social insurance card. The police officer looks at the identification and then radios dispatch, "Hi, we have a 10-12 and are requesting a 10-7 on a..." The police officer walks away and gives the name listed on Dragon Dagoth's identification so that Gav is not able to hear the name. He returns to the room shortly after.

"Sorry sir, I am sure you understand why I had to verify your address."

"Yes, I understand."

Dragon Dagoth walks to the door as the police take Gavrilovich to their police car and then drive off. Giving no second thought of remorse or care, he shuts the door behind him knowing he is now free to pursue what he has always longed for.

"Yes they are to launch the attacks tomorrow. There is no question about it, and our boss wants it done now," Rashidi informs his employee on the phone, nervously swinging his pen back and forth between his fingers while he awaits a response.

"Okay, I will inform the others," the voice on the phone replied.

"I want the strikes to hit the World Trade Tower buildings first so that the focus will be shifted there, and then attacks on the Whitehouse can go through successfully. Lastly whatever happens, I want to thank you and Khalid for all your help and support. I shall send you funds once the task has been completed. Allahu Akbar! WaAleykum al Salam, Osama."

"That has been the plan all along, my friend. Do not worry. Our men are well educated. I handpicked them myself. They will get the job done right, my friend. Once again, I am sorry for the loss of your cousin. I was a very good friend of his and not only was he a benefactor of Al-Qaeda, but also a shaheed for Allah in this jihad bis saif. He will be greatly rewarded after judgment day. Allahu Akbar! Wa Aleykum al Salam, Rashidi."

September 11th 2001

The ring of the alarm clock annoys Christopher. Turning over he shuts the alarm clock off and tries to pull himself out of semi sleep. Sitting up in the bed, Christopher looks around for his remote control. He can't find it, and so uses his powers to turn on the television set and switch the channel to CNN. He waits.

Half an hour of watching the television passes by and Christopher grows impatient. He is expecting to see something happen, and it is not happening yet. Suddenly breaking news cuts into normal programming as President Bush speaks to public school students at the first founded all black school, Booker Elementary. A commercial airliner was shown going through one of the twin towers of the World Trade buildings in the state of New York, America.

While Christopher continues watching the television, another airliner flies through the next of the twin towers leaving a mushroom cloud of smoke soaring high to the heavens. The unfolding incidents seem like a movie; however, the events on television are very real.

After forty five minutes of watching the breaking news on CNN, a news reporter announces that there has been an attack on the pentagon. The last of the attacks is thwarted when passengers of flight 93 take out the Islamic extremists who hijacked the plane to crash it into the Whitehouse and deliver a death blow to the United States President. This part of the mission was a double failure. For one, Dragon Dagoth's men failed by not driving the plane into the Whitehouse, two had they succeeded and sent the plane into the Whitehouse, the President of the United States of America was in Sarasota, Florida, far away from where the assassination would have taken place. As he continues to stare at the television set, although he is let down by their failure to kill the President, he feels and knows this could still work to his advantage and smiles.

It was time for Dragon Dagoth to complete his next mission; he would continue using the Muslims to do attacks around the world until the day would come that he would get elected into power.

Stretching his arm across the bed to place on top of his newborn son, Mohammed, and further over to his wife, Rashidi feels nothing but an empty space on his bed, sheets and covers. Opening his eyes, he looks at his alarm clock, "1:54 A.M." Not giving it much thought, he assumes his wife Khaterah is breast feeding his son downstairs and turns over to fall asleep once again.

No more than half an hour later, Rashidi turns over and wakes himself up, subconsciously fearing that he is about to roll over onto his son, when he realizes Khaterah and Mohammed are still not in bed. He looks at the time, "2:21 AM". "Khaterah?" Rashidi's voice is barely above a whisper, shaking off being so tired. Rashidi takes a deep breath and calls his wife again.

Getting up and putting on his slippers while still half asleep, Rashidi walks down the stairs and into the living room. What he sees, stops his heart for a few brief seconds. The very embodiment of evil is sitting on his couch, carefully holding his son Mohammed while caressing his baby's hair with his free hand. His fingers nails are painted with black nail polish, something he has never noticed about the man before. Just looking at the cloaked, dark black figure sends shivers up and down Rashidi's spine.

"You failed me Rashidi!!!"

"My Lord, we did not fail. We did as you asked. We destroyed the World Trade Centre and attacked the Pentagon. I cannot explain why the Whitehouse did not go through but you must understand the implications of such things. Please give me my boy."

Dragon Dagoth does not look at Rashidi as he speaks to him. He continues to caress the boy's hair, "Ah, your son is beautiful. Mohammed is his name, right?"

Rashidi carefully nods his head yes. If only there was a way to take his son from the Ibliss' hold. He looks at his wife. She is in a deep sleep. She is under Dragon Dagoth's spell.

"Yes he is. Please hand me Mohammed. Please give him to me. We did not fail you."

"Oh, that is strange?!" Dragon Dagoth's deep voice bellows, and the baby in his arms starts to get agitated by not being in his mother's arms and starts to cry out a little.

"Shh, shh, shh…" Dragon Dagoth lifts his head looking at Rashidi. His face grows cold and distant. The atmosphere in the house shifts quickly.

"The American President still lives! You have failed me! The attack on the Pentagon was supposed to be done with an airline, not a cruise missile. There weren't supposed to any survivors. You assured me personally that you could accomplish this small feat without a hitch and this is what I get?!" Dragon Dagoth's powers begin to rage uncontrollably. The furniture in the living room begins to shake and rattle. The glass on the family portrait pictures crack and break. Debating whether to toss the baby across the room or not, Dragon Dagoth calms down. The baby has nothing to do with any of this. Then again, neither did his son while he was a boy, and his son was brutally murdered by people just like Rashidi.

Dragon Dagoth stops caressing the boy and looks at him, growling at it like a wild beast. Rashidi takes a few steps forward. He cries out loud, "Please my Lord, my dark Ibliss, the great Shaitan. I beg of you, please do not hurt my son. He is just a boy! Take my life. I am the one you feel has failed. My son has nothing to do with this, please…"

"My son was killed by people just like you. He was just as innocent!" This was a different type of loss of composure, highly unusual that he would have a personal outburst expressing his feelings about his loved ones to those under his control. He rolls his eyes and walks over to the sniffling man, grovelling before his feet, bowing down worshipping him as if he was a god. Rashidi prostrates himself before a man he thought was Shaitan. Dragon Dagoth bends over and hands Rashidi his cute baby boy.

"My Lord, I did not fail you. You are the great Shaitan. Use your powers and see that my men did use an airliner to fly it into the Pentagon. They are all dead! We have only failed on the assassination of the American President, and even if we took out the Whitehouse, the President was not there."

Standing erect once again, Dragon Dagoth stretches out with his mind. Rashidi is telling the truth. An aeroplane crashed into the Pentagon, and his men were dead. "So it appears you are telling the truth; however, you have still failed to kill the President. I can still make this work. Next time I expect results, not excuses. I will not be as pleasant if you fail me next time, Akim! You will need to move far away from your homeland. I would suggest informing your men to head to the Kingdom of Saudi Arabia. There you will wait in hiding till this 'crisis' abates the Western world, then I will deliver further instructions."

As Dragon Dagoth, the Dark Lord walks by, a shiver goes up Rashidi's spine. The door shuts and he collapses to the floor. Thoughts of fear racing through his head, he does not sleep at all that night as he holds onto his son for dear life, and watchfully awaits the waking of his wife, Khaterah.

10

The president of The New Order Enterprises Incorporated, Max Diamond, has been hired by an anonymous source, Dragon Dagoth, and is standing before a slew of cloning experts, technical experts and construction specialists. Each of them has been paid handsomely to come to Max Diamond's special meeting.

"Good afternoon ladies and gentlemen. First off, I want to thank you all for coming here today and on such short notice. Next, I have asked you all to come here today because I want to embark on a mission that will give us each a special place in history. We will be as pioneers to the global engineering of the world. What I have before you, Michelle, if you please." Max waves his hand for his secretary to remove a curtain behind him to unveil a few prototypes of what he is talking about.

"Here are the prototypes of cloning pods, and robots from our sponsor who is endorsing all this, the New Order Enterprises Incorporated. The New Order Enterprises Incorporated's mission is to supply military forces with these technical specialised robots that will be able to tell the difference between allies and foes on the battlefield. The reason for the cloning pods is simple, our sponsor. The New Order Enterprises Incorporated wants us to create clone blood, tissue and flesh for these robots. That way these robots will look real, smell real and our robots can be involved in infiltration missions.

"Basically the New Order Enterprises Incorporated respects and values human life, and after these unfortunate terrorist attacks on our neighbouring country's civilians, the United States will be planning an allied invasion of Afghanistan and Iraq. It is their primary duty to keep as many of our troops alive as possible. With your help you will be creating the future wave of warfare and hopefully this will lead to saving hundreds, if not thousands, of our troop's lives. The downside to all of this is that this is a top secret mission. You are called here because you are the most elite of your positions, and you will be called out for at least a year or however long it takes to complete this mission before you, whichever is less time. Afterwards, the New Order Enterprises Incorporated will compensate you all with three million dollars in U.S. currency."

Many of the attendants feel as if this job is a dream come true. The money would help dearly or in fact give them enough to live out the rest of their lives comfortably. Others were sad that they would have to leave their families for a year but the thought of so much money in their hands afterwards, was good enough make the decision an easy one.

"For those of you that are ready to embark on this bold new direction for the future, please follow my assistant Michelle as she takes you to the back parking lot where you will be escorted to vehicles that will take you to the secret location where you will be living, and may I ask the others who are not leaving, to stay behind as you will be asked to sign some waivers and then you can be on your way."

Half an hour passes and many of the attendants are shipped off to Dragon Dagoth's base and the others that stay behind, a few shy of twenty in total, wait impatiently for the waiver forms to come in so that they can sign them and leave.

Dragon Dagoth visits the hotel and watches as the trucks drive away, and then walks to the shadows of the parking lot, peeking in through the ballroom windows. Locking all the doors to the hotel reception area by remote, while watching on a live feed he is able to see the people rushing to the doors and scrambling for a way out. Pressing a button he detonates the explosives in the reception area. The entire lower level of the hotel is blown apart, leaving no traces of evidence for his plans behind.

While at the base, Max Diamond leads his new employees to the time portal, and takes them back fifteen hundred years in time, setting the coordinates to the base in Britannia. This is the same time era that Dragon Dagoth was coming back from war against the Saxons, and will be able to save his wife and son from certain death.

Through the help and backing of The New Order Enterprises Incorporated, Max takes his time helping transport everything the experts will need in order to work on Dragon Dagoth's inventions. Partial parts of the base including a park, are equipped with homes and have miscellaneous shops. The base is total utopia, and a complete simulation of the outside world to relax them for the time that they will spend working on the robots that will be programmed with the most sophisticated software of the time, that they had ever seen. However, access to other parts of the base are only accessible by Max Diamond or Dragon Dagoth.

Dragon Dagoth keeps to the shadows as he rushes quickly to the forest near the area he remembers his precious Annex being attacked, and he waits until morning, hiding in the outline of the trees. The longer he waits, the angrier he becomes waiting for his prey to show up.

It is not long before the soldiers show up. He watches as his wife runs through the field, and a few soldiers follow quickly behind her, and then he notices one of them bending over to pick up a stone. "No!" Dragon Dagoth shouts out as he rushes into the open field. Using his power, he makes his wife fall to the ground just in time to see a rather heavy stone avoid collision with her. Using his power, he sends the stone off in another direction and raises his gun up to the soldiers rushing his way. Looking through the cross hairs of his scope, he opens fire, killing the soldiers easily.

Annex continues to lie down on the ground screaming, and covering her ears from the deafening sounds from the gun. She then looks up to see a man in front of her who is dressed in garments that frighten her, and she struggles to her feet, doing her best to back away from the man.

Putting his assault rifle behind his back, Dragon Dagoth reaches for his hood and takes it off so that she can see his face.

"Ethel?" she cries.

Cynric searches everywhere for his mother. He does not know where she is but he uses the powers his father has been training him with, to locate her. Axe in hand, he runs down the dirt road to find her. He feels her presence all along the trail as he keeps an eye out looking for her everywhere along the path.

At last, he sees a few soldiers in the thick of the field, and they are dead, smoke rising from their wounds. In the distance, he sees a man clad in black with thick, long, dirty blonde hair tied back in a ponytail, extending his arm out to pick his mother up. Cynric reaches out and is able to feel that this man saved his mother. He can also feel that this man is his father, but how is this possible? He does not recognise him at all.

"Ethelwulf, how may this be so? Thou hast been gone only for a few full moons and thine appearance hath changed so much, and what contraption is this ye wield?" Annex says.

"Cynric is on his way here. Once he comes here, we will have to go. I have no time to explain. We must head to your old village."

"Even thy tongue sounds strange unto me. Art thou my Ethelwulf?" Annex asks, while cupping her hands on Dragon Dagoth's face. He has changed. What he has seen and experienced within the last few hundred years was beyond any amounts of explanation that he could give to his wife at the moment.

Cynric cautiously approaches his parents, curiously staring at his father, wondering if he is his father.

"We need to go now before the other soldiers come."

After informing his family to wait inside the barn that he used to take refuge in while he was a child from his adoptive parents, Dragon Dagoth carefully places remote mines across the village, where he knows or anticipates the other soldiers will trace them to, and then he creeps back into the barn, waiting with his family, hiding on the upper level of the barn.

A few minutes pass by and Britannian soldiers rush into the village on horseback following the dogs' trail of Annex, Cynric and himself. Dragon Dagoth pries open a piece of plywood and aims his assault rifle, equipped with a silencer, at the Dux Bellorum. He watches the Dux barking orders at his men. Focusing on the Dux in the crosshairs, he pulls the trigger, taking him out, and then quickly shoots down a few more unsuspecting soldiers who do not have the faintest idea of what is going on. As the soldiers hide behind their horses, reaching into the inside pocket of his cloak, Dragon Dagoth pulls out a small transmitter and touches a small red button.

Outside the barn, several remote mines blow up, taking out the majority of the soldiers and most of their horses, as well as well blowing apart some of the hand built houses that are around the mines. Dragon Dagoth rushes out of the barn and towards the remaining soldiers who are fearful of who this person is.

They pull out their swords and move to attack the person that seems to be unarmed, not knowing the weapon he is holding is greater than any sword created.

Dragon Dagoth shoots the soldiers down, save two fresh soldiers that are rushing in through the field, which are Drake the Goth, and his former self.

Ethelwulf draws his sword and Dragon Dagoth removes his hood revealing his face. "Stop please!" Dragon Dagoth shouts out towards himself.

As Ethelwulf rushes closer to the dark man, he slowly comes to a halt. As he walks towards the dark figure with his sword to his side, he is curious to know who this person is and curious as to why he did not kill him and Drake like the other soldiers. Yet, the closer he gets he cannot help but see the resemblance to himself, of the man before him. Is this his father Joshua? Or was this his brother? Or could it be another relative of his? What's more, he can feel the strange power emanating from this person. "Who art thou?"

"I am you. I learned how to travel through the depths of time. Now, I want you to listen to me very carefully."

Ethelwulf looks at Dragon Dagoth intensely. His friend Drake stands by his side and is just as curious as Ethelwulf, recognising the resemblance of his friend Ethelwulf in the stranger.

"Hello Drake," Dragon Dagoth says to his friend.

"Who art thou?"

"I used to go by the name of Ethelwulf, which was until you were murdered by these soldiers here. I took my revenge and killed Palmyra, Annex's mother for betraying her daughter and my son, but that was in another time frame. I have just altered the present. Anyway, I took on the name I had nicknamed you. Instead of calling myself Dragon the Goth, I took on Dragon Dagoth as my new name. I also go by another name as well Max Diamond. I no longer use Ethelwulf.

"Ethelwulf, your senses were correct. These men came here to find our family. They were burning on stakes. Annex was dead by the time you killed off these soldiers. Cynric was burning to ashes. He is like us. He cannot die unless his head is removed. That is our weakness as long as we keep our heads on our shoulders we can live eternally. Seeing the pain Cynric was enduring you eased his pain and sliced his head off. Before you could kill off the rest of the soldiers, you noticed Drake."

Dragon Dagoth lifts and aims his gun at Drake, indicating that he was talking to him "Drake was held captive by the soldiers. They tossed you both off that cliff over there." With Dragon Dagoth's right hand, he points towards the cliff. "With that said, it is imperative that you do as I say to you, okay?"

Ethelwulf falls to the ground while listening to the story. It is too much to bear. His wife burned to death by the orders of her own mother over Christianity? His friend killed when they were tossed off a cliff? For crying out loud, he was talking to himself, and not just in his head. He was talking to himself face to face. Composing himself, Ethelwulf's thoughts transferred back to his beloved wife Annex and son Cynric. If that had all happened and he had returned from the future to save them, where were they now?

"They are in the barn Ethelwulf; however, I cannot allow you to see them again. You need to go to a place that I will instruct you to go to and kill off some soldiers from the future. From there, you will travel to the future and meet a police officer who will help you. Let the future play its course. Once she betrays you, I will know and give you further instructions. Go now with this knowledge I have presented to you and do what must be done."

"No," Ethelwulf raises his sword. There is no way that he would just leave his son and wife to this person claiming to be him from the future. "No, I shalt not do as thou hast said unto me. I shall slay thee here and live an abundant life with mine wife Annex and mine offspring Cynric!" Ethelwulf leaps towards Dragon Dagoth and swings his sword at him.

"No, please don't!" Dragon Dagoth begs, jumping out of the swords way and running backwards away from Ethelwulf. "I can make Annex immortal like us. I have the knowledge to do it, and I have more power than you do. Allow me to do this. You will eventually be with them in the future!" Dragon Dagoth keeps running from Ethelwulf who is chasing after him. Fed up, Dragon Dagoth aims his gun at Ethelwulf's kneecap. "Stand down!"

Ethelwulf does not listen and keeps pursuing Dragon Dagoth. Dragon Dagoth continues to back up, while keeping his gun aimed at Ethelwulf, and then finally, he blasts holes in Ethelwulf's knee caps, dropping him instantly. Drake unsure of what to do, rushes to Ethelwulf's side.

"Please Drake my friend, this is between me and myself. He has to listen."

"Do not listen unto him Drake for thou art my friend. He wishes to keep me away from mine wife. Slay him!"

Drake raises his sword and slowly approaches Dragon Dagoth.

"Please don't do it. You were like a brother to me. If things play out properly, you can have a place by my side in the future. Together with my family, we will rule the world! Please my brother, listen to me!"

Drake lowers his sword. Dragon Dagoth is very convincing. There is a ring of truth to everything he says, no matter how bizarre it sounds. But his loyalty is to Ethelwulf; yet, if this person is truly Ethelwulf from the future, his loyalty should be to both of them, all too confusing.

"Drake, he hath born falsehoods unto thee as well as I. He is not me! Kill him!"

Knowing that he shouldn't take the chance, Drake raises his sword and charges towards Dragon Dagoth. Without thinking twice about it, Dragon Dagoth raises his gun, Drake still charges towards him, waiting to see if Drake will swing his sword. Dragon Dagoth keeps his finger steady on the trigger, and there it was.

Drake swings his sword back for momentum, and then brings it forward. Dragon Dagoth squeezes his trigger, shooting Drake in the head, leaving himself with a new memory, on top of the older ones he had. Firing more bullets, this time in Ethelwulf's ankles, Dragon Dagoth slowly walks back for his family, to the barn he spent the majority of all his childhood in, and then he leads them to the base.

1 year later: 556 A.D.

A great deal of excitement is circulating among the scientists and programming specialists. It has been a year since they've had the opportunity to speak with their families, many of whom are becoming angry and frustrated, but after a year of hard work they would soon see them.

Some of the scientists are a little put out that they are being given frivolous tasks while they wait for the technical programming specialists to complete their secret tasks, which is programming voice recognition for the machines to recognize Max Diamond's voice and commands, as well as Dragon Dagoth's, which those specialists thought is strange seeing that these machines are supposed to replace soldiers. Either way they are being paid to work and not ask questions.

The machines are very life-like. They pass for humans, although their movements are choppy, and they act like dummies. Max will provide the specialists with whatever they need to make them the most sophisticated computerised machines, and give them whatever they need to correct these glitches.

The machines are all programmed to take orders from Max Diamond alone, and the machines are all programmed to get their orders from a central processing server within the base, and they would all follow their orders in unison, unless some are given individual missions, assassinations, infiltrations etc.

All the hard work is finally done, and almost everyone is celebrating their impending return home. The experts unveil one of the machines in all its perfection before Max Diamond.

He takes his time walking around the machine. He is proud of the hard work the experts have performed. Walking around the machine, the machine turns each time Max walks it to keep its eyes or sensors on him, which thoroughly impresses Max all the more.

"Affirmative... task completed... on standby... awaiting further instructions."

Everyone is confused as to what the machine is saying. No one has given it orders but perhaps this is just part of the show. It even sounds real, although it did speak quite simply. Max frowns a bit, and shrugs it off. It does not matter. This thing is so magnificent; it looks identical to a human. Who could tell the difference?

"Hey Tom! Take a look at this. The server is taking control of itself. I can't get the system back," Taylor says, as she tries to re-enable her account, while half eavesdropping on the unveiling party.

Tom rushes over to the computer dashboard beside Taylor and tries rebooting the system. The system does not reboot. He then tries to enter access codes to override the system, thinking that an outside source has taken over but all his codes are denied.

A machine walks into the server room and raises its gun at the couple, "You are to report to the main lobby. This room is now restricted."

Not about to argue with a robot holding a light machine gun rifle, Tom and Taylor quickly leave the server room and join the others rounded up and held inside the main lobby by the machines. Tom and Taylor murmur between themselves, wondering if they made a fatal error in the programming somehow, and then another turn of events unfolds before their eyes. They watch as a frightened and defenseless Max Diamond is dragged into the main lobby by one of the machines. The machine grabs Max Diamond by the throat and then it whispers a set of instructions in his ear.

"Ladies and gentlemen, I am sorry that it has come to this. You are all to provide a DNA sample and you are all to be cloned. After your clones are created, you will be ordered to train these clones after which you will be returned to your families. A shareholder by the black ops name of Dragon Dagoth has now assumed complete control of this facility. He will be giving you all further instructions. This is the last instruction I have for all of you. I am deeply sorry for this."

After Max finishes his speech another machine walks through the frightened crowd and grabs Max Diamond, taking him out of the immediate vicinity. No one saw this coming at all. In fact, they all thought they were participating in a noble cause and they are now prisoners of their own work.

Not wanting to waste his time on any frivolous pyramid meetings to get to know the top sellers of arms within the biker gangs, Dragon Dagoth sends his assassin machines to have meetings with some of the middle men. They in turn provide the loyalty that the top gangsters are looking for to provide some proof that Dragon Dagoth is serious about his purchase plans for arms, regardless of whether or not he could get them overseas.

After a couple of years, Dragon Dagoth is finally allowed to meet with some of the higher end warlords that run the Toronto area for weaponry and drugs. Dragon Dagoth's initial meeting proves to be quite the situation.

Dragon Dagoth is escorted behind several of his transport trucks after he leaves his limousine. His armed machines hop out of the vehicle, alarming everyone there. The gangsters pull out their guns and order the machines to drop their weapons.

"We are unable to comply. We protect Dragon Dagoth, just as you protect who is in charge of you. Our boss has arranged a meeting with the good intentions of having further transactions in the future. If you will not permit us to protect our boss as you do yours, we will leave and you will not see from us again nor will you profit from us."

There is a few minutes' silence as the bikers speak with their boss over the phone. Eventually, they wave Dragon Dagoth and his crew, inside the warehouse.

"I want to meet this man personally," says Rex, the bike gang leader. "That way I will know who to kill if this guy turns out to be a cop."

The biker gang leader's entourage pull out their guns and escort their boss Rex to Dagoth's limousine.

"My boss only wants your boss to see him," one of the gang says to the robots. "I assure you that no harm will befall him. Please stay standing where you are now."

Rex waves off his men but signals them to wait at a comfortable distance away. As the chauffeur opens the door, Rex takes a step backward as he feels an eerie presence inside the limousine.

Rex has met cold bloodied killers before. He has met the most terrible of men. He has foot soldiers working for him that just do not care about anything, and not one of them has made him flinch with unease before. Dragon Dagoth is the first man who has ever brought a sense of fear to him. The man resembles the character death. He can feel the evil reaching out to him from within the limousine as he stares at the man with disbelief.

"Get inside," Dragon Dagoth bellowed towards Rex, while keeping his eyes off him, and monitoring something on a television inside of the limousine.

Shaking off the uneasy feeling, Rex sits down as the chauffeur shuts the door behind him. Dragon Dagoth makes no gesture to shake the President of the biker gang's hand or even look at him as he continues to stare at the monitor in front of him. He is using a remote control to go through what appears to be a slideshow of other gangs, some of which Rex recognizes, and on some other slides he notices that his face is included with other close personnel that are high up in ranks.

"What's this?!" Rex snaps, undecided on whether he should pull out his gun and blow a hole through this person's head.

"These are pictures of all your rivals including yourself. I know of a Politician who knows all of you. In fact, he is been willing to make you an offer, one that will keep you out of jail indefinitely. You see, my soldiers have been running a sting operation for him and have damning evidence on all of you. All you have to do is place in a bid for freedom. It will be one bid. It's quite simple really. The highest bidder wins their freedom, the others go down. If you do not bid high enough, you go down as well."

Rex's blood begins to boil. How he could have been duped like this? Everything within their operation had been close circuit. Everyone that entered, if there was enough of a trust built up, had to kill someone as initiation. All of this would be placed back on him. If he killed this Dragon Dagoth, he would definitely go down, but how much had the other rivals bid? Was this evidence damning enough to put him away for a long time? While Rex thinks this over, Dragon Dagoth flicks the remote and shows him live digital feeds linking him to executions of rival gang members as well as participating in major drug deals. All of the slides point to someone in his organization being a police informant!

"On the seat beside you is an envelope. You will make an electronic bid using the portable interac machine inside. Use the phone here if necessary to find out how much you are willing to bid. Remember others have bid before you so this may give you the advantage. I implore you to use any means necessary to win your bid."

Rex snatches the envelope on the chair and pulls out the portable interac device. Before Rex starts to provide a bidding amount, he recalls what Dragon Dagoth said to him: 'Remember the others have bid before you so this may give you the advantage. I implore you to use any means necessary to win your bid'. After careful consideration Rex picks up a phone inside the limousine and calls each of his gang chapters in Toronto and informs them to sell all their assets immediately, and informs them that the cops are on to them, and that they have less than an hour to comply with his orders.

Dragon Dagoth shuts the monitor off, and turns on some classical music, which invokes the eerie feeling inside of the limousine again.

After an hour Rex calls his banks and merges all his accounts into one, closing all the other accounts and provides Dragon Dagoth a handsome bid. After he is done, he tosses the interac machine aside and lets out an exasperated sigh, leaning deep into the cushion of the back seat.

"Leave. I will either inform you of the results or you will be arrested in a sting operation if you have not won the bid. If you try and sniff out the leak within your entourage, I will know and instruct my servant to kill you all. My servant is a well-trained assassin and is quite capable of such a feat. Now leave!"

Rex stares at Dragon Dagoth. The anger boiling within his veins nearly compels him to pull out his gun and repeatedly shoot him. In fact, Rex desires it so much that he envisions the cloaked black figure begging for his life each time he pulls the trigger, but eventually calms down. "How the hell did you appear from nowhere and have such control over us? Our gangs have been in power for decades and here you come, no one has even heard of you until just recently and you have full control?! This could only be done if you are the police or in the law enforcement agencies, somehow!"

"I assure you Rex I am not affiliated with the police, however, I will have complete dominance over them in time as well, and nothing will be too great a task that I will not be able to complete it. Now leave my vehicle before I get angry!"

Rex opens the door and hops out of the vehicle and stares at his entourage as he shuts the car door. All of those men standing in front of him, the most trusted individuals of his gang, have been reduced to nothing in his eyes, within the blink of a short conversation with an absolute stranger!

As Rex walks away from the limousine, he faintly hears his loyal guards following behind him. Rex stretches his hand up high in the air for them all to see, and extends his middle finger, "Don't follow me. Stay here. In fact, just go home for the day. I don't want any of you around me right now."

"Our task has been completed. Let's leave," Dragon Dagoth commands his chauffeur.

"Ah yes, come in," Max replied to a knock on the door from the Toronto Chief of Police and a few of his other officials.

They walk into the sparsely furnished Liberal's office one by one, to see why the Mayor of Toronto has invited them.

"Good morning everyone and thank you all for coming on such short notice. The reason I have called you here is of grave importance. I was recently contacted by a trusted anonymous source who gave me information that will lead to the arrest and convictions of just about every known organized crime syndicate in Toronto which will possibly lead to other chapters spread out through Canada, the States and perhaps worldwide."

Trying to be polite, the Chief of police speaks up, "Sorry to bring this to your attention Mr. Diamond but our police sergeants have their own informants. They are the ones that deal with these type of situations."

Max quickly counters the Chief of Police, "Ah yes, I am aware of that, however my informant wants to be sure that he is going to a trusted source, and they do not feel the police are. I am certain you understand my informant's position." Max takes an edited version of the crime syndicates' information and puts it in a DVD player, turning it on. "Please watch."

Twenty minutes pass by in silence. Feeling they get the gist, Max shuts the television off. "You see my friends, these people have damning information on just about every crime leader in Toronto. What do you intend on doing with this evidence that I have?"

There is still silence as the police are dumbfounded by a goldmine of evidence.

"I have several copies of unedited versions that may appeal to you guys more. I want you to take it, but I wish to be credited in taking down these criminal organisations, to boost my next political campaign." Max walks over to the Chief of Police and hands him several documents. "Once again, I thank you all for coming here on such short notice. I know that your hands are probably full but I am sure this will help. I shall be informing the media of your valiant efforts in helping crush organised crime and keeping our streets safe. I must let you all go for now, for I have other pressing matters to attend to at the moment. Thank you once again."

Within a few hours, the Toronto police organise the biggest sting operation in Canadian history. The police cripple organised crime. Within a matter of hours, nearly every hard core gang is brought to its knees.

Drug labs are raided, contraband, and other accessories seized. This could never have been accomplished before without the help of the new media-made celebrity, Max Diamond. Over the following years, Max captures the attention of multiple Politicians throughout Canada, all seeking his aid in ridding their streets of crime.

"Cynric."

"Yes, father?"

"Listen to me; in the years to come, I want you to keep practising all I have taught you in case one day people rise up against me. I want you to secure everything that I have worked hard to achieve as your own. In the meantime I must get back to work. I am working hard at devising a plan that will ensure I become ruler of this world."

"Dad?"

"Yes."

"Your plans, they sound as if you're the Anti-Christ."

"Listen son, Christians will point their fingers at anything that scares them. They will kill anyone that is against them, and stop the progress of all things that are not according to scriptures, and these scriptures were written thousands of years ago by bronze-age people living in tents. Anyone worthy of recognition that so happens to go against scripture, Christians will refer to as 'the Anti-Christ'. I must stop the oppression of the Christians, Jews, and Muslims. I will eliminate them once and for all. I must trample all religions, destroy their entire holy rite, and secure a place for people like you and me.

Think of what people would do to you, heck, even me, if they found out we could lift a penny with our thoughts. They would be threatening to kill us, or mob us and surely kill us. Can you only imagine what would happen to us if we were caught using our minds to lift a car?"

"Yes father. I see all that but do they really need to be killed? I mean you came back to save us right? So there really isn't a need to avenge us anymore right? And what of all the innocent people you'd be killing in the process? Dad, I think it's high time you let go of your hatred and just enjoy having mother and I in your life again."

Dragon Dagoth turns from his son. He does not want his child see the anger welling up within him. Trying to contain the anger in his voice, he speaks in a casual dark monotone voice, "The only good Christian is a dead one! If they had the power to, they would kill us without thinking twice about it. We'd be dead, just like the memories that haunt me about your deaths over a millennium ago."

Cynric rolls his eyes and walks away from his father. Why does it matter so much to him? After all, Christianity is no longer the threat it once was. The belief system is controlled by most governments around the world.

"Off topic, I've created a system that will be able to track my father down. Perhaps we can learn more secrets on how we can command our powers. If I am to exact any of my plans in future we must take down the Russian Empire, striking at the heart of Taras Ivanov."

"You mean *the* Taras Ivanov, the President of Russia?"

Dragon Dagoth nods his head. "Yes, I feel he is the one responsible for creating these time machines and I feel he has created a future where he is in dominant control over everything. Somehow I feel he had used me in the past to destroy others like us, and alter a future that he was not in control of. I shall do the same and gain control over the world and then execute my plans without him standing in the way.

One last thing before I go, I am sure you will be pleased to know I have scientists working on possible brain transplants. It's a clone to clone procedure for now. Your mother will eventually grow old and die, and I hope to be able to grant her eternal life."

Cynric is happy to hear the news, but is not certain how well his mother will take to living forever. He does not even know if he enjoys the thought of his own immortality.

"Well Cynric, I'm leaving. If anything happens to me in the times to come, I have left instructions for you to follow. I've also programmed a couple of machines that are not on the grids server, for you and your mother, to be your loyal guards." Dragon Dagoth gives his son a warm-felt hug before leaving, stopping a couple of times to smile, happy to have his son in his life once again.

More often than not Rashidi expects to meet Dragon Dagoth unexpectedly. This time, it is not the case. This makes Rashidi's nervous. The Dark Lord is so unpredictable and volatile, that he knows it could be his last day on earth at any given moment, that or the Ibliss will kill his family at any given moment. These are some of the reasons he remains in Dragon Dagoth's servitude, and why he betrayed and murdered his own cousin.

Approaching the Dark Lord, Rashidi reluctantly bows before Dragon Dagoth, and then after a brief second, rises. "Why have you summoned me, master?"

"I have new orders for you. Return to Afghanistan and set up base. Once you are there I want you to contact the others who were involved in the other missions that I have given you. I have your instructions in this envelope."

Rashidi watches as Dragon Dagoth reaches inside his dark black cloak. Initially thinking he was reaching for a weapon, he breathes a sigh of relief when he pulls out an envelope just like he said he was going to do.

Rashidi reaches for the envelope and then respectfully bows before Dragon Dagoth once again.

"Do not fail me, Rashidi!"

"I don't understand, Hamasa. Why do you favour me over the other students? Are they not just as smart? Do they not deserve as good an education as I am getting? Or is it because you are my good friend or because my father has money?"

Scanning Mohammed's actions, Hamasa searches for an appropriate response, "Yes, we are good friends and yes, your father pays a great deal for your education. Perhaps it is my friendship with you that makes me favour you. Does this bother you?"

After thinking about it, Mohammed shakes his head, "Yeah, it makes sense I guess." Mohammed cuts himself short when he notices Reichana walking down the hall outside of his classroom. "You will have to excuse me professor. I just saw someone that I need to get hold of." Mohammed does not wait for a response and grabs his duffle bag and rushes out of the classroom.

"Hey."

Reichana smiles, turns around and rushes to meet up with Mohammed, wrapping her arms around him. She gives him a peck on the cheek. "Why do you consistently speak to Professor Hamasa?"

"He is the smartest professor in Umm al-Qura. I don't see why everyone has a problem with him. Yeah, he is a tad strange but I learn so much from him."

Reichana grabs Mohammed's hand and leads him down the hall, "Others say he speaks with the Jinn Ibliss, you know?"

"I am just as Islamic as the next person but come on, really. Do you really believe that. I mean, have you any proof that Jinn exists? Perhaps such things are metaphors or symbolic?"

After leading Mohammed outside the university, she takes him to a bench and together they sit down on the grass, continuing to hold hands. "Listen Mo hun, my father is a rich man. You know that and of course I know that, and if we are to get married, he wants to know everything about you and your family. I am sure you have even heard rumours that your father has been involved with the Ibliss?"

"Yeah and that is one of the stupidest things that I have ever heard."

"Okay Mo, I am just going to drop it. I just want you to be careful for me if not for yourself, okay?"

"Yeah, alright. Listen, I have to get back to class." Mohammed says as he stands up, straightening out his trousers. Although Mohammed is a bit annoyed with his fiancée, she stands up and cools him off with a warm hug and kiss.

Throughout the rest of the day, Mohammed intensely watches Professor Hamasa teach the class. He can barely focus on his schooling. He is trying to see why so many people think this way of the man. He cannot come up with any conclusions except for his lack of humour, his vast knowledge of just about everything, his extensive memory and how he could quote the entire contents of any encyclopaedia if he wanted to. Well at least that is what he thinks, joking around with himself. But nothing points to the man being an agent of evil.

After class is done, Mohammed doesn't leave right away, and although the Professor never pays much mind to this, he approaches him regardless. "There is someone who would like to meet you. Your father works for him. He is also the major reason that you are here today. It is quite a coincidence that you were asking such questions before lunch today."

"Yeah, but I normally take my fiancée home after school. Can I meet with him later?"

"You will find out that your father's boss does not like to be disappointed. I strongly suggest that you meet with him now."

This is disappointing to Mohammed, but he nods his head and agrees. Before leaving, he explains the situation to Reichana, and they make alternative plans for meeting up at a later date. They drive far into the outskirts of Mecca until they arrive at an isolated area, mainly desert lands and highway that stretch for miles on end. While they wait, Mohammed carries on a conversation with the Professor until they notice an entourage of vehicles heading their way over the horizon.

Mohammed's first impression is that the vehicles belong to one of the many Princes of the Kingdom of Saudi Arabia; however, his initial thoughts change when he notices that the chauffeur of the Limousine is a white man with a very muscular build, possibly American.

"Mohammed, come with me."

Mohammed feels something strange as the chauffeur opens the car door, waiting for him to enter the car. Eyes widened and terrified, Mohammed's mind races like it never has before; his father does in fact work for the Ibliss!

"Get in!"

Terrified, Mohammed jumps inside the Limousine, doing his best not to anger the man who he feels and senses is the very embodiment of evil, emanating to each and everything he sits on and touches.

"So your father has trained you well. I understand when you were younger you were a weapons specialist. Now you have been studying at Umm al-Qura for quite some time now, so I assume you are smart as well. You will begin working for me now. I have your first mission instructions in an envelope on the seat."

Mohammed promised his father beforehand that if his boss ever contacted him, he would never kill him, and although he has no weapons on him, his impulse to jump across the seat and break his neck with his bare hands is overwhelming. But a promise is a promise, and he also knows that if he kills the Ibliss, the Ibliss' friends will kill him and the Professor afterwards.

"I will not work with you!"

Still not bothering to look at Mohammed face to face, Dragon Dagoth turns on a monitor, showing a local Mosque that Mohammed attends at El-Gumah, "I will finance your wedding and shower you with more riches than you can ever think of. Should you refuse me again, I will cut your bride's head off in front of your eyes!" Dragon Dagoth then shows Mohammed a picture of him together with Reichana as well as some other photos of Reichana either by herself on the University campus, or with her family near their home. "She is beautiful. I don't think she would look the same without a head, though. What do you think?"

Mohammed grits his teeth, and does his best to conceal the tears forming in his eyes. It all makes sense as to why his father had done his best to not have him involved with his work or even share anything about his work with their family. But how did his boss know about him? Perhaps with the amounts of money that his father had, this man probably had ties to everything and knew everything they did and everywhere they were. Thinking quietly to himself, he knows the best way to win is be compliant with his new boss; yet, find out everything he can about him so that he can turn the tables around and place the Ibliss in the same situation. "Fine, I will serve you. Just don't hurt her."

"I am glad you see things my way."

The Professor stays with Dragon Dagoth and his men while Mohammed takes the long, quiet trip back home. He turns up the music on his radio so that he can drown out the voices of his father's boss, threatening to kill his fiancée. Each time he hears the man's voice inside his head, he grips the steering wheel tighter and tighter, gritting his teeth in anger and screamed out trying to vent out all his pent up frustration. He feels trapped. Once he arrives home, he informs Reichana that he has to take a trip to Afghanistan and that he will explain why, when he returns, without fully knowing how he can explain to her that she had been right.

The flight back home is not that long, a couple of hours, seeing they make a few other destination stops along the way. At the airport, Mohammed follows the instructions and meets with a few other people at the airport, including Professor Hamas. Each one of them has different instructions and they are to combine what they know together and then carry out the mission as a single unit.

They leave in a couple of taxis to go to a hotel where they will work out their ideas, based on the plans that they have. Once they are there, they realise that the plan to be carried out are not all as bad as they expected. In fact, they are in honour of Islam. They are to execute some Islamic extremists who have brought a bad name to their religion that work for their new boss, whose name did not show up on any of the documents.

That night they all share their stories about their initial meeting with the man in the black cloak in the Limousine and somewhat all agree that they will do their best to kill him if given the chance, once they complete their mission.

"I don't feel comfortable with killing him."

"Why is that, Brother Akim?"

"Did he not show you pictures of a loved one that he will kill, if we do not do as he asks?"

"They will be in Allah's hands. You worry too much, brother Akim."

"Well yes, I am in love. I am to be married, and my father had warned me about this man and then he appears in my life, in all of our lives, with threats against the one person I cherish more than life itself."

"If it makes you feel uncomfortable brother Akim then we shall kill him ourselves and part ways after this is done."

Almost everyone agrees to kill their boss, save the Professor and Mohammed.

It is the following night, and the party arrives at their destination. They wait for their targets to arrive to what appears to be a terrorist base of operations in the midst of reconstruction. The wait is long, and the men lie prone behind objects to safeguard their invisibility. The sun sets and the cold of the desert night starts to get the better of them.

A point man spots a few vehicle headlights down on the horizon and signals the other men. Mohammed and the others begin to ready their weapons and the cold night air no longer seems to bother them, seeing their nerves are getting the better of them.

As the last of the trucks drive over the remote mines, one of Mohammed's associates detonates a mine, blowing the truck to pieces. Another member in the group fires an RPG at the first truck in the queue, blowing it apart and trapping the other vehicles in between the first and last of the vehicles that have been immobilised.

Without thinking twice about what just took place, Mohammed rushes towards the trucks, shooting at anyone jumping out, and other shadowy figures that he does not recognise from his entourage. The rest of his team follow suit, shooting down the Islamists. Mohammed catches sight of Professor Hamas who seems to have no regard for danger, as he puts his life in the hands of the enemy, shooting as many of them as possible, brazenly in the open.

"Follow me men!" Mohammed shouts as he joins the Professor. The others rush to help out Professor Hamas, each one looking out for the other.

"Mohammed!" A body in the shadows desperately calls out above a whisper.

"Who are you? How do you know my name?" Mohammed shouts out as he rushes over to the dying foe, his gun aimed at the enemy's head as he inches his way closer, trying to adjust his eyes to the darkness.

"Oh Mohammed, he has got you to betray me."

"Father?!" Mohammed half questions as he rushes to his father, dropping his gun. "Dad I had no clue. I did not know. Your boss approached me and said he would kill Reichana if I did not do as he asked. He never said you were a part of the terrorist attacks!"

Rashidi doesn't reply to his son, not that he doesn't want to. It is because of the pain. He applies pressure on one of the painful bullet wounds and tries to gain some energy, regardless if he can feel his energy fading away.

"Father, I swear to Allah the most beneficent that I did not know that it was you! Oh, I am so sorry!"

Startled, Mohammed turns around to screams of his companions. As they yell and cry out, he realises that they have all shot or killed a loved one of theirs. Some victims are past recognition; yet, they understand the possibility that they too have killed someone they know and love.

"I failed in one of my missions, and he has sent my only son to kill me, Mohammed." Rashidi begins to cough up blood, and then grimaces to block out the pain.

Mohammed cradles his dying father in his hands and cries, "I am so sorry, dad."

"There is no time for that now, son Reach into my pocket. What I am about to give you, trust no one with. I have uncovered something that can possibly gain your freedom from him. Read this, only when you have spare private time. Dragon Dagoth is very cunning and powerful, and I fear he can read minds, so act without haste. I am the source of this information, so it is to be trusted. I love you, Mohammed."

Rashidi looks into his son's eyes one last time, and then dies. Mohammed quietly mourns the loss of his father and holds him in his arms one last time before they meet Allah on Judgement Day. He reaches into the sleeve of his father's coat pocket and pulls out an envelope containing the secrets of his father's find. A Limousine casually drives to the site, with its lights off. Dragon Dagoth and some body guards leave the vehicle and overlook the chaos that can be seen from where they stand.

Mohammed looks over at the Devil who he killed his father for, and then gazes at all the mourning people who serve him. Professor Hamas is also on alert, watching everyone carefully. Mohammed blanks in and out of extreme rage as he grips his gun tight; yet, his conscious self-control keeps him from pulling the trigger as he does not know what will happen to Reichana.

"What do you intend on doing to the boss?" Professor Hamas asks.

"Nothing. I will do whatever he asks of me!" Mohammed replies in a hostile tone.

The Professor casually walks over to the others. They begin yelling and screaming, and then threaten to kill Dragon Dagoth for what he has done. Professor Hamas opens fire shooting each of them down, and then walks back over to a Mohammed.

"What the fuck! Why did you kill them? They are on our side!"

"There is only one side, and that is to serve Dragon Dagoth. You have passed this mission. They were going to betray and attempt to kill Dragon Dagoth. I could not allow that to happen."

"Didn't he kill your family as well? Are you not upset?"

"I am one of his loyal guards, and I have been monitoring you for quite some time. Now come with me. My master would like to speak with you."

"Reichana was right about you all along!" Mohammed screams out. Letting out all of his bottled rage, he swings his fist at Professor Hamas' face as hard as he can. His knuckles crack and break on the Professor's brick hard face, and the Professor does not budge, or so much as flinch.

Feeling bitterly defeated, betrayed and severely upset about killing his father, Mohammed knows his only choice is to obey. Trying to hold back his tears, desiring not to give Dragon Dagoth the satisfaction of seeing him cry, he stands before the Dark one, the monster that came out of nowhere and gained all control of his life.

"You have done well, Mohammed. Rashidi failed me before, and I hope for your sake that you do not fail me! I will be in contact with you on a regular basis. As for now, you are to find yourself a crew that you can rely on. It seems the others did not want to share the benefits of serving me. If you decide in future that you are to turn your back on me, keep in mind that I have eyes and ears everywhere and it will be most unfortunate for the ones you love, if you rise up against me."

With that, Dragon Dagoth leaves Mohammed to think about what he said, and each of the horrors committed this night.

11

"Well it's confirmed. She was extradited by the Russian empire, and it seems only Christopher knows the reasons why. Every trace on Christopher and Gav has disappeared from provincial and federal systems. However, we have information from the prison; she had no priors, was an outstanding police officer, but left the force sometime after her partner was murdered. Her disappearance to Canada sparked interest in the ongoing cold case file of her partner, so we can only assume that Christopher is behind all of this, and that he set her up to go to prison for a crime she didn't commit."

"It all seems to add up, save these visions and dreams you have, but the risk of going up against our former master is not worth it."

"I've already set the plan in motion" Gefallener Klon states, straightening out his posture and conducting himself as a leader amongst his fellow clones. "I was in love with our mistress, and she saved us all. I am more powerful than our old Master. I can feel it, and soon we will get our revenge!"

"He is our creator, our maker. Is it really worth killing him?"

Gefallener's posture weakens, and his confidence wanes. He folds his hands around his body in an insecure posture, "I don't know? And I didn't say anything about killing him. I said revenge, and I said I set the plan in motion. It doesn't mean I am doing anything personally."

Gefallener feels reassuring hugs from two of his brother clones.

"Also think of it this way, not only will he always be our maker, he will always accept us as we are. We've studied humans and their relentless cruelties. We're copies of one being, while we all feel like we are human beings, and homo-sapiens will never accept us as human. We won't have the same rights as them, or even animals for that matter."

Gefallener nods his head slowly, "We've come too far to reconsider or take anything back. I am sorry my brothers but we must move forward."

"I could do this forever!" Annex says cosily cuddled underneath her husband's arm. Her accent is still strong but she has taken to speaking in modern English quite well, but has not adapted as quickly as their son Cynric.

She takes comfort as her dear Ethelwulf strokes his fingers through her hair. They sit together on the couch watching modern wonders on some technical device called a television. "I remember when our Kings and Magistrates declared such things. Since when do the people decide who is in charge?"

"Oh my love, a lot has changed over time; it's called 'voting'. Voting allows the people to decide who the best candidates are, and they are the decision makers for a limited time."

"Is he the person thou hast been talking about?

"You mean, 'is he the person *you have* been talking about'. Yes, he is."

Annex giggles and slaps her husband playfully on his chest.

"Ladies and Gentlemen of Ontario, I thank you for all the support you have given me, however I feel I can best serve the public by joining the New Order which is being financially backed by their very own company. I hereby resign my position as head of the Liberals and will pursue my political career with them and run for Prime Minister in the upcoming election."

The response is electrifying. Ethelwulf smiles as Max Diamond gets a standing ovation for announcing that he will start running for office in the Federal election. The reporters discuss the shocking revelation during a time of defeat and are sceptical about Max's optimistic approach in running for Prime Minister.

"This calls for a toast. Dinner should be just about ready." Ethelwulf says, as he holds Annex's aged hands and helps her to her feet.

"My back... sorry dear. It's not what it used to be."

"Why does this call for a celebration, father?" Cynric asks, coming to his mother's aid, and helping her to the kitchen as his father opens a bottle of wine. "Didn't you want him to win?"

"Oh, I am glad you're home, son. Just in time for a toast. Remember your training, buddy: it's all about manipulation of the masses. Max entered Provincial office way too late, but look at the overwhelming amount of seats and support he got in that time, second place. He announced his intentions and will take the government in the upcoming election."

"Whatever. Politics and politicians bore me no end."

Ethelwulf cracks open a bottle of rich red wine and fills a trio of glasses on the table, and they toast to what he feels will soon be a brighter future. They somewhat entertain his happiness but are in the dark as to the reasons that compel him to be so in tune with politics, save the connection between Max Diamond, and his secretive business.

During dinner, Cynric watches his father hold his mother's hand. His father does not care about the wrinkles on her skin, or what can be perceived as a massive age difference, and there is only love between the two. "Dad, are you going to tell mom about your plans with her?"

"Oh?" Annex's face lights up with enthusiasm, but the news comes at a time when Ethelwulf is not prepared to share the information.

"Umm, I am still working on it, Cynric."

"Working on what, my dearest?"

Without knowing the best way to say it, Ethelwulf speaks candidly, "I have the ability to create copies of humans using science. The term is cloning. As you know, Cynric and I will live forever, but unfortunately you will... well you know. I can attempt to prolong this fate; I can save you from death. Cloning you will not be a problem. I am experimenting with brain transplants. Actually the details you don't really need to know, but just know that we have a chance at having you live with us as long as possible."

Gently sliding her hand free of Ethelwulf's, Annex holds her dinner plate and takes another bite of food. She looks at her husband through the fog of watery eyes, while repeatedly chewing the same bite of food in shock. Cynric and Ethelwulf can pass for brothers. Neither age, neither will die.

"Thou dost not find me to your liking?"

"Of course I do, love."

"Thou shalt have me become young looking like thee? I am but an old hag and thy sorcery maintains thy youth, your youth."

"No, love," Ethelwulf says as he gets up from his seat and wraps his loving arms around his wife, and gently rests his head on her graying hair, snuggling into her, and embracing her with dear love. "It's not that at all. I love you more than life itself. Since you and Cynric have been back in my life, I've never been happier."

Ethelwulf cradles Annex in his arms. Cynric feeling a little uncomfortable at their signs of affection, excuses himself from the table, and heads to the living room.

"Baby, can't you see I love you, and you are perfect to me no matter what you look like. I love you so much. I love you with all of my heart. I just can't bear to think what life will be like without you ever again. I won't let it happen again. Together we can do the impossible and cheat death! I will defy death so you can be with me until the ends of time. My powers have grown. My wisdom has grown, and soon I am sure I can make you immortal like me. Until that time, I must do what it takes to keep you with me forever!"

Letting go of her plate and fork, Annex raises her hands and holds her husband's arms, "I love thee, my dearest Ethel. It's just the things thou speakest of, frighten... speak of, frighten me. What if it doesn't work? What if something horrible happens? Wilt thou be able... I mean, well you know what I mean; wilt you be able to save me should your technical magic fail?"

"Of course."

"I've actually been meaning to ask you about that place."

"What about it?" Ethelwulf asks while running his fingers through Annex's greying hair.

"You're not the Ethelwulf I remember growing up. You're much darker. You are angrier. And you seem so focused on spending time away from me in that base you took us to when you travelled back from time to save us. I have not been included in your private affairs in this secretive base of yours. You are training our son to fight and develop his strange powers which you also have. I am learning now about brain transplants, what else goes on in this base of yours? What are you actually doing? Please do not keep this from me."

Ethelwulf looks into Annex's light green eyes and doesn't know how to answer her. His initial impulse is to use his power on her and make her think about something else, yet the human side of him feels that such a thing is wrong. Should he lie about what he does? That is equally wrong.

"Are you thinking of a story you can make up to me? Why all this secrecy? You've confided in me since we were children. I want to know why all the secrecy."

"For centuries I have building an army of robots who look human. I have cloned scientists, and technicians who build these robots, train other clones to take their place when they expire. They have also been mass producing weaponry and weapons of mass destruction. This is why I have been keeping it a secret."

Annex folds her arms and rapidly taps her toes underneath the table on the floor while looking away from Ethelwulf. "I asked you why the secrecy. You're evading the question. There is a reason you're doing this and I want to know what that reason is!"

"Baby please is there a reason you need to know?"

"Ethelwulf of Londinium! Art thou not mine husband? Wilt thou be a man and divulge thy secret unto me! Or shall I come back in time when thou hast grown to be a man?!"

"Where will you go?"

"Anywhere but here. Thou hast three seconds to speakest thine secrets. One, two."

Over the years Ethelwulf lost any form of human compassion, remorse, empathy, and feelings. He did not feel any of these emotions when he severed his mother's head clean off her shoulders. The only emotion he felt was rage after he learned hundreds of his workers, that built his base were Christian, and Catholic. And happiness knowing that he slaughtered them all personally. Yet, it is his childhood sweetheart who makes him feel guilty for withholding information from her. And who makes him feel ashamed for these types of behaviours.

"I've created the army because I intend to kill each and every Christian and other religionist in the world. That is why I am investing so much time away from home. Seeing your dead body years ago, and sparing Cynric from agony has left me scarred for hundreds of years. I admit I have nothing but happiness having you back in my life, and our son. But they must pay for what they did."

Annex takes a few steps backwards, she can't believe what she is hearing. Everything another man proclaiming to be her dear Ethelwulf said is true. But how can she share this with this wretched man who proclaims to be her husband?

Annex quickly gets these thoughts out of her mind. Should her husband read them, there is no telling what he may do to her. "Who are you referring to when you say 'they' need to pay?"

"Christians!" Ethelwulf says. His lips are curled, and he addresses those of faith with utter contempt.

"My dearest Ethel we are alive thanks to you. Do you recall we spoke of getting away from all of this? We are one thousand years more in the future. There is no need for this evil obsession of yours anymore and I will not have it, nor will I be a part of it."

This conversation is frustrating Annex was not the one who had to see him, or their son die. "What would you do if you watched me die, or Cynric?"

"If I travelled back in time and saved you I'd thank all the gods and goddess in the world that I have you both in my life again! Ethelwulf of Londinium dost you thee hear yourself speak? 'They' have been dead for over a thousand years. These Christians that you speak of are not the same people from that time. Since you were able to travel back in time did you kill the people who harmed us?"

"Yes."

"Was my mother there?"

"Yes."

"What did you do with her? She is a Christian you know. Would you kill her? Did you kill her?"

No longer able to contain his frustration a plate on the table levitates and smashes against a wall. The bottle of rich wine implodes, and its contents spill on the dark brown oak table. Ethelwulf glares at Annex fiercely. Then quickly releases his gaze. He does not want to project any dark angry thoughts toward her over mere petty Christians. She simply does not have the capability to understand his thoughts.

"You killed my mother?" Annex says clasping her hand on her chest growing faint and weak.

"I did not say anything! What makes you think I killed her? I am just upset that we're defending the very people who killed you and our son!" Ethelwulf walks over to hug Annex.

"No please do not touch me. I do not want you to hold me right now. You haven't answered my question. Did you kill my mother?"

Ethelwulf grips onto the kitchen counter, his long wavy hair dangles across it, as he thinks of another way to avoid her question.

"You killed her, that is why you're not answering me. You're trying to think of an aversion to the question so you can worm your way out of telling me that you killed her. Tell me Ethel how did you kill my mother?"

I thought I was the mind reader Ethelwulf thinks to himself. "She told the soldiers to kill you, and our son, her grandson."

The news is too overwhelming to behold. Annex begins to sob. The dear sweet boy she grew to love more dearly than life itself has become the monster he so despised just on the opposing side. "My heart can't take this any longer. I don't want to live forever with you knowing what you've done. What you're about to do. How can I live with this knowing you will do the exact same thing to others which has happened to us? Our family! For the gods sakes Ethel please, leave it behind!" Annex begs.

"Father! I sense something bad is about to happen!"

"I know, she is upset and I am..."

An explosion rocks the house, and a couple of masked men jump through a hole where the front of the house used to be. Cynric is partially ripped in half, his intestines and blood are covered in the debris and dust from the explosion. One of the armed men shoots Cynric in the head while the other rushes into other parts of the home. The search ends as the other masked man finds a man who appears to be dragging his mother to safety.

The assailant opens fire, shooting Annex several times in the stomach, a few times in the face and head, and continues raising the gun, opening fire on Ethelwulf, hitting him in the chest a few times. The shots cease as he hears his partner screaming in agony. The gunman runs into the living room and watches as streaks of lightning course through his partner. Unbeknownst to him, a transference of power is taking place.

The gunman runs back into the kitchen to finish his job. To his shock, the man he shot stands up, with a look of immense hatred and rage. The gunman raises his gun in the air. The man continues to stare at him. He tries to pull the trigger but can't; it must be shock. He tries again. The trigger must be stuck. He realises that for some reason, he is not able to move at all, as if something is controlling him. His arms extend straight forward, while the man growls in anger. He watches as the man grits his teeth like a vicious animal.

Dragon Dagoth stares at the intruder who killed his beloved Annex, and he senses the life of his son has been snuffed from this world. No matter, he will go back in time and prevent this from happening. Nothing will stop him from being with his family. He looks hard at the man that killed his beloved wife, and uses his powers to bend his arms at the elbows in opposite directions. The bones rip out through his shirt, and the man screams in pain.

With a final surge of power, he wills the man's ribs to cave into his chest, killing the man instantly. Dragon Dagoth grabs a knife and walks into the living room and looks at his dead son, and the man beside him who just encountered a transference of power. Dragon Dagoth plunges a knife into the man's spine and leaves him handicapped, and paralyzed on the floor. He walks off, to return a few minutes later with a sword. He uses his powers to levitate the man and throw him against a wall out of the neighbours' view, as they are all walking around in the street to view what is taking place in their once quiet neighbourhood.

"Who sent you?" Dragon Dagoth growls out!

"I don't know."

Looking at the debris, Dragon Dagoth wills a brick up from the rubble and sends it hurtling at the intruder's ankle. The impact is so vigorous that it crushes the man's foot, breaking the ankle inside of the wall. "Who sent you?"

As the man screams in agony, he repeats himself only to meet the same fate with his other ankle. "I said I don't know. Okay! Okay! I got a box mailed to me. I opened it up and there was a black plastic bag taped up. I opened it and it had a hand inside of it. There was a picture of masked people and my little girl who was missing a hand, in an envelope. It said they will mail me her other hand tomorrow if I didn't look at the other envelope. I looked at it, and it had your three pictures in there with your address, and the words: 'Kill them, your daughter lives'."

Dragon Dagoth reads the man's mind. He sees the images that the intruder is referring to. He searches the man's mind some more and can see that his ex-wife is the one with primary joint custody of their daughter. After searching more, he can see his daughter's face, on the weekends that they share together. He feels her essence through him. He can feel the little girl's pain with her missing wrist, and he can see that the men are masked, where she is being held captive. He becomes one with the intruder's daughter and squeezes her heart with his mind until it pops inside of her nine year old, frail body, and life ceases to exist within her.

Dragon Dagoth comes to. "As you can see, I am a man with magic abilities. I've just killed your daughter."

Before the intruder reacts, Dragon Dagoth slices the man's head off and releases his telepathic hold on him, and the body crashes to the ground along with the man's severed head. He tosses his sword aside, and walks into the kitchen to see if Annex is still alive. The bullets caved in her face. Blood is everywhere, and Dragon Dagoth collapses to the floor and screams out in pain.

The street is secured by emergency task force officers who close in on the house. Some of the officers inspect the van in front of the house. Judging by what they see inside the van and how badly damaged the front of the house is, whoever brought the van to the house was preparing for a small war.

Walking on top of the debris and making their way slowly inside of the house they see a few bodies, and then make their way into the kitchen, to see a man holding and mourning over a body shot beyond recognition.

A bitter and defeated Dragon Dagoth looks up at the officers who've made their way inside of the kitchen. He makes no effort to part from his dearly beloved Annex.

"Hands in the air. Step away from the body."

In a hostile manner, Dragon Dagoth darts his eyes up at the officer making the demand.

"Wait!" Another ETF officer pipes up, listening in on a radio frequency, while placing his hand on his partner's gun. "Why? We have the site, and subject contained. Please advise." There is a moment's pause as the ETF officer receives further instruction. "Fall back, men."

"Why do we have to fall back? We can bring in the subject and be done with it"

"As you heard, I asked the same thing. The reasons are classified and we have our orders."

"Why were we called out of there?"

"Here is why. It is because you were never here, in fact none of you were. If word spreads that any of you officers were called here tonight, you will deny such allegations. There will not only be dire consequences for your actions if you choose not to comply, but for your families as well."

The ETF officers raise their weapons at the gentlemen in front of them. They appear to be decorated soldiers, yet neither of the pair is wearing their name badges. "Lower your weapons, gents. You're only embarrassing yourselves. Go home and forget this all happened. This is now a top secret classified mission."

The soldiers walk inside the war torn looking house, and into the kitchen where Dragon Dagoth holds his dear wife. He glares at them as they walk inside the kitchen. "Do you need a moment, sir?"

"My wife and son are dead."

"Our condolences, Christopher."

Dragon Dagoth raises his eyes with curious intent at the soldiers' motives for being there, "That is not my name."

"Do you prefer Ethelwulf, or Dragon Dagoth?"

Dragon Dagoth glares at the soldiers once again, contemplating what he should do, but then dismisses their actual knowledge on him, and fixes his gaze back on his beloved wife, once again.

"I am sure Annex, and Cynric meant a great deal to you. We'd be just as devastated if we lost any of our family."

Gently placing his wife's body on the ground, Dragon Dagoth rises to full height, "Does this have anything to do with the person that broke into our home a few months ago?"

"Initially, we ruled her out until an anonymous source sent us a detailed report. This report gave us information on underground bases, time machines, robots created for war, and clones. This brought us to the discovery of one of your mistakes."

"All of that sounds absolutely insane, and you choose to come here and harass me with this insane bullshit after my whole family has been slaughtered? You guys need to get the fuck out of my house now!"

General Keri continued while chuckling (it did sound insane he thought to himself), "Listen, you're good, hands down. You're not just good, you're one of the best if not the best. But I'd like you to talk us through a problem we're having. How is it that you are here mourning the loss of your wife and son when you're at the elections ... Mr. Max Diamond, is that what you prefer to be called?" The General gave the go ahead for Commander Soleman to approach Dragon Dagoth with a mobile device showing him a live feed of the after election ceremonies.

After taking a glimpse at the live feed, Dragon Dagoth stares at both of the soldiers. It would be so easy to end their pitiful meaningless lives simultaneously, but it takes more than his reserve energy to stand up and part his newly deceased wife. "What do you want with me?"

"We came here to offer our help. We want your cooperation; in return we will do our part and ask the courts to show you lenience."

"Amazing, I will take my hat off to you both. Amazing that you have got this far and made such insane accusations..."

General Keri raises his hand, "Stop. We know who you are, and we will help you. We will travel back in time and save your wife and son should you cooperate with us. If not, we can do this the hard way. It's really up to you."

A dark rage fuels deep inside of Dragon Dagoth. He begins to snarl at the men like a wild beast, and the taunting laugh of the General increases his rage.

"Before you go and do something stupid like try and kill me with your magic, consider the fact that we have your house surrounded. You will die, and your family will never have the opportunity to live again."

Quickly considering this, Dragon Dagoth puts his rage into a far place inside of his mind.

"I give up. Just help me save my wife and son, and I will do what you want," Dragon Dagoth says as he buckles to the floor and reaches for his wife's hand. "Since you know so much about me, do you know who did this to us?"

Commander Soleman walks over to Dragon Dagoth with a pair of cuffs, "We're working on some leads, and we..."

"Commander, due to the nature of who we are apprehending, I suggest you keep those answers to yourself."

"It's pointless placing cuffs on me Commander, and the General's life is limited. Pledge your allegiance to me and I will spare you."

"Respectfully Mr. Diamond, we have more on you than you have on us. With that said, we suspect Islamic terrorists are behind the attack. Do you know anything about this?"

"Thank you. Take me to my base. Everything is coded with my physical presence and voice commands with sophisticated technology that is years beyond anything known now."

They travel an hour to the outskirts of Toronto, and drive into a remote field. After a five minute drive into the field, they approach a house, and then leave the vehicle. Dragon Dagoth knocks on the door. A gentle warm muscular looking old man opens the door, and looks at Dragon Dagoth then the army officials and other men behind them, "Code in."

"Eagle."

The old man nods and allows Dragon Dagoth and the rest of the people to enter the home. Dragon Dagoth escorts the men to a secret room where they wait for an elevator to take them to the base.

"No funny business, alright," says the General.

Dragon Dagoth does not pay the General any attention, and he enters the elevator when it comes. The doors open and to his shock, the hallway looks like a warzone. Lights are flickering or broken out of the ceiling from gun fire. What's worse are the litter of dead clones each shot repeatedly and finished off with a bullet to the head along the hallway.

They reach the time portal room. All of the time machines are destroyed. Dragon Dagoth buckles to his knees, and all hope of being with Annex once again is crushed.

"Master?" a voice says.

Dragon Dagoth turns to see a clone in a pool of blood, "You survived? What is your number and what happened here?"

"Number Sixteen, sir. I think we were attacked by Muslims. They rushed off before they could finish the job on me and Number Fifteen."

Commander Soleman reaches for his phone and tries to call for help, "Shit, I am not getting any reception down here."

"Why?" Dragon Dagoth sneers at the Commander.

"Your men could use the medical attention."

"We have our own doctors ... but thanks." Looking at Number Sixteen again, he notices that the clone does not appear to be hurt, "You were shot?"

"Yes?"

"Your wounds appear to be healed."

"Yeah, I found that odd as well." Gefallener states, while pretending to be oblivious to his powers.

"So, your clones are useless. You have an army of robots that don't know how to defend your base, and you were overrun by terrorists. This is a joke and so are you. Can someone handcuff this piece of shit so we can get back home and call it a fucking night?" General Keri states angrily, feeling his research has all been but a waste.

Defiantly making his voice known, Commander Soleman turns around to face the General, "We need him."

"Arrest the Commander if he impedes my instructions any further."

Obeying the General's commands, the handful of soldiers move forward to arrest the unarmed Dragon Dagoth.

Commander Soleman stands in front of the few soldiers attempting to make the arrest, to no avail. They cuff him, and then cautiously make their way to Dragon Dagoth. In a fit of rage, Dragon Dagoth extends his hands and wills a dark force to pull their eyes from their sockets.

The soldiers start screaming and drop their guns, putting the hands against their eyes in futile attempts to prevent their eyes from being yanked out. Each one of them can hear the ligaments of their eyes stretching, tearing and popping. General Keri reaches for his gun and aims it at Dragon Dagoth. Sensing danger, Dragon Dagoth notices the General and controls his mind, inhibiting him from pulling the trigger, and then wills the General's index finger to bend in the opposite direction until it snaps in half and the bone in his finger tears through his flesh.

"Give your allegiance to me and kill them all, Commander Soleman!"

Frightened by the outcome of refusal to Dragon Dagoth, Commander Soleman shoots down each of the soldiers and the General.

Dragon Dagoth cracks a small smile at the commander's compliance, albeit the dreadful sadness at losing his wife and son, "Commander Soleman, I want you to train my clones. This embarrassment will not happen again!"

Gefallener keeps his rage contained, and diverts eye contact from his master to the commander and reads the fear coming off his mind. But he also learns that his master is playing several different roles, and will use the commander to his advantage.

"Sorry master, it will not happen again!"

"Silence!" Dragon Dagoth barks out. "See it done commander. Number Sixteen, I want a full report on what transpired here. Have it on my desk in a days' time! In the meantime, I must hasten my plans and set them in motion. The time has come for me to exact my revenge!"

Max does not waste time implementing his ideas as he represents his company at a meeting in parliament. He introduces a new chip, a tracking device that will be inserted into the skulls of regular, everyday citizens. However, Max does not release full details about his idea as a shift of dead silence consumes the audience. Max quickly assumes control of the situation and people's emotions, while doing his best to change the shifting emotions that people are starting to have over the controversial Chip idea, "Ladies and Gentlemen, these proposed Global Tracking System Chips will be ideal for predators being released into society. The public needs to be guaranteed that these people will not go around our children and if they do and they take our children for their sick pleasures, we will be able to immediately track them down!"

"I think this is absurd. Really... inserting chips inside people's skulls; have you gone mad?"

Max Diamond chuckles a bit. The room is still in shock at Max's proposal; thus far he did not seem to be swaying anyone's minds, "Mad, Mr. Clarke? Funny you should say that. According to Corrections Canada, most sexual predators cannot be cured. Over ten percent of criminals are sexual offenders. Now don't you think that is a high quota? Additionally, over fifty percent of these predators are on parole. Furthermore, twenty percent of these sexual predators commit pedophilia. Many of these same offenders are let back out into the public, and they frequent neighbourhoods with public schools, just like your daughter, Chantelle's, school.

"Are you aware that it has come to my attention one of her classmates, whose name I won't bring into this, was taken home by one of the caretakers of the school? You can use your imagination as to what happened. Oh and by the way, did I mention that this caretaker was a predator? I did imply that if you weren't clear before, right? You see, Mr. Clarke, if parents want to have these chips implanted into their children, and if it is mandatory for high risk offenders to have the Chips inserted, poor innocent children can and will be rescued from sick, twisted perverts like the caretaker who not only traumatised, but scarred this poor kid for life!"

A pin drop could echo in the dead silence that filled the room, yet again. Mr. Clarke could barely get his next words out of his mouth, "You mean this happened at my daughter's school?"

"Yes, Mr. Clarke. Oh and guess what, because of our laws at the moment, the public can't track who is a predator in the neighbourhood. They can't see what these predators are doing. This is why we need to vote in favour of these chips. High risk offenders need to be monitored at all times!"

Max Diamond had got his wish. His party had won a bill to insert the global tracking devices into all high risk offenders, in addition making the Chip marketable for Doctors.

12

The votes of the election have been tallied and Max Diamond is now sworn in as the new Prime Minister of Canada, and quickly works on his ulterior motives for becoming the ruler of Canada. He feels that this feat of becoming the ruler of a country is a significant feat, and he is amazed at how he has accomplished this task in such a short time. After his swearing in, he works on his visions, implementing his changes in parliament, which will also affect the rest of the world.

Max Diamond wages war against organised crime, crushing it with Canada's All in One Card, a new form of currency that has replaced paper money currency. He also makes it mandatory for all federal offenders across the nation to have incisions of the Global Tracking System Chips. Additionally, Max Diamond signs another bill to merge all Canadian identification into the All in One Cards. Many other countries begin adapting his patented All in One Cards.

Now it will only be a matter of time before he locates his father and learns more of his powers, or murders him and takes that power, as he is feels Joshua is responsible for all those years of agony, being abandoned and left at a Christian home, tortured, killed, watching his beloved family die, and left in solitude for all those years. Max also desires to obliterate the world of all religious people, including their children.

Nothing will ever diminish the pain he feels regarding the loss of his dear Annex, and son Cynric for a second time, and the pain eats at his heart knowing the Muslim terrorists that attacked his base destroyed all of the time machines, meaning he cannot go back in time to save their lives, until he figures out a way to rebuild them.

Feeling empty and longing for death, Max returns to his home which was recently rebuilt, and stands above his wife and son's graves.

Lightning rips across the sky and thunder rumbles throughout the quiet night, shaking the ground. Commander Soleman walks up and stands behind the Prime Minister. He has shown up unannounced and remains silent while the Prime Minister mourns the loss of his family.

"I am taking our country in a new direction. In order to do so, I cannot allow the people to have a say. They can no longer have a voting system. I must abolish the Charter of Rights."

Commander Soleman treads with care in his response, "Mr. Prime Minister, I do sympathise for the loss of your family, but surely you must understand if you intend on doing something the people disagree on, they will stop you."

"Then I will force them to see what I have planned my way!" The new Prime Minister growls out. "I am going to replace the Canadian army with my organisation's robots. I will also disassemble the Canadian government as a whole to make way for a new future. I just want to know if I have your support."

"That doesn't really answer my other question, sir," Soleman responds.

"I will be more direct. With an army of robots all under my direct control, if the populace challenges my direction and future of the country there will be minimal threat to stop me with humans out of the equation."

"I don't mean to piss on your parade but several families will lose their income due to the loss of jobs. The Army is their livelihood. You will hurt a lot of people by doing this!" It doesn't matter what display of magical powers the Prime Minister can conjure up, or how bad he can physically harm him, as a fellow soldier he could not stand idly by while the Prime minister gives away his plans to destroy the lives of honest hardworking Canadian citizens.

"Relax Soleman, I intend on giving the same salary they are making now to attend a University or College of their choice, and study whatever programs that will get them into the workforce during this transition. If they already have certificates or degrees of some sort then I will grant them a year severance package."

"All that will cost money, tax payers' money. How do you intend on doing this?"

"Mind your place, Soleman. Leave the politics to me! Now since you're here, how are the clones progressing?"

The Prime Minister observes the Commander's hesitation but allows a few seconds to pass before he considers probing his mind for thoughts the Commander may withhold.

"Remarkably well. In fact I've never seen humans adapt as quickly."

"But..."

"One of them... seems defiant. In fact, each time I speak about you I can see the animosity in his eyes, and he glares at me with ill intent each time I refer to him by his number."

"What clone is this?"

"Number Sixteen."

"What else?"

"I suspect they are covering up something about the Muslim attack on your base. I personally feel it was an inside job which points back at them, and the report by Number Sixteen doesn't add up."

The Prime Minister pauses for a brief moment, "I will deal with the Muslims I feel may be responsible for the attacks, to be on the safe side. I still have a use for the clones. After they have fulfilled their purpose, I will close down the clone project. Now if you will excuse me, I would like to be alone."

Max Diamond turns away from Soleman who leaves to attend to other duties. Max leans down toward the tombstone of his dear wife, remembering their childhood together, laughing, playing, and the dark times, the times when Christians and Muslims alike murdered her in cold blood. "I will avenge you, my dearest love. Every religionist will suffer for what they have done to you and our baby boy!"

"But you do realise that Prime Minister Max Diamond is in the process of creating a worldwide government? As I stated if you grant my brother and I asylum, we will provide you pertinent data to aid you against an upcoming economic, political and superpower takeover."

Taras Ivanov stares at the two clone brothers, one of which he is able to read the mind of, as if he is an open book. The other is not as transparent in thoughts. "I am supposed to trust either of you? You're traitors to your nation. Even if you what you say is correct, why are you so convinced that the might of the Russian empire can be defeated by this mere Prime Minister who rules over a second rate country such as Canada?"

Gefallener Klon senses an unusual feeling, trying to reach into his mind and read his thoughts. Nagging thoughts cross his mind as he searches his thoughts in a way to betray his former master, and keep any relevant information about him and his brother clone away from the Russian President.

"Sir, with all due respect, I have no reasons to trust you. I came to you with Intel. I've destroyed much of what you've ordered me to do. Our trust is warranted!"

Taras dismisses Gefallener's statement, leans into his desk, sliding apart his folded hands and placing them firmly on his desk. He shoots the clone a dark look. "Empires are created through pseudo forms of trust. They are created through power, deceit and treachery. You betrayed your Prime Minister for me. It has worked in my favour, but why should I trust you? How do I know that this is not some scheme of his to gather intelligence on me by doing trivial, irrelevant acts that have no bearing on my Russian Empire?"

"Joshua."

Taras leans back in his chair studying the clones. "You're wasting my time. I think you should both leave."

"Oh, Joshua means nothing to you? You are his father isn't that right, Satan? And if you're his father, that means we are clones of what your grandchild is. Technically speaking, we're your grandchildren. Are we still wasting your time?"

Perplexed at the whirlwind of information conveyed, Taras leans forward in his chair and studies the two, "Ah, Dragon Dagoth's clones. I knew I recognised you. It was over a thousand years ago or so since I've seen you or him. So that is how you knew of time machines and destroyed them. Where is your master now?"

"I am Gefallener Klon. I have no master. I am 'The Fallen Clone'."

"And so you are. Where is Dragon Dagoth, aka Ethelwulf?"

"Seems you want something from me now. We should discuss your trust in us..."

The oil refinery worker does not stop violently thrashing his arms and legs as he tries to fight off his assailant Mohammed, who keeps his hand wrapped tightly against the oil refinery worker's mouth. He vigorously cuts through the worker's neck. Mohammed quickly and desperately cuts through flesh and bone before he is noticed by anyone in the refinery. He feels the warm blood pour onto his hand, and the oil refinery worker's screams moderately echo out in the immediate area, causing Mohammed to panic. Mohammed realizes his victim's vocal box is exposed and the screams are coming from the gaping hole in his neck. Mohammed panics and drops the worker's body, and puts his hand on the gaping wound in order to keep him quiet. He repeatedly stabs the man in the chest, bending his dagger on the man's ribs in the process, as he vigorously stabs the worker in order to kill him swiftly.

Tears roll down the sides of Mohammed's cheeks. This is the first time he has killed someone. His mind is in utter chaos, and he cannot keep his eyes off the innocent refinery worker. The sight of the oil refinery worker is revolting, and Mohammed regurgitates on his vomit. He feels chunks of his dinner slide back down his throat, and he is left with a warm, bitter aftertaste. Looking at the dark blue overcoat uniform he reads the name Ben in French style script, and wonders if the man had a wife and children, or friends and loved ones that cared about him. If the man did, he just took this special person away from them all. All this to do the Dark Lord Dragon Dagoth's bidding in order to save his own family, and self.

Feeling sick to his stomach, Mohammed says a quick prayer for the man, and tries to get the frozen images of his slit throat, his pulsating voice box moving up and down screaming for help, and puncture wounds in his chest, out of his mind. The images are maddening; yet, he has done it. Mohammed is ashamed knowing that the Holy Qu'ran specifically states that if you kill one man, it is as if you've killed the entire world. Weak at the knees, and dizzy from this earth shattering experience, Mohammed keeps in mind that he must complete his task otherwise the same fate will befall his beloved Reichana and their baby.

Mohammed's crew quickly assemble in the shadows of night behind pillars, and slowly sneak deeper into the oil refinery grounds. With Mohammed not that far behind them, they breach the oil refinery's security room and shoot everyone there.

Among five hundred and twenty recruits of Mohammed's travelled to America in order to assist him with the destruction of twenty six listed oil refineries that

Dragon Dagoth earmarked for them. The recruits install blasters on the support columns in the oil refineries all across Texas and wait for further instructions from Muhammad. The majority of the recruits believe they are to fulfil the will of Allah and avenge their countrymen who have fallen at the hands of the American infidels.

"Why are we doing this Mohammed? I mean Americans or not, this is wrong. They are innocent people. If we kill one person, it is like we have killed everyone in the world."

"Do you think I do not know the Holy Qu'ran?!"

"So why are we doing this?"

"You agreed to come here I cannot give you any more details than that. You knew what we had to do. You knew the risks involved and ... fuck, why are you asking now? Fuck, they are against Islam for fuck sakes. We must uphold Islam!"

"I am just saying, I have never seen anyone kill another man, and we travel to another country to destroy their buildings and kill innocent people? For what?"

"If you don't shut up, I am going to kill you too!" Mohammed shouts, barely able to contain himself. An epiphany strikes him: 'the monster has created a monster within him'. Dragon Dagoth has turned him into an animal, an animal that will do whatever it takes to protect his loved ones. Mohammed notices the bewildered look on his friend's face and apologises, "I am sorry. There is just more than meets the eye, and I cannot expect you to understand. I am cursed too and I am sorry I can't tell you more."

Mohammed's cell phone rings. He answers, and the recruit informs him that they have installed blasters in each of the other oil refineries, and are awaiting further instructions.

"I am sorry my friend. Are you with us?"

"Yeah..."

"Go and set the charges then. Let me know when you have set them up. As for now, I must go and make a video statement to America." A lie, Mohammed knows that he cannot have any of them return to Afghanistan with him. The others are not aware that Mohammed controls each of the blasters with a master detonator. He drives off to a safe distance and detonates the blasters, ending thousands of lives and completing the Dark Lord Dragon Dagoth's task.

Calls flood the Prime Minister's office, every agency from the F.B.I to the R.C.M.P. to other North American agencies inquiring about information on who is responsible for launching the terrorist attacks in the United States of America with regard to the oil refineries. The Prime Minister, Max Diamond, immediately increases border security and other security measures across the nation and other provinces that were once independent nations prior to surrendering their sovereignty to Canada, in his efforts to make a one world government.

Max Diamond quickly addresses the American nation and implores them to combine forces and become another province of Canada, to hand their independence to the growing of Canada so that they will have added security and protection within Canada's ever growing empire.

"Citizens of America, my heart goes out to the people who have lost their lives in this tragic attack on your nation and you have my deepest sympathies. Today I mourned the loss of your people after being informed of these tragic attacks that took place in your nation, in the name of tyranny, for the sake of religion! As you know, I have lost my family due to these religious extremists. They have taken a vital resource from you today, and killed thousands of people, some of whom were dear to me, and more of which were dear to you. You called them son, daughter, father, mother, brother, sister, or best friend."

"I implore you to see a way to reaching out to your President and becoming a province of Canada. It is through us that you will find the protection you need, and a constructive presence around the world that has been improving the lives of many since my time in office. I know America is a sovereign and independent nation, however, I cannot bear the thought of seeing your nation attacked anymore. If reaching out to your nation's President does not change matters, I ask not, I beg of you to motivate in favour of it. I swear it upon myself to do what it takes to protect you as my people and to help re-establish your mighty nation as our mighty nation, as our mighty people!!!"

Max Diamond's speech is hit with heavy criticism, and he is accused of using similar tactics to Russian President Taras Ivanov during the Second World War in order to gain power. Some even went as far as to say that he was helping orchestrate the terrorist attacks. His meeting with President Ballard is met with more scrutiny as he proposes plans to merge the United States of America into a Canadian province.

America would not be taken in. This was not about them giving up; this was about them striking back. The only time America had turned away from a nation that attacked them was when Russia led a massive attack, and occupied their homeland after the end of the Second World War.

President Ballard would not fold to the ever increasing influence of Canada's fake kind heartedness. He assumes Max Diamond is a tyrant, and does not want to be known as the President that gave up America, believing suicide is a better alternative.

Yet, during the meeting the President keeps his cool, as does the Prime Minister. The meeting quickly wraps up, seeing Max's conventional means of persuasion do not work on the President of America.

Max tries to contain his tension while leaving the Whitehouse; he cloaks his anger and respectfully answers questions the media ask him. Thinking about it further, Max knows this will give him the opportunity to win the hearts of the Americans, knowing that if America ever hands their sovereignty over to him, and becomes another province of Canada, he should do his best to make people want to become a part of Canada before the day comes when they will be.

A politician from the Republican Party walks over to meet the Prime Minister after the journalists are done asking their questions. He is vibrant and full of life, and immediately Max senses that the young man has an emphatic desire to express his sentiments toward him and praise him for all the work that he has been conducting. Max also foresees that this man will be President much sooner than expected.

"Mr. Prime Minister, I have been a fan of yours for a long while. I have read all of your books and have implemented what you have written into my political strategies and it's paying off. I have waited a long time for this moment to meet you sir. You are a great inspiration to me and others."

Max reaches out his hand to shake the Republican candidate's, "No need to be so formal sir, you can address me as Max, and you are?"

"Oh, thank you sir. My name is Gerald Yonge."

Max pats Gerald on the shoulder as he nods his head. As he leaves the Whitehouse, he asserts with a warm smile, "I hope when or if you become the President, you will listen to the people and give them their wishes. Your people are in a state of need, my friend." Max stops and plays his celebrity like status with the Politician, "If you were the President would you not do what is best for your people in this time of need, knowing what position your country is in? We are, after all, in a state of emergency. Don't you feel that it would be beneficial to take us up on our offer?"

"Well, with all due respect Mr. Prime Minister, we are a country of pride. Would you do the same with Canada, if asked?"

"You're answering a question with a question and avoiding mine, but I will answer yours. Yes, of course I would. Even if I was the most hated man on earth after, I would have done it to protect my people ... and their children. I am sorry. It truly was a pleasure meeting you Mr. Yonge and good luck with your political endeavours and career, my friend."

Max smiles as he leaves the Politician to his thoughts, (which is part of the plan based on what he has foreseen regarding the young impressionable mind of Gerald), having reinforced the last memorable thoughts he will have which will motivate him all the more to become President. Qs Herbert W. Ballard cannot be reached by conventional means of persuasion. This will be the alternate route to acquiring America.

Mohammed is wary of the impending meeting with Dragon Dagoth. He fidgets with his ghutra on his head and walks around the abandoned palace, impatiently looking around for the Dark Lord. He notices that he is being called out to more meetings than his father ever was when he was a young child, and is beginning to wonder if one day, he will share the same fate as his father, or if Dragon Dagoth has plans in mind to keep him permanently.

With him are highly trained snipers. They are just outside a town called Tykrit, in Iraq. They wait for Dragon Dagoth to provide them with details on their next mission. Leading up to the time of this meeting, Mohammed was diligently training trusted individuals as ordered by Dragon Dagoth for this upcoming mission they are to carry out.

As they wait inside the palace, they are taken aback by the smell, due to the lack of upkeep of the surroundings; there is also the eerie, uneasy feeling of something that was not good about the place at all. The wait seems to last an eternity. Mohammed notices up above on the second floor, Dragon

Dagoth, as he casually strolls out, clad in his black cloak. He places his hands on the banister, and watches as the men scramble to collect themselves. Frightened, a couple of the snipers aim their guns at the black-cloaked Dragon Dagoth who does not budge in the slightest at the cocking guns. Mohammed screams at his men to stop what they are doing at once, and that Dragon Dagoth is the contact. They argue that the dark-cloaked man is Shaitan, and fearful emotions cloud the room. Dragon Dagoth glares at the men down on the lower level and feels utter contempt and repulsion for the weak fools aiming their guns at him.

"Mohammed, are you going to get your monkeys in order so that we may get to business?"

Mohammed looks at Dragon Dagoth, angry that he is being admonished while trying to get his men in line, while silently hoping that one of his friends disobeys, and shoots the Devil man. Once he calms everyone down, Dragon Dagoth begins to speak.

"Mohammed, I have your reward same as usual."

"You stupid man, how am I to be rich anymore? Canada seems to have screwed the world's currency over; paper money is going to be like toilet paper, you know!"

"Interrupt me again and I will cut your head off with a dull butter knife! Got it!!" Dragon Dagoth growls out. To show his intent and power, the ceiling begins to split and crack. Small pieces of rubble fall to the floor, and Mohammed and his men cringe in fear. "I have an All-In-One card for you. I want you to go to America with your friends and assassinate President Herbert W. Ballard. Time is of the essence. As always, you will be rewarded." Reaching into his cloak, Dragon Dagoth brings out an envelope which contains All-In-One cards for Mohammed and his crew, and then tosses them to the lower floor.

"Does this also include the payment for the other assassination?" Mohammed casually asks as he bends over to pick up the yellowish brown envelope containing the cards.

"What other assassination? All I am commanding you to do is assassinate the President."

"Max Diamond and his family, you know the one where we captured people's family members and fathers to kill the Prime Minister of Canada and his family. We got the wife and son. We still need more time with the Prime Minister, but have not heard from you regarding the matter."

Dragon Dagoth leaps from the second floor to the ground below, "What did you just say to me?!"

"Are we to carry on with your orders to kill the Prime Minister as well? As well as kill the President of America? You seem displeased. We will kill him. I am sorry things did not go according to plan."

For the first time since Dragon Dagoth had entered Mohammed's life, he lowers his cowl and glares at Mohammed, "Did he look like me, but with a short military hair cut? And smoother face?"

"Sir, he was you, same face. I could not see him too well like I never see you too well until now, but I could tell he had long hair. The man you are referring to is definitely you."

Dragon Dagoth reaches for his cowl and positions it carefully on his head once again, "My memory is foggy. Help me recall something; did those orders include attacking a secret base?"

"No, that was it Ibliss."

Dragon Dagoth nods, looks around the lower level of the complex at the small crew Mohammed has gathered, and then marches off without his usual parting words.

"We will be paid for that assassination? That is correct."

"You will get a special reward for it." Dragon Dagoth growls his words out, without looking back to address Mohammed, as he walks off into the black of night.

Mohammed picks up the envelope and hands out the cards. "How did he get my picture?" he rhetorically asks.

"Perhaps the Canadian secret service, the American F.B.I., or Russian Empire my friend. I am not certain. What I can tell you is that it scares me to know how connected this man or Devil is. What scares me more is not being in the know. Something is not right and he looked worried about something," one of the snipers speculates.

"I noticed that as well, we can use that to our advantage."

The trips back and forth to America have taken a toll on Mohammed. His latest terrorist attacks on American soil have been eating away at his conscience, and he knows that if the time comes where he is ever caught for those horrendous crimes, he will surely face capital punishment. However, Dragon Dagoth has been quiet, withholding his identity, and he is looking forward to what seems to be his final reward for all of his services throughout the years.

The perplexing question plaguing Mohammed's mind is how Dragon Dagoth acquired forged All-In-One cards, seeing The Canadian Prime Minister, Max Diamond, made these cards to help combat crime. His assumptions lead to him feeling that Dragon Dagoth has connections to people within the Canadian government, but what is the motive in having him assassinate the American president? Is Canada at the brink of war with the United States? And if Canada attacks an occupied territory of Russia, will those two nations be at loggerheads?

President Herbert W. Ballard is set to give a speech at the first pre-season football game of the year in public to show that they are doing their best to combat terrorism. Dragon Dagoth's orders are to have him assassinated at this speech, and strike fear back into the heart of the nation.

Mohammed has barely slept since he was given his orders. Assassinating a political leader of a country is not the same as destroying buildings. How they would pull it off was not the question. How they would get away with it is another story.

The past few weeks leading up to now consisted of endless planning, studying the stadium, finding out where to purchase illegal weapons, and where to hide them within the stadium. A few of Mohammed's men were hired as low end workers within the Red Skins stadium. They helped with taking photographs and finding areas to take a sniper shot at the President.

On the last night, time drags by reviewing the plans over and over again to make sure that nothing is out of place. This does not alleviate any tensions either. Lack of sleep is apparent as Mohammed has difficulties keeping his eyes open which seemed to be a challenge in itself as he walked towards the stadium. Thankfully, the electric energy of the crowd seems to rub off on Mohammed as he makes his way towards the stadium, carrying an American flag, blending in, humming hip hop tunes which he couldn't care less about, walking in sync with other patriotic Red Skins fans to the stadium to watch the football game, and pay their support to their country and President.

After finding his seat amongst the sea of Red Skins fans, Mohammed looks around the stadium to see if he can see any of his friends that left at separate times and locations for the game, and then to see if he will be able to spot the one who will be shooting the President with the high powered 50 calibre American Barrett sniper rifle. Of course, he was unable to spot him.

Cheers from the home fans escalate as the home team rushes onto the field. Mohammed follows suit, waving his

American flag in the air a few times to compensate for not having a home team flag.

Mohammed stands up with the rest of the home team fans, waving his American flag and looks up, and around the stadium to see if he is able to catch a glimpse of his crew, and as expected he notices a few secret service police canvassing the stadium, as well as a few secret service snipers.

Everything about this mission spells disaster. At this point, Mohammed feels the urge to run away, through the midst of the crowd, and be with his love. This has all been too much already; yet, flashes of his father being murdered indirectly by Dragon Dagoth are etched deep in his mind. If Dragon Dagoth could do that to someone that had worked with him for all those years, he would not hesitate to kill him and his family, something Dragon Dagoth kept constantly reminding him about.

Mohammed will do anything to keep his love out of harm's way. Doing these tasks, helps ease Mohammed's mind. He feels that each time he does the Dark Lord's requests, it is a chance to save not only his life but the lives of his family. Regardless of how many people he kills, the affairs of the heart have and always will be justified concerning his family.

Keeping up the façade of pseudo excitement throughout the football game proved to be a tedious task; additionally, having seats next to obnoxiously loud diehard football fans grows overwhelming. However, Mohammed had studied all he needed to know about the Washington Red Skins, and the basics of football. The obnoxious fans continue to jeer, and crack callous jokes about Mohammed's origins, and interrogate him about the game and football. This was not something that he had in mind when creating plans to assassinate the President.

"I am sorry I just don't know as much as you do about football."

"Only diehard fans go to a Pre-Season football game. If you aren't a diehard fan, what the fuck are you doing here? You didn't get lost on your way here thinking that this is that Paki prayer place, uh what is it? Mecca, is that what your kind fucking call it? You know the place with the big block of shit you guys pray to?"

"That would be a 'No true Scotsman fallacy sir; I am a fan of football, albeit I may not know as much as you do. I do enjoy getting out of the house and watching such events. This is much better than paying to watch it on the television. With that said, I did not anticipate meeting someone of your rather intriguing intellect, and I feel that the American education system has done an injustice to you. To have clever quips about that would be more appropriate, not something as trivial as what people pray to, and where they do it."

"'Fallacy?' What the fuck does that mean? You're some university dude, aren't you? You don't get pipes like these pushing pens and books around." The man rolls up his shirt and tries to intimidate Mohammed by his show of muscular attributes. After his encounters with Dragon Dagoth, he is far from impressed or intimidated.

"Thank you for emphasising my point. I will continue watching the game now. Please excuse me."

"Suit yourself guy, this isn't the Taj Mahal or one of them fancy places you Arabs have back where you live where I have to shut the fuck up, just to let you know, uh huh!!!"

Mohammed bites his tongue. He has a job to do and is already getting more attention than what he bargained for by carrying on a conversation that didn't need to take place with one of the local fans. The first half of the game comes to an end, and this is Mohammed's cue to get ready. He inserts a headset in his ear and begins communication with the others. Trying to be to inconspicuous, Mohammed pulls his hood over his head and listens for the others to check in.

"Huh?! It's eighty six degrees out in the shade today, boy. Why are you placing on a hood? Not hot enough for your kind, boy?"

Ignoring the obnoxious individual beside him, Mohammed pulls out his digital camera and begins to stream live content for one of the snipers. In order to save being interrupted any further by the individual, he leaves his seat and walks down the aisle past the rowdy bunch of football fans, and walks down the stairs in order to pretend to take photographs of the President. The atmosphere within the stadium changes dramatically once the President steps on stage during the half time show and walks over to the podium in order to give his speech.

"Alpha here, I have the mark in my sights, waiting for a green light."

"Omega here, I have the mark in my sights, waiting for a green light."

The President begins his speech, and the crowd shows their respect by becoming silent. The President addresses how the nation of America will combat terrorism.

"People of America, and fellow allies across the world, we have not suffered such tragedies since the attacks of nine eleven; suffice to say that does not make it any less tragic. My heart ... my heart goes out to the families of those who lost their loved ones. America we must stand strong in the face of adversity, and we must unite together to continue to flush out the remaining terrorists that stand to threaten democracy, and threaten our freedom," President Ballard states hypnotically while looking around the football stadium.

"Boss?"

"You have the green light."

John Craig   241

Mohammed's knees threaten to buckle and his heart pounds, anticipating the shot. It does not get any easier terminating someone's life.

The people cheer during the President of America's long dramatic pause. Red, white and blue flags are waving in the air, held high by the proud patriot American citizens, and naturalised citizens, proud to call themselves American. The President wobbles, and reaches for his chest after jerking back a couple of footsteps. Mohammed zooms in with his digital camera examining what is taking place with the President, and then another bullet tears apart the President's skull. Blood sprays out of his head like a fine gentle mist. The President's knees buckle from under him and his body falls to the ground, knocking over the podium before him.

The feedback from the microphones screeches and cackles as they slam to the ground under the President's dead weight, and then are finally cut. This is the first successful Presidential assassination since John F. Kennedy.

The crowd in the stadium screams in horror or express their shock in some way after witnessing the assassination. Some of the President's armed guards frantically try to help the President but it is too late. Mohammed turns around and rushes for the exit through a sea of body traffic.

Running down ramps to get out of the stadium, he reaches the exit and continues to run towards Prince George's Plaza, and enters the subway system in order to get out of the state which was part of the plan. From there, he would board an airliner to get into Canada.

It takes less than a few hours to reach the hotel that Dragon Dagoth informed Mohammed and his team to rendezvous at. After his arrival, he waits for the others, hoping that they made it out of the state safely.

"I just received a call from one of them now. Before you make the arrest, I need to know where my clones are. I think they are responsible for my wife and son's deaths."

"Your clones haven't reported in for days, sir."

"And where might they be?"

"Russia."

"Why are they in Russia of all places?"

"That is their last known location. I don't know the reasons behind why they are there, sir."

"So you mean to inform me that they've disappeared from the grid and that the G.T.S.Chips are not being picked up?"

"That is correct, sir."

"Notify all friendly airports to detain them the moment they appear on grid. Send a team to apprehend them once they are found."

"Affirmative, sir."

As Mohammed tries killing his nerves waiting for the others to show up, he rents the banquet hall in the hotel to alert Dragon Dagoth of his presence, and to get rewarded for their services.

After Mohammed's friends show up at the hotel and settle in, they all wait impatiently for the Dark Lord to show up.

"I cannot believe that you trust and believe this man Mohammed. How do you feel you can trust this man?!"

"This man has been funding our organisation for years and has worked with my father, so leave it at that, my friend."

As several thoughts race through Mohammed's and the rest of his team's minds, the banquet doors to the reception area burst open, and Canadian Special Forces rush inside, aiming their guns at Mohammed and the rest of his team members.

Mohammed instantly feels sick to his stomach. Had they been tracked down to this area? How was that possible? It was too soon for the law to have tracked them down; it was literally impossible!

Mohammed walks over to one of the Special Forces officers with his hands in the air, showing that he poses no threat to them, "What is the problem officer? What is going on? We are tourists."

"Shut the fuck up! You are under arrest for the assassination of President Herbert W. Ballard."

Amidst the screams and curses of Mohammed's friends yelling in Arabic at him for placing his trust in a man that they felt was the Devil himself, Mohammed staggers backwards in utter shock. There is no way that they could have been tracked that quickly! They were not caught for anything before, unless his men got sloppy and were followed to this location. "Shut up fools. Let me speak to the officers!"

"There is a mistake. We're tourists."

"Shut the fuck up! Hands where I can see them, Mohammed!"

Betrayal! If he was going down the best way to protect his fiancée Reichana is too inform the officers of everything that had been going on up to the assassination. If he was going down he was going to bring down the man that had indirectly killed his father and who would still pose a threat to his beloved wife. There was no way that he was going to let anything happen to his fiancée under any circumstances.

"I am responsible for the murder of the American President Herbert W. Ballard. I am taking orders from a man who uses the name Dragon Dagoth who will be here shortly."

"Drop your weapon before I shoot!" the officer yells at Mohammed.

"Don't be silly. I have no weapon. Here are my hands, see?"

At that particular moment, Mohammed has an epiphany and realises that Dragon Dagoth is in control of everything. Additionally, he realises that there would be no other way for Dragon Dagoth to give him and the others legitimate All-In-One cards if he was not a part of the government. Moreover, there would be no way that he would have been able to successfully get away with carrying out all the other missions without getting caught if Dragon Dagoth was not in direct or indirect control of the government.

Everything that he had done was for his family. He closes his eyes and pictures his beautiful fiancée, and envisions what their wedding would have been like, while trying to picture Reichana's face for the last time. He recalls each time he left for a mission, her words telling him to be careful, and that she wished him luck so that she could see him again, and to have and hold him in his arms, and maybe one day when this was all over, they could raise their family together.

Today, that was not going to happen. Mohammed realises Dragon Dagoth has been using him as a pawn for a much bigger game that he is playing, a game that he does not know anything about and will die for, without ever knowing. The last thing Mohammed hears while he has his eyes shut is the cocking of the officer's gun. The officer executes him. He shoots Mohammed point blank in the chest several times. The rest of the terrorists are taken to an undisclosed detention centre to await their trial.

Just as Max had foreseen and planned out, Gerald Yonge becomes the next President of the United States of America. He uses this very opportunity to address the Canadian people in regards to the capture of the terrorist and places his next plans in motion.

"My fellow Canadians, it scares me to see all these terrorist acts taking place on our beloved continent. I have done much good for our people because I am like you, and I am for us, the Canadian people. However, it scares me to even fathom the thought that all I have worked so hard to accomplish for us could be ruined by another Prime Minister taking my place in office.

"This is a time of crisis for the Canadian people. We are in a state of shambles. I feel that it is my primary duty as Prime Minister to continue making a better system which I have spent countless years making for all of us. This includes restoring and bettering our health care system, and saving the lives of people within our new provinces. These people are the brothers and sisters of our relatives that used to be in other countries that I have helped you reunite with. Now we are faced with the sad truth that terrorism is on the rise and it has been through me that I have captured the terrorists responsible for killing my wife and son, and the President of America.

"While there are still more on the prowl waiting to hurt us, I feel that it would be in our best interest to announce a state of emergency in Canada, and for me to stay in term for an indefinite period of time until we have hunted down and captured all the terrorists that would dare harm us!!! I will continue to carry on my work in hunting down these criminals!!! After I have accomplished my goal and when I see that our country is in good hands I promise you that I will return our country to its original political state.

"From there, I would like carry out the rest of my life helping the needs of children through non-profit charities, and organisations. Believe me I see no other alternative in declaring myself as supreme leader of Canada."

Over the course of the next few weeks, Max uses his influence over the young American President and Gerald Yonge signs over American sovereignty to Canada. After Max had issued a state of emergency, he orders all religious institutes and organisations to close their places of worship, setting up the next stage of his plan, an insurrection.

With the ever growing populace of Canada, Max decides that it is best to commence the other phase in his plan, the first global government of the world. He orders all soldiers within the ever growing empire of the New World Order to be replaced with highly sophisticated robot soldiers. Additionally, he signs a bill making it mandatory for all citizens within the

New World Order to have the Global Tracking System Chips surgically implanted in them to help counter terrorism.

To counter all of the violent protests that are taking place throughout the New World Order, Max Diamond issues a ban on any media publications on government affairs. If anything is to be released it will need to be approved by the government first.

One of Max Diamond's appointed officials sends word to remaining countries that have not turned themselves into a province of Canada, that it would be in their better interests to surrender to the New World Order and share a one world democracy, in order to help deter and obliterate crimes worldwide and help unite the world and be as one.

Some leaders want no part of it, while others surrender and swear allegiance to the country once known as Canada. The people of Canada feel betrayed by their supreme leader, and so do some of the other countries that swore their allegiance to Canada, and not a New World Order; however, Max Diamond remains far removed from the emotions of his citizens, persuading his people with otherwise.

Max Diamond continues to win the hearts of many people in the free world, implementing more changes and giving the New World Order more control by the day, further imposing laws against religions using the guise that it is so that terrorists can be singled out.

Citizens of the New World Order, protest and take to violent uprising against the Supreme Leader's actions; however, the people no longer have a say. The voting system has been long abolished. Further impositions are made law which in include citizens being forbidden to wear anything that represents religion in any way, and new laws stipulating churches, temples, mosques or anything resembling a place of worship are not to be entered during this experimental ban on religion.

Max terminates all paper currency, continuing to carry out his guise that he is flushing out terrorists the world over, and that the best way to find out criminal transactions would be to monitor everyone's spending habits.

This has been hundreds of years in the making, and the once pure, loving Ethelwulf is a dead and gone shell, hiding behind Max, a man who lies about his good hearted intentions, to the people of the world. Soon, he will move on to the final stage of his plan and get the vengeance he has patiently waited for all these years and kill each and every religionist that is now under his grid and under his watchful eye. He will make them all suffer and account for what they did to his beautiful son and wife. Soon, he will remove the mask of Max, and strike fear into the hearts of all religionists across the world when he removes that mask and declares himself Emperor Dragon Dagoth!

ERA
The Religious
Holocaust

13

"Holy shit, dude! I can't believe what's happening outside man." William says, exhaling a cloud of smoke from his cigarette, astonished by what he is observing on the news. His friends Jody and Joshua nod their heads. "See dude, this is what I was talking about. There is going to be another Taras Ivanov!"

Joshua interrupts William, "Unlike Taras Ivanov, the Supreme Leader is doing this to Catholics, Muslims, Christians and anyone else who worships a god, not invading other countries."

"Seems that way," William says, exhaling another cloud of smoke, as he reaches across the coffee and snuffs out his cigarette. "Listen Josh, it's a fucking cover up! Think about it man, these are Jew based religions man, so Max Diamond is just like ... finishing off Taras Ivanov's work. What do you think, Jody?"

"I think that it is wrong to kill people over a religion, but we don't know that this is happening. Who is to say that some of these people are not terrorists. They can't all be terrorists."

Since Max Diamond became Mayor of Toronto to Prime Minister of Canada, Joshua has followed all of the world events surrounding the former Prime Minister of their old country and now Supreme Leader of the New World Order. Years ago when Canada was still a country, the Prime Minister crushed their money laundering business; they acquired their funds through a drug and arms trade.

He is very convinced that there is something strange about Max Diamond; the Supreme Leader is able to get whatever he wants when he wants. He remembers back over a hundred years ago when Taras Ivanov who he knows is Satan, caused WWII, in order to find him. He used the same cunning, hypnotic spell over the people of the land and tracked him as far as America until he went into hiding and sneaked across the border to Canada.

All of the Gods are dead, and Satan killed the rest of the Devils, so whoever this Max Diamond is, presents a grave danger, which is part of the reason he will not get his mandatory G.T.S chip.

Getting his mind off things, Joshua turns to his friends and contributes to the conversation, "To be fair, everyone was told not to go to church or other places of worship, so they had it coming. You wouldn't go inside a building that is seconds away from being demolished and sit on the dynamite then say they should have known someone was inside. This is just ridiculous!"

"All I know is, I am not getting that fucking chip stuck inside of me, that is for damn sure," William says.

"You have to get the chip dude. If you don't, your All-In-One card will be confiscated and you will not be able to do anything at all. If you do that, I suggest growing your own food and raising cattle in the middle of nowhere, because that is the only way you're going to eat," Jody counters William.

William nods his head and agrees with Jody. There really isn't a way out of the situation.

"Fuck, Jody is right, guy. It's like the Supreme Leader has all of his bases covered. We're gonna be fucked if we don't get those chips."

For well over a thousand years, Joshua has done his best to stay off the radar and not attract any attention, however, in order to survive, there does not appear to be any viable alternative other than succumb to the Supreme Leader Max Diamond's system. The best way to avoid certain detection is having William help him acquire a new identity.

"Hey buddy, I need to speak with you in private."

The two excuse themselves and walk into another room.

"Will I need to pretend to be your brother, and assume your last name as part of my new identity? As you're aware, I am in serious trouble with the law right?" Will nods as Joshua continues speaking, "I can't be discovered. If I am discovered, I will be killed, more than likely."

"Exactly what are you wanted for if you want me to vouch for you as my brother, guy? If they come looking for you and find you, they're more than likely going to arrest me for helping you. You know this, right?"

"Keep this a secret between us. I am not sure how I will be able to break this to you so I will just be as blunt as possible. I am not human. In fact, I've lost count but I am close to two thousand years of age. There are other beings such as myself that roam the world, and they are some of the most powerful beings on this planet. We went to war with each other years ago. They killed my father, and I also believe they killed my wife. Since that time I have been living off the grid, and keeping to the shadows so that I am not discovered."

"Dude. you know what? I can't do this for you, man. I ask you one simple question and you can't even give me a straight forward answer. I would have probably agreed but since you wanna make up a bullshit story, you can go fuck yourself and get the damn chip like everyone else has to!"

Joshua glares at William. There is not much he can say to prove his story. In fact, if he was in William's shoes right now he'd probably be thinking the same thing he is.

"I understand what you're thinking and how odd this sounds, but I have no reasons to make up anything to you."

"Like I said, I am not helping you!"

"The future is not clear. Whoever is after me has clouded my vision. The Supreme Leader will no longer be in charge, and there will be a new system in order. Dragon Dagoth will assume control, and come after me; he will kill your mother, your friends, and everyone close to you, just to watch you suffer. You need me more than you know."

"Are you fucking threatening me?!" William asks, as he reaches for his gun and aims it at Joshua's chest.

"Listen, I am not bullshitting you, nor do I have any reason to threaten you, unless the reason you're not going to do this for me is because you're scheming to take over our crime syndicate? Secondly, this being came after me around fifteen hundred years ago, but if you've lived as long as I have trust me all the years seem to be a fucking blur. I don't really remember how long ago it was! Next off, I am demi- immortal, you will not be able to kill me with that puny toy of yours!"

Without a second's hesitation William pulls the trigger. Before the bullet is able to leave the chamber of the gun, Joshua races over to William, grabs the gun and places his fingers on William's temple sending flashes of his memory of the past to William.

"Because you have fought gallantly under glory and honour of Rome, you will be given a soldier's death under the Caesar's decree."

"Tis not my fault, I cannot explain unto thee why I do not age, all of ye must understand I serve the one God, Caesar and his will, and Rome and all of her glory. There are nought pledges or pacts made with the Devil and abomination of the One God!"

In slow motion, William sees the memory a soldier walking with a broad sword behind Joshua, and then Joshua's face falling towards the ground, followed by dark black. Another flash of the memory shows a man clad in a black cloak, looking at Joshua as he opens his eyes again.

"Joshua, son of Sharon, ye are demi-immortal; come with me and I will show thee secrets beyond thy wildest dreams."

"I felt the blade go through me and into my insides. Yet, I live? Hast thou tended to my wounds? Who art thou?"

"Ah forgive me Joshua son of Sharon. My name is Satan. Forget those who have betrayed thee and learn what I have to teach

unto thee. Unlearn what thou knowest, for that which I have to teach and pass on to thee, is ultimate power."

As William continues to grip his gun, more of Joshua's memories flood his mind. He sees Joshua learning all sorts of magic with other Devils. They teach him the art of melee combat. In that time he meets a sweetheart Elizabeth, and she conceives his child. He is warned by Elizabeth and the others not to take revenge on those who took his life. He does not listen and heads to the army outpost where his aggressors and executioner are camped. He slaughters them all along the way to meet his executioner sword in hand. He also demonstrates his magic power combusting some of his potential attackers into flames, turning others into stone, giving heart attacks to those who run after him, until he approaches the one who drove his sword deep inside of his rib cage through his neck.

"Thou hast accused me of making a pact with the Devil. Now I have come back from the dead and I have made a pact with Satan the Devil! Thy life ends now!"

Joshua roars out like an angry beast in rage and swings his sword downward, splitting open his executioner's rib cage and opening his abdomen. His execution holds his stomach for a few brief seconds until his innards fall on to the ground, his knees buckle, and blood pours out of him until he dies.

The memories continue. Joshua is at his estate and Elizabeth is not there. Satan smiles at the pain and rage he endures knowing that his wife with child left him. There are many hostilities, and the five beings are at one another's throats and start a war amongst each other. In the midst of battle, a warrior carrying an assault rifle emerges on the scene followed by other warriors who all look the same as the one leading the way. They shoot down a few of the Devils. Joshua escapes the battle.

From that day forward, Joshua searches for his wife and son and they are nowhere to be found. He takes to his other passion and fights with the Britannia soldiers, and then leaves so as not to arouse suspicion that he is demi-immortal. He travels to Northern Africa to escape the crusades, and then back to Europe to avoid detection. He fights in arenas and amphitheatres to earn coin for his travels. He fakes his deaths in battles. Eventually he moves to the west, the North American continent and is an early pioneer, lurking in the shadows. He fights in the civil war, World War 1, and World War 2, and laid low since the Russian invasion of America led by Taras Ivanov. William then sees Joshua saving him in a gang fight where they first met; all takes place as the bullet slowly leaves its chamber and speeds its way down the barrel of the gun. Joshua lets go of William's temple and the sound from the gun echoes throughout the room leaving a ringing noise in either ear.

Looking around the room, William does not notice Joshua and then realizes the gun is not in his hand and is in Joshua's as he spins to his side and notices him there. "What the fuck?"

"You're going to help me, correct?"

Archer walks inside the quartet's home and notices Jody running into William's room, which he surmises is more than likely something to do with the gunshot he heard before entering their home. As Jody rushes into the room, he notices Joshua holding a smoking gun, "Sorry, I accidently pulled the trigger?"

"You fucking stupid man. Last thing we need are pigs here," Jody says, referring to the police.

William takes advantage of the situation and leaves the room and does not answer Joshua. He is frightened to death. He does not know how Joshua grabbed his gun nor does he know how he blanked out for a second, and now he has several images of Joshua's past stuck in his head, but feels it is no more than auto-suggestion.

"Oh, hey Archer. You're home. You sell the crate of arms?"

"Yeah, were you guys firing the guns off in the house?" Archer curiously responds to William.

"Joshua did. Anyhow, I need to clear my head, and by the way Jody ordered pizza earlier. It's on the counter."

The Toronto West congregation of the Worldwide Church of God sings hymns inside high school hall at West Humber Collegiate, despite the new law imposed by Max Diamond against congregating for religious purposes.

"Hallelujah praise god, the eternal shall reign; he shall reign for all ages, our king and our god."

At the end of the chorus the minister addresses the congregation, "Everyone please bow your heads for the opening prayer: Oh heavenly father and blessed God who sent your only begotten son to die for our sins, we are gathered here today at our last meeting in this school as the great tribulation in the book of Revelation that you have so warned us about, arises. We pray oh heavenly father, that you convince the people whose faiths have waivered, to you let them see the signs of the times, oh heavenly father, and to understand that this is all just part of your heavenly plan coming to a close. We also ask that your son Jesus Christ will take us to our place of safety. We humbly ask these things of you, in the name of your great son Jesus Christ who has died for our sins, oh great and mighty heavenly father if that is your will oh lord, in Jesus Christ's name. Amen."

The congregation mirrors the minister and chants "Amen." The minister addresses the congregation, "Brethren, today as you may be aware we will be changing the format of our services. Instead of having a Sermonette followed by announcements, and closing with a sermon, we will just have our announcements conducted by Mr. Goldstein, and then a closing hymn and prayer. Mr. Goldstein, please come to the stage."

The minister leaves the podium, as the district's Head Pastor Mr. Goldstein walks onstage and heads toward the podium. He does not resemble the strong leader the congregation is used to seeing. He appears to look weighed down, carrying a heavy burden; he speaks slowly and aloof seeming, while addressing the congregation. "Brethren, as you know the great tribulation is upon us, and Satan the devil is doing his part in destroying us. He is aiding the Muslims through the acts of terrorism on our nations which has brought forth the Anti-Christ Max Diamond who is doing all he can to stop us from gathering together on Sabbath days. As you all know, we can no longer meet on church premises; however, I am glad that you have placed your faith in the Lord God to save us from anything which may be brought upon us. The Pastor General will be informing us where the place of safety is soon, and we will relocate in order to be saved and be where the Lord will watch over us throughout the next few years."

The auditorium doors swing open, banging against the walls and breaking Mr. Goldstein's hypnotic speech. The member causing the commotion shouts frantically, "Mr. Goldstein, Mr. Goldstein! They are here. I think they are surrounding the school. They have guns!" The lady rushes into the auditorium, clutching her baby close to her chest, nearly tripping over her long flowing dress as she runs down the centre aisle.

The congregation begins to speak amongst themselves; sentiments of panic and dread are shared with each other on the church lady's revelation of what may be in store for them. The panicked talk amongst one another escalates, and turns into frantic panics and screams.

"Please, everyone remain calm. We are not violating the law. We are only holding a meeting. I am sure I can explain this to them regardless if today is the Sabbath. I assure you that none of us will be taken into custody today. I will head outside, speak with whoever is in charge, and rectify the situation. I speculate the caretaker informed the police that we are gathering here for a church meeting, when in fact we are just conducting a few announcements. I shall return momentarily."

Mr. Goldstein walks away from the podium, off the stage and heads outside the auditorium, leaving behind three hundred worried members. A few moments later the sound of heavy machine gunfire erupts, followed by silence. A few moments later, sounds of glass shattering from the entrance of the school echo into the auditorium as soldiers march into the school, and march throughout the corridors outside the auditorium. A few people within the auditorium cry, while others feel it is best to escape. They run out of the auditorium and are shot down just as quickly. Screams of terror fill the auditorium; people begin to climb over one another in order to escape. The doors slam shut around all the exit and entrance points to the auditorium. Several more gun shots echo throughout the hallways. Inside restrooms, classrooms and everywhere else, church members run to hide or escape.

A soldier from outside the auditorium addresses the congregation using the school's public address system, "You are all in violation of the Supreme leader Max Diamond's decree. This is a terrorist meeting which is a capital offence, and you will all be punished accordingly."

Frantic screams from church members inside the auditorium, echo in the hallway outside, some pleading that there are innocent women and children inside, and none of which are answered. A few minutes later, from inside the air conditioning duct, the scent of something similar to pesticide seeps into the auditorium, Zyklon B.

"Mom, Dad let's get out of here. I know a way out through the back of the stage. I hang out there sometimes before and after services," Mark says, keeping his voice down so other church members do not hear him.

"Mark, they are shooting everyone outside the auditorium. Can't you hear them?"

"Mark, your mother is right," Mark's dad, Paul, says, coughing a few times in reaction to the airborne chemical agent, while placing a warm hand on his son's shoulder and thinking of an alternate way of getting out of this situation alive.

"Guys, listen to me there is a swimming pool area behind the stage. A door leads to it. We can get out through there and hide there if necessary. Let's go! It's either that, or we die here and we don't take the chance," Mark says as he proceeds, heading up the first steps towards the stage, covering his mouth and nose with his hand. His two younger siblings, one brother and sister, follow suit. His baby sister is cradled in his mother Victoria's, arm. She turns around and watches the church members throwing each other out of the way, clawing at the auditorium doors, breaking their finger nails off, and gasping for fresh air between the cracks of the doors.

Together they rush onto the stage, and run behind the curtain as everyone in the auditorium is screaming in dire pain. The Zyklon B. begins to take its fatal effect on the weak, old and young inside. The others find the pain unbearable as their flesh begins to burn and they bleed from their ears and foam at their mouths until they drop to their knees or fall down on other victims where they choke to death in their final moments.

Mark and the rest of the family enter the pool area which is unaffected by the fatal gas seeping into the auditorium; Mark shuts, and locks the door behind him and his family.

"Mark, we should inform the others that this is a way out. We can help save their lives. That isn't very Christian of you! Why would you condemn them to die like that? Open the door at once!"

"Screw you! You think I am going to be hunted down like the others we heard out there. We can at least save ourselves! If we try to save everyone else we will all die! Let's get in the pool and just wait for the soldiers to leave." Mark says in an angry whisper.

"Mark, do not yell at your mother like that!" Paul angrily demands like the authoritative father figure he is. But he does not care that there are soldiers searching the hallways for stragglers.

"The gas seems to be in here as well. Let's just get in the pool. They have oxygen tanks in one of the rooms. Hold on while I get a few."

Mark runs into the change room, quickly grabs a few oxygen tanks and runs back to his family. Each of the family members adjusts the oxygen masks on their faces. Since his mother is pregnant he helps her hide in the change room and wraps her, and his sister Penny in a fire blanket. He runs back to the pool and slowly submerges himself into the pool.

A soldier grabs hold of the swimming pool area door and gives a few short tugs. Noticing that the door is locked from within, the soldier does not realise a chain is wrapped around the handles of the door.

"Noise was registered inside," the soldier shares with the others.

The soldier scans the door and gives a final tug, fragments of the door splinter across the deck of the swimming pool, and the chains locking the doors, break apart like fine glass. The soldiers use their heat scanners and detect a couple of faint heat signatures in the change room. Armed with an assault rifle the soldier followed by a few others, walks inside of the change room, and finds a terrified mother clutching onto her baby.

"This must be the last of the survivors," the soldier states, as he aims his gun at Victoria and shoots her in the head. A mist of blood sprays the wall and still has enough force to go out of the other side of her cranium and break a chunk of the brick wall behind her. Victoria's baby daughter Penny rolls out of her mother's limp, dead arms and hands, and then falls on the floor, along with the oxygen tank attached to her. The impact from the fall on the floor leaves an egg-sized bruise on the little baby Penny's forehead.

The soldier walks over to the infant and scans the baby. With one swift and mighty motion, the soldier hoists its leg into the air and sends it down on the baby's head with a mighty crash, crushing the baby's skull and causing parts of brain matter, and blood to splatter across the white ceramic floor in all directions. The soldier turns around and without emotion, leaves the room with the other soldiers.

Around nightfall, Mark and his family hoist themselves free from the pool, and quietly look around the immediate area. There does not appear to be any trace of soldiers in or around the outside of the school. Paul screams out loud as he finds his wife Victoria and newborn baby dead inside the change room. Paul runs to his dead wife and Miriam runs into the room following her father's screams. She notices her mother and baby sister and begins to cry. She picks up her baby sister Penny. As she does, her baby sister's head which is stuck to the floor from the impact of the blow from the soldier peels off her neck. Miriam drops Penny's lifeless body, regurgitates and then vomits in her oxygen mask and then vomits again at the smell of vomit in her mask, chunks of vomit still logged within her throat.

Miriam's brother, Simon, rushes to her aid while fighting away tears. He gently removes Miriam's mask and wipes away the warm puke that clings to his finger and her face in strands. He wipes it on his clothing and takes the remainder off Miriam's mouth and chin. He looks at what remains of his baby sister Penny and his knees buckle from the shock and horror. *This cannot be true. This is a nightmare,* he thinks to himself, and he also tries to wake himself up, slapping his cheeks. The shock is too much to fathom but this is reality.

Mark slowly walks into the change room after canvassing the area for soldiers, and has a knot in his stomach, unaware of the reasons that the rest of his family are upset. However, he discovers the reasons all too soon. The last thing he recalls saying to his mother was "screw you". Now she lies dead, straddled in his father's arms. Mark rips off his oxygen tank and walks slowly over to his mother's corpse; he is not able to process the reality of her murder. He kneels down next to his father, holds his mother and kisses her cold dead lips. The coagulated blood on her cool lips sticks to his. The taste is bitter. Emotionally distraught he does not care that his father ever said "boys don't cry". Mark weeps and kisses his dead mother repeatedly.

"How could God let this happen to his followers? How could he let this happen to my mommy and baby sister! Fuck you God! She was just a baby!!!" Mark screams, and he cries and grips his mother's dead body tighter.

Paul angrily stands up, letting go of his dead wife's body. Her head thumps limply backwards against the wall and excess blood pours from her skull onto the bench he was sitting on. Paul's mind slips and let's out an emotional outburst, punching his son Mark directly in his mouth. Mark topples, and slides across chunks of his baby sister's brains. Paul runs over and kicks Mark in the ribs. He feels the crunching of bones from the impact of his foot in his son's midsection. "It was God's will. We can't question the will of God, you blasphemer. God must have something in store for us."

Mark angrily yells back at his father who towers above him, while Simon and Miriam cry watching their father yell, and violently beat Mark.

"I fucking hate God and I hate you too! I fucking wish that was you who got killed and not mom! You fucking cocksucker!"

Paul punches Mark once more in the mouth, and Mark falls flat on his back. He presses his knees down on Mark's chest and repeatedly punches Mark in his head. Swinging his arms back and forth full length, Paul's fists ram their way onto Mark's head with such forceful impact that some of his knuckles break on top of Mark's head. Paul stands up with the stinging pain in his fist and the realisation of what he is doing to his son, albeit he is deceiving himself in refraining from the beating, knowing that it is the pain from his broken knuckles which has stopped him from beating up his son, "It was God that chose to work through you and save the rest of us. God has chosen not to spare your mother and sister. God works in mysterious ways and he has chosen you to save us. You should be thankful. Not everyone has the opportunity to have God work through them!"

Mark, sore, bloodied, and bruised is not in the slightest mood to respond to his father's insane remark, nor is he in the mood to have another one-sided fist fighting match with him.

"Let's just go home," Mark says, as he wipes streams of tears from either side of his cheeks.

The Parkinson family walks through hallways of the school together. They note the litter of bodies shot down, and bullet holes in the walls. They notice chains on the auditorium doors with pad locks interlocking the chains together. An eerie chill creeps through all of the family members.

Together, the family walks into the coat check room to rummage through the dead church members belongings to find something dry to wear. The coats still have the scents of cheap cologne and perfume freshly sprayed for this week's Sabbath day on them.

They head to a restroom after finding dry clothes to wear from the corpses and coats from the coatroom. As they take turns using the hand blow dryers to dry out their hair, Miriam cries out, "I want mommy." Simon quickly cuddles up to her, and does his best to alleviate her suffering, giving his little sister comforting hugs.

They leave the school and look for their car in the parking lot. As they do, a few black armoured vehicles drive into the school's central parking lot, and then head towards the front of the school doors. Dump trucks follow behind the armoured vehicles. Paul, Mark, Simon and Miriam duck down into their seats inside the minivan in order not to be seen by the soldiers. A few hours later, the dump trucks leave. As they drive out of the school parking lot, they notice limbs of some church members dangling over the sides of the dump trucks.

"This is just horrible," Paul says, as he shakes his head. "Children, let's bow our heads and say a prayer."

Mark shoots his father a look of utter contempt and disgust while Miriam and Simon both lower their heads.

"Our father and all wise Lord, we give thanks for your many blessings, especially today. We give thanks that you have spared us from Satan's agents of evil..."

Mark rudely interrupts his father's prayer with his harsh words, "I saved you Dad! Not your invisible friend who does not exist! If he exists then he is the one responsible for my mother's death, and my sister's death. I was the one who knew about the door to the pool area. I saved you, not that fucking fairy tale God of yours!"

Paul unbuckles his seatbelt, and reaches for Mark who ducks. He finds a lock of Mark's hair and interlocks it in his fingers and pulls him up by the hair, and punches Mark in the face repeatedly, while Mark holds his hands up trying to parry off the punches. It is enough. In a violent fit of rage, Mark defends himself and punches his father back square in the nose, forcing Paul to let go and gasp in pain.

"Seems like you think you are God! You seem to be the one doing his punishments and dirty work, is that it? Paul. Are you God?! "

"Why, you rebellious little brat. Wait till we get home, you're going to get it!" Paul yells at Mark, and then carelessly turns on the ignition to the van without thinking about who may still be around the school grounds. Fortunately no one is there.

As they drive up to the school's parking lot exit, it is barricaded with cement blocks. Fortunately there was a way around it. They drive down the street, and head for home. The family remains silent save the sniffles and muffled cries of Miriam. Simon and Mark reminisce, and try and block out the horrors that took place throughout the course of the day. As they drive down the street, the family notices a building on fire. No fire fighters are putting out the blazing fire.

They notice a few shot down people sprawled across the lawn as well as some bodies hanging out of the building's windows. The sign outside the building appears to have Jewish writing on it, and the building seems most likely a Jewish synagogue.

Simon averts his eyes from the devastation, and looks at his father who is just as frightened, "Dad, why are those people dead?"

"They are Jewish, son. They go to church on the same day we do. The same people that killed the people at our church must have killed them as well."

"Why is this happening, daddy?" Miriam asks through her sobs.

"These are the end times that were prophesied by the prophet St. John in the book of Revelations, honey. This is the great tribulation against the men and women of God."

"But Daddy I thought God only does good things?" Miriam's inquisitive nature questions the motives behind how an all loving God could allow such horrible atrocities to take place.

"He does my little pumpkin; he does good unto those that obey and keep all of his commandments."

"What about mom and Penny?! Explain that one, Paul!" Mark says, while half contemplating jumping out of the moving van and running away from home, and telling the police about the numerous times his father has beaten him over the years, but worried in the same sense that his father may not go to prison and will take his abusive behaviour out on Simon and Miriam without him to beat.

"I don't want you to say another word until we get home Mister. You're in enough trouble as it is at the moment," Paul snaps back.

"O yeah, I forgot God," Mark sighs, and then he hyperventilates and cries, remembering the horror of his last memory with his mother and baby sister. How will he ever be able to erase these images from his mind? Mark desires to scratch his eyes out of his head so he can stop seeing all the death around him. Miriam copying what Simon did for her earlier, cuddles up to her big brother Mark, and pats him on the back.

"Don't worry, Mark. One day we will see them again at the resurrection," Miriam says with a smile on her face.

"Whatever Miriam. What if that is just a fairy tale like Santa Claus," he brushes his little sister's arm away from his back.

Paul drives into a gas station and heads straight to the liquor section for a bottle of whiskey. This day has been tremendously terrible, and the only thing that will temporarily alleviate how he feels is getting drunk. He nods and waves to Sarah and Frank, the owners of the store behind the counter. Before he gets a few feet inside the station, Sarah motions for him.

"Hey Paul," She whispers. "I suggest if you are going to buy anything it should really be only for emergencies."

Paul nods his head and turns around, not without caring about what she said.

"Paul, I know you're a Christian. That is why I say that. It's quite obvious you didn't go to church today or you would be dead. The government said that they caught several religious organisations holding meetings in schools, convention centres, churches, mosques, synagogues, you name it. I know you guys go to church every Saturday at West Humber Collegiate. They said there was a shootout at the school and because of this and other terrorist plots, any person that belongs to a religious organisation, meaning anyone who checked off that they were religious when they applied for their All-In-One cards, are now suspected of being a terrorist. The Supreme Leader Max Diamond has decreed all terrorist suspects shall have all but twenty debits seized from their All-In-Ones, and all credit on the cards are frozen. The Supreme Leader is giving suspected terrorists a week to liquidate all but $500 debits worth of assets. Seems stupid if you ask me because they're more than likely going to seize four hundred and eighty dollars on your All-In-Ones, before you are all shipped off into ghettos."

Paul shakes his head in disbelief; he only came inside of the store to get a bottle so he can get plastered and temporarily drown away the last memories of his wife and daughter, and now contemplates adding an additional bottle to that equation.

Frank leans across the counter adjacent his wife, "Go home, Paul. It's not safe for someone like you to be on the streets. They will shoot you on sight if they see you out past your curfew. This new law came into effect immediately at nine o'clock. Go before your whole family gets killed."

"They killed my wife and my baby; they killed everyone else at church, even the children!"

"They are just targeting people of religions that they feel they are terrorists."

"You talk as if you're on their side, Frank. What is wrong with you. I just sat here and told you they killed Victoria and Penny. They also murdered everyone at church. Frank, you have known me for five years now. Do I look like a fuc... do I look like a terrorist pardon my language, that was very un-Christian like of me."

"Listen Paul," Frank leans closer in on the counter and brings his lips close to Paul's ears and whispers, "We are terribly sorry about Victoria and Penny. I feel for your loss, my friend, I seriously do, but I don't know what to say? I am not religious; yeah I think it is bad what they did to you guys and all." Frank pauses and thinks about whether it is a good idea to discuss the matter further. Paul has been through enough already, and the last thing he feels Paul needs is for him to be sharing his opinions any further regarding the matter. "You know what Paul, take what you need for now. It's on us. Just let me shut off the cameras first. Anyone caught aiding and abetting a religionist will be found guilty of being a terrorist as well, and will be punished severely. Just take what you need and hurry home."

Paul nods his thanks and grabs a couple of bags of groceries from Sarah once Frank shuts the power off. Paul thanks the couple and scuttles out of the store.

He hops into his vehicle and quickly explains to his children, what Frank and Sarah conveyed to him. Paul notices the lights inside the store turn on again though his rear view mirror, as he drives through the parking lot and heads off the property. In an instant, he slams his foot on the brake pedal. An armoured army vehicle has stopped directly in front of him and soldiers exit the vehicle with their assault rifles aimed at him. Paul raises his arms in the air as a sign not to shoot him and carefully moves his left hand down to roll down his window, while the soldiers approach his vehicle.

"I need to see your All-In-One card for identification purposes, sir."

Paul gasps and reaches inside his back pocket for his wallet containing his card. "May I ask what this is about, officer?"

"We are seeing who is in direct disobedience of the curfew. Identification now, sir!" the soldier demands.

Paul pulls out his card quickly. "Sir, to be quite honest with you, we just learned of this curfew, and we are on our way home now to abide by the law."

The cocking of guns sends an eerie feeling into Paul's stomach. The faith in his Lord and one and only true God is temporarily replaced with the fear of his children's lives which are at stake.

"So you're Christians then?!" the soldier asks Paul.

He finds it hard to swallow and even find words for the soldier, knowing how quickly and efficiently they slaughtered the entire Toronto West Congregation of the Worldwide Church of God earlier, and if he lies about being a Christian, he knows that he will be breaking God's commandment about lying. However, there is a chance that in doing so, he can save his family. The thought makes him sick to his stomach. There is no way he could do something as immoral as lie! God will watch over his family. "Yes sir, we are Christians."

"I hate God! I don't believe in that crap! And I am not a god damn fucking Christian, Paul!"

The soldier looks in the vehicle. He notices a rather angry teenage boy who does not appear to be over the age of eighteen. "Is there a problem, young sir? Are you being held by these terrorists against your will? Show me your Identification," the officer looks at the rest of the children. "All of you."

"Yeah, there is a fucking problem alright. I am sick of when Paul speaks for me. I am not a kid anymore! Fuck I'm seventeen, and I am not a little kid like he tries making me out to be!"

"Understood," the soldier scans Mark's eyes in order to detect any hint of lies through facial expressions or pupil dilations. None are registered.

The rest of the other soldiers continue aiming their assault rifles at the family, while another other soldier takes Mark away from his family's interrogation. The soldier takes the identifications and runs a check on the Parkinson's. A few brief moments later, the soldier walks back over to Mark.

"No, you can't speak with him. He is my son. What are you going to do with him?" Paul says.

"Place your hands on top of the steering wheel and stare forward. You are a known terrorist, Paul, who I might add is out past curfew. We will extract any information that we need from Mark."

The soldier walks away from eavesdropping range and speaks candidly with Mark, "I have changed your status on your All-In-One card to non-religionist, if that is okay with you, sir?"

Mark's eyes widen with excitement, "Why I don't know what to say, thank you very much!"

"Tell us where you and your family were, and where you are heading now. I must also remind you everything you say may be used against you in a criminal proceeding."

Mark's look of excitement drops just as fast as the expression came on his face. "Well... " Mark looks down, thinking of an answer that would not get everyone in trouble, "We went swimming with family. After we left, dad pulled in here to buy something. I am not sure what he got? Some groceries? The groceries are in the vehicle and then I think we were heading home, I am not sure."

"Your father still has twenty debits on his All-In-One card, therefore, he could not have bought groceries! Let me remind you that you're under oath. Let me rephrase my question. How do you explain that he bought anything from the store?!"

"I don't know? He just came in and out with groceries. Ask him," Mark replies desperately.

"I read your file. You have a mother and sister. Where are they now and why aren't they with you?"

Mark continues to hang his head low while methodically thinking of a rational lie to explain where they are, aside from inside a dump truck.

"Oh yeah," he says, holding back his emotions, (he has to, as the rest of his family's lives are at stake), "They went to church without us today. They are probably at home waiting for us with a nice cooked meal on the table for when we get home. It's hot dogs and French fries tonight," Mark says, bottling his rage as he stares at the asphalt. Then up at the officer.

"There is blood on your face. What happened?"

Mark sighs, "Ah, my father and I have been disagreeing about a few things such as his bullshit religion and well, he hit me earlier today."

"Do you wish to press charges against him?"

"Nah, it's just bruises. I'll live."

"Okay, get your family home. Your father and siblings are in direct violation of the curfew but your story pans out. If your father is in violation of the curfew again, he will be subject to a criminal conviction, and may be imprisoned or receive capital punishment if it is proved that he is out endorsing terrorist activities. I suggest you inform him for future reference. Your home is within a fifteen mile radius so we will give you twenty minutes to get home."

The soldier turns around and walks to his vehicle, hops inside, and then backs up to allow the Parkinson family to leave, so they can head home.

After the Parkinson family drives away, the soldiers walk to the gas station shop and approach Sarah and Frank. "Why was the power out in your Station?"

Frank looks at the soldier in a peculiar way, and has a funny feeling Paul informed them about the groceries but quickly shrugs the thought from mind seeing they were allowed to drive away safely, "Oh, the power goes out like that from time to time. Nothing unusual."

"I have a non-religionist witness statement saying that you aided a terrorist with food rations. I am of the belief that you shut off the power after a man in question Paul Parkinson entered your premises, and might I say anything you say may be used for and against you in a criminal proceeding."

Frank looks toward his wife Sarah whom he has been married to for over forty years. How could he have been so foolish to have helped out someone, only to have endangered his beloved wife Sarah.

Sarah scrambles to move away from the soldier who is strikingly intimidating, as a fourth soldier walks into the station, pouring gasoline from the pump on the floor of the shop. Her stomach sinks as fear engulfs every fibre of her being. She watches as the soldier pours gasoline on the shelves, over the food, and splashes the gasoline on the walls of their shop.

The soldier motions for his team to leave the shop and then lights a match and ignites the gasoline. The fire spreads instantly inside the gas station, and as the soldiers walk out of the shop they chain the doors together, and then wait and watch the couple frantically run around and scream inside. As the flames spread, it scorches their clothes which quickly catch fire. Their hair singes as the flames burns their hair off their scalps. The smoke suffocates them and they collapse on the ground in foetal positions, gasping and coughing for air, as their skin melts like candle wax. Their flesh bubbles up, and the blood underneath their skin grow to a point that it is boiling. Eventually their skin blisters and pops in multiple places. The elderly couple do not have the strength or endurance to withstand the pain, and they scream as the fire engulfs them. They die next to one another and the flames continue to burn their lifeless corpses.

"I don't know what you're so upset about? I saved us once again. He was going to kill everyone if it wasn't because I said I wasn't a Christian, and do you want to know what? I never lied. Aren't you cluing in dad? Hasn't it already registered inside of your pea-sized mind yet? That maybe you're on the wrong side of the fence?"

"No son, you're right. You are seventeen now. You're not the little boy I keep thinking you are. You're almost a man now. You are old enough to make your own decisions now and if you don't want to be a Christian that is your decision and a consequence that you will have to live with on your own. I just feel bad that I have not guided you as well as I thought I had done. Where did I go wrong Mark? I don't want to see what happens to you when Christ returns."

Paul makes his son a cola and whiskey mix, taking the small glass. Mark shakes his head and gives his father a look of uncertainty, "Dad listen man, Mom and Penny were just killed. I want, and need to be alone. If all you care about is God go hug your bible in a corner somewhere, or preach to Miriam. Her young, impressionable mind seems to adore that crap you're forcing into her mind like a pacifier. All I know is if God was really real, and really did care about his people, he would not allow such things to happen to my mother and sister or any of his other followers today. Those people were loyal to God's law and if he is real, he just watched them all die for his own fucking personal amusement! Now leave me alone. I wanna be by myself."

Mark sits down and holds in his tears and then bursts out crying. Tears stream down the sides of his face. He stands up. He is angry and confused, thinking to himself *real men don't cry* due to his father's lack of empathy or shred of care. If God is real perhaps slitting his throat or wrists will bring him closer to his mother and baby sister Penny, but if God is not real, killing himself will be for absolutely nothing. He screams out and cups his hands over his face as he cries in pain at the loss of his mother and baby sister. The images of his mother's crushed head and flap of the back of her skull dangling by a flap of muscle and skin are images he only longs to erase from his mind. He grabs a knife in the kitchen and desires to jab it in his father's throat, remembering how his father punched him out hours ago and how he slid on parts of his little sister's brain. He screams and tosses the knife aside, wiping his skin trying to get the psychological eerie feeling of the brain matter off him.

"Fuck sakes!" he screams out loud

"I will not tolerate that language inside of this household young mister. When you get a job and can afford to live on your own then you can say whatever you want, but while you're underneath my roof, mister, you are subject to God's rules and mine!"

"Fuck you!" Mark mutters under his breath.

"What was that, mister? Speak up. I didn't hear you."

"I said 'I thought of you', umm yeah sorry; it just came out, sorry," Mark passive aggressively takes into consideration the beating he endured earlier and how drunk his father is getting now, and does not want a repeat of what happened after church.

"That didn't sound like that. You think you're a tough guy now that you punched me. Shall we start from where you left off, if you think you're so tough? I have God on my side. Who do you have, Devil worshipper?"

Reconsidering the outcome, "Dad, what did I say, come on please. Honestly I said 'I thought of you'. What did you think I said? You know I love you, and I know you're going through a hard time. Sorry if I said the F word sakes earlier."

"Oh, I thought you said something else after sorry son."

"Lucky I don't fucking kill you, bitch," Mark mutters, not wanting to exacerbate the situation by speaking loud enough for his father to hear.

14

"My Lord, we have found a DNA match. We have found Joshua. Well, his DNA strands match yours, sir, so we assume this is the Joshua you are looking for. He of course, is not using that name. He is using the alias John Curthy. He is posing as William Curthy's brother. 'John Curthy co-owns a home with a few other people: Jody Knoiky, his wife Phuong Knoiky, Archer Komodo, and William Curthy. They are also co-owners of a restaurant business, and we have the local police informing us the owners are trafficking drugs and weapons from inside their restaurant. They've tried to figure out the modus operandum of their business but without that, are unable to obtain a V.I.P. pass to their restaurant, in which their informants are allegedly claiming deals take place. Our sources who have surveillance around their home, say there does not seem to be any illegal activity in and around their house, so we are certain that they don't have the drugs there, and we are unable to get a search warrant to apprehend Joshua. Lastly, Lord Dagoth, I believe the senate of the New World Order have plans to throw Max Diamond out of power, as they feel the recent bills which he is passing go against human rights regarding creed. They wish to abolish any form of Supreme Leader and have the senate claim power over the New World Order. Please advise on how you wish us to proceed."

Lord Dragon Dagoth's sordid dark face breaks into a smile; at last he has found his father Joshua. This time he will not allow his father to escape his grasp, and he will capture Joshua at all costs; however, a more pressing matter is at hand. In order to rid the world of the religious, he needs to ensure his final plan to secure himself as the world's first emperor does not get scuppered.

"You have served the New World Order well, General Soleman. Additionally, this news regarding Joshua is most excellent. I will be there personally when you capture Joshua. As for the senate, we must act quickly. Max Diamond's veil must be revealed. Kill them all. I have measures in place that will secure our power.

The Supreme Leader Max Diamond calls a special summit together for the Group of Five nations. Taras Ivanov does not attend neither do a few other political leaders on such short notice, or knowing that Max Diamond desires to honour the late American President by emulating lack of security protocols. All senators within the provinces of the New World Order are required to attend or they will be fired.   Max Diamond desires to convey his intent to return his supreme powers to the senate and restore religious freedom in the wake of the uprisings and declare the war on terrorism over for the first time since September 11th 2001.

The senators and other world leaders arrive to the G5 meeting, and take their seats at the Toronto Convention Centre. As world leaders and other politicians take their seats, the robots created for the regime of the New World Order surround the convention centre, shooting bodyguards of the world leaders with silenced weapons and quickly discarding the bodies in nearby trucks. A chemical airborne agent is released inside the Toronto Convention Centre which starts to take its fatal effects on everyone inside. The senators begin to drop dead due to asphyxiation from the chemical weapon, and realising there is not much time to go, Max Diamond quickly addresses the inhabitants of the New World Order, appointing Dragon Dagoth as his successor.

There are no senators left to share the mantle of power with, and at a later date Dragon Dagoth announces that he is now Emperor Dragon Dagoth, the first Emperor of the world, and no longer has to wear his false identity, Max Diamond. He no longer needs to hide in the shadows which he had been doing for centuries, and now has the power to do as he pleases. As his first duty, he rids the Empire of the senate so that there is no one left in place to take away his absolute power and so that there will be no Empirical successor. Hundreds of years ago, he watched Christians burn his dear son Cynric, and beloved wife

Annex, at the stake. Now the time is at hand for him to pass a law stipulating a cleansing of all religionists from the Empire; a religious Holocaust!

Landing on a strip of runway with a private jet supplied by Taras Ivanov, Gefallener Klon and Schatten exit the jet and enter a car that they built together with the latest in technical gadgets, onboard computers and equipped with evasion devices and some weaponry. Although access to the Empire's database has been severed for the clones, Gefallener installed a backdoor program command to access top level security at any given time.

"Appears our access has been denied. Dragon Dagoth knows we have gone AWOL."

"What do we do from here, Gefallener?"

"Appears there is a high alert for Joshua our father. They've located him so we should get to him before Dragon Dagoth does."

"Are you really going to bring Joshua back to our grandfather Satan?"

"No, Schatten you are going to kill Joshua. I will help you, and together both of us will be able to defeat our old master and Satan. You know as much as I do that if Satan kills Joshua he gains his power. You need that power. It is up to you if you want to kill our old master. I don't know if I can, he is our creator."

"But he killed Gav. Weren't you two…"

"Yes, we were… I just simply do not know if I can kill our creator, which is why I leave the decision up to you."

"Guys we can't go back to the house. There is grave danger there. Pull the car over. Pull the fucking car over, Phuong!"

Phuong angrily pulls her car over to the side of the road, "What the fuck are you shouting at me for you asshole!?!"

"Yeah, fuck Josh, give it a rest. What's your fucking problem?" Archer parrots Phuong's anger in contempt, desiring to get home and have a shower and call it a day.

"I have foreseen our deaths. We cannot go back to the house or we will be killed there, all of us!"

Archer laughs rather uncontrollably although his laughter is an expression of his rage, "Josh, just get out of the fucking car. I want to go home to shit, shower and shave. I have no time for this bullshit, honestly!"

Joshua has no emotional attachments to either of his companions. The only particular reason he has some sort of connection with William or Jody is for monetary gain and so he will play the part to keep either alive. Therefore the decision to let Archer and Phuong act on their own inclinations, will only benefit his pocket book provided they fulfil his vision and return to the house. Taking a brief second to think things through, he opens the car door and salutes them thinking to himself that they can die for all he cares, and then he slams the car door shut.

Shaking her head, Phuong extends her middle finger to Joshua and drives away. Phuong and Archer pull up in front of their house, and she pays no thought to Joshua's silly premonitions, and warning.

"Oh, look at me. I am Joshua. I should have got into the psychic business, not a crime syndicate," says Archer.

"Shut up, Archer. It's bad enough Josh is an idiot. I don't need to hear your fucking mouth too!" Phuong says snatching her purse, turning around to walk towards the house and then she stumbles on the hood of her car.

Archer collapses to the ground, and the thunderous sound of sniper fire echoes throughout the air. Snipers on a rooftop across the street have opened fire and shot out the back of Phuong and Archer's kneecaps, popping out the ligaments, cartilage and breaking away chunks of their kneecap bones. They scream in utter pain and terror as they realise they've been shot. Secret Imperial army personnel drive into their parking lot, leave their vehicles and cock their weapons. Making the situation even more horrific is a man who resembles death walking towards them, Emperor Dragon Dagoth.

"Where is Joshua?" the Emperor growls over their frantic screams.

"We don't know any asshole named Joshua, fucker!" Phuong shouts at the strangely dressed man, wondering whether Joshua orchestrated this attack, or wondering if he knew that someone was after him at the same time. However, the unbearable pain of her kneecap hanging by threads of skin and the loss of blood are her immediate concerns at the moment.

"If I tell you where he may be, you will let us go?"

"I will kill you if you don't!!! Now tell me at once."

"Don't say anything Archer or I will fucking kill you."

The Emperor reaches inside his dark black cloak, pulls out his broad sword, and vigorously swipes it at Phuong's neck, slicing her head off with a single blow. He walks over to Archer and steps on his chest, and penetrates Archer's throat with the point of his sword. "I only ask once."

"Guy, he had a vision down the highway about this, and wanted out of the fucking car, man. He is somewhere down the 401 highway hitchhiking, for all I know."

Dragon Dagoth thrusts the rest of his sword into Archer's neck. After the blood stops squirting out of Archer's neck, Dragon Dagoth pulls the sword free from his victim's lifeless body. "I will let you go now."

He says to General Soleman, "General Soleman, take any pertinent data that will assist us in capturing Joshua then burn down this house, their vehicle and destroy their remains. I want a team to assist me at their other known location, their restaurant. Find Joshua's other companions and send a team on the highway to investigate Joshua's alleged whereabouts. And remember, I want him alive!"

As the sound of vehicles rush past him and he feels the wind push him from their speed as they veer down the highway, Joshua feels the deaths of Phuong, Jody's girlfriend and Archer, a mutual acquaintance of theirs as their lives fade away. He stops walking along the shoulder of the highway and uses his power to appear at their home in order to view what is happening.

Imperial vehicles are littered across his lawn, along the road and in their parking area. Using his power, he glides to a couple of bodies. One of the bodies is wearing the same clothing Phuong was wearing; regardless if the body is headless, it can only be her. The other is clearly Archer. He glides around and sees the man that attacked him hundreds of years ago with Imperial soldiers, and recognises the man, or being, as none other than the new Emperor, Dragon Dagoth.

He stops using his power and becomes one with himself and runs as fast as he can off the highway and to a payphone in order to call the restaurant, however, there is no answer. He retreats to a storage facility where he has had a room since the building opened a few decades ago.

A slew of black Imperial vehicles speed down the street past Jody as he drives home. Several more drive in the opposite direction, all of which exceed speed limits. Jody drives his car into a far off neighbour's driveway and powers off his vehicle. "Dude, what is it?" William asks curiously.

"Something is wrong. Those are Imperial vehicles. We should walk somewhere close to our house and see what is going on."

William smiles wryly, "Yeah okay, sure go ahead and do that while I wait here and you know, not get arrested."

Jody leaves William in the car and walks down the sidewalk until he gets to a comfortable enough distance to observe what he can from where he is standing. He notices soldiers on his property watching fire burn his home down. Immediately grabbing his mobile phone, he calls the fire department, "Hello 911, my house is on fire."

"Is this Mr. Knoiky?"

"Yes!"

"Head towards your house and wait for firefighters to arrive."

Jody runs back to his car and urgently gets inside.

"So what's up, man?"

"Imperial soldiers are burning down our fucking house."

"What? Are you fucking shitting me?

"Does it fucking sound like I am?"

Crouching down in their seats, they look in the rear view mirror, noticing more Imperial black cars and trucks race down the street. They quietly leave their car and watch the Imperial vehicles drive to their house down the street. The soldiers surround the house, armed with assault rifles. They search for Jody in response to his 911 call.

"We have to leave and get far away from here!" William says, as his complexion turns white as a ghost, fearing what will happen if they're caught.

Joshua walks into his storage unit which he has been renting for several decades. The room is spacious and contains many valuables that he's collected over the past thousand years, including sentimental items. He finds an open frequency to the local police on an old truck CB scanner that he was given years ago. There are no discussions about anything transpiring at his house. He sits down and meditates on his vision, and sees nothing has changed. Trying to look into the future, he is not able to see the fate of his friends and despite his power, he is not able to look into his own future regarding this. Strangely, he is able to sense Satan, who has nothing to do with what is taking place. Breaking free from meditating, Joshua snaps his cell phone to pieces and takes some much needed items, leaving the storage facility to investigate the matter more closely.

"My Lord, we've received a call from Joshua's friend, Jody Knoiky. He informed us that he will wait for us at his house. Our soldiers have canvased the area, and have not found him during the search."

"Soleman, I am not interested in telling you how to do your job. Find them or I shall hold you personally accountable for your mistakes!"

Emperor Dragon Dagoth ends the call just as they arrive at Joshua's restaurant, The Gold Rush. He leaves his Limousine followed by his robotic soldiers and together they smash their way into the building searching for Joshua, and secondary targets, William and Jody. After a thorough search, they're not able to locate the trio of fugitives. However, they lurk around the premises hoping the alarms will attract their attention, and bait them to the restaurant.

Jody and William's mobile phones ring simultaneously. They both answer and are informed their restaurant has been broken into and police are on their way.

"Do you think Joshua knows about the imperials that are after us, and broke into the restaurant in order to hide?"

"No, I don't think so. He spoke with me in confidence saying that he was in trouble and needed me to vouch for him as his brother. I had no fucking clue that he meant he was in trouble with the fucking law though!"

"And you just vouched for him without asking questions?"

"To be honest, I swore I shot the fucking guy that day. I mean I pulled out my gun, pulled the trigger, and the next thing I know, faster than I could blink my eyes, he had my gun in his hand and I had flashes of his life all in my head. The fucking guy freaks me out man; I wasn't going to say no after that."

"I would have said 'no', guy."

"I seriously doubt you would have."

"Well, perhaps you were just imagining things, and blacked out. I was like that when I killed someone my first time. It happens, just got to get used to it. Fuck man, I will kill Josh myself if I find out he is behind the authorities clamping down and around our house."

"We don't know what is going on. Someone could have been caught and dropped the dime on us. We don't know."

William notices soldiers moving down the streets, banging on each of the house doors and searching the inside of the houses, cars, driveways and garages.

"Jody I think we should quietly get out of here?"

"I think your right."

They slowly sneak down the street inconspicuously, hiding in the shadows, and staying clear of florescent lights which illuminate everything.

General Soleman follows the Emperor's orders and takes his team of soldiers and searches the neighbourhood again for Joshua, coming up short. Resorting to desperate measures, he extinguishes the fire on Phuong and Archer's corpses, and finds their mobile phones, semi intact. One of the robotic soldiers is able to extract all text, and other numbers from the mobile phones which include the trio of fugitives. The robot searches the New World Order database and is able to acquire the addresses of Jody, and William's family members, and they send special force robot soldiers to kidnap the family members. General Soleman contacts Jody using a ghost number that uses Phuong's cell phone number.

"Baby is that you? Are you okay?!" Jody frantically asks, finding somewhere private to talk.

"Phuong, did I pronounce her name right? Anyway she is dead..." Before General Soleman is able to continue, Jody yells, screams and curses and pleads to know what happened.

"Jody, how about you meet up with me and I will be happy to answer all of your questions. I don't know where you are but I am going to tell you where I am. Do not tell anyone otherwise I will kill your family members, starting from the oldest to the youngest."

"Who is this?"

"I am General Daffy Soleman of The New World Order serving for his Majesty Emperor Dragon Dagoth. Now do I have your cooperation and will you come in so that we may discuss urgent matters?"

"You mother fucker. I saw you assholes at the house!" Jody shouts, peaking William's interests who walks over, concerned about Jody's welfare. "I'm going to kill you, motherfucker!"

General Soleman presses his phone against Jody's brother's ear, "Jody I'm okay. Don't listen to him. Save yourself. They're going to kill us anyway!"

"Des? Are you okay?"

"Glad I got your attention. Will you come in and meet with me? Rest assured I will not do anything to your family if I have your full cooperation and you come in so we can talk. However, try anything and I will kill all of your family that happen to be here."

Ignoring William, Jody walks back to his car while trembling and shaking, as a mixture of fear and anger course through his body and his mind frantically races with worry. He speeds off down the street, following General Soleman's directions.

It's been over a week since Paul sold his house; fortunately Mark was able to buy the house and keep all the belongings due to the fact that he is a non-religionist.

Life takes another turn for the worse for Paul as he is fired from his warehouse job due to more restrictions imposed by the new Emperor Dragon Dagoth. His All-In-One card is debited by his former employer; however, he is only topped up to his $20 debit limit, regardless if he is owed for the last two weeks of work.

"This is ridiculous," Paul says as he slams his pay stub on the table. "How am I supposed to feed a family of four with twenty dollars, twenty freaking dollars, what is this?! I am sick of eating soup with vegetables. Even no name Kraft dinner seems to be a rich man's food. Why are they doing this to us? I think I am going to have to lie to the government. I think I am going to go into the office where you get the All-In-One cards and say that I am a non-religionist."

"Dad, no one has been allowed to do that since last Saturday. There have been over a billion reports of people trying that online, and in person and they are all being denied. Now they have soldiers stationed at the offices to prevent any hostile entanglements. Rumour has it that they are building ghettos for religious people to move into, as of October thirty first."

"Are you joking?! Are you playing some sick kind of a joke on me?! That isn't funny, you know!"

"Dad..." Simon interrupts his brother and father. "I saw it on the news too. We have to move into a ghetto, every Muslim, Catholic, Buddhist, orthodox Jew and other religionist that checked the box when applying for their All-In-One cards need to relocate."

Mark gloats; he has a smug look on his face and flaunts how he was right in front of his father, after his brother's confirmation. "As I was saying before I was rudely interrupted, The New World Order knows where every religionist is due to our G.T.S. chip implants. If you guys fail to comply with the order, you will have your leg sheared off from the hip down as a symbol that you tried to evade the Empire and that includes babies that belong to religionists."

"That is not true. They can't do that!" Paul argues, and then sits down trying to process everything that he is being told.

Ever since the first Supreme Leader of the New World Order, Max Diamond, was assassinated along with the rest of the old senate, life had been turning horrible ever since this tyrant was appointed Max Diamond's successor, this Dragon Dagoth who claimed the title of Emperor. Max Diamond was going to give religionists their rights back but this new Emperor has made life way worse than Max Diamond's old cautionary measures.

"Have you heard from anyone in the church yet? Has there been word about going to a place of safety?" Paul asks with a little glimpse of hope.

"There was one lady who called, Mrs. Fraser? I think that's what she said her name was. Anyway she was wondering the same thing and said that she hasn't heard from anyone since Saturday. She said she was sick and couldn't make it to church that day of the attack and I was the only person she had gotten hold of. I told her about the massacre, and I think she went into shock. All she kept repeating was 'oh my god', and then hung up the phone. Dad I think we are probably one of just a few people that has defied the law, went to church that day, and survived. I don't think there is anybody left in the church except for a couple of us."

Paul ran his fingers through his short, blonde hair in disbelief, wondering how God could let such a tragedy happen to his chosen members and second guessing his faith that God knows all. The church always warned its followers about keeping a keen ear to the end times. Now it seems within the blink of an eye the entire church had been wiped out.

"Maybe we should go to a government building and figure out if the head members of the church are still alive. That may give us some hope and then we can fly to the church's headquarters. Mark you will have to sell my house."

"Hate to break it to you dad, but I bought this house fair and square off you for five dollars, all you were allowed. It's my house and I am not selling it. Next off, you can't go into public buildings anymore let alone the airport. You will be shot and killed."

Each time Mark speaks, Paul feels a nauseating presence in his stomach, and it almost seems as if his very own son is taking pleasure giving him news regarding the Empire's new policies.

"Okay guys, I need to lay down. I am going to bed. I feel sick to my stomach. I need to think about things."

"Oh dad, it's against the law for Christians to lie down in a bed. It has to be a floor without carpeting."

"What! No now they are going too far. I am not going to sleep on the floor in the comfort of my own house!"

"Correction, my house. Yeah, you can sleep in the bed. I was just joking about that last part. There is no such law."

Paul's face turns beat red with anger at Mark's cold joke, and he storms out of the room deciding not to punish his son for mocking God's people during the tribulation.

October 31st 2048

"Dad, you can't let Simon and Miriam go. I will do my best to hide them."

"Mark, don't worry. God will be watching over us. He has this far. I hope you place your faith back in God and realise that he is all knowing and all wise and that this is part of his plan."

"Dad... Paul, I don't give a fuck if you believe that shit till you drop dead, but nothing good seems to be happening regarding your faith. I don't want to see my other sister or my brother go either. I will take care of them! They aren't going to that fucking ghetto!"

Paul sighs as his son breaks the fifth commandment: honour thy Father and Mother, on their last day together. Shaking his head at the lack of respect from his disobedient son, he realises he is too weak to punish Mark, and has a long journey ahead of him. He is hungry; not just hungry, he is starving, and the only thing of nutritious value he's had to eat the entire month has been vegetable soup. This past week has only been boiled water with salt sprinkled in it for flavour. Paul weighed himself the other night and he is an incredible one hundred thirty two pounds from one hundred eighty five, fit and good looking.

Everything that Paul, Simon and Miriam are allowed to bring is downstairs. The house is filled with bitter sadness at the fact that they will soon part ways with Mark. Simon, who has the closest connection and attachment to his older brother, has always admired Mark, who is five years older than he is. Miriam runs over to Mark before Simon is able to and wraps her arms around Mark's back, hugging him goodbye.

"Mark. aren't you coming with us?" she asks without fully understanding why he isn't coming.

"No Miriam, you guys have to go. I will do my best to save you guys somehow."

"It's okay. Daddy says Jesus will come for us soon."

Mark continues holding onto his little sister and cries. His tears stream down his face as he squeezes his brother and sister tight. He doesn't want to let go. He struggles to let go. He knows this is the last time that he will ever see them again.

Simon, sensing this, somewhat pushes Mark away and smiles, "Yo bro, don't worry. This is only temporary, guy. Don't worry, man. We'll be out of there and back home before you know it, bro. The Emperor just needs to make sure no more terrorist attacks happen especially after all the attacks and the assassination of the Supreme Leader Max Diamond."

Simon places a firm hand on Mark's shoulder and tries cheering him up with a pseudo smile, despite how terrified he feels. The smug, happy and confidant look disappears from Simon's face, "Okay Mark, in all honesty I am starting to believe you about God. If he is real and knows how much I love you and always wanted to be like you ... if God is real... things would be just like you said. He wouldn't take me away from you. I hate God too, Mark. I hate him. I hate him. Why do we have to go? Why?!"

Both brother's push Miriam aside and hug each other once again, crying in one another's arms.

"Simon, Miriam, it's time to go. Where are you guys?"

Paul walks up the stairs to see all his children crying and holding each another. They have to leave now. He feels that everything will be okay. God will see them all through this; whether it be life or death, they will be united in the kingdom of heaven.

"Well Mark, this is it my son. Don't worry, I have taught you all that I could and it seems you have chosen your own path. It's not my place to cast judgment against you for only the Lord may judge us, but for old time's sake, would you like to join Simon, Miriam and I in a final family prayer before we part from one another?"

"I am not praying to a god that doesn't exist!"

These are the words Paul would expect from Mark; however, Paul, Simon, and Mark turn their heads in shock.

"My little girlio! Now why would you say something like that?"

"Mark and Simon don't believe in him and I have never seen him do anything for me. You told me God can do anything. I will believe in him if he brings back Mommy and Penny!"

"Kids, we have to go otherwise a very real military will come in here and sever our legs if we don't," Paul says sighing, bitter and defeated.

Paul walks up to Mark, not knowing whether to shake his hand as a form of adulthood respect, or hug him as a father should his son, but it is Mark who hugs him and says, "Dad, I love you."

"I love you too, son. Take good care of yourself while we're gone. Pray for ... I am sorry. I don't mean to ..."

"It's okay, dad. I will pray for you guys."

For the first time since his wife Victoria and daughter Penny have been murdered, he smiles at something Mark said.

Thousands upon thousands of people walk down the streets to a mega ghetto constructed for housing the religious. The Parkinson's follow suit down the street. They notice dozens of murdered bodies sprawled out on sidewalks. They overhear and eavesdrop on discussions about how these people were killed for walking on the sidewalks, as religionists are forbidden the public luxuries. Animals must be herded down the city streets, and this is the Empire's degrading process. Others too weak to walk to the ghetto, fall from fatigue and seeing they lack the medical attention required to save them, they die slowly or are trampled on by others walking to the ghetto.

Each major city hosts a mega ghetto in the poor parts of the cities within the New World Order. Each ghetto was created to ensure that it was big enough to support the prisoners of the neighbouring suburbs, towns and villages; yet, the homes inside the ghettos were not built to be accommodating in size.

The outer walls are fifty feet in height to help prevent escapes and help prevent people from tossing over food or other supplies.

After the last of the religionists enter the ghettos, an electronic door seals the ghettos shut. Inside the ghettos, there are several apartment buildings. Each apartment has tiny three by six feet of space for each room. The kitchens are only equipped with tiny portable electric stoves good enough for one pot or pan. One washroom in each apartment building that houses four hundred people per building, and these washrooms contain four holes in the ground, which are good enough to squat in and do your business where toilets should be. There are four shower heads all of which have no privacy booths. There are no laundromats in any of the buildings. Those fortunate enough to get a shower are able to wash their clothes while taking a shower; however, it is strongly urged not to use any detergents seeing the water is never recycled and residents will be drinking from the same water they showered, and do their toiletries with.

November 1st at the stroke of midnight, soldiers systematically walk down each city street within the Empire, and break into houses, apartments or other places to capture religionist fugitives who are evading the Emperor's order to report to the ghettos. Millions of fugitives are captured and the soldiers sever a leg per fugitive, and drive them to the appropriate ghettos.

People who used to be doctors or nurses before they were ordered into the ghettos rush out to help the victims risking their own lives out past curfew to save the wounded. Unknown to the doctors and nurses, the soldiers are programmed not to shoot down the violators of the curfew. It gives Emperor Dragon Dagoth great pleasure to know they are suffering.

In rougher parts of the world, the New World Order capture proves more difficult than on the continent of North Canada (formerly North America). Several people band together and fight the Imperial soldiers; the soldiers make short work of their duty and shoot all aggressors down and bring the remaining fugitives to the mega ghettos minus a leg each.

Mark has a terrible time adjusting without as much as a phone call from his family. All that remains in his house are memories, painful memories. Mark no longer desires to live another night in his house and leaves to go to the bank in order to sell his home which he has lived in all of his life.

"Oh wow, son. Your father must have been one real smart man selling you his house. Here's why," the overweight man who is a bank manager adjusts his seat to speak more in confidence with Mark.

"You see, each house is still currently under the title holder's name and the government hasn't changed any rules as of yet, so you can turn around and sell your house and buy other houses. I would suggest the ones previously owned and up for sale by terrorists. Sorry Mark, but it is a term that I as a manager of the national bank have to uphold, regardless if they were, do you know what I mean?"

Mark hangs his head, "Yeah I understand how my baby sister who was just six months old was killed for being a terrorist. The Supreme leader must have been pretty fucking petrified she was going to throw her pacifier at him or something. That goes double with my brother and other sister who are in a ghetto at the moment. I really understand how they pose a threat to the national security of the first one world government and Empire. Makes perfect sense to me, how about you?"

The overweight bank Manager squirms in his chair a bit after Mark's reply, "Listen son, everyone that is outside of those walls is in the same position as you. My wife had to go to the camp as well. I haven't spoke to her in days, but listen to me, son. I am trying to help you because I am doing the same thing for myself. Sell your house valued at three hundred thousand debits and buy a terrorist's house at no more than twenty debits. Don't buy it from other people that aren't religious otherwise it will more or less be classified as just a trade and you'll have to either pay out debits or you'll just get a few thousand debits in return and you don't want that. Buy up all the terrorist houses that you can resell them and with what you get afterwards, you'll be one of the wealthiest people on earth, I promise you this."

Mark laughs. The news sounds way too good to be true." All I have to do is sell my house and buy all these houses at less than twenty bucks and resell them? Is that what you're telling me? Why isn't anyone else doing this? Like come on, I may be a kid but I am not daft. What is the catch?"

The overweight man looks around and continues speaking in a low voice while leaning forward on his desk, "Son, the rich don't share their secrets. Why should we compete with the poor? Does that make sense to you? I am helping you because you're young and alone now. Only certain people in banks are aware of this. I went from making fewer than fifty thousand debits a year to being a multi-millionaire in less than a week. I can't thank the new Emperor Dragon Dagoth enough for this. I am so filthy rich!"

"You got the filthy part right. I thought you said your wife is in the camps?!" Mark asks in a hostile tone. He can't believe the manager does not seem to care about anything other than money and that he seems oblivious to the fact that his own wife is in a ghetto.

"She is son, but I bet after making all this money, it will be so easy to bribe a soldier into letting her out. With this kind of money I can buy anyone, their children and their grandchildren, maybe even a ghetto and release the prisoners. Do you understand this?"

Mark thinks hard about what the man is saying. He has nothing to lose and his whole family to gain. "You're right. I think I will do it."

As Paul tucks Miriam into the bed which he made for her on the floor, he places clothing and bed sheets around and underneath her so she will not get sick from the cold concrete floor. As Paul tells her a bed time story, a loud noise bangs at the door and flood lights from the top of the ghetto walls shines into the ghetto.

"Dad, the door is locked! What's happening?" Simon says, as he runs into the room that his father and sister are in.

"I am not sure. Stay in the bedroom with your sister, while I make sure things are okay."

Paul rushes into the living room for lack of a better term and tries opening the door to the building. "It's locked?" He rhetorically says to himself, and then walks over to the window to see why the flood lights are turned on. The ghetto wall begins to open and armed soldiers march inside. Once the wall is fully open, a couple of guards stand and keep guard adjacent the exit. The remaining soldiers walk inside the apartment buildings.

One of the first buildings is the one the Parkinson's reside in. Gun shots are heard downstairs. Paul cringes in fear. He runs to the door and keeps his body weight pressed against the door to give the soldiers a hard time if they try to come inside. Miriam begins screaming. "Simon, keep her quiet!" Paul yells frantically, shifting his body weight against the door again hoping whichever new way he tries, holds the soldiers off as long as possible.

He hears someone's footsteps running up the stairs, Paul's heart feels as if it is lumped inside his throat. He feels lightheaded and expects the worst. The lady inside the hallways is screaming and pleading for her life.

"Help me, someone please help me! Open the door they are going to kill me! Open the fucking door! They are going to fucking kill me!"

The lady bangs on every door on the floor. More footsteps follow in pursuit of the unknown lady.

"You are in direct violation of the nine o'clock curfew and have now been convicted of conspiracy to commit a terrorist plot."

"I was using the washroom and I got locked out! I am not a..."

A gunshot echoes throughout the hallway, and the sound of a body slaps onto the concrete floor. The sounds of footsteps proceed down the stairs while fewer gunshots echo throughout the ghetto.

As the sounds of gunshots fade away, it is not long before they hear the electronic wall closing shut. Paul cups his face with his hands and begins crying out loud, and Miriam and Simon run to their father who is still pinned against the door as their protective hero. As Paul still sits pinned up against the door, he feels warm blood from the victim saturating his trousers from underneath the crack of the apartment door.

"Did they kill her, daddy?"

"Don't worry yourself about it, pumpkin."

Trying to sleep that night is horrible. There really isn't much sleep, if any. The poor woman's screams for help and being powerless to save the lady, leaves Paul sleepless the remainder of the night. Each moment that he tries to sleep, he keeps rehashing her cries while imagining trying to do the best he can to open the apartment door to save her.

He watches Simon toss and turn on the cold concrete floor throughout the night, which leaves a sore spot in his heart. Perhaps tomorrow night Miriam and Simon can share the clothes on the ground in the bedroom when they go to bed, if they're able to both fit inside the bedroom.

The doors in the building simultaneously unlock at seven in the morning and the flood lights shut off. An alarm which sounds like an air raid rings in all the buildings inside the ghetto for five minutes, and then shuts off.

I guess they want to make sure everyone is awake, Paul thinks to himself. Looking inside his bag of belongings for food, he finds a bag of vegetables for breakfast and there was only a quarter bag left to feed the three of them. Paul shivers at the thought of trying to cook the food with the nasty tasting water, as the plumbing for the building was designed without septic tanks and other filters to manage human waste.

There is a knock at their door, Paul cautiously opens the door to see a couple of in-shape men stand adjacent one another with pens and a pad. "Do you mind if we come in sir?" One of the twos asks, speaking in a soft tone.

"Do you mind telling me what this is about? I have done nothing wrong and I have been here all day looking after my children."

"Oh sorry sir, I don't mean to alarm you. This is Rick and I am Sunny. We are looking for people with traits that could be useful while we are imprisoned here. There has already been a string of robberies and break and enters, and since we will be living here we could use some strong men and women to help police the ghetto. We have several sick and injured people inside the ghetto who could really use doctors' help, or anyone with medical expertise. Basically, we're looking for everyone to pitch in and give a helping hand. We need to establish order while we are living here, even if that sounds absurd due to our circumstance."

Paul lets out a sigh of relief. These people are in the same situation, and are just like him. They're not Imperial soldiers, and they're only thinking fast for the greater good of everyone in the ghetto. It would be a good idea to help the public; however, his children need his protection. "Well, I am all my children have and they need me to watch over them."

"Our wives and girlfriends will help the workers watch the children. They will be establishing a free daycare for the children while we are doing our moral duty sir. They will be in good hands. You look like a strong person. I shall mark you down as a peace officer unless you have another skill that you would like to share with us that may be useful? If not, please report for duty tomorrow morning at the front of this building."

Paul nods his head. He is not thrilled that he has been given little choice in the matter; however, he will do it regardless, as there are people in the ghetto that would probably benefit from his services.

He reports for duty the next morning, bringing his children along with him. There were fewer killings last night, but enough to have another horrible night with lack of sleep. His initial duty as officer is working on establishing a place of detention, inside the same building as they will use as a hospital.

"Men and women, you will be upholding the law and not abusing it. Your duties will be limited to important stuff; such as break and enters, thefts pertaining to food, assaults with weapons, murders and rapes. We are not able to attend to everyone's personal problems so I ask you all to use your better judgment in handling these affairs. Firsts things first, you will be working hard all day, so you will need to eat. We have cooked some meat in the cafeteria for before and after work. Keep in mind there are no refrigerators in any of our buildings so don't be modest! Eat as much as you can before going out on duty."

The officers leave for the cafeteria and eat the breakfast that has been prepared for them. As the officers are eating, one of them breaks his tooth on a bullet, another bites on a bullet. Fortunately he does not break his teeth like the other police officer in the café.

"Hey, how'd you guys get guns in here? And where are the animals? We have no food at home I need to know where these animals are if I am going to be working for you guys so I can help feed my kids," A lady says in the crowded cafeteria, followed by others wondering the same thing.

"We're eating dead people!" screams someone in the café after she notices a wedding ring on part of what was once someone's finger. She starts vomiting her meal up, trying to get undigested parts of whomever she was eating out of her system. Other people mirror her actions horrified they're eating the remains of other prisoners the Imperial solders kill at night. However, while some others are disgusted by the discovery, they continue eating trying to block out the mental aspect that the food was once another person, in order to fill their stomachs.

"People, calm down. Yes, you are eating the remains of people, but they were the victims of the previous night. We need nutrition somehow, and face it, many of us have not eaten any meals in several days and if any of us have been eating, it isn't much of a meal. There only seems one way of getting any type of food at the moment. Trust me when I say this," Sunny addresses the crowd.

"You fucking Muslim. This is all your fucking people's fault, and now you fucking terrorists are feeding us people. I am going to kill you!!!" an angry Christian in the crowd yells as he rushes Sunny, grabbing him and swinging his arms back and forth, trying his hardest to give Sunny a knockout punch.

Rick jumps on the attacker, tossing him to the ground. He struggles to get the man's arm behind his back in order to keep him from fighting.

"It wasn't Sunny's idea. It was mine and he is right we need to eat, and this goes for everyone here. Hear me when I say this: we all have different religious backgrounds. Discrimination against another person's religious beliefs will not be tolerated!"

With the National Bank manager, Jeff O'Neil's help, Mark makes millions of debits flipping assets in a relative short frame of time. He learns the real estate ins and outs with Jeff's diligent help and has become one of the youngest and wealthiest entrepreneurs in North Canada, let alone the New World Order and all of its provinces.

With Jeff's tutelage he buys baseball, football, and hockey stadiums, business corporations previously owned by religionists, and other assets that quickly bring in a massive fortune. Despite his success, there is only one thing Mark truly cares about.

"Jeff, when are we going to do this? I know it would hurt me to give up everything for my family back, but I would gladly do it. I miss them more than life itself."

Jeff fidgets with his pudgy fingers, quickly trying to think of an answer to manipulate the kid into helping him make more money before replying to his broken hearted friend, "Okay son, tell you what; let us take a drive to the ghetto. We'll buy our families back okay. I am sure we have more than enough to make any soldier's life happy for as long as they live, and their children's children right? Of course that's right!"

An eerie feeling comes over Jeff and Mark as they approach the ghetto. This is the first time Mark has ever seen the fifty foot tall ghetto wall which sends shivers up and down Mark's and the chauffeur's spines.

"I hate coming here." Jeff says, a little more used to seeing the prison than the others.

"Gentleman, I shall park here so that we can remain inconspicuous?" their chauffeur states, hoping they agree, as he is not wanting to get any closer to the ghetto than they have to.

Jeff looks at Mark then the chauffeur "Yes, here is fine. Thank you, Gordon. Mark, you wait here while I go fishing for a guard."

The chauffeur opens the back door of the limo and Jeff hops out, wiping the sweat off his brow with a handkerchief, as his nerves are getting the better of him. He approaches the mammoth-sized prison. Despite the size of the wall, he is able to hear the groaning and wailing of inmates begging to be let out.

Oh how horrible, Jeff thinks to himself.

Two soldiers standing adjacent a barracks fence aim their assault rifles at Jeff as he approaches them. "No one has business here. Leave now!"

"Oh, please no don't shoot me. My name is Jeff O'Neil, and I work at the National bank. I'm also one of the wealthiest real-estate owners in the Toronto region. I am here to speak with someone in charge. I buy and sell real estate. Surely you have heard of me?"

The soldiers do lower their guns, change their facial expressions, but continue giving Jeff cold blank stares.

Jeff realises it will take a lot more to peak their interest, as he gazes at their cold dark stares. Everything about the pair of soldiers is eerie and frightening, from the silver metallic chuck-skull cross bone emblems on the front of their black army uniforms, to their incredible size and stature, to their bright red occult symbol of an upside down pentagram on the sleeve of their black uniforms, to the assault rifles pointed at his chest with laser guided sights.

"We have heard of you, yes. You still have no business here with us. Leave now!"

"Sorry my good sirs, but I am looking for a few terrorists and I have enough money to make both of your lives worthwhile?" Jeff says with clear uncertainty his bribe may not work. But the pair of soldiers say nothing in response and he takes this as a cue to continue.

They must be listening, Jeff thinks to himself. "I am willing to pay you both one hundred million debits per terrorist. I am looking for four people."

"Bribery against the Empire where terrorists are concerned is punishable by death. You are in clear violation of that law!"

"Wait, wait. Hold on wait a minute here. You guys are mad. This is in between us. I am talking about a fortune for the both of you here and now, four hundred million debits! What do you make a year as a soldier thirty, forty thousand? This is madness!"

"You have been charged and convicted by the corruption and disobedience act section 121 which states as follows; everyone who commits fraud on the government, anyone who directly or indirectly gives, offers, or agrees to give or offer to an official or to any member of his or her family, or to anyone for the befit of an official, or part four a claim against his majesty the Emperor or any benefit that his majesty is authorized or entitled to bestow whether or not in fact the official is able to cooperate, render assistance , exercise influence or do or omit to do what is proposed, will be punished for an offence under this section and is guilty of a capital offence and is liable of a capital offence if in fact they are trying to liberate a terrorist." a soldier says.

"Woe, wait you can't do this. No wait, we can work something out. Don't be foolish. I can debit your accounts immediately. Wait! I will pay each of you four hundred million debits. I am good for the money. Consider this a golden opportunity!"

Both soldiers open fire on Jeff. Bullets fly in and out of his body, and he falls to the ground like a rag doll, twitching on the ground like an epileptic having a seizure. Before Mark is able to instruct the chauffeur to drive away, a sniper shoots the chauffeur in the head, and his head explodes like a fragile vase.

Mark screams in horror and opens his door to run away, as the sniper fires off another shot from its M14 rifle ripping a chunk of metal away from the car door Mark swung open. As he runs down the street, screaming and pleading for his life, and not to be shot, Imperial soldiers surround Mark and order him to drop to his knees.

"Bribery against the Empire where terrorists are concerned is punishable by death. You are in clear violation of that law!" a soldier says, while it approaches Mark.

"I was going to buy some office buildings! I worked for that man. What the fuck did he say to you? We were just going to buy buildings!"

The soldier tries to scan Mark's eyes; however, Mark continuously keeps his head down as he continues to cry, and plead for his life. The soldier yanks Mark's head back and presses his gun against Mark's head. The soldier is still not able to scan Mark's eyes because they're closed.

The soldier lets go of Mark's hair, "Your friend was a traitor to the Empire. Be careful in who you select as company. Acts of treason are punishable by death. This decree has been handed down by Emperor Dagoth himself. No one has business here. Leave now!"

Mark runs away, fearing they will take his life.

15

Millions of robotic machines designed to look every bit as human as humans, leave the Emperor's secret base of operations where they were created, and head to military bases across the New World Order's provinces around the world.

"What do you mean we don't work here anymore?" in his native Spanish tongue Jose questions one of the soldiers that have come to relieve him and others from duty.

"By order of his Excellency Emperor Dagoth, all military personnel are to be replaced. Each of you has fifteen minutes to pack your belongings and leave. Religious military personnel are to come with us, or face the consequences."

"We're not going anywhere, mister and you are not touching any of our religious personnel who have been loyal and served our country before our President sold out to this pathetic New World Order, so you can all go back home and tell your Emperor we're not going anywhere!"

The soldier does not respond and leaves Jose to comply with his orders. The soldier stands with his fellow machines and waits for the humans to comply and leave the base. The robotic soldiers intercept instructions from Jose to the other sentient beings on the base to gather weapons and take a stand against the Imperials.

After intercepting and eavesdropping on the human militants, the robotic soldiers perceive the humans as a threat, turn on their thermal imaging to confirm the actions of the sentient soldiers, and ready their weapons in return. "By the authority of Emperor Dagoth, all soldiers in this base and others throughout the empire are dismissed. You are hereby ordered to leave immediately!"

They march into the base. There are no emotions, no fear, and no concerns of injuries as they approach the humans who have rallied together and are hiding behind trucks, walls and other inanimate objects throughout the base property. Gun fire erupts. The human militants take aim and fire, Jose's best friend Pedro, who served with him for fourteen years, looks around a corner to open fire on the imperials and as quickly as he does, a bullet rips his chin off and the remaining teeth he has, dangle on his tongue as he drops his gun and tries to scream.

Jose comes to his aid and with futile attempts, tries to re-attach his friend's chin. Knowing that his efforts are in vain, he drags his friend to safety and while doing so watches the other soldiers do their best to repel the Imperials.

The Imperials make short work of the rebels as they close in on the remaining soldiers in the base, including his. Jose jumps up and tosses his gun aside, surrendering as the Imperials near him; a robotic soldier quickly fires his gun, and puts a hole in Jose's head. To Pedro's horror, he watches his best friend fall on the ground next to his hip as he continues to sit on the ground, desperately trying to re-attach his chin, and keep conscious at the same time. When he is discovered, the Imperial's shoot him in the face, and they continue shooting down the remaining rebels on the base until it is clear of all threats.

The Imperial robotic soldiers shoot down any rebelling soldiers across the globe in the same manner, and those smart enough to take their severance pay, are able to leave without incident. The machines also deal with religionists that have been escaping the ghettos. The soldiers find them using the database which is able to determine their locations across the New World Order by tracing their G.T.S. chip, and they execute each of the religionists, drive their bodies back to the ghettos and impale their bodies through their rectums, with poles long enough to penetrate through all of their organs and out of their mouths. Their bodies are displayed in the middle of the ghetto streets to serve as an example of what happens to those who defy the Empire.

"My Lord, you will be pleased to know that we have dealt with any potential rebel forces in our Kingdom and you will also be pleased to know that I have captured Jody Knoiky,

Joshua's friend. He is in our custody as we speak," General Soleman informs the Emperor.

"Good, you have served the Empire well General, and for all of your loyal services I have credited your All-In-One Card so that you may live comfortably in your retirement."

"What? Retirement? Sorry your Excellency, I do not mean to speak out of turn but this is my livelihood; surely your grace can bestow me the honour of remaining a loyal part of the Empire?"

"If you're able to apprehend Joshua, I will provide you a bounty for your time and efforts," Emperor Dagoth casually says after a moment's thought and walks to the interrogation room, as the ex-General is escorted from the premises.

As Dragon Dagoth walks into the interrogation room he is surprised that Jody, unlike so many others does not fear him, and stares him directly in the eyes as Dragon Dagoth walks closer.

"Jody, it appears that I can help with the release of your family. It is easier than you think, really." Emperor Dagoth tosses a pile of papers on the table in front of Jody, and then waves his hand over Jody's handcuffs. Jody's handcuffs fall from his wrists to the table, unlocked.

Emperor Dagoth finally feels Jody's fear. Jody feels an unknown presence of power coming from the man who entered the interrogation room and he tries to conceal his fear from the person he mistook as a man. Now he wonders who this demon or Devil is.

"Go ahead, look," Dragon Dagoth softly asks Jody.

A bit shaken, he acknowledges the Emperor and picks up a few of the papers on the table. To his surprise, they're not papers. They're photographs of Joshua, William with Joshua, and some photographs of the three together. "I want to see my lawyer. We haven't done anything."

"Selling drugs is illegal; therefore, you have done something wrong."

"We have a restaurant and a good chef, and our clientele pays top dollar for our food. Our competitors talk shit about us, and make up stories about the money we make because they're jealous. You have nothing on any of us," Jody says, trying to figure out who has informed the police regarding their illegal business endeavours. "You said I can get my family back, so how am I going to do that, asshole?"

"Your illegal doings are of little concern to me at the moment. Joshua is the one I seek and I want him flushed out and apprehended. It has come to my knowledge that Joshua co-owns this business of yours, and is deep into illegal doings. I want you to merge your business with every gang that you affiliate with so Joshua has nowhere to turn, as I suspect he will avoid you and your friend at all costs now that he is aware we're after him. When he comes out of hiding, you will bring him to me otherwise I am not sure I can guarantee the release your family. In turn, I will greatly reward you and allow you to run your business. As an added incentive, I have the power to bring Phuong back to life. Get Joshua for me and you will see Phuong again."

"She's dead. You motherfuckers killed her! Now you're going to stand there and try and bullshit me to my face. How about you and I take a walk out of this interrogation room? I bet you're not so tough without the protection of these soldiers and police watching your ass, you fucking dick!"

The Emperor smiles and raises his hands, "Is that a threat?"

Jody leaps to his feet and curls his fingers into fists and rushes towards the Emperor who raises one of his hands levitating Jody. He telekinetically throws Jody lightly against the back of the room's wall, and then uses his other hand to show Jody his raw display of power and levitates the table bolted into the ground and telekinetically launches that at Jody.

The legs of the table break into the wall either side of Jody, buckle and bend until the table top is at Jody's throat.

The Emperor grits his teeth in an awkward smile and addresses Jody's hostile sentiments, "As you can see, I have the power to do what I will, and if I desire to bring your girlfriend back to life I will. Tempt me no further than this or she will forever remain one of the dead!"

The Emperor lets go his telekinetic hold of Jody and the table, dropping either to the ground, without caring if Jody is injured in the process, and says, "I don't see why you wouldn't do it? After all she would not be dead if it wasn't for Joshua. He could have turned himself in to me years ago. Now, not only is your girlfriend dead, your family may join them. The reason I bring this up is because I read your thoughts and you do not want to 'rat out' Joshua. That is perfectly fine. I will start killing your family. Your grandmother seems like a sweet lady. I will start with her first!"

"No wait! Please!" Jody pleads, screaming out desperately. "If you can do that for me, I'll fucking get him for you. I'll kill the son of a bitch myself."

"I want him alive, Jody. Alive."

Bitter and defeated, Jody returns to his restaurant and sits at one of the booths. William takes notice and approaches Jody, stepping over mounds of broken debris in order to get to his depressed looking friend.

"Will, I need your help finding Joshua; we are to capture him at any cost."

Lighting a cigarette and taking in a deep breath of smoke, William stares at his acquaintance, wondering if he ratted Joshua out to the Imperial soldiers, and he turns his stare into an intimidating gaze.

"I am not capturing our buddy. What are you talking about? We would not have this place if it wasn't for him!"

Knowing that he is not able to physically harm William, Jody returns William's stares with a look of utter contempt. He could pull out his gun and shoot him in the face; however, he doesn't feel compelled to spend the rest of his life in prison for shooting one of his friends, especially when his family's lives are at stake.

Bumping his way into William, Jody walks past him into a small cluttered back office room, and starts contacting his rivals, letting them know that he wishes to merge his business with theirs, offering incentives and large percentages of business stocks.

"Did I seriously over fucking hear you? Are you seriously calling up rival fucking gangs and shit telling them how we are besting the Empire and offering them stakes in our business? Tell me why I shouldn't kick your fucking ass right now, and when Josh gets back and I tell him, tell me why both of us shouldn't go to the hospital I am going to put your crippled ass in and we both beat you some fucking more?! What are you fucking doing, you fucking fag?"

"Listen, you white fucking cracker, just shut the fucking hell up, stop moving your big fat fucking obese mouth for just two fucking seconds before I shoot it off your fucking face, you fucking knob gobbler!"

The pair stand in a confrontational position to each other, both with clenched fists and ready to swing at the slightest flinch of the other.

"That shit you told me about earlier, Josh."

"Yeah, what about it, fuckhead!"

"Fucking true man, the New World Order Emperor is after him. He holds me hostage. He shows me pictures of my family. He tells me if I do not help him, he will kill my family."

It takes a few moments for Jody's words to register, and William vaguely remembers some of the details of what Joshua conveyed to him before their house was burned down, but it was not making sense as to how Jody got to see the new Emperor, or even why the new Emperor would even remotely be interested in kidnapping civilians.

"He's the Emperor. What in God's name would he want or need you for?"

"He knows about our illegal business operations. He is willing to let it continue. All we need to do is turn Joshua in."

"So wait, let me get this straight. The Emperor of the New World Order knows that we have an illegal business, and says, 'Oh yeah, I know that you are a drug lord, but hey who cares. Get me Joshua and you can go home, sell guns and drugs. I don't really care about any of that. I just want Joshua?' Are you fucking kidding me? Call Hollywood guy, you've just got yourself an Emmy winning performance for the biggest crock of shit ever told."

"They fucking have my family, you cocksucker," Jody says, eyes diverting from William's focus so that he can conceal any amount of tears forming.

"The Emperor will supply us with whatever manpower we need if we discover his whereabouts. Are you going to help me save my family, William?"

This is the first time he has ever seen Jody so desperate, in need of a back brace to keep him up, so down and withdrawn. Jody's story is so convincing anyone would be compelled to believe it; however, who could he tell about what happened to him when he tried shooting Joshua? That is a farfetched story of its own regardless if it is true, no one in their sane mind would believe it if he shared the story with them.

"I'll think about it," William says, as he leaves Jody to himself. William leaves the restaurant in order to get some fresh air.

It takes a few weeks of persistence, contacting all of his rivals some of whom make tentative agreements with Jody, and together they agree upon a new name for their organization: The Order of the Snake. All hierarchy in the mafia will have matching tattoos of the Chinese Zodiac symbol of a snake on their arms to match the mixed race Chinese and Thai tattoo Jody has inked on his left arm.

Jody also makes all those who agree to work with him promise to bring Joshua in at all costs; however, the bounty is beyond his means of payment which gives others rise to suspicion that he may not be good for the money. A business associate of his informs him that she is able to set up a meeting with an up-and-coming wealthy boy, Mark Parkinson and Jody agrees to have a meeting with the young real estate agent, if a meeting can be set up with him, and negotiate talks in person with this young fellow.

"A bunch of us are planning on escaping. We just can't find a way past the guards. I honestly think the guards in the booths are nothing but ploys like cameras designed to look like guards," Paul's new friend, Samantha, says, as she looks up at the fifty foot tall wall at one of the booths where one of the guards is situated, to validate her point.

"Like have you noticed they don't go out for breaks or leave for lunch, go home at night or do much of anything other than turn their heads from one side staring at one part of the ghetto to the other side periodically, like a camera watching us from side to side. Also these same guards have never left their posts whatsoever. I've noticed this since I've been here."

Paul looks at his new friend Samantha. *What courage*, he thinks to himself. However, he is not in a position where he can escape and ever since the soldiers brought the last batch of escapees into the ghetto, there is no way he is willing to take the risk and jeopardise his children's lives.

"No, I haven't taken the time to notice that sorry, but I did hear rumours circulating last week about several gunshots at the south end of the ghetto. They were coming from the outside. One of the guards in the booths was said to be using a sniper rifle."

Samantha nods her head, acknowledging the news. "I have heard the rumours as well, but we need more than rumours. We need facts and more importantly, we need freedom. Look at us. We are living the good life patrolling the ghetto, you know, a good meat filled breakfast in the morning and evening. Of course we would not be eating if it wasn't for people stupid enough to be outside after curfew, but I want a real meal again. I don't want to be eating the ass out of someone I just shook the hand of the previous day, you now?"

Paul laughs. Samantha has quite the way of making a dark situation light; however, his attitude quickly changes. A couple of weeks of living in the ghetto and they are reduced to savage beasts. How appalling.

"Paul, do you actually believe in God?"

Stopping dead in his tracks, he turns to face Samantha. The look of uncertainty clouds his facial expression, and he does not know how to answer her question.

"I mean, you know when I filled out the All-In-One application, I checked the box saying I was Christian because you know that is what everyone does, unless you're a Muslim or something. I think I have been to church a couple of times when I was younger, for a wedding and funeral, but I didn't go all the time like some bible thumpers or whatnot, you know?"

Paul lowers his head. All his life, he has been a devout Christian and has passed on what he knows about God, Christ and the Holy Spirit to his family, just as his parents did for him. Thinking hard about it now, all that he has ever accomplished is gone because of his belief in God. His house, his wife, his newborn daughter murdered because of their faith and belief. His oldest child Mark, who he taught to believe, hates him because of his belief; however, it is not for him to judge Mark's path. He only hopes that his son Mark is doing the best that he can to survive in a world full of Satan's evil agents.

He looks around. This is where his belief in God has got him, a ghetto. To wake and see a litter of dead bodies each morning, to casually stroll down the streets not even paying attention to the foul stench of bloated and rotting bodies of people that have either died of starvation or malnutrition, or who were in desperate need of medical assistance, maggots eating away at their carcasses, is a common sight.

Inhabitants inside the ghetto pleading for their lives, screaming not to be shot after curfew, used to make him feel uncomfortable, and make his heart fall into the bowels of his abdomen. Now it is nightly entertainment. He counts how many people get shot each night with his children and they even have a name for the game.

Do I believe in God? He questions himself, wondering if he can truly answer Samantha's question. Perhaps, not a night has gone by where he has not stopped praying for God's kingdom to come. He still tells his children bible stories each night; however, he has nothing to be thankful to God for.

"I don't know, Samantha. I used to go to church every week on the Sabbath, then on Wednesdays for bible study. Now I ask myself where my faith has brought me, to this place. Not even my children believe in God anymore, especially my oldest. That is what saved him from being here."

Paul sighs and hangs his head, fighting off tears welling in his eyes, wishing that there was some way of knowing, or finding out how Mark is doing.

"Don't worry Paul. We will escape, hopefully nothing bad has happened to your son and you can re-join him."

Paul nods and smiles.

"Keep your voice down. I know we are safe to speak here, but you never know," Stacy peers around a corner to make sure no one is eavesdropping, and then continues speaking. "So what you're telling me is he was going to offer those guards four hundred million debits and they just killed him? That doesn't make any sense to me at all!"

Mark nods, "I know. None of this is making any sense. I know he offered them money because they told me and they were going to kill me as well. It is a capital offence to bribe the Imperials."

"Those guards must be insane. Who wouldn't take that kind of money?"

Stacy lowers her head and lets out an exasperated sigh, and then looks back up at Mark, "That's a crying out loud shame. Jeffry was a good man. They are trying to make it sound as if he was some notorious criminal all over the news. I have connections in the media telling me that they are given transcripts of events that are government related, to justify their acts and now they are doing the same to Jeffry. If they refuse to say what is written on the transcripts, I'd hate to see what the outcome would be for them."

Mark holds Stacy's hand. Both are miserably sad, and heartbroken, mourning over Jeff's loss. "I just wish there was something we could do, if not us someone," Mark says, wiping away his tears with his free hand.

"I miss my family and my dad will probably die thinking I hate him. I wish I could save them, if not save them talk to them at least one last time. Someone has to do something, and if I ever get a chance, I will do something."

Stacy leads the way to her car with Mark, urgently. "You're right about someone doing something and now you're being watched carefully."

Stacy notices Mark's perplexed look on his face and continues speaking, "Mark your new found wealth has attracted the interest of some people of note that are in the underground."

"Stacy, are you talking about criminals? Why are they watching me?" Mark wonders, nearly scared out of his wits.

"Excuse me Mark, are any of your family members 'criminals' or 'terrorists'? This is a new age, an age where we do not have rights. We gave up those rights when we all got mandatory chips in our heads. We gave up our rights when we merged all of our cards into one card, controlled by the government, now Empire. We are not able to go anywhere without being tracked. We cannot buy anything without the Empire knowing what it is. Now tell me who are the real criminals? Your family was targeted as terrorists because they believed in a god. Regardless if he is real, it is everyone's right to believe in what they want so long as it does not harm anyone else, but the Empire has done away with our human rights. They broke the law, and they are the real criminals!"

Mark grips his face with open hands and sobs. His initial impulse is to freak, yell and scream at Stacy; however, he knows better.

"You're right. You're right," he says in between sobs. "So why are these people watching me?"

"Easy Mark, try and understand something; because of their differences they are criminals. Everyone who believes in a deity is a criminal. These people that are in the underground justify what they do, however, they are criminals. But you can steer them right, give them purpose, and perhaps pay them to help take down the Empire, so that maybe, just maybe, one day you can be reunited with your family again. Do you understand where I am going with this?"

"Yes, I think I do?"

"Well, seeing that you have an abundance of money, you can help finance the war against the Empire. Donate some of your buildings to help support the underground movement against the New World Order. Someone has to do something, right Mark? Once we defeat the Emperor you will be reimbursed, and your name will never be brought up if we are not able to succeed, or are caught in our plot against the Empire. What do you say?"

A sudden realisation shows in Mark's eyes. He is being led astray by Stacy. He opens the car door in utter contempt of what she is manipulating him into doing against the authorities. He steps out of the vehicle, regardless if the law is drastically different from when he was younger. He pauses for a moment as he realises that everything has changed, and perhaps he should hear her out in order to get his family back. Perhaps the Empire which he chooses to blindly obey is far worse than the criminals that she is proposing he speaks with.

"Mark, all you have to do is speak with them. That is all I am asking you to do. It is your decision what you want to do or whatever route you choose. I am not asking you to put yourself at risk but how many more Jeffrey's, need to die?

How many more people like your family needs to be put into custody?"

"The Imperials killed my mother and baby sister," Mark says, entertaining Stacy's words a little more. "I take it all I have to do then is pretend to rent out some of my spaces while you guys do your thing?"

"It's not a bad thing Mark. We all want a shot at getting our family members back. That is why this underground movement is spreading so fast. The underground as you may know it, is not all that bad. Please we could use your help."

"I love my family, and I will do anything to save them."

After nine o'clock, the flood lights turn on and all the apartment doors in the ghetto slam shut. The infamous wall begins to crack open. Waiting for the soldiers to make their rounds, is a small band of potential escapees led by ex-soldiers, and police who are leading the expedition.

Over the past few weeks they have trained those who are physically able and desire to leave the ghetto, how to fight in hand to hand combat, or by using whatever weapons they are able to get their hands on inside the ghetto which will be used against the soldiers when they ambush them.

The ones who are confident enough to fight will immobilise the first wave of soldiers that come inside the apartment building they are hiding in, take their weapons, and then kill as many soldiers as possible when the next wave of soldiers rush to their aid.

Kendrick, the leader of the escape is highly experienced at taking out the enemy in stealth and in hand to hand combat. He served the Canada armed forces in many hostile terrorist zones, and was frequently called in to clean up the mess before the times of the New World Order's Empire.

As the wall creaks open, the roar of army vehicles are heard outside the apartment building. A soldier walks inside the first apartment building where the escapees are hiding, and one of Kendrick's best trained fighters rushes the first soldier, and thrusts a knife as hard as he can into the neck of the soldier.

To the escapee's shock and horror, the soldier faces him and punches face. His skull is crushed inside the muscle and skin holding what is left of his face together, and a pool of blood falls out of his mouth as he crashes to the floor, due to the severe fatal traumatic contusions to his brain. Blood pours out of his ears and nose while he lies on the ground epileptically twitching, after the instant death blow.

A couple more escapees rush in and try to fight the soldier, and they are thrown against nearby walls. As they try to get up, the soldier shoots them both in the head, blood hissing out of their skulls as they fall to the ground, this time permanently.

Kendrick runs into the universal bathroom and grabs a gun that he smuggled into the ghetto. *That fucker thinks he's a hot shot knocking everyone around with a knife in his jugular. I will put a bullet through his head. Let's see how tough he is then.* He thinks to himself.

The soldier walks into the washroom, and before it realizes anyone is in the washroom, Kendrick fires his gun twice, once in the soldier's stomach to wind him, and then in the head to finish him.

The soldier stares at Kendrick, who in turn unloads his clip into the soldier's head. Kendrick drops his gun, and his mouth hangs open while he stares at the soldier's forehead. There are several bullet hole craters on the soldier's head where Kendrick shot him, and trickles of blood running down the soldier's face.

Continuing to stare at the soldier's wounds, he notices some sort of metal.

"Un-fucking-believable. That's impossible! You're a fucking robot." Kendrick says, coming to the epiphany that the rest of the soldiers that replaced him days ago are also robots.

The soldier shoots Kendrick in the centre of his face. The front of his face caves in and the bullet breaks out the back of his head. A pile of broken bone, blood, and brains fall and pour out of the back of his head, as his face falls open mouthed directly into fecal matter on a hole where prisoners have to squat in order to do their business. The soldier walks over to where Kendrick's lifeless dead body is and confiscates the gun before other escapees acquire it.

The remaining terrorists run into the open with solid metal tables in order to deflect bullets. The plan works. Twenty men, women and children run around the corner of the last apartment building to reach the gate. Two guards start shooting the terrorists in mid stride as they make good their escape. The bullets deflect off the tables with great force; however, they keep pushing forward until they reach the gate to freedom. Five of the escapees are shot down in the process by the sniper in the tower at the opposite end of the ghetto.

After running into the outside world, the terrorists drop the heavy metal tables and run for their lives, dodging and ducking anywhere they can find for cover as the soldiers lock onto their G.T.S.Chips, pursuing the fugitives. The soldiers inside the ghetto run to their vehicles and speed off down the busy downtown Toronto city streets, locking in on the terrorists' positions.

Prisoners witnessing what is transpiring, try smashing out their bulletproof windows in order to jump out and run to freedom while the ghetto gates remain unguarded. Some prisoners on the lower levels are able to smash through their windows and jump out of their windows and hobble towards the gate; however, they are shot down by the snipers in the towers. Other prisoners on the upper levels of the apartment buildings jump out of their windows and break their legs on impact. Some have their femur bone rip through arteries and out of their skin, blood squirting onto the ghetto streets. Others try and break their fall with their arms and hands, only to have their forearm bones pop through their elbows and rip through their flesh, and split their faces open, fracturing their skulls on impact.

The ones who have broken their legs, crawl out of the line of sniper fire, and wait in dire agony while they watch other prisoners get shot as they try and drag themselves to the gate. They wait until the sun comes up which seems like an eternity; some live through the pain and are brought to the hospital and are given the best archaic treatments available.

Paul leans close to his window in order to see the death toll once the alarms sound throughout the ghetto to wake the prisoners. He shakes his head. There are way too many corpses to count on the ground outside; however, he is extremely happy for the ones who were able to escape. As he continues to hear gunshots echoing throughout the ghetto in the free world, he immediately falls to his knees in prayer, "Oh merciful Lord God, and almighty Father in Heaven, please watch over your brethren as they try and escape our persecutors, and guide them through this turbulent time if this is your will. I ask this in Jesus Christ's name. Amen."

"Dad, what's going on?"

"I think some people escaped, Simon," Paul says, extremely excited.

Simon doesn't share the same optimism, and Paul's smile vanishes from his face, as he asks, "What is it, son?"

"Dad, they are all going to be killed. G.T.S. chips, remember dad? The government can see wherever any fugitive runs to, or tries to hide. They will all be killed. No one will be able to escape and live in the outside world."

All glimmers of hope and faith vanish with Simon's unfriendly reminder about the chips. This unfriendly reminder confirms the reason why Paul will not make any attempts to escape with his children. Only by the loving grace of God, will God set them free.

Air raid sirens wail throughout downtown Toronto. Screeching, squealing tyres gives an estimate of how close behind the soldiers are to the men and women that escaped the ghetto, fleeing for their lives. Although these are some of the most physically fit prisoners from the ghetto, they can only burn so much energy due to the lack of nourishment they've had. And it doesn't seem to matter where they run, the soldiers are always heard zeroing in on them.

"We are going to have to try our luck in the subways," Felix motions for the other prisoners to follow him as he runs down the stairs and inside Eaton Centre to lose the soldiers that are tailing them.

"One of us is going to have to get a transfer in order to get more transfers from inside so we can find a bus somewhere to get on without paying."

"Good idea. I will do that," Abigail states while running inside of the mall to see if she is able to see any useful transfers on the ground, so she can get the other escapees into the subway.

As Abigail runs around looking for a transfer, she notices the stares of innocent civilians gazing at her as they walking to and fro in the subway. She hears a couple or the passengers refer to her, or ask their parents if she is a Christian. She moves quicker and more efficiently and then finally finds a transfer on the ground, and then runs into the subway to get enough transfers to get her companions inside.

They hear the soldiers upstairs and vehicles come to a halt, despite the level of noise downstairs from the passengers walking to and fro talking amongst themselves, using mobile devices and the sounds of trains periodically coming into the station. Together all the terrorists run towards the subway together, and show the transfer slips to the attendant.

"Excuse me. You can't use that transfer at this station."

"Yes sir, I just got off at the wrong subway stop with my friends here," Felix says desperately looking behind him to make sure the soldiers haven't located or noticed them yet.

"Well sir, you're going to have to pay another fare. Those transfers are no good here."

"Sir, I am sorry but we need to get back on the train. Please, we got off at the wrong stop," Felix says, looking back again noticing the soldiers are pushing people out of their way and getting closer.

Other pedestrians in the line are getting fed up with the hold up, and start to convey their bitterness at the entourage of homeless people; unbeknown to them the people are terrorists.

"Let me see your All-In-One card, sir. The fare is just twelve dollars and fifty cents in debits. I am sure you have that! Let me see your All-In-One card, sir!" The attendant yells loud enough for the soldiers to hear.

Felix, Abigail and the rest of the terrorists run past the attendant and into the subway system.

"He's a Christian. They are all Christians. Stop the Christians get them, get them! They are dirty Christians! Soldiers over there. Christians get them!" the attendant yells and points the soldiers in the direction they are heading.

Pedestrians scream at the sight of the Christian terrorists, or move clearly out of the line of fire from the ruthless and remorseless soldiers in pursuit of the terrorists, as they run for dear life into the tube. The soldiers occasionally shoot at them once they enter the dark tunnel. A train is heading down the tracks and the terrorists cross over onto the other set of tracks to avoid the oncoming train.

As they hop the tracks, some of the soldiers follow suit; however, they are not programmed to understand the mechanics of the subway system and some of the soldiers step on the third rail. Sparks fly out of some of the soldiers, and all they're able to do is watch the terrorists run to safety before they are smashed into by the train. Parts of the soldiers fly down the railroad tracks, and the other soldiers stop pursuing the terrorists in order to clean up the mess and conceal what they are. They send signals to other soldiers but seeing they're underground the Empire's database is not able to pick up on the signals and transfer them to nearby soldiers to continue with the pursuit.

The terrorists walk the next train station and notice that there are more soldiers looking for them, so they walk back down the tube and find an underground exit. Army vehicles are driving up and down the downtown core of Toronto's city streets looking for and waiting for the terrorists' signals to appear on their scanners.

Realising they are not able to blend in with regular citizens because their clothing is worn due to the elements of the ghetto, some of the males in the group have over a month's worth of facial hair on their faces, and the women who are wearing shorts have the same growth of hair on their legs because razors are forbidden in the ghetto for suicide reasons. The best course of action to blend in is steal some clothing, scissors and razors to give one another make overs.

They smash their way into a nearby store and grab clothing and hygiene products, discarding what they were wearing, in the store. As they head to the exits, they notice that the soldiers have arrived.

As Stacy rings Mark's doorbell, a well-dressed butler answers the door and allows Stacy and a few of her associates inside to meet Mark.

They are seated inside a banquet area inside Mark's illustrious mansion, and they quietly talk amongst each until Mark walks out and introduces himself to his guests. After the greetings, they get straight to business.

"Yes it is true. I was the president of a known biker gang. Once Max Diamond was voted in, everything we worked so hard to achieve was destroyed overnight by this man. Emperor Dragon Dagoth or whatever he calls himself is turning a blind eye to crime, well certain types of crime. I am sure if he knew we were going to do something to help out Christians, he would kill each and every one of us for some strange reason. Anyway, apparently someone by the name of Jody is an inside man that has a direct link to the Emperor and this Jody is looking for every old Mafia, biker organisation, and any other crime syndicate to help capture someone named Joshua, who goes by the alias John Curthy. Point being, we can run our organisations until this Joshua is caught. Hopefully, after that happens we can still run our businesses; however, that is just me speculating," Rex says, looking for other people's opinions on the matter.

"So why isn't she here? And does she need our help as well?" Mark asks curiously.

A well-dressed Asian man, Tseng, who is listening intently to the conversation, speaks on Jody's behalf, "Yes sir, umm Jody is a dude, but yeah sure he needs a warehouse which we can store our ... supplies."

Mark quickly interrupts the man, "Okay, this is all fine and dandy that you guys wanna sell your drugs again and whatever else you guys used to do, but how is this going to be an uprising against the New World Order. I don't understand how selling your drugs will help get our families back!"

"Well Mark, we're going to do it. We just need that drug money to finance our war against the Empire; furthermore, we need to spread word and find people on the front willing to fight and die for us to get our freedom back, as well as liberate our families and at the moment, selling drugs and firearms seems to be the only way possible way we can do it. Once we have enough money and manpower then we can wage war against the Empire." the ex-President of the biker gang says.

"May I say something, sir?" a stern-looking man with short, white hair pipes up.

"Umm, yeah, sure. Okay, go ahead."

"I was a lieutenant colonel under direct command of a Commander Soleman until we all got our severances and were fired from the army and replaced by a new regiment of men and women that look like they eat steroids for breakfast. I will cut to the chase, sir. There are quite a few of us who lost our family members and dear friends, and they're living in these ghettos. I have organised a tactical assault and recon team. Our first plan of action is taking out the ammunitions depot, but I would suggest you buy that instead of risking the lives of our people? That would greatly be appreciated. We could use all the supplies we can get our hands on. Next off, there are buildings that we could use within range of the ghetto where we can set up a perimeter and use that as a tactical striking advantage against the ill-reinforced ghetto. After all hostiles are neutralised, we can perform a recon. I would suggest you purchase some birds ... sorry sir, helicopters to go to an extraction point that we will set up once inside of the ghetto. Once we're inside the hostile zone we can get the friendlies out of the hostile zone and to a safe extraction point that I suggest you own sir, or purchase for this operation."

"I support that idea; however, I will not entertain or support the sales of narcotics. You can do that on your own time and own property."

"Might I speak candidly, sir?"

Mark looks back at the Lieutenant who is eager to speak once again, "Candidly?"

"Sorry sir, freely, openly. I will just get to the point. The narcotics dealers can give us quite the tactical advantage with numbers and recruits. We're always... we were always trying to recruit children for the army. It starts off with having them watch Sunday morning cartoons, cheering for their favourite soldiers, and then they play video games as soldiers when they're older. We developed these video games because they are so fascinated by war, and by the time they are eighteen they are making that commitment to join the army. Using these drug dealers, we can do the same thing using their cause in order to recruit the manpower. In any case, their men can be trained to help on tactical assaults and help liberate the ghetto."

"I love what you have to say. Thank you for coming by so that we could have this opportunity to meet. You've given me a lot to consider. I will keep in touch or Stacy will inform you regarding my decision."

16

Soldiers smash into the store and throw hand grenades inside. Explosions tear the lower level of the store to pieces. They run to the escalator and try shooting the terrorists fleeing on the upper level. The soldiers run up the escalator to the upper levels opening fire again, smashing apart televisions in the electronics department, and narrowly missing the terrorists running for their lives.

The terrorists run inside the mall, looking for any exits along the way. The soldiers relentlessly open fire and bullets break chunks of tile on the ground near the terrorists. Soldiers flank the terrorists on the upper, lower, north, south, east and west entrances, closing off all means of escape as they close in on the escaping terrorists.

A hand grenade knocks some of the escapees from their feet. Abigail feels something strike her face, assuming it is debris from the impact of the explosion. She attempts holding her face with her hand to comfort the sharp pain when she realizes that she is not able to move her arm. It is laying on the floor twenty paces behind her.

"My arm, where is my arm?" she frantically asks the others.

"Abigail, get a move on before they kill us!" Felix shouts at her before he is hit by a bullet in his calf and drops to the ground in agony.

Abigail notices her arm in the distance. Not thinking clearly she runs back to pick it and tries connecting her arm back in its socket. "It has to go back on." she says, before she buckles from the loss of blood hissing from her socket and spraying the floor. She is hit a by a few rounds of bullets and dies before her face splashes on the ground in a pool of her own blood.

Felix runs head first into a women's shoe store. Glass partially tears through his chest as he dives on the floor. Trying to block out the pain, he limps into the back of the store and to the employee exit which connects to the street.

The remaining three terrorists jump to the lower floor so they will not be shot by the Imperial soldiers running their way. They land in the food court down below. One of the three snaps her neck on impact. One of her neck bones penetrates her jugular and tears through her flesh, squirting blood out in all directions on some of the patrons running for safety.

Another breaks his leg in half as he lands on a chair; his leg from the kneecap folds in the complete opposite direction like a patio summer chair. The other falls and rolls on the ground and does not sustain any injury. He runs out of sight of the soldiers who are running down the escalators, zeroing in on the G.T.S. chips. He looks behind him as he is running away and notices the prisoner that broke his leg from the fall, slump over after a soldier shoots him in the head.

Malcolm turns his head to see where he is running but is unaware that soldiers are countering this move. As he runs around a corner, a soldier standing directly in front of him and shoots him in the head. His skin screeches, as his dead body skids across the freshly polished floor inside Eaton Centre.

Felix hobbles his way down Yonge Street, and then down a side street, hoping that he is not seen by anyone. He doesn't hear any vehicles, which is a good sign. He takes a moment to relax, and figure a way to keep pressure on his wound. Fortunately no major arteries have been hit; however, he knows that he is in need of medical attention. Perhaps finding a veterinary clinic to help give him stitches and patch the wound will suffice, because no hospital will allow a Christian inside.

As he struggles to get up, he uses a nearby wall for leverage, and then lunges forward. He feels as if he has just been hit in the back with a baseball bat. A loud noise follows the impact on his back. Felix looks down, and notices a hole in his abdomen. His intestines start to slowly fall out of the hole and then dangle between his legs. *How'd that happen?* he thinks to himself while reaching for his guts attempting to insert them back inside of his gaping hole. Another shot follows suit, penetrating the back of his head and breaking through the front of his face. Felix topples over dead.

"I don't care where your employees have to go. They just can't be here, and they can work in the stairwells for all I care. All I know is we have a job to do. If you want to pursue the matter further, I will just call your boss, and you two can straighten things out?" Gregory informs Elena, a supervisor who is putting up a fuss regarding losing productivity in her office.

"Fine, just do what you have to do," Elena responds.

"I am. Paula cut the power we need to get this over and done with now. We are behind schedule as it is."

"Already done, sir," Paula replies.

"I am going to speak to your supervisor and have you fired for this; furthermore I am going to send a letter of complaint to the owner of this establishment to make sure he never contracts your company again!"

"You can do that, however, I do not think that will go over well with Mr. Parkinson who has hired us to do this job. Now, please leave."

Elena and her staff leave without further incident, leaving Gregory and his team behind to do their job. Once the last of the staff leaves the office, Gregory and his team over-turn desks, shut blinds and establish radio contact with their other teammates who are waiting for further orders, in other buildings and on rooftops.

Gangsters, hoodlums, bikers, mobsters and other criminals line up in position in the city streets while Gregory's experienced ex-soldiers fortify the rear.

"Is everyone in position?" Gregory asks and waits for confirmation in order to give the orders to commence attack.

The others cue their confirmations and the uprising begins. Gun fire echoes throughout the downtown core and Imperials exchange gun fire. Gregory orders his snipers to open up fire and shoot down the enemy sniper. The sound of sniper rounds is deafening inside the small office room.

"Sir, I swear I shot him."

"I don't need a fucking narration on your job. Just take out the fucking snipers so the other men can advance on the perimeter!"

The sniper keeps shooting the Imperial snipers, once, twice, five and six more times, "Sir, I fucking hit him. He's not going down, sir."

"What the fuck did they teach you in basic training, soldier?"

"Sir, with all due respect, I have shot him, but you have to take a look at this. Oh shit..."

The Imperial robotic soldier spots Gregory's sharp shooter, aims and fires. The sharp shooter's head breaks as a bullet penetrates his skull. His body falls onto the office floor, and blood pours from his open wound across the blue carpet.

Imperial robotics soldiers hone in on the rebels and head to the office building where the gun fire is coming from. Paula grips her carbine scar-h gun, running in a crouching position to fire at the soldiers approaching the building. She shoots at one of the soldiers in her sights but does not take precautionary measures as she hangs out of the window, firing upon the soldiers below.

After emptying her magazine, she leans back and reaches for another clip on an office table beside her, when a sniper opens fire narrowly missing upper body; however, the bullet tears her arm off from the bicep down.

She screams in pain and falls on the floor, pressing her back against the wall underneath the window so that she is not fatally wounded. Noticing his partner screaming in pain, Gregory crouches and quickly manoeuvres his way to her and wraps an electrical cord above her wound to stop the bleeding.

"My arm!" she utters.

"Keep pressure on the wound and we will get you patched up in no time," Gregory says, as he rushes to get back into position.

As he runs to get back into position, a propelled rocket from a SMAW blows away the wall where Paula was seated behind, killing her instantly. Her head rolls to Gregory's feet, bloodied and with the same sad expression she had on her face realising she lost her arm.

With the impact of the propelled rocket, a partial amount of the ceiling gives way, crashing down to the level Gregory and some of the other rebelling soldiers are, offering cover fire. Gregory falls into a prone position, wriggling his way to a nearby exit.

Another SMAW propelled rocket blows apart a decent amount of office space. Brick, glass and debris scatter across the room. Dust, fire and smoke along hot winds from the rocket, have asphyxiating effects to the remaining few that survived the blast. Gregory, one of the survivors is tossed against a wall by the blast. He shakes the debris off and slings his M60E4 otherwise known as the pig, around his shoulder and tunes out the pain he has endured, while entering a nearby stairwell for safety.

"General, sir. Come in! We can't hold our ground. They are coming at us with incredible resistance. It's like they have steel fucking plates as full body Kevlar, sir!"

"Why is this such a fucking problem for everyone?!" Gregory yells into his radio, "Stand your fucking ground with everything you have and advance on the fucking hostiles. That's a fucking order."

Waving his hand angrily, the soldier Dave who Gregory just finished speaking with, gives hand signals to his squad members to ensure they hold their position. "Understood, I'm just going to let you know that I am not happy with your command!"

They take aim and fire at the soldiers who are swiftly approaching them, to no avail. One of Dave's squad members throws a few grenades which explode near the soldiers, severing some of the soldiers' legs and other body parts. "Move in, move in, move in! That's a direct hit."

They run towards the fallen soldiers, guns at the ready, and to their horror they are still alive and shooting at them, forcing Dave and his squad mates to duck for cover.

Wondering if the soldiers have died, Dave peeks his head around the tyre of a burning car he is hiding behind and notices the metal, wires and other technical hardware on a few of the soldiers, leaving no room for doubt they are not fighting humans, they are fighting machines.

Everything makes perfect sense now after seeing who and what these soldiers are. Dave realises this is why all the soldiers are the same height and weight, and why they all had the same frame, manner and gaze to them. He recalls the new regime walking into Gregory's base and informing everyone that they were dismissed. There were no apologies, sympathy, empathy, no heart felt emotions or concern for the dismissed army personnel, each of whom had families to support.

Humans would not be able to relieve others of their command on such a grand scale. Nor would they would be able to carry out such orders and put friends and family members inside the ghettos, the very ghettos the humans are liberating now. Dave realizes that these robots will follow the Emperor's orders without flaw or emotion; they will not hesitate when orders are given to shoot down anyone, from an adult to a child religionist.

The question plaguing Dave's mind as he watches these complex looking robots with real human flesh, muscle, tissue, and complex hardware, is how could The Emperor Dragon Dagoth ever possibly created a mass army of machines of such stature, programming and testing these machines behind the government's back without their knowledge, and mobilising them in the relatively short time it took him to take office.

Was it possible that Max Diamond was a part of this? Dave thinks to himself, mesmerised as the soldiers regroup and take the fallen broken soldiers away before they are discovered. And even if that is true, Dave thinks to himself, it would have taken several years beyond Max Diamond's political career to create all these soldiers and program them to perfection. These machines are not beta machines, they are the real deal.

"General, sir! We have a situation here! Emergency, sir. We have a situation here!" Dave yells into his radio device.

Gregory rolls his eyes, infuriated that they are not advancing on the soldiers as they're regrouping. The Imperials' defence zone at the ghetto is weak. The enemy is regrouping and his soldiers are hiding behind cars and walls for cover.

"What the fuck is it? The only emergency I want to hear is, 'Commander Sir, my men are all down!' Make it fucking good, Dave," Gregory storms up the last few stairs, opens the roof door and jumps back as he sees fighter jet missiles screeching their way to the ground, followed by explosions.

Shit, Gregory says to himself, "Dave, come in. Dave are you there?"

"It appears as if everyone in close proximity to Dave has been killed, sir."

Quickly grabbing a pair of binoculars, Gregory crouches near the edge of the roof and watches the commotion unfold on the ground. The Imperial hostiles have gained ground; Dave and the rest of his squad are dead.

"Alright everyone, we need to clear these rooftops. That jet will be back any minute now. Whoever is within range, fire your SMAWS and blow a hole in that ghetto wall. Send all immediate reinforcements through that wall. We are going to commence Operation Exodus immediately. Have the choppers on standby and ready to land in the ghetto on my command."

"Yes, sir."

Gregory runs back to the stairwell and hurries down the stairs. The thunderous boom of more explosions on the ground echoes inside of the stairwell, as his team fires rockets at the Imperials. Another thunderous explosion echoes throughout the stairwell, this time rocking Gregory and his team off their feet and into walls inside the stairwell.

Gregory's ears ring from the deafening explosion overhead. Rubble and debris hit some of the troops. Getting to his feet, Gregory looks around and helps his squad to their feet, making sure that everyone is okay.

"My fingers are broken, sir."

In utter contempt and disbelief, Gregory's eyes open wide and his mouth drops in utter disgust, "Is it your trigger finger, soldier?"

"No, my pinkie and ring finger. Take a look sir. Oh god, it hurts so much."

"I just picked up Private Paula's arm and handed it back to her moments before she was blown to smithereens and she didn't say shit. Now I have you whining like a little school girl over a couple of broken fingers? Give your fucking head a shake, asshole. Get in the game. Get out there and fucking fight, you pussy!"

"This is chopper L19-13 to General Gregory Reynolds. There is no way we can land our choppers in the ghetto to commence Operation Exodus. The roof tops have spikes on them and there is nowhere to land due to the dense population of high-rises. Request to perform this recon elsewhere, over."

"I'll figure something out and get back to you in five," Gregory says clutching his assault rifle tight while running down the rest of the stairs, out of the building and towards the gate area, keeping a lookout for Imperial soldiers. "Fire more SMAWS at that gate. I want that gate turned into rubble!"

"Sir, I have an aerial visual on hostiles advancing on your perimeter with heavy M1 Abrams tanks and some anti-aircraft BUK M1s. We are not going to be able to hold this position much longer. I repeat, we are not going to be able to hold this position much longer."

The SMAWS tear out chunks of the fortified wall, and the rebels rush inside the ghetto wall to commence Operation Exodus.

Frightened men, women and children scatter as the rebel forces blast their way through the gate. On a loudspeaker, one of the friendly soldiers shouts instructions to the prisoners that they are there to rescue them.

The heavy Abrams tanks explode on proximity mines as they drive towards the ghetto; however, more are behind the first line of tanks and drive around the destroyed tanks along with more Imperial soldiers; they are a few miles away from the ghetto where rebel forces are liberating the prisoners.

"We are looking for the Parkinson family," Gregory calls out on a loud speaker multiple times.

"Dad, you hear that? They are calling for us," Simon says to his father Paul, as he runs out of the apartment door.

"Simon wait. Miriam come," Paul picks Miriam up and tails behind his son. As he exits the building, he loses track of Simon in the ever growing crowd of prisoners who are desperate to be rescued.

The prisoners determined to escape, punch one another in order to get ahead, and throw each other out of the way. Paul screams out for his son, mute cries among the desperate pleas to be rescued, and the deafening sound of helicopters overhead.

A soldier grabs Simon, pins him on his stomach, and ties his wrists together. After picking him up, he runs Simon to a nearby helicopter, "Any signs of the other two, private?"

"No sir!"

"Climb aboard then. We have to get out of here."

As the chopper lifts up into the sky Simon gazes into the crowd below looking for his Father and sister; yet, only sees a blur of prisoners, fighting to be saved. He is too scared to say anything, and does not know who these people are or why they've taken him. His thoughts race and he is not able to distinguish whether these people are the good guys or the enemy, until an older man with stern features, a battle hardened man sits beside him and places one of his hands on his shoulder.

"You're Simon, right? Well I was sent to get you. We are taking you and the others to an extraction point. The others can go as they please but we have somewhere classified to take you. Don't worry, son. You're in good hands now. I am the General who led this strike to help you and the other civilians escape." General Gregory shouts over the noise of the helicopter.

Simon nods his head. He is still uncertain about everything and is torn that he ran from his father but he does not care for long as he is free of that wretched ghetto, and living nightmare.

A tank opens fire, blowing apart a transport vehicle that is escaping the ghetto with prisoners in the trailer. Limbs and bodies bounce off what is left of the trailer as the truck itself rolls multiple times down the street, dispersing people along its way. A BUK M1s opens fire on straggling helicopters that are evacuating the ghetto, sending everyone to their deaths. Only a few choppers are able to take the prisoners to safety,

Imperial soldiers open fire, shooting the remainder of the escaping terrorists into ribbons. Some of the terrorists contemplating escape see what is happening to their fellow inmates and run for dear life back inside the ghetto, as bullets hiss and snap off walls next to them or ground below them, and some manage to duck into their apartment buildings for safety.

Some of the survivors wipe the blood splatter, and remains of loved ones from their clothing when they reach cover, figuring they've been shot somewhere and then realizing it was someone they loved that was murdered behind them.

Others fortunate enough to escape, clutch onto sockets where their legs or arms were shot off, or hold loved ones and mourn over their losses. Paul looks out of his apartment window as he covers Miriam's eyes and sees prisoners ripped in half, others putting their mutilated intestines back inside of their bodies, as they throw up blood over their own faces.

He continues to watch in horror as mothers running for safety, clutch on to their infants only to notice blood gushing out of a socket where a baby head should be. Some mothers grip their babies so tight, as they run for safety, that they crush their toddlers' rib cages, piercing their vital organs.

Imperial units close in on the rebels fleeing the ghetto. Some of the experienced rebels attempt to repel the Imperials and exchange gun fire but to no avail. None of the rebels have ever encountered a battle like this in their time of service.

A halo of bullets engulfs the ghetto back and forth in the suicidal mission. Aerial bombardments tear apart some of the buildings terrorists retreat to. Even innocent civilians are killed by the desperate religionists taking refuge amongst regular citizens.

For the rebels who manage to liberate the terrorists without incident, they remove their army clothing and dress in regular clothing so that they're not detected by the Imperial soldiers. They also discard their weapons and leave on their separate ways.

As General Reynolds drives back home, he notices that his house is surrounded by Imperial soldiers. A man approaches his vehicle with an outstretched palm, motioning for Gregory to stop. To Gregory's shock, it is Commander Soleman. "Commander?"

"It's General now, Lieutenant Reynolds. I am pretty sure you have heard about the attack downtown today and well, that is the reason I am here!"

An uneasy feeling creeps over Gregory as he continues to firmly grip his steering wheel. "What attack? I thought the terrorists had been dealt with? And why would that bring you here? Besides, I thought our whole regiment got dismissed? Why are you still working?"

"I was among a few people that have close personal ties with Emperor Dragon Dagoth. He contacted me personally and credited me considerably to come here to question you. The reason I am here is because of your minced words with me about taking back 'our' country, on top of which I would like an explanation as to why men from our regiment were amongst the rebels found dead fighting against us and some of the tactics used were tactics that I trained you to use on the battlefield?"

"I can't answer for what they do, can you? They were also a part of your squad. You do realize that right? I have things to do. Are you arresting me or can I go?"

General Soleman leans into the car window so that his words will be clearly understood and not taken lightly, "No you're not being arrested; however, at the moment, I am not going to put you into a position that would make you further incriminate yourself. The New World Order has its eyes fixed on you as of now, and rumour has it arrests will be a thing of the past. These soldiers that took over the other incompetent soldiers are judge, jury and executioner. Be careful!"

Mark walks into his lead underground bunker underneath his house which he recently constructed with his newfound wealth. Satellite signals are not able to reach mobile phones, nor can G.T.S. chips be located. In the reception area where Simon waits, he notices his brother Mark and runs over and showers his brother with loving affection, giving him a hug and kiss. Mark holds his younger brother dearly in their joyous reunion.

"Where's dad and Miriam, buddy?"

Simon lets go of his brother and hangs his head. He is scared to admit that he lost them while running away, and feels that it is his fault they're not with them now.

"Simon, what's wrong? Is everything okay?"

"No, they're still at that terrible place; it's my fault I should have waited for them!"

Rather disappointed at the news, Mark consoles his younger brother, holding him close and tight. "It's not your fault, buddy. I will try and figure another way of getting them out. In the meantime, sit down. Our maids are about to bring us dinner."

"Maids?"

"Yes, a lot has changed since you've been away. We'll speak more about it over dinner."

The two are seated and dinner arrives shortly after. Mark slices a bite of meat off his steak. Each bite tastes like paradise. Simon eats his vegetables, and other side dishes, but ignores the steak.

"Simon, steak is your favourite. I made sure that this was prepared for your arrival. Dig in, bro."

Simon regurgitates and shakes his head. "You know I made a friend Karla while I was at that place with Dad and Miriam. After nine o'clock at night, they lock your apartment doors and if you're caught outside, the army kills you. There was one morning I looked out of my bedroom window and saw Karla on the ground dead, still holding on to her stuffed doll, her brains splattered on top of her teddy bear. Guys in the camp came and picked her up and took her dead body away. I asked where in the hell they were taking her because believe me when I say this Mark, there isn't any place to bury the dead in the camp except for the garden area but no one wants to bury anyone there. He looked at me and said we have to clean her up for dinner. You know at first I thought they had lost their minds she was fucking dead how could she eat? But I thought about how in the hell was dad bringing home food or 'steak' every night after work. When dad came home that night, he brought home a barbequed steak and gave Miriam a Teddy bear. He said, 'Don't worry honey, I will try and wash the blood off your new doll later. That was Karla's stuffed doll."

Mark nods his head as he tries to envision the extreme conditions his brother was in, and understand how scary it was for his brother to see dead people, especially friends that he met. "It's okay, Simon."

"The steak was Karla. In fact, I found out we had eaten quite a few of our neighbours who did not obey the curfew," Simon went on, interrupting his brother.

Mark stares wide-eyed at his brother and then vomits over his plate, and then pukes through his fingers as he tries to get up, holding his mouth to run to the washroom.

Simon fiddles with the steak on his plate with a fork, wondering if the steak is from a cow or someone from the ghetto. The scent of the steak is appealing; however, so was the steak in the ghetto, which was until he realised the meat was Karla and other people that they were eating in the ghetto.

The recent attack on the ghetto has inspired many New World Order citizens to fight against the Empire. Word of the growing underground movement and news of the recent attack financed by Mark Parkinson, spreads to Jody Knoiky and William Curthy.

Jody takes the initiative to set up a secret meeting with Mark, and Jody travels to Mark's estate. Both Parkinson brothers notice several tattoos on Jody's arms as he walks into the estate and greets them. One of the tattoos is a snake which trails up beyond the sleeve. They also notice that that Jody is not just some average street thug, judging by his sharp clothing; however, they're both terrified of him and the dark persona either see in his cold dark gaze.

"I used to bring my brother everywhere with me as well, for meetings and such. My brother is my best friend."

Not knowing what to say, Mark wonders if Jody's brother is in the ghetto but does not want to offend him and press the question.

"Is he in the ghetto?" Simon asks.

Mark holds in his anger from the direct, bold question his brother just asked.

Jody looks at Simon with his cold, dark gaze but has no ill intentions towards the young child. "No, he is the Emperor's prisoner. The reason I am here is to offer you guys a deal. Help me capture someone by the name of Joshua Curthy, and I will give you guys anything you want, and that includes family you have in the ghetto."

Mark laughs as he recalls Jeff telling him the same thing once before, "You'd never be able to get my sister and father out of the ghetto."

Jody pulls a cigarette out of his gold cigarette case and offers one to Mark.

"We don't smoke and there is no smoking permitted in this house."

Jody shrugs his shoulders and lights his cigarette, "I don't talk shit, guy, and if you want your family back, help me capture Joshua Curthy. Josh can only work in the crime world seeing he cannot be on the grid, and I know that you have a lot of criminals who are eager to help you. He may be employed by you, and I need him alive. If you find out where he is, capture him or contact me immediately and I PROMISE you both, I will get your sister and Dad back. I will also get my family back from there. We can team up with our organisations and take down Dragon Dagoth."

Jody takes a long drag from his cigarette and turns to leave, yet pauses. "You may be wondering how I can do this eh? Well I personally work for the Emperor and he is the one who wants Josh. You get him and you will be reunited with your family. Let me know when you have found Joshua."

Jody flicks his cigarette at a corner of the wall and then heads out of the estate. Mark would have said something at Jody's blatant disrespect, but he just stares at Jody as he leaves, frightened to death of the Asian gangster.

"Mark, you have enough money. You can easily find who he is talking about."

Mark smiles at his younger brother's train of thought, "Simon buddy, if it was a matter of money finding Joshua, the government definitely has more than enough money to find him. Anyway..."

"I want to take my chance helping Jody. Does anyone have any reason to believe that he can't get my family back?"

After an awkward silence from everyone in the room, Stacy speaks up, "Well Mark, Jody seems to have rallied quite a few people to his cause. That has to give him some credibility. He must be keeping some promises. You really don't have anything to lose by helping him find Joshua and if you do happen to find him, you have the choice of going before the Emperor yourself to get your family back, or you can help Jody as well and have Jody deliver Joshua to the Emperor, your choice."

"Thank you, well this is a lot to take in. I am going to ask you all to leave while I think this over or whether we should launch another attack on the ghetto and get my family back that way. I have Simon now and I still want to take the chance in getting my dad and sister back."

One by one, Mark's friends and associates leave, save General Reynolds. "My friend I will gather what troops I can to search the streets for Joshua and we will bring him before you. If we capture him we can see for sure if Jody lives up to his word. This will be a lot easier than sending hundreds more to their deaths on another suicide mission, pardon me when I say this, for two people. We will get Joshua for you. I don't want to see more people die."

Even though he wants to be reunited with his family, he understands what Gregory is saying. He does not want more people to die either.

Several soldiers surround Mark's mansion. Tanks smash through the gates and walls and tear up the lawn as they drive towards the mansion, and a few helicopters hover above the mansion ready to fire upon anything that moves. The soldiers smash open the locked door and hustle their way inside the house, looking for trap doors, or anything that fugitives can hide inside of.

Mark runs out of his room in his pyjamas and is greeted by a soldier with a blank expression on his face. "May I ask what you guys are doing in my house?"

"Fugitives have escaped the ghetto. We suspect you of harbouring one, and we have a warrant signed by the Emperor himself to search your premises, as well as any other properties that you own," The soldier stares at Mark for a brief moment, and then pushes him aside, smashing his gun through a nearby wall and scanning the contents.

Mark suspects the soldiers are looking for traces of lead and leaves the soldier to do his business. He discreetly alerts his live-in servants and maids as to what is happening. They wait downstairs as the soldiers tear apart the house looking for any missing fugitives. The Imperial soldiers are not able to find anyone and leave the house, informing Mark to alert the Empire if he is ever in contact with fugitives.

The sun is bright and beats its sweltering heat down on the prisoners at noon high, adding to the already uncomfortable elements they're in. As Paul and Samantha patrol the ghetto, their foul body odours prickle at their noses. Already feeling dead inside, neither are truly embarrassed. Prisoners inside the ghetto, male and female alike, stroll around topless so the stench akin to stale urine does not make them any more nauseous.

Samantha looks hard at Paul opposed to giving him quick glances since his son Simon escaped the day the rebels liberated as many people as they could from the ghetto. She could see that something was on his mind other than Simon, "Are you feeling okay?"

"Yeah, I think God wanted my sons to both be free from this place so he has sent them his blessing. I just know something good is going to happen today. For some reason, I know. I might sound crazy but..."

Paul stops in mid-sentence. *More false hope; nothing good has happened since the Prime Minister Max Diamond was assassinated. Nothing good has happened at all for anyone who is religious and believes in Christ or other gods*, he thinks to himself.

Samantha quickly turns her head away from Paul, she hates these awkward moments where Paul ends up breaking down, crying and hugging her for comfort. She is annoyed that he is taking the loss of his children as an excuse to get a quick feel on her; she is sick of it, and his behaviour. She is sick of the ghetto, seeing corpses lying around on the streets or slumped against apartment buildings with flies eating away at their bodies. She hates seeing spoiled corpses that are not edible, or good for consumption. She hates knowing that the only edible thing to eat is other humans. She hates it all. Long gone are the days talking to her friends, going to clubs on the weekend, chatting with her friends on Facebook. She screams and takes her Billy bat, smashing it on the ground.

Paul places his hand on her shoulder, "Are you okay?"

"Don't fucking touch me, you dirty old man!" she screams and then bursts into tears crying.

A few prisoners look at Paul but are too weak to come to Samantha's aid; they lower their heads and continue to die within themselves. Paul wonders what he has done wrong and feels rather uncomfortable as he stares at his young friend who is in tears. However, he cares for her and wraps his arm around her shoulder as she quivers and cries while crouching in a foetal position.

The rebuilt gate wall opens up and Samantha stops crying. Soldiers drive into the ghetto, which is an odd sight as they've only come inside at night to kill those who do not obey the curfew. Once they are inside, they drive to the far end of the ghetto where the garden is and set up stakes, tents and barriers. They order the prisoners to clear the immediate area, and the ones who do not comply are shot down.

Samantha and Paul both run over to help enforce the Imperials commands, keeping the other prisoners back, and to help prevent suicide by Imperials.

"All children under the age of twelve are to report here for vaccination shots, and other necessary shots. Your children will not die of illnesses here because of your terrorist beliefs. Bring your children to the garden area to be treated. Parents who violate this order will be executed," a soldier announces on a P.A. system that alerts the entirety of the ghetto.

Several parents bring their children, babies and toddlers as quickly as they can. They are given food and candies which alleviates the parents' initial fears. The Imperial soldiers lead the children to the enclosed tent areas.

"I have to find Miriam. Watch my post okay, Samantha?"

Sunny puts his hand on Paul's chest, "No she will be fine. I need you here, bud. Don't worry about it. It's just a shot; she'll be fine. She is fine with needles, I hope?"

Paul starts to panic, "What if something bad happens?"

"Don't worry she will be fine, hun. Listen, I am sorry about what I said earlier but look, you are right. Something good is actually happening today. Hey, I might not be being helped today, but at least your daughter is getting a vaccine shot. Many of us could use them but at least they are thinking about the children. You know because of you, I am starting to believe in God again. I watch you and see how things just go well for you. There is definitely someone watching over you and your family," Samantha reassures Paul.

For the first time in a long while, he smiles and his faith is restored. He feels God's Holy Spirit is working through him and shining off him onto others in these dark times, this great tribulation. *It will not be long before the Lord Jesus Christ returns to punish these wrong doers*, he thinks to himself. He leans in towards Samantha who holds him tight, and they stare affectionately into one another's eyes. His heart pounds as he is aroused holding her, believing that she likes him despite what she said earlier out of frustration. He feels if he pursues her that she will be a good mother figure for Miriam. What is more, is she is beautiful and reminds him of Victoria. He leans in close and tilts his head to kiss her.

Samantha stares at Sunny. Her posture begs him to say something.

"Get back to work, you guys."

With a sigh of relief, she pats Paul on his arm and then slips into the crowd, pretending to meet anxious mothers who are not quite able to squeeze through the crowds to help their little toddlers get to the front, shaking off the eerie feeling of Paul trying to kiss her. *What was he thinking?* she thinks to herself. He isn't bad looking but he just gives her the creeps and he is not her type.

Inside the tent, the children are restrained by the Imperial soldiers as Emperor Dagoth walks back and forth, staring at the frightened children. He feels nothing but utter contempt for these disgusting religious children. He blanks in and out of anger as he recalls the memory of holding his son Cynric whose burning body was so hot it cooked his own hands and arms, as he held his dying son.

"Look, he's a stupid Devil," one of the children says, laughing and pointing at Emperor Dagoth, and some of the other children giggle at the little girl's humour.

Walking over to the little girl, Emperor Dagoth smiles sadistically at her while running his fingers through the little girl's knotted hair. "My son was about your age and he was once in the same situation you're about to be in," he says in a gleeful, condescending manner.

"Tell me princess, how old are you?"

"Eight."

"Awe, how cute. My son's name was Cynric. What is your name, cutie?"

"What a stupid name for a Devil's son. He has a stupid name you know. I don't care about your stupid son, and I am not your princess. I don't talk to strangers."

"Scissors," Emperor Dagoth says to one of his soldiers.

The soldier complies and brings the Emperor a pair of scissors. Emperor Dagoth wraps the little girl's hair in his hand and lifts her off the ground and she begins to scream.

"Shh," he says, using his power to silence her.

She hypnotically stays under his spell as the Emperor inserts the pair of scissors into her mouth and begins to cut her tongue off. The tongue is hard to cut. She dodges it from side to side as she feels the sharp blade go underneath her tongue and

are shot in their kneecaps by the Imperial soldiers. Eventually the mass amounts of screams lead to a frenzy of panic among the prisoners. To add to their horror, the soldiers take down the tents and curtains and give the parents the horror show.

The parents see exactly why their children are screaming and the reason behind the smoke. The parents' screams match their dying children's screams as they vigorously try and fight their way past the rule enforcers.

Samantha turns around to see what in the hell all the commotion is about, and with her initial glimpse, drops her Billy bat in sheer horror.

"What have we done?" she cries, allowing the screaming parents to push their way past her.

The soldiers do not kill the parents. They aim their guns at the prisoners and shoot out the knees of the parents with incredible precision.

In front of the burning, impaled children is Emperor Dagoth, smiling at the inundated mass of religionists' futile attempts to run and save their children's lives. He occasionally looks behind his shoulder to see their little bodies wriggle as they try to get fresh oxygen, as they burn to death.

Paul turns around, still glowing from the words of Samantha and drops his Billy bat on the ground. His eyes stare wide in horror, "Miriam! Miriam!"

He rushes towards the impaled and burning children on the stakes. He notices that the children's skin is bubbling up and catching on fire. He notices babies who are not old enough to be impaled are chained to stakes while the fire dances, soaring high burning their tiny little bodies. Some of the babies slide down the stake in their chains and become like logs kindling the fires.

Everything is in slow motion for Paul as he rushes towards the burning children screaming in pain. Paul screams out loud as he feels his leg give out and then he falls down on the ground. The Imperials shot his knee. Fragments of bone and cartilage stick out of his filthy trousers. Grimacing in agony, he proceeds to drag himself towards the burning children, ignoring the pain, "Miriam, Miriam! Don't worry. Daddy is coming!"

He is not able to see his beloved Miriam, not that he would be able to recognize her body burned beyond recognition at this point. He looks up and tries to see if he can see his daughter through the fire and smoke which proves difficult. As he continues to drag himself along, the Imperials walk through the crowd of parents who are crawling to find their children and shoot out their elbows to prevent them from getting any closer. Paul screams in agony as he feels bullets break through his elbows.

Many parents who are either too weak or know better than getting shot down, watch their children from a distance burn alive, and either faint at the sight, or helplessly cry.

17

In Tehran, Moscow expresses hope that upcoming meetings of the Russian Empire Atomic Energy Agency (REAEA) with Iran will help deter an upcoming war against the New World Order, provided Moscow resolves the future of Tehran's nuclear program, Ambassador Pavlo Ovsianikov to Russian head of state, reports.

"We are hopeful we can reach a deal over the next few weeks' meetings between REAEA and Iran, and will begin concrete efforts to see this through. Our aim is to strengthen ties with the Islamic Republic and we feel that this is a positive step forward concerning the Iranian nuclear program," Russian Ambassador Pavlo Ovsianikov tells the press at a conference.

Iran and other Islamic nations are under direct threat, by namely the World Order, who is making it adamantly clear that all other nations must hand over their sovereignty and surrender any religious stragglers. No deadline has been set.

Searching for Joshua has been tedious work, living in their state-of-the-art stealth vehicle for weeks as they've staked out every known address of Joshua, and his friend's houses, without turning up any luck thus far, until now.

Just recently Gefallener Klon, and Schatten broke into a hospital facility where Joshua had a G.T.S. chip installed as John Curthy. They were able to find out the doctor who performed the procedure, Corey Lafleur. He had had run-ins with the law in his youth, and gave video recorded statements, shifting the blame on someone named Joshua who was never able to be located for questioning by Toronto Police authorities.

Gefallener Klon shuts the car radio off as he waits for Schatten, very intrigued to learn that Satan has taken his advice and is plotting counter-measures from a potential New World Order strike against Russia.

Non-lethal darts stick into a pizza delivery agent and he shakes and falls to the ground unconscious. Schatten looks at a list of places and who ordered what types of pizzas and administers a sleeping toxin for the pizza that is to be delivered to Corey Lafleur's house. After administering the toxin, Schatten runs into the pizza store, "Hey guys! I think one of your pizza delivery guys fainted near the trunk of his car? I noticed this while I was coming in here for a slice. You guys should check it out."

Frustrated, the store manager asks a few of his employees to check out the issue and then sends another pizza delivery agent to deliver the pizzas to the address that the other driver was supposed to do.

"Hi, what can I get you?"

"Just a peperoni slice, thanks."

Swiping his counterfeit All-In-One Card, Schatten pays for his meal and watches as the employees bring in the unconscious driver, and the other driver speeds off to do the deliveries.

"Thank you for letting me know about our driver. Here is a free pop and dipping sauce on the house."

"I prefer water, and thanks but your gratitude is not required. I was just doing a good deed."

"It's the least I can do. Here is your slice, water and dipping sauce have a good day and once again, thank you. It's nice to see good citizens in these dark times."

"Sure," Schatten says, as he leaves the store and heads back to the black stealth Imperial vehicle parked off the property out of sight. Before entering the car, he throws away the fast food as he is not used to such impure tastes from the outside world.

"It is done."

"Good, it should only take a few moments for the toxin to settle in."

The clones drive to Corey Lafleur's house and turn on their thermal imaging scanners. There is one body lying motionless at a table and another lying on the floor.

"Let's do this," Gefallener says to Schatten.

They pick the lock to the house and Schatten disables the security alarm with his mobile scanner. Gefallener takes a DNA sample of Joshua and runs it through his mobile computer, confirming the body is John Curthy, and then injects more sleeping toxin into his arm, and together the clones drag Joshua outside to their car and they drive off to an abandoned warehouse. They strap him to a metallic table with a sheer device attached to it. Should Joshua make any attempt to use his powers or escape, it will sever his head.

After the sleeping toxins wear off, Joshua realises that he is no longer at Corey's house, and realises that he is in danger. Just before he uses his power to free himself of his restraints, Gefallener advises him against doing so.

"Should you act on what you're thinking, that device will sever your head."

Turning his head to the side Joshua tries to read the thoughts and minds of the two people close to him. They are like him but not quite. One is extremely powerful and is clouding Joshua's ability to read his thoughts. The other appears to be trained to hide his thoughts and empty his mind.

"Who are you?"

"Right to the point. I like that. The name I have given myself is Gefallener Klon, German for Fallen Clone. My clone brother is Schatten, German for 'shadow'. The host body we come from is your son Emperor Dragon Dagoth, also known as Max Diamond."

"My son? The Emperor is not my son."

"Or so you believe. Elizabeth was your wife or partner, correct?"

"How do you know these things? Have Jody or William put you up to this? Is it because they want my business?" Joshua growls out, visibly angry while thinking of a way to escape.

"Stop thinking about escape or I will cut your head off and gain your powers."

Joshua relaxes and reaches out to Jody and William's minds. Jody is extremely angry with him and is searching for him to hand him over to the Emperor. However, Jody is not aware of either of these two men. William has informed Jody about his past but does not know about these clones.

"Are you satisfied?"

"Hmm?"

"Do not play coy with me. You probed your friends thoughts. Are you satisfied that we have not been sent by them?"

"Yes, I am."

"Our former master and host body, your son Emperor Dragon Dagoth has been searching for years for you. We travelled back in time to capture you. Prior to doing so, our grandfather, your father Satan, informed us of your location."

"Ha well, my father is Belial, and no one can travel back in..." Joshua quickly remembers the war against the other Devils and recalls another being with an entourage of soldiers joining the battle shooting both Lucifer and Leviathan in the battle.

"Yes that was us. You killed some of our brother clones, technically your children."

"I'm confused. Are you here to kill me, or are we going to talk. Where is my son now?"

"Your son killed your wife. His mother is technically our mother as well. He is angry that either of you abandoned him at birth to Christians. I don't know why he is searching for you. Our orders were not to kill you."

"You've stated that you're a fallen clone. Does that mean you're no longer working with him?"

"He wants us dead. I have foreseen this. I am confused as to what you have to offer us and why Dragon Dagoth finds you so important. Perhaps we should just hand you over to your father Satan, or we kill you and gain your powers?"

"I don't know why you keep saying Satan is my father, Belial is! And Emperor Dragon Dagoth is not my son. He can't be. My son's name is Ethelwulf and as far as I remember, he was a fierce warrior. I met him over a thousand years ago, more or less in one of the amphitheatres. When he discovered who I was, he was eager, if not desperate to learn everything about me, where we come from, how to use our powers. We shared the same story about people from the future coming to get us. He was shot in the knees by this person. This same person killed his best friend Drake 'the Guttan' and kidnapped his wife and child; my grandson. I was more than willing to help him, but he certainly didn't want to kill me, nor tried to. As far as I heard, he died in the arena."

"Parallel alteration of time," Schatten rhetorically says to himself, chiming into the conversation. "When our former master travelled back in time for his other wife, he must have altered something. I bet he communicated with himself, shot his other self, and took his wife and son. Which means Ethelwulf knows about us somehow and framed us for the death of Max Diamond's family, which is why Dragon Dagoth wants us dead! This is very confusing but logical at the same time."

"What are you two? The fucking Hardy Boys? Get me out of this contraption. I am willing to speak with either of you. I can train either of you. If you want to know about where we come from, I can teach you that as well. I can show you how to use your powers, but other than that, I really have nothing more to offer you. What I would like to know is why Emperor Dagoth is after me?"

After unhooking the IVs, restraints and other gadgets to secure Joshua, he gets off the table without incident and he gazes at the clone.

"You both look good," Joshua says circling both of the clones. "Sorry, do not mind me. The last time I saw you, or my real son was a thousand years ago, like I said."

"We are your real son," Schatten says, a bit angry at the implication that neither of them is real.

"Yes, you're real. That isn't what I meant. The Emperor created you. I created my son, but you're the same which is more than remarkable," Joshua notices that either of the clones feel upset that he is inspecting them as if they're science projects, and sympathises that they have probably been ill-treated their entire lives, and he stops.

"Alright sons, what will you gain by handing me over to Satan or the Emperor? But first explain why you think Satan is my father."

"DNA matches link us to Satan; therefore, Belial lied to you. According to Satan, Belial was turning soft and in an effort to rise against Satan, he manipulated others into turning against Satan and you into believing that you were Belial's son, and that way Satan would not have someone as ruthless as he is for his travel back to Ares."

Joshua relaxes. So many years have passed by, he barely remembers Belial, or if Belial was trying to manipulate him and the others to side with him against Satan, although he thinks the possibility is certainly there with the revelation that he is Satan's son. "No one can argue against DNA evidence. Well alright, let me go and I will help you both out. How does that sound?"

The clones signal that they must speak in private and walk out of earshot from Joshua, keeping an eye on him to make sure that he does not escape. In the meantime, Joshua meditates and feels his surrounding and does his best to foresee the future and what will take place when the brothers return.

The two return to where Joshua rests comfortably silent on the contraption they've built for him. Gefallener hands the device over to Schatten and then approaches Joshua, "We are going to war with Satan and Dragon Dagoth. It will be a quick and hostile takeover; thus, we've agreed to allow you to help us out."

"Thank god. Fuck man, get me out of this thing," Joshua says and then immediately senses danger recalling the looming doom that presides over his future.

"As you wish!" Gefallener says and motions for Schatten to press the button.

Schatten presses the button on the device to behead Joshua and the contraption jerks in a swift and quick motion to behead the once great warrior of Britannia.

Sensing the danger, Joshua uses his power to smash the contraption to pieces and telekinetically thwarts the shear about to sever his head, in the opposite direction, while using his power to thrust Gefallener across the room. Joshua levitates in the air above the table.

"You fucking fools!" Joshua yells, while levitating and choking Schatten from the ground. "Do you take me for some weak and helpless mortal?"

After skidding across the floor, Gefallener scrambles to his feet and pulls out his gun and aims it at Joshua, who pulls Schatten into the line of fire and roars out laughing, and uses his power to disassemble Gefallener's gun.

"Did either of you replicas of a humanoid think you were a match for me? You beheaded a Devil so now you think you have what it takes to defeat me who has seen war, who has trained with the Devils?" Joshua yells at either of the clones.

He thrusts Schatten to the ground and slowly Joshua lowers his feet onto the table and roars again with sardonic laughter and watches as Schatten rises to his feet and takes a sword out of his sheath with one hand and a pulls a gun from his holster in the other hand.

Gefallener watches in horror as Schatten is possessed by Joshua who opens fire, shooting Gefallener once in the chest and another clipping the side of his cheek as he throws himself behind a wall in an adjoining room. Concentrating on his wounds, Gefallener heals them, "Have you fucking gone mad Schatten?"

"I welcomed you scientific test tube babies as my children, and you seek to kill me, you fucking freaks?" Schatten says, as Joshua places the thoughts into Schatten's mind to say. Joshua continues to laugh sardonically while controlling Schatten's words and actions like a puppet on strings.

Using his powers, Gefallener tries to tap into Schatten's mind and possess Schatten as well; yet, Joshua overpowers him, locking him out of Schatten's mind. He gets to his feet and pushes the bullets free from his cheek and chest and his wounds close and heal up.

Testing his power, Gefallener creeps around the corner and focuses his power and maintains control of Schatten's ability to fire the gun at him, and then runs out with his sword drawn to attack Joshua.

Using his power, Joshua summons the shear once part of the contraption to be Gefallener's demise and grabs it from thin air, and together Schatten and Joshua rush to fight Gefallener.

Gefallener looks above at the ceiling and commands the hydroponic lamps above to crash down on Joshua. One after another, they repeatedly fall from the ceiling. This catches Joshua off guard and he releases his hold on Schatten to deflect the lamps falling down from overhead.

"Now!" Gefallener cries to Schatten.

Schatten opens fire as he desperately tries to make himself at least barely conscious and shoots Joshua in the centre of his throat. The bullet penetrates and exits the back of his neck.

Snarling in rage, Joshua telekinetically hurls the gun free of Schatten's grip as Gefallener leaps through the air to bring a death blow to Joshua and sever his head. Joshua suspends Gefallener's movement while in midair and slices Gefallener's mid-section open with the shear in his hand.

Breaking free of Joshua's spell, Gefallener screams in dire pain as he falls to the ground, clutching at his gaping open wound and noticing his innards pulsating. Fortunately the shock blocks his pain and he heals himself before Joshua delivers a death blow of his own. Narrowly escaping impending death, he rolls to his side as Joshua's shear sends sparks off the concrete floor of the warehouse.

Schatten runs to save his clone brother and Joshua parries Schatten's sword with his shear. Metal on metal chimes and echoes loudly throughout the abandoned warehouse. Joshua battles the highly trained assassin with little difficulty, parrying each blow and delivering small slices and gaping cuts to the assassin in return.

Running behind Joshua, Gefallener swings his sword to bring this fight to an end but is met with Joshua's shear. Joshua kicks him in the mid-section and the two exchange a few strikes, sword meeting shear, and shear meeting sword. Joshua uses his power while exchanging blow for blow, and creates a howling wind which sends Schatten toppling backwards. Gefallener sees this and is helpless to do anything about it.

Another being materialises. It is another Joshua who appears before Schatten. As Schatten gets to his knees in order to return to the fight, the new Joshua severs Schatten's head.

"Noooooo!" Gefallener screams aloud.

Joshua thrusts his shear into Gefallener's stomach, and smashes his head into Gefallener's jaw. Gefallener topples over as Joshua yanks the shear free from Gefallener's mid-section and angrily swipes and slices open Gefallener's throat as he falls back, severing his head.

The image of Joshua severing Schatten's head was a horror which threw Gefallener off the course of battle.

"Empathy, such a pathetic weakness, and now your undoing!" Joshua sneers as he looks at the ghost white clone writhing in pain at his feet.

Gefallener smashes his free hand into the ground, causing an earthquake which sends Joshua off his feet as he swings his sword to cut the rest of his head off. The might of the earthquake brings the part of warehouse they're in, down to the ground, collapsing on all three of them.

As the building smashes down upon him, Gefallener uses what little power he has left and shields himself, and senses where Schatten is and tries to protect his brother. Moments later after coming to consciousness, the effects of asphyxiation with the rubble on top of him cause dire pain. Gefallener regains his strength and uses his power to smash through the rubble, turning it into fine dust. He emerges free of the stone, wires and metal beams.

"Schatten!" Gefallener cries out, trying to sense where his brother is.

Staggering on top of the remnants of the warehouse below his feet, trying to keep a steady balance, Gefallener coughs while trying to not inhale the settling dust from the building.

"Schatten!" He tries again.

He senses a faint hint of life; however, the hint of life is too faint to determine whether or not it is Schatten or Joshua's and could be one of Joshua's sorcerous ploys to fox him. The life force grows stronger and as it does, Gefallener recognises it as his brother and runs at a steady pace on top of the rubble to where the life source is. He uses his power to levitate and remove the pillars of stone, casting them aside.

To Gefallener's horror, as he levitates one of the stones, he sees Schatten whose body is crushed and mangled. One of his legs is bent backwards, a shin bone sticking through the back of his leg and blood caked and coagulated on the skin and dusty ground beneath him. A metal pole sticking out of a stone is penetrated deep inside one of his rib cages, and one of his arms is beneath the stone crushed and mangled, dangling blackish and blue with freshly broken bones poking free of his flesh from his arm.

Horrified, Gefallener staggers backwards, not sure if his next efforts to remove more stone would be the death of his brother.

"Did you kill Joshua?"

"I think so? I've only been able to sense you."

"So you're not sure?"

"Who cares about that right now? I need to save you!"

"No find him and kill him. Come back for me when it is done."

"He's dead. I do not sense or feel him at all. I am not leaving your side. If he comes, I will deal with him when he gets here."

Grabbing a stone, Gefallener reaches his foot down and keeps balance as he tries to find his footing to get inside the crater that he made, levitating the debris away. Gefallener feels his way down until he is on balanced, sturdy footing and looks for a safe way to remove the stone from his brother.

He kisses Schatten on his forehead, and then hugs his brother's head tight, "I want you to know that I love you, bro. I'm going to get you out of here safely but just in case anything happens, I want you to know it has been an honour serving with you, and I will always love you."

"Everything will be okay. You've been my inspiration, brother, and you've given me a name, not a number. If it means anything, you're my father figure and not our former master."

With that said, Gefallener uses his power to levitate the stone. His brother grimaces and yells aloud while gripping onto one of the free steel poles next to him. Blood squirts out of some of Schatten's wounds as the stone is lifted free from his body and the poles slide out of his wounds.

"Stay still. I will heal you."

Gefallener touches his brother's leg and his brother's leg bends back into place and Schatten screams as he is being healed. The shin bone is reconnected to its other half of the bone. He moves his hand up to his brother's other wounds and seals the holes. He collapses after his power is depleted from healing his brother.

Schatten rises to his feet and smiles while his brother kneels before him trying to gather his energy and he says, "As I said once before, empathy shall be your undoing!"

"Joshua?!" Gefallener gasps as Joshua thrusts the steel pole in his hand through the mouth of Gefallener smashing in Gefallener's teeth, piercing his tongue and the pole penetrates through his back breaking the through his spine and out of the back of his neck.

As Gefallener convulses at the tail end of the pipe, Joshua rips the pipe out of one side of Gefallener's neck, half severing the head of the clone while still using his brother's appearance and says, "Who else?"

Joshua swings the pipe to behead Gefallener completely and then staggers as Schatten lands adjacent him, gripping his sword tight. Joshua looks up and notices storm clouds gathering and then realises what is taking place. He staggers backward and holds the steel pipe in his hands in a defensive position to fight Schatten.

His voice calls out clairvoyantly to the clones, snarling, *Nooooo* in wretched anger. He tries to turn Schatten into stone, yet fails. As he staggers backwards, his body starts to rise and he fights what is taking place. With one last clairvoyant call, he reaches out to Satan whom he senses is speaking with his son Ethelwulf, and warns his father that he is being betrayed.

As his body levitates from the ground, his head rolls off his shoulders. Lightning penetrates his body and his powers are transferred to Schatten.

Lightning streaks and repeatedly strikes Schatten who let's go of his sword screaming as he feels a surge of power rippling throughout his body until finally the transference depletes and fades away. An immense sense of power like never before courses throughout Schatten's body, and the urge for more power courses throughout his veins. In one last fleeting attempt to possess Schatten, Joshua's fading presence tries to take hold of Schatten and he looks to the ground and levitates his sword into his hand.

Schatten shakes free the spell of Joshua once and for all and looks at his dying brother, blood gurgling out his mouth, and his weak and pathetic brother's arms flailing at either side as he gasps for air. A menacing look creeps over Schatten's face as he hungers for more power. One last slice to his brother's head and he will be twice as powerful. He shakes his head and comes to, and uses his power to heal Gefallener.

"What kept you?" Gefallener asks.

"Nothing, just that strange feeling that overcame me after I killed Joshua."

Gefallener rises to his feet but doubts the integrity of his brother's reply, yet says nothing to question it as he is already aware of the urge to be the most powerful being that Schatten is more than likely feeling. Schatten sheathes his sword and helps his brother to his feet.

Sitting opposite one another, Russian President Taras Ivanov discusses his disposition to the New World Order's Emperor Dragon Dagoth constructing nuclear weapons. He informs the Emperor that this is clearly a violation of Russian law against the Americas.

Emperor Dagoth argues that whatever holds or sanctions the Russians once held over America are no longer in effect as the New World Order is a worldwide government and Russia has no jurisdiction over the New World Order.

The heated discussions carry on into the late afternoon when Taras Ivanov asks the media to step outside to give the Emperor and himself some time to speak privately.

"What is the meaning of this? Why have you sent them away?"

"I felt my son, your father's death."

"Joshua?"

"That is correct."

The Emperor bottles his rage while keeping his thoughts to himself. He reaches out with his powers to tap into what Satan may have sensed.

"There is no need to do that. One of your clones killed him. I felt the transference."

"So you've set this meeting up so that they can kill him for you?"

"They did not act on my accord," Satan says nonchalantly. "If anything, I'd be questioning why they came to me in the first place and secondly why their loyalty in you is shaken enough to act against you by coming to me and then killing your prized obsession."

Satan rises from his chair, "It seems you have a lot more to worry about than our trivial game of politics in front of these petty humans. I have my reasons for not allowing you to build nuclear weapons, so don't do it. Also, I want you to focus on coming to my home world Ares with me. Under my domain you will have more power than you can ever dream possible than here on this petty primitive world. Refuse and I shall coerce your clones to come, and I will kill you; your choice."

"You just informed me that your son is dead and all you can think about is going back home and telling me not build weapons of mass destruction?"

Straightening out his suit, Satan pays Emperor Dagoth no mind and heads to the door. Dragon Dagoth tosses his chair aside and grabs Satan by the shoulder, "Answer me!"

"Okay. Joshua was weak and unworthy of the title 'son'. I don't want you building the weapons because I want you to come to Ares with me. I already said this. Who cares what these monkeys worship?"

"I do! Unlike you I actually care about my wife. Unlike you I actually care about my son, and I will avenge their deaths!"

"Again, who cares? They were weak, and like Joshua, deserved their fates!"

Swinging his fist, Emperor Dagoth tries to strike Satan in his face. Satan grabs Emperor Dagoth's fist in mid swing and crushes his hand. The bones pop and break inside Satan's vice grip hold. Emperor Dagoth growls out and tries to use his power against Satan and telepathically throw him across the room which has no effect. Satan smiling, mirrors what the Emperor of the New World Order did and tosses him into a desk across the room. "Appears you're just as weak. I suggest quitting while you're ahead."

Satan exits the room leaving the Emperor to will his wounds back to normal and decide on what he must do.

In the city of Kermanshah, Sayid rushes to a screaming Reichana who has just learned that her husband, Mohammed who has been missing for several years, was killed for the assassination of President Herbert W. Ballard.

Sayid removes Zamyad from Reichana's arms as she mourns the loss of her fiancée, Mohammed.

"Mohammed is a martyr now Reichana. I know you mourn for him. We all do. Listen I do not care if you are upset that Mohammed is now dead but you know Allah detests a woman who mourns too loud."

"Allah you say? I don't care what Allah likes or dislikes right now! Mohammed swore repeatedly to me that he worked for the Jinn Ibliss Shaitan, who I bet was responsible for his death, so guess what? He wasn't the perfect Muslim either!"

"Watch your tongue Reichana!"

"I will be right back. I am going to lay down, Zamyad."

Feeling lightheaded, Reichana sits down while reminiscing over the last times she ever saw her fiancée alive and how increasingly worried he was becoming. He was not like any man she ever knew and she loved him more than anything in the world, save their child Zamyad who she loves just as much. Now it is confirmed that he is gone for good; however, she will do whatever it takes to avenge his death and kill Dragon Dagoth or have him killed.

In lieu of the unfolding events in the Western World, Reichana decides on a whim that she is going to take the remaining members of her late fiancée's organisation and train them for a possible war against the New World Order Empire. In order to carry out her plan of attack, she considers a contact and acquaintance of hers in the Western World, albeit she has seldom had contact with him since the rise of the New World Order.

Putting her whimsical thoughts into action, she phones her contact, Jody Knoiky and they discuss an appropriate time, date and location to meet. During their initial call, he is reluctant to meet as he is entangled with pressing family issues, until she discloses the news of her late fiancée and informs him who she believes is responsible for Mohammed's death.

"Well I should just get right to business," Jody says while straightening out his posture.

"As you may or may not be aware, as of now the Emperor of the New World Order is executing each and every religionist in the New World Order. I also know he is planning a full scale attack on any country not willing to ban religion and to execute the religionists within their countries as a means of allowing these countries to keep their sovereignty. Furthermore, I am aware that the Emperor used to work with Mohammed before he was betrayed and murdered. I feel we can benefit from one another and join forces when the time is right to take down the Emperor. I hear from my sources that your fiancée left you with a substantial amount of wealth as well as assets, plus weaponry? An organisation I created, 'the Order of the Snake', will be forever grateful and in your debt if you were to join forces with us."

Reichana is horrified to hear what Jody is saying to her! Here is a man she only knows as an acquaintance sitting in her living room who decides to be open and tell her that he is working for the man directly responsible for her fiancée's death? She is not afraid to show Jody a look of utter contempt no matter how fearsome he may appear to be. She turns in her chair and motions for a bodyguard. She grabs her bodyguard's gun from his holster and aims it at Jody.

"Woe lady! After full well knowing that the Emperor ordered the execution of Mohammed, do you think I would be stupid enough to come into your house and inform you that I am working with Dragon Dagoth just to get myself killed? I have come here in good faith. Maybe you should learn to ask questions before you start waving that thing around like that, especially around me. I came here to help you."

"How do I know you're not playing double agent? A spy of his trying to get everyone else involved with my late fiancé not husband? We were supposed to get married but that never happened. Dragon Dagoth, the Shaitan took him from me," Reichana snaps, while keeping her gun steadily aimed at Jody.

Jody slowly reaches for his wallet and pulls out some photographs, handing them over to Reichana. She looks at the photos and then back at Jody.

"That woman was my wife and Dragon Dagoth killed her personally. I would love to kill him and avenge her death but he has kidnapped my family. They are being detained as we speak. He's also done the same with my friend, William's family. So why am I here? It is because I felt that you may want to help out someone that has been in a similar situation. I need your help building an army to bring down the Emperor and the New World Order."

"I understand," Reichana gives the gun back to her bodyguard and then hands the photo of Phuong and Jody cuddling in each other's arms with a decorated heart around the couple, back to him.

She lets out an exacerbated sigh while contemplating her future course of actions. "Our country is under Islamic law and same with our bordering and neighbouring countries. Do you really think it will come to war? You know I was so happy when America lost its power to the New World Order. Now I feel that they are even worse than America."

Growing a bit restless, Jody reaches for his pack of smokes and inserts one in his mouth. Reichana's bodyguard informs him that there is no smoking allowed in the house.

"It is okay. Hush now. Give me one too, Jody. We will smoke together."

Jody lights her cigarette, "Since I've created The Order of the Snake, we've amassed quite a loyal following. All our members have been affected by having their family members shipped off to ghettos. I remember when this all started happening, the government executed every single religionist that had defied the law and went to church. They were burned to death, shot down or killed by chemical agents.

"In a sense, I feel the Emperor is unstoppable. It's like he has planned for all of this for a very long time. He knows who everyone is and where everyone is at all times. Those who refused to get his G.T.S. chips will likely die from starvation or already have, unless they're living off the land. I guess the point I am trying to make is I would seriously like you to consider joining my forces. Gather what men and women you have and go into hiding, far away from your country and anywhere else that is not a part of the New World Order and is under Islamic or Christian law to stay clear of nuclear blasts zones. Gather whatever weapons you can and I will do my best to keep in contact with you. When Dragon Dagoth wages war with your country, I can only hope that you took my advice and travelled far away from here. After his focus is directed elsewhere, I will call you then we can plan for war against The New World Order."

Standing up and straightening her hijab, Reichana extends her hand to Jody and they shake on a deal, "I don't know how else to thank you Jody. After his use and betrayal of my fiancée, I too seek revenge. Thank you for your kind words to me, and sharing what the Emperor intends on doing. I will join the Order of the Snake, but what are your plans after you take down your Emperor? Are you going to assume control?"

Taking a final drag of his cigarette and savouring the flavour of rich tobacco, Jody cracks a smile and hugs Reichana, "Great. I am glad to hear that. Well my ambition is to find and free my family if they are still alive, and then hopefully make things the way they used to be before Emperor Dragon Dagoth. I would probably hand the government to people who are best qualified to lead. I'm not a Politician."

Reichana returns Jody's smile with one of her own as she has a deeper sense of his character. He is not in this for power but to make life better for those who deserve it. She escorts Jody from her mansion, and the pair share small talk along the way.

In the following weeks, the Russian Empire issues several warnings to the New World Order Empire, stating severe repercussions and counter measures will be exercised if any soldier's boots touch any Islamic nation's soil. Also issued are warnings that if the New World Order uses nuclear weapons against the Islamic nations, not only will this be a violation of human rights but they will counter strike civilian populations at the heart of the New World Order.

During the course of political tensions between the world nations, Reichana prepares her people and secures weapons and food shipments for their overseas destinations, which Jody secured through the Parkinson Enterprise Inc. One of the major issues she faces during this time is convincing her people to avoid Government drafts for their national army in preparation for what may be an inevitable war against the New World Order.

"The guards were working on something again last night, after hours in the basement of the kitchen. Sounded like construction. Everything they've done so far is no good; I don't think the construction is going to benefit us," Samantha says, bringing Paul some soup.

Over the past few weeks since Paul was shot and his daughter Miriam murdered, she has been doing her best to bring Paul to health, combatting his fevers and making sure that he doesn't starve to death. He continuously speaks about suicide and she does her best to console Paul in his time of need while trying to coerce him to escape, once he is better, in order to find his sons in the outside world. "I'm still sore, but you have done a great job in taking care of me. I guess I knew I had to be ready for tonight. Is it still going to happen?"

"The others are concerned that you will slow them down when we leave this place tonight."

"I am not anybody's responsibility Sam. I don't need to be babysat while we're escaping. I know I am ready and I need to find my other children to make sure they are okay."

"No, they're not going to babysit you. I am just thinking in terms of your own wellbeing. I don't want to see anything happen to you!"

The last of the soldiers leaves the ghetto and the infamous wall closes behind them. Paul slowly opens his door and smiles at Samantha, "It worked! The piece of metal stopped the door from locking."

"Okay, let's be careful and quiet as we go."

The two run down the stairs and to the corner of their building. It is dark there and hidden from the flood lights which illuminate the ghetto streets. They rush around the corner of the building and wait. No gunshots, and the snipers are looking elsewhere.

They meet with the others who are escaping, at the designated waiting area and then proceed to the hospital area where the soldiers were doing their construction. They walk down a flight of stairs and head to the basement where they have been doing construction of their own. Over the course of a few months, they've dug a tunnel that stretches to the lakeside area of the downtown Toronto.

"Is this thing sturdy?" Marcy asks Dan and Ron, the ones primarily responsible for making the tunnel.

"It should hold unless excessive weight is placed above it. We should be okay. If not, anything is better than 'living' here."

"Alright everyone, this is the moment you've all been waiting for. A word of caution, act as inconspicuously as possible. Once you're in the outside world, find whatever you can
that can be used as a weapon. Most importantly, pray that we're not captured! If this works, we will come back and try to rescue the others or at least get someone to help us rescue the others. Remember only a few people should escape each night for the safety of the others."

Samantha holds Paul's hand and kisses him softly on his cheek.

"That is for good luck," she says while they crouch together and manoeuvre as best as they can down the tunnel. They reach a sewage tunnel and jump into the fecal waste. The stench is unbearable; however, the overwhelming possibility of freedom leaves little concern for waste they're in.

"Wait. Wait," Jenifer says.

"The chips implanted in our skulls. What about them? Won't they catch us the moment we leave the sewers?"

"Jenny, I thought that was only if you reported someone missing they would use those chips to locate people. If no one reports us missing then we should be fine. Anyway how would they know we are missing if there is no one to report us missing?" Shawna replies.

Paul continues holding Samantha's hand, and occasionally squeezes it for comfort. He feels the urge to indulge his feelings for her and occasionally glances her way but feels that vying for her heart would be more appropriate when they're not waist deep in human waste.

"Ah, Jennifer, my son said, 'the government could track the people that don't abide by the new decree and leave for the ghettos' when we were first ordered to go. I guess the same rule applies for those who escape?"

"Yeah, the government knows who all the religious people are. They're going to know that we've escaped and find us. Once they know we have escaped, they will track us down and we will be in trouble."

One of the AWOL prisoners, Tyrone pushes his way past everyone, while ignoring the debate, "You're all a bunch of idiots really. They will kill you if you stay. Look at everyone that had children. I would hate to see what they have in store for us if we stay. I will take my damn chances on the outside world, chip or no damn chip. I will kill any motha fuckin soldier that comes near me. I was the hardest Nigga among my peeps. I was the hardest Nigga on my cell block, the hardest motha fuckin Nigga in the ghetto and I be damned if those fuckas going to cap me cause of a damn chip stuck in my head. I will fuck em up! You watch, I will get back with my boys. Get me a gat and let's blast these motha fuckin bitches!"

"Excuse me sir, but why were you in the ghetto in the first place? You sure don't sound like a true Christian to me?"

"Shut the fuck up, you byatch ass white cracka! I'm just as Christian as any of you peeps. I spent the same amount of time in there as any of you fools, and you wanna say I ain't representin Christ? Who da fuck are you? Ya know what? Fuck you all, bitches. I am out of here. Ya'll can worry about whether or not you gonna get killed up by this motha fucka while I get me some freedom, and a damn fine hood suck from some phat ass bitch."

"Tyrone is right. Who knows what they will do to us in there. We have to get out of here," Samantha says to Paul.

"Wait a minute Samantha, you understood everything that foul-mouthed little boy was saying?"

Letting go of Paul's hand, she starts walking through the sludge, "O Paul give it a rest. We need to get out of here and Tyrone is right. Besides, if anyone wants to stay in the ghetto they can just go right back."

Catching up to Tyrone, Samantha reaches the end of the sewer and stares at the beauty of Lake Ontario. The city lights glisten upon the rippling water and the sight of freedom takes her breath away, "You know Tyrone I never thought I would be so happy to see city lights, Lake Ontario, or be so happy to have shit splashing off me, but I can say I have never been so excited in my life."

Laughing, Tyrone wraps his arm around Samantha's shoulder, "Yeah, I feel ya. I never thought I would be so happy to be standing next to a gal covered in shit, who smells worse than a homeless bum, while we staring at a lake, myself."

Samantha places her hand on Tyrone's chest and giggles just as Paul catches up to them. Holding in his jealousy, he glares at the couple while bottling his rage at Tyrone, figuring it is pointless getting into a fight with him being so close to freedom. He turns back and notices that the others are catching up to them.

"Wow, looks like this is it, everyone. Now that we have our freedom where do we go, and what do we do?"

Tyrone laughs at Danny. "You should have thought about dat before you left the ghetto, fool. Whatchya thinking we gonna do, babysit your white ass? Man, you trippin nigga. Every man and woman for dem selves, ya hear!"

"See ya around Tyrone and take a shower whenever you get somewhere safe. You smell like shit," Samantha giggles, giving Tyrone a final hug.

"Yeah I feel ya, comin from the chikita that smells like roses," Tyrone responds while winking at Samantha and leaving the sewer and then walking along the beach to freedom.

The others hug and kiss each other goodbye before heading their separate ways into the night. All that remain are Samantha and Paul, and they share a few last words with each other, "You know Samantha, I must thank you for taking care of me in our last few days in the ghetto and for being a good friend while we were in there... together. You know I have a house that you could come to if you have no place to go?"

Samantha smiles uncomfortably. She just wants to go home and have absolutely no reminders of the ghetto, including any friends that would bring back the ever so pleasant nostalgic memories of residing in the ghetto. She does think it over. She was living on her own. Her rented suite is most likely gone, and without a means to travel back home to Vancouver to her parents who might have also been shipped to a ghetto, the thought is appealing, "Alright, I'll come with you."

Hearing their doorbell chime, Layla walks over to her door and looks through the peephole and notices two homeless looking people.

"Who is it?" she asks, curious as to why they're at her door.

"Can you open the door, please? It is Paul, Mark's father."

"Give me a few seconds please."

Layla runs over to her husband, "Ron, I think there is a couple of Christians at the door. What should I do?"

Ron rolls his chair away from his computer, perplexed, and thinking that he misheard his wife, "What? How is that even possible?"

"I don't know, Ron but the scary part is they know the landlord. Do you think they escaped? What if they are looking to kill the landlord? We should call the police!"

The doorbell rings again, and is followed by a few loud knocks.

"Mark, are you there? It's dad. Hurry and answer the door before someone sees us."

"Oh my god, Layla. I don't know if it is a good idea to call the police on our landlord. It seems like this person is Mark's father. What if Mark finds out we called the police on his father? He might kick us out."

"I will take my chances with that. He'd have to explain to the rental tribunal that he is kicking us out because we didn't let his terrorist father in a house that is ours. There is no way I am taking any chances speaking to him when we both know what the Imperials do to those who associate with terrorists, Ron."

The doorbell is pressed repeatedly. Ron grabs a baseball bat and answers the door, opening it at chains length. "My wife is calling the police on you guys. You're Christian right?"

"No wait, you don't understand. This is my house. What are you guys doing?!"

"No this is my house... well we're renting it from the Parkinson Enterprise Inc."

"Parkinson Enterprise Incorporated?" Paul repeats curiously.

"Wait a minute, you don't know Mark at all. You're just a filthy Christian looking for his house back. Layla call the police!" Ron shouts, slamming the door shut.

Grabbing Samantha's hand, the pair of fugitives runs away into the night.

"Mark sir, there is someone in the lounge to see you. In fact, it is a couple of people sir. You should come quickly."

"Thanks Ralph," leaving the game room inside the underground palace constructed for his brother Simon, Mark walks into his estate, and into the lounge room. He is taken back by who he sees.

"Stacy? Jody? What are you guys doing here?"

Running over to Mark, Stacy gives him a big hug. She is excited to see him, "Mark, I have some great news. There was an escape in the ghetto a few hours ago. My sources at the news station inform me that they are withholding information that your father was among the few who escaped."

"That is great. My father is alive! Oh Stacy, thank you so much for telling me. I love you so much. Thank you, thank you, thank you. I can't wait to see him again. I need to find him and let him know that I live here."

The couple's mood instantly changes when Mark reveals his enthusiasm to find his father.

Stacy continues, "Word is the Imperials are going to wait for him to contact you. When he does they are going to kill you both."

Tears cloud Mark's vision as he paces back and forth in the lounge and then he explodes, releasing his anger, kicking over furniture while screaming. He smashes whatever is mobile that can break.

Rolling his eyes, Jody looks at his young partner and biggest financer with utter contempt. *At least his father is free from the ghetto and can find a safe place to hide, unlike my family,* he thinks to himself.

"Mark, who knows when the Emperor will no longer require our service. He has my family and may kill them at any given moment. You need to think about the future of everyone who has their families imprisoned in the ghettos. Do you save your father or let him fend for himself and save yourself, as we need your help liberating these people the Emperor's tyranny. We need to take him down. I've had the opportunity to gather sources overseas who are willing to join our cause. Please advise me on your decision."

"What! Are you fucking mad? What would you do if you were in my position?"

"Sir, you have an urgent phone call. It is a collect." Ralph interrupts the meeting as he brings Mark the phone.

Gazing at the ceiling in disbelief that Ralph has the audacity to interrupt the conversation, he yells at his butler, "Ralph, can't you see that I am a little fucking occupied at the moment. Take a fucking message."

Ralph bows his head, and hands Mark the phone, "I insist that you take the call. It is Paul, your father, sir."

Feeling weak and shaky, Mark grabs the phone and contemplates what he is going to say in lieu of the information about the Empire's plans to kill them.

"Sorry, Ralph," Mark says while analysing the situation and gazing hard at Jody. "Dad?"

"Hi, son! I went to our old house but you don't live there anymore. Whoever is living there says they're renting it from the Parkinson Estates Inc. Son, I have some good news. I've escaped! Please listen to me. I have a friend with me. Her name is Samantha. We escaped together and when we went to our old house, the couple said they were going to call the police on us. Tell me where our new place is so that I can come home quickly before the police find and arrest us."

"Yeah dad, sure. Umm yeah, I live at 1 Parkinson Estate in Woodbridge. Is Miriam with you?"

"Come on Mark, this is no time for jokes. You have to tell me where you live, and Mark, just in case I don't make it there alive, I have to tell you over the phone so you will know the truth. No, she didn't make it. They killed her a few weeks ago along with every other child in the ghetto. Your brother Simon escaped a couple of months ago. Is he there with you? Address please. I can't stay here much longer."

Mark clutches the phone tightly as tears stream down either side of his cheeks and drip to the floor. Stacy shakes her head from side to side, sympathising with Mark and his predicament while wiping away tears of her own.

"Miriam is dead, how? Oh my god, why? What could she have done to be killed, dad? I loved her so much. You should have been protecting her!"

A dead silence is periodically broken with Paul's snivelling. He knows his son is right. He should have been watching over both Miriam and Simon instead of playing police officer for a bunch of people he didn't know, "I know Mark. You're right but what can I do about that now? What can I fucking do about that now? I asked you a question. Did Simon make it home?"

Collecting his thoughts, Mark wipes the rest of his tears away from his face, not wanting to embarrass himself any further with company around by looking like a cry baby. He glances over to Jody and Stacy who are making small talk on a nearby couch and he comes to a decision, "Dad, come home. We need to talk, and no Simon never made it. I guess you should have kept a better eye on him as well. At least you're safe, and we have each other. I will prepare a meal for you and your friend. Don't forget 1 Parkinson Estate in Woodbridge." Mark hangs up the phone and thinks about his next course of action.

Paul and Samantha walk past a gate which leads up to a swirling driveway and massive home which is further down the driveway. The couple walks hand and hand towards the mansion until Paul stops and turns, facing Samantha.

"Paul, what is it?"

Leaning in, Paul kisses Samantha, bringing his hand up to cup her face, and running his fingers through her auburn hair. Their tongues swirl and flick off one another's in their passionate moment together. Samantha's heart pounds as he brings her closer, her breasts pressed tight against his chest. After a few minutes of lovingly embracing one another, Paul pulls away and smiles, "I just wanted to thank you for your good luck kiss earlier. I think I love you. I can't wait for you to meet my son. I love him so much. I have missed him so much, and here we are. What a great night. First we get our freedom and now thanks to you, I am reuniting with my son."

Walking hand in hand, they reach the door. Excited, Paul turns the handle, smiling as he looks forward to seeing his beautiful blonde-haired, blue-eyed son, "Hello? Mark? Dad's home!"

The sound of vehicle tyres screeches up the driveway near the couple before they enter the home, and they turn around to see speeding black Imperial vehicles surrounding the driveway where they are. Other soldiers already on the property, flank either side of the couple, cock their guns and order them to remain where they are.

Mark watches from a distance while his father returns his gaze with a bewildered look. Fighting off tears, he watches the soldiers grab and thrust his father to the ground along with his friend.

"You're a terrorist, Paul. You shouldn't have come back here especially with another terrorist. And what were you thinking? You couldn't just come here knowing what the government is like and endanger me. It's bad enough Miriam is dead because of you! I am just glad that Simon is alive and well, you fucked up dad. You fucked up," Mark says.

"Simon is okay?" Paul asks, short of breath and struggling to remain calm as the soldiers apprehend him, wondering if he heard his son right.

Mark acknowledges his father with a slight bow regarding his question.

"You are being tried for these very serious offences: Prison Breach as contrary to the Criminal code one forty four, escape and being at large without lawful excuse. Paul Parkinson, Samantha Hudson, how do you plead?"

"What is this? This is no court of law! We are pinned down by your feet in the middle of nowhere and you are giving us a trial here? Well, if this is a trial, I want a lawyer!"

A soldier then picks Samantha up and hands her over to another soldier, "Samantha Hudson, you have been found guilty under section one forty four Ghetto Prison Breach. Anyone who is under subsection A, by force and or violence breaks out of a Ghetto to set liberty to herself or any other person confined therein and subsection B, with intent to escape forcibly, break out of, or makes any breach there in, an apartment holding cell, afterhours or other place within the Ghetto that is to be confined, is guilty of a capital offence where sentencing is to commence immediately and section one forty five, one subsection A   Escape and being at large without excuse, everyone who, escapes from Imperial custody and B anyone who escapes before the life term set forth in the confines of the Ghetto to which she was sentenced in or out of the New World Order without lawful excuse, the proof lies within her, is guilty of a capital offence in which sentencing is to commence immediately."

After reciting the sentencing, the soldier cocks his assault rifle and opens fire, shooting her multiple times in her skull. Her lifeless body collapses in the other soldier's arms as Paul screams in horror, witnessing the new love of his life murdered at the hands of the Empire. As the soldier takes Samantha's corpse to one of the vehicles, another soldier grabs Paul and repeats the sentence given to Samantha, "You are being tried for these very serious offences: Prison Breach as contrary to the Criminal code one forty four, escape and being at large without lawful excuse. Paul Parkinson; how do you plead?"

Paul keeps his gaze fixed on the ground while his son watches from afar. Not understanding why his very own son called the Imperials on him, he accepts his fate. As soon as this is over and done with, it would only seem like the blink of an eye before Christ resurrects him and he is one with God in the Kingdom of Heaven: "The LORD is my shepherd, I shall not want. He maketh me to lie down in green pastures; he leadeth me beside the still waters; he restoreth my soul. He leadeth me in right paths for his name's sake. Even though I walk through the darkest valley, I fear no evil; for thou art with me; thy rod and thy staff they comfort me. Thou hast prepareth me a table before me in the presence of mine enemies; thou hast anointed my head with oil; my cup runneth over. Surely goodness and mercy shall follow me all the days of my life, and I shall dwell in the house of the LORD my whole life long ... Mark, I love you."

Mark's mouth drops open, overhearing his father's prayer; such dedication, and loyalty even in the midst of his final moments.

"Paul Parkinson, you have been found guilty under section one forty four Ghetto Prison Breach. Anyone who under subsection A by force and or violence breaks out of a Ghetto to set liberty to herself or any other person confined therein and subsection B with intent to escape forcibly breaks out of, or makes any breach there in, an apartment holding cell after hours or other place within the Ghetto that is to be confined, is guilty of a capital offence where sentencing is to commence immediately and section one forty five, one subsection A, Escape and being at large without excuse. Everyone who escapes from Imperial custody and B anyone who escapes before the life term set forth in the confines of the Ghetto to which he was sentenced in or out of the New World Order without lawful excuse, the proof lies within him, is guilty of a capital offence in where sentencing is to commence immediately. And blasphemy against the Emperor Dragon Dagoth under section two ninety six sub section one offence, everyone who quotes any blasphemous material as quoted therein of terrorist books as a means to defame the mighty New World Order Empire or his royal Majesty himself, is guilty of a capital offence in which sentencing is to commence immediately."

"Dad, I love you with all my heart," Mark says and then Mark runs into the confines of another room.

"I love... " Before Paul is able to say his last words, a soldier shoots Paul in the head multiple times.

As Paul's body falls to the ground, and his face slaps against the concrete, blood pours out of his skull and hisses out of his carotid arteries.

Stacy consoles her dear friend Mark while Jody, indifferent to the situation, lights a cigarette and heads for his vehicle.

"I'll wait outside," he says while Stacy holds Mark and does her best to console him and express her sympathies, and then she heads to Jody's car and leaves, promising to return the following day.

"Well, here is your house, Stacy."

"Thanks Jody," she says, staring uncomfortably at her house.

Jody puts his hand on hers, "Don't worry. He won't find out about what we are doing unless you tell him, and well, sometimes sacrifices need to be made."

Stacy shakes her hand free of his and gives a look of utter contempt to Jody, and then fidgets through her purse for her house keys, "Yeah, I know. I guess we are no different than the government then, are we?"

18

"You have both failed me, I gave either of you a simple task: track down Joshua, your friend and bring him before me."

"How'd we fucking fail you? We're doing our best!"

"He's dead."

These are not the words that either William or Jody desire to hear, knowing that the Emperor is keeping their families held hostage. Unlike Jody, William already feels his family is not a bargaining chip and assumes the worst. He has no inclination to fawn over the Emperor for their lives.

"Well, sorry to hear about your loss. Can I take my family home now?"

"My loss is your loss!"

Lights turn on in the adjacent room. Dragon Dagoth stands in the middle of Jody's and William's family members who are strapped to chairs. The rooms are separated by bullet proof glass and thick walls. There is no way for either Jody or William to get to their family members.

The Emperor takes an X-Acto blade and holds William's grandmother by the hair and penetrates her skin with the blade and carves the knife around the outline of her face. Amidst her and William's screams, the Emperor casually smiles before he peels her face off and then presses it against the window.

"I'm going to kill you, you motherfucking fucker. You're dead. You're fucking dead, do you hear me?" William repeats multiple times while banging his fists against the bullet proof window, trying to break the glass and get inside the room.

The Emperor repeats the same course of action with Jody's grandmother. Jody, in turn rushes towards the window cursing and screaming, pleading for the Emperor to stop. The Emperor holds both of the elderly women's faces in the air for both to see and presses the flesh of their faces together, mocking a romantic kiss between the two before tossing them into the waste.

"Silence!" Emperor Dagoth yells amidst their screams, using his power to make their cries go silent.

"I still have use for you yet. Your grandmothers will more than likely die from shock; however, you can save your other family members. There are two of my clones on the loose. They are responsible for Joshua's death, and ultimately, these two beautiful ladies," the Emperor backs away from the window and shows William and Jody who he is referring to, as both of their faceless grandmother's writhe and twitch in their chairs in agony.

Returning to the window he continues, "Bring them to me dead or alive and I will return your families to you," the Emperor summons a couple of his royal soldier guards who bring in two more family members. The soldiers push the family members to their knees and the Emperor takes his sword out of his sheath and severs their heads while both Jody and William are powerless to scream in lieu of the Emperor's powers silencing them.

The Emperor leaves the room and orders that Jody and William be taken from the base back to their respective homes.

"Your Excellency, your flight awaits you."

Emperor Dagoth arrives in the New World Order's province Italy near the Vatican City's border, and sits inside of a VDV Buggy with his sword drawn, "Commence attack on the Holy City. Destroy everything in sight, but leave the Apostolic Palace intact!"

A few tanks drive into the Vatican City followed by one hundred robotic soldiers who set foot on foreign soil, this being the New World Order's first declaration of war. Surprised citizens watch as New World Order forces open fire on several hundred year old buildings and they run to safety.

"Stop the vehicle," Emperor Dagoth snarls. He draws his sword and takes in a deep breath, "Kill them all. Leave no survivors. Save the Pope for me, and do not allow anyone to escape!"

The soldiers open fire, shooting down Vatican City citizens who run for cover. Citizens who run near Emperor Dagoth are cut to pieces by his sword. In the distance, a helicopter proceeds to take off and is struck down by a surface to air missile. There are no further means of escape by air left. Soldiers smash in doors and execute priests, cardinals and other clergymen of the cloth.

The Emperor walks inside of the Apostolic Palace in search of the Pope with a few royal guards near his side, and to his surprise they are greeted by Pope Celestine VI.

"Please we are a neutral country, rich in tradition and heritage. We are a peaceful nation. Please call off your attack!" he pleads.

Turning to his royal guards, Emperor Dagoth issues a few commands, "Program the soldiers to burn all historical text books, scrolls, and anything to do with the Christian Catholic history and faith. Burn their library to the ground."

Turning around to face Pope Celestine VI, Emperor Dagoth's face twists with bitter rage, "You are a country that slaughtered its way to neutrality. You are rich off the wealth you've stolen from other nations that did not believe in your peasant non-existent god, and I recall the type of peace that was ordered by men under the papacy's command when they burned my beloved wife Annex to death, and my ten year old son Cynric, my little boy, my pride and joy, both of which were my life!"

"I beg your forgiveness and please excuse my confusion, but the last time someone was executed was over two hundred years ago, 1826 if I recall correctly. There must be some mistake. The Church has long since seen the errors of its ways."

Without a moment's hesitation, Emperor Dagoth walks up to the timid Pope and grabs him by the back of his white hair and shoves his sword inside of his mouth enough to cut through the Pope's tongue. He tosses his sword on the ground and reaches inside the bloody mouth of the Pope and pulls the remainder of his tongue out and tosses it on the ground.

"I am the Emperor. I did not give you permission to speak did I?!" taking a deep breath and composing himself, Emperor Dagoth continues. "I am well over one thousand years of age. I make no mistake in telling you, I watched with my own eyes the murder of my beloved wife and son."

Emperor Dagoth turns to his royal guards, "Seize him, and bring him to the stake where Catholics burn!"

The Pope is forced to remove his clothing, and Emperor Dagoth approaches the Pope and inserts a foot long dildo inside of the Pope's anus and secures it in place by nailing either side of the end to the inner sides of his buttock cheeks with rusty inch long nails.

"That is to avenge all of the young boys who were violated by priests under the papacy's command over the centuries!" Emperor Dagoth says in a calm state, while the Pope screams in anguish, gagging on his blood due to his missing tongue.

Taking his sword, Emperor Dagoth holds the Pope's genitals, moving aside the Pope's shaft, he cuts off the Pope's testicles one by one, and then severs the shaft. The Pope continues screaming, fading in and out of consciousness.

"Lift him up!" the Emperor commands his soldiers. "Begin filming."

Emperor Dagoth looks into the camera. Filmed by his soldiers, he addresses the provinces of the New World Order, "Citizens of the Empire, and all other people across the globe, for several months The New World Order has captured all terrorists who are known to be 'religious'. They have been shipped into major parts of our cities until this very moment today.

"Today marks the end of religion and a new era in humane and civil society. As of today, it is a capital offence to be a terrorist, otherwise known as a person of religion. All those who are religious are guilty of treason. Today marks the end of the papacy and Pope lineage and end of religion for a more safe and secure society. Thus, we hereby officially declare war on the Vatican City, the Islamic Republic and other countries who do not outlaw religion which will only be referred to from this day forward as terrorism, including The Russian Empire and any of her allies that do not abide by our Empire's decree!"

The Emperor shows the camera a lit torch for a brief moment and then walks over to the Pope, "Do you renounce your belief in terrorism and accept there is no god but me?"

Weak, in pain, and suffering from loss of blood, the Pope makes no effort to even attempt to answer the Emperor who tosses the torch into the kerosene drenched logs which quickly light fire and begin to burn the Pope. He watches as the Pope writhes in agony, shaking violently back and forth on the stake. Using his power to keep the Pope alive, he also makes sure that the Pope's nervous system remains intact as the flames burn his body so that he does not go into neurogenic shock that makes the pain all that much more unbearable. Eventually, the Pope dies at the stake and the flames continue to consume and burn the last Pope's lifeless body.

Enough time had passed since the extermination of the children in the ghettos, took place. Emperor Dagoth turns to his soldiers after they finish filming the execution of the Pope and programs them to torture the religionists in the ghettos, to death.

Across all the provinces of the New World Order, soldiers enter the ghettos with several instruments of torture devices and begin severing, or dismembering the adult prisoners' limbs. Arms, legs, hands, and feet are pulled from the prisoners sockets during the torture.

Prisoners in hospitals have the medicine in their intravenous bags, replaced with bleach; water in the showers is replaced with sulphuric acid. Over the period of a few weeks, all remaining survivors are systematically shot dead.

Some Middle Eastern countries leave the Islamic Republic, become provinces of the New World Order and liberate their provinces from Islam, exterminating those who do not seek asylum in other countries or renounce their faith. These new provinces face open ridicule and humiliation from neighbouring Arab nations.

In the wake of war, the Islamic Republic regimes attack the Arab provinces of the New World Order on crimes of apostasy; however, they are obliterated when Emperor Dagoth orders a nuclear strike on them, crushing their rebellion with ease.

Before the annihilation of the people of Islamic nations, Emperor Dagoth travels to Saudi Arabia's province Mecca and storms Ka'ba the most holy mosque in Islamic tradition. He orders his troops to hose down the mosque with swine excrement and blood before taking to the slaughter of countless Muslims, and the order to strike the nation with nuclear bombs.

Reichana, her troops and followers, watch the nuclear explosions which annihilate their countries as they travel to safety. The first few nights are horrifying as the night turns to day in the wake of the explosions. They grieve and mourn the loss of their fellow countrymen and women as they travel to the continent of North Canada.

During their travel, food runs sparse and word is yet to be brought from Jody or The Order of the Snake. It is a few weeks later when they receive Morse code messages with regards to a safe docking port where they are able to arrive.

"Listen, everyone. Today, we will be docking in the Nova Scotia Province of the New World Order. I must remind you about the deaths of our loved ones and family members. My fiancée used to tell me that he had contact with a Jinn, and that Jinn's name is Dragon Dagoth. He is also the Emperor of the New World Order now. I will find this man and personally execute him so I must thank all of you for helping me in our quest to rid the world of this injustice he has meted out upon those who blaspheme Allah and his ways. In order to carry out our mission, we must act as if we are westerners who are not religious."

Reichana lowers her head and removes her Niqab and hijab which shocks some of the Muslims who are accustomed to seeing modest women, "You all must do the same by removing what is sacred to Allah in order to kill the agents of Shaitan. I seek refuge in Allah from the outcast Shaitan. In the name of Allah, the Most Beneficent, the Most Merciful, Allahu Akbar, Allahu Akbar, Allahu Akbar, praise be to Allah, the Lord of the worlds!"

One by one Reichana's followers reluctantly remove their religious attire in order to pre-emptively avoid suspicion while on foreign soil.

After weeks of preparation, searching through Imperial databanks, finding those on the Empire's most wanted list whose net worth will be beneficial to them, the clones Gefallener Klon and Schatten find and convince young Mark Parkinson and coerce him to donate several warehouses to them. They also strategize a plan of attack to overthrow the Emperor. They drive to a nearby base and approach one of the guards.

"It is time."

"Agreed," Schatten responds to his brother, as they approach a base of operations.

"Allow me entrance."

"Code in."

"Cynric."

The robotic guard recognises Gefallener Klon's voice as Emperor Dagoth's and allows both Schatten and him to enter the base. They walk into the elevator and down into the base. As they enter the underground city, they see various scientists scurrying to and fro, interacting with one another, and hurrying to work in between shifts, breaks or leisure time.

There are a few robotic soldiers standing guard within the underground city. Gefallener leads the way to one of the soldiers, "How many active soldiers are within the base?"

"There are three million on reserve, ten million on standby, and an unaccounted number being created, your Excellency."

"There is a conspiracy against the Empire. Execute the following orders: kill all organic life in this base save myself and my partner beside me. Destroy any and all new robotic soldiers that are being created. You will arrive at the coordinates which we will provide you with. Once there, new orders will be uploaded to you. It is imperative that these orders are carried out within the Local Area Network and not within the entire intranet infrastructure. Commence orders in Time equals 00."

As soon as Gefallener finishes speaking the robotic soldiers execute all of the scientists and otherwise citizens living inside the base, as they upload all pertinent data from the Empire's base of operations to their own and zero the database and hard drives, completely erasing all information after the data transfers are complete, erasing everything that took place within the base.

"May I speak with President Ivanov, please?"

"May I ask who is calling?"

"Gefallener Klon."

"One moment, please hold."

Schatten overlooks the devastation inside the base as Gefallener nods his head while on hold on the phone. Screams from more civilians are snuffed out and the echoing sounds of gun fire fade away in the background.

"Thank you for holding Mr. Klon. Unfortunately President Taras is unavailable at the..."

"Make him available."

"Pardon me, sir?"

"Did I stutter?"

"No sir, you did not; however..."

"If you do not make him available now I will have you killed as I am doing to thousands of people at this given moment. I am sure you can find him. For your wellbeing, I think it is imperative that you do."

"Might I remind you that this call is being recorded for quality assurance and security purposes. Now may I ask if you are openly threatening me?"

"No, not at all." Gefallener says as he reaches out with his power, figuring out who the lady is at the opposite end of the receiver. He uses his powers to cease her breathing.

After a minute of her asphyxiating, her fellow secretaries try to aid her. Gefallener releases his hold on her, "Oops, you were saying something about a threat. I don't threaten. I follow through. Get the President."

After a few short moments the President is on the phone, "You killed my son Joshua. I have no further interest in speaking to either of you test tube freaks of nature."

"Dragon Dagoth mistook us for sycophants who blindly worship, serve and obey him, just as you're doing now. We've acquired a force powerful enough to render either the Russian or New World Order empires inoperable. It would be in your best interests to tell us why we should not obliterate the New World Order and obliterate the Russian Empire instead."

Satan chuckles on the other end of the phone finding it humorous these mediocre beings are actually trying to threaten him, "Young fools, I've obliterated countless worlds, home to trillions of sentient beings. I am unable to tell you how many beings I've killed with my own hands. So, with that said, do you understand how asinine your threats appear to me?"

"You only impress yourself, Satan. You've conveyed to us that you're making the trip back to your home world. We will destroy all the vessels you've built and that Dragon Dagoth has built for space exploration, keeping you here longer than you'd probably desire. We'd obliterate your military targets, and while we do that we will destroy your time machines to prevent you from altering what we're doing."

"You have my attention. What do you want?"

"Gavrilovich, wife of Christopher was detained several years ago. She was wanted on murder charges and extradited back to Russia, for the murder she committed in England. We were having an affair. She is my lover. I want her back."

"You've gone through all of this trouble to get an aging monkey in a skin suit back? Is that all?"

"No, we'd like to accompany you on your trip to Ares, and you will teach us how to effectively harness our power along the way."

"What is stopping me from killing you and your test tube brother when we return?"

"We've killed your son. We've outwitted you and your grandson. Do you really want to dispose of us when we have already proven ourselves to you?"

"That remains to be seen. Launch an attack on the New World Order and kill my grandson Ethelwulf, Dragon Dagoth or whatever silly name he is using nowadays, and you will have my support."

Before Gefallener Klon could refuse, Satan hangs up on the other end of the phone, "He wants us to kill our creator."

"Let's get to work then."

"We can't kill him. I will go as far as destroying his empire but I will not kill our maker!"

Schatten raises his eyebrow, while looking at his brother clone in a condescending manner, "Just because he created us does not mean he is automatically entitled to our respect and loyalty, nor does that mean we don't have the right to kill him to fight for our own survival. You taught me that Gefallener. You taught me the importance of living my life, and I will choose my life over his any day!"

"There is an alternative, Schatten. Without his empire, he poses no threat to us. It doesn't have to be his life. I will not stand for it, for who? Satan?"

"You gravely underestimate our former master. He created an army of robots. He created us, and he created the first world government and took the world over and became the first Emperor. Do you think it is a logical thought that he will passively stop and fade away after we destroy the empire? No he will hunt us down, and he will kill us or die trying. He's had a one-thousand-year-old-plus obsession with finding his father whom I killed; therefore, it is not logical to think that he will merely stop any pursuit of finding us. I will kill him. He must die, and I will gain his power as it should be, and then perhaps we can face and kill Satan."

Gefallener grimaces, and then turns away from his brother and takes a moment's time to think of a response, a response that is not clouded with anger, "I need time to think about this."

"Your compassion for our former master is not required, and it is illogical to have empathy for him. Empathy is a weak trait among humans and we are superior to them. We've had such flaws removed from our being.   The only logical conclusion is to act now."

"No!"

Schatten takes in a deep breath, quickly assesses the situation, and then deems his fellow clone incompetent, logically flawed, and inferior, "Machine, mission critical, red alert! It appears one of the fugitive clones has assumed my identity and is acting as Emperor. Locate and kill him immediately."

"I said no!!!" Gefallener yells out loud, drawing his sword and swinging to attack his brother clone who jumps back quickly out of the way drawing his own sword, heart racing, wild-eyed and angry that his brother Gefallener, who taught him to think for himself is now controlling his very thoughts.

Gunshots suddenly cease as Muslims in Ka'ba evade the bloodshed. Some hold hands and pray to Allah to save them from the injustice which has befallen them.

Sensing grave danger, Emperor Dagoth tries to pinpoint the immediate source of the threat using his powers. Gunfire erupts once again. His royal guards are shot down and destroyed, and bullets fly in and out of the Emperor's body, killing him, and ending his tyrannical reign of terror in Mecca.

The soldiers leave the body behind and evacuate Saudi Arabia, while the Muslims celebrate the death of the Emperor by dragging his lifeless body throughout the city streets, whacking his face with their shoes, spitting on his corpse, and celebrating the day by praising Allah.

Jody leans in on Stacy's desk and looks around to make sure no one is eavesdropping. He is upset Stacy is not trusting his judgment, and is taking this moment to clarify how he feels, "No I don't have any emotions left. My feelings for people changed when my wife was brutally murdered and my family was taken hostage. I really don't give a fuck about anyone besides my family, and all I am doing is trying to ensure their safety. I would only hope that you can see that I want what is best for me first, and our organisation. I have a chance at getting my family back and the Emperor has promised me that he could bring my dead wife back to life. There is something about Dragon Dagoth. He is different. I know he has the power to bring her back, so I will do whatever it takes for me to get my family back and have my wife brought back to life, even if it means betraying a couple of people here and there. It will be for the greater good of society!"

"Sometimes Jody, I don't know whose side you're on!"

Stacy says, without caring who overhears them.

"I am on my side, and I only work for me. People like you work for me, and if you don't like the way I work then don't." Jody finishes signing papers and while speaking, employees run past Stacy's cubicle cheering out loud and running down the hall.

"Stacy hun, you have to come here and see this!" one of the employees says, vying for her attention.

"In a minute; I am with a client."

"The Emperor was assassinated in Saudi Arabia. He was killing Muslims at Mecca and while they were praying to their god Allah, all of a sudden he gave them a miracle and the Emperor's soldiers stopped killing them and shot the Emperor dead! Life is going to be so much better now."

Stacy jumps from her chair and embraces Jody with a warm hug, "I wish I could say we did it Jody, but it's all the same. Looks like the Muslims saved us."

Deflated, Jody half-heartedly smiles, lowering his head. He is happy to know that he will get his family back; yet, he is upset that he will never see his wife again. That is, if the Emperor was telling the truth when he said he could bring her back to life.

"It appears either of us is no different than our host body. It's a shame you're an inferior product, Number Sixteen," Schatten gloats.

Gefallener charges Schatten. Years of training and daily experience show in either of the combats, as their swords sing and chime off each other's swords. They dance with each other, shifting their legs, moving side to side, bobbing and weaving to avoid death's embrace.

Within the first few seconds, Gefallener makes a quick slice, severing tendons above Schatten's forearm and between his bicep. Schatten drops his numb arm, parrying a few more blows in the time that it takes his arm to regenerate and heal completely. Stumbling backwards, Schatten summons his new found power and throws dust Gefallener's way, catching his eyes.

Before Gefallener is able to wipe the dust from his eyes, Schatten leaps to his feet and swipes his sword, while embracing the rage and hatred which courses throughout his veins. The sword punctures and slices its way through Gefallener's jaw. The highly skilled combatant drops his sword and clings onto his face. His knees buckle, and he drops to the floor, screaming in agony.

Taking quick advantage of the situation, Schatten thrusts his sword through Gefallener's left collar bone and pierces his heart, "The last memory you will have before dying shall be of you fighting to save someone you hate. Pathetic. Such a human characteristic. You are such a flawed clone!"

In the time it takes Schatten to pull the sword from Gefallener's body, Gefallener grabs his side arm weapon and aims underneath Schatten's jaw and pulls the trigger.

Tossing the gun to the side, electricity from inside the warehouse snaps and crackles and shocks Gefallener. All the knowledge from Schatten and Joshua, flow into him as he experiences the transference of power. Once the transference is complete, he falls to the ground.

A few moments later, he comes to and feels his new found strength and power, course through his veins, "I am different, brother. I believe in our creator, and one day he will accept me. It will take time and patience, but there is no need to kill him."

Bending over slightly, Gefallener closes Schatten's eyes and then calls the President of Russia, "The Emperor is dead."

"You're clever manipulating your brother clone, killing him at the same time the Emperor is shot down in Saudi Arabia so that I can feel the transference take place. I am rather impressed. I have a confession though; I sensed your weaknesses when you were here. While I commend you for trying to rise up against me, you needed to be taught a lesson. So I allowed you to believe you had control over me. I gave you some options and I am assuming you told Schatten about the option to kill the Emperor. He bit the bait, you guys fought, and you're the victor."

An uncontrollable dark power and rage fills Gefallener. Electronics around him begin to spark and smoke. He releases his rage, breaking and exploding many of the devices around him, feeding his temper, "I am going to destroy ... "

"You're not going to do anything to me, or your sweetheart 'Gav', I will cut limb from limb. What you're going to do is find and kill Emperor Dagoth, and if you even so much as think for a brief second about rising up against me, I will start cutting your sweetheart to pieces."

There are several people speaking Arabic in what appears to be another room. Dragon Dagoth bumps his head as he tries to sit up. Feeling the cold temperature around him, and the weird object on his toe, he is perfectly clear on where his surroundings are. *A morgue, brilliant,* he thinks to himself.

KSA agents open his drawer so that reporters can take photos of his body. Smiling, Dragon Dagoth sits upright, "Go to sleep people."

The KSA agents, reporters and morticians fall on the ground in deep sleep. He strips one of the reporters of his clothes and wears them as his own, and leaves the mortuary undetected by any of the other authorities or anyone else.

After driving to an airport he uses his power to force a pilot to fly him to Fiumicino airport so that he can return to the ruins of the Vatican City, the focal point of interest for the new capital city of the New World Order.

"Unbelievable! I can't believe the body of the Emperor cannot be found. I bet the terrorists faked the whole thing just to make it seem as if they are the most powerful," Stacey says, twirling her straw in the contents of her coffee cup.

William nods, "I know. Listen Stacy, Jody found out the Emperor is alive and has decided to help him. I hate the Emperor. I want him dead, and I am thinking of starting my own organisation to kill Dragon Dagoth. All Jody cares about is himself. All he wants is his family back. I'm not stupid enough to believe they're still alive. We need to start worrying about ourselves. We need to create an organisation dedicated to ridding the world of the Emperor, and saving its citizens from the empire. Are you in?"

"William, in all fairness Jody is going to be worth a few billion, and yes, he will get that from betraying one of us. But do you think for one moment he is just going to let us get away with betraying him? And to do what? What are we going to do? Start recruiting people, already in his underground organisation and lead them with no money?"

Jody gathers the remaining leaders of his underground organisation to one of Mark's many locations, for a clandestine meeting in lieu of the Marshal Law.

"You people are all that remains of the loyal followers I have in this immediate region. As you are all aware, William and I have had a falling out. He has irresponsibly created a rogue squadron called 'The Christians' to solely launch attacks on the Empire and to set himself up as the next Emperor. Some say this is good. Others feel this will bring more attention on us.

"Because of his irresponsible actions, our secondary mission is to take out William and the rogue soldiers at all costs, but not at the expense of carrying out our primary mission of taking down the Emperor. Any questions?"

"I have one!" Reichana says, as she approaches Jody. "You and I have had plenty of conversations since our arrival here, but I cannot help but see your lack of motivation in avenging our friends' and family members' deaths. Perhaps William is more motivated than you. Face it, your most loyal friends have turned on you, William and others, even your own General Gregory. With him gone, this gives his organisation a tactical advantage. So my question is when are we going
to attack the Emperor? If you don't give us a time soon, I will lead my people to fight against the Emperor myself, especially after what he did at Mecca!"

Jody exhales. Although he's visibly angry with Reichana, he knows she is right, "Well Reichana, that is why I have asked all of you here now. Right now at this very minute we are setting up a strike on parliament. Believe it or not, it is not very well guarded. Infiltration will be easy."

One of Jody's friends Tyrone, a former prisoner in one of the ghettos, recruits friends of his to serve Jody, and the Order of the Snake. His friends have been in plenty of gang wars, and are a beneficial asset to the organisation.

Unfortunately due to the G.T.S. chip implanted in Tyrone's skull, he is unable to come out of hiding and shares residence with Simon Parkinson in a secret underground house so that he will not be caught by the government. A warrior at heart, he is upset that he cannot fight alongside his friends.

Stealthily, the members of the Order of the Snake take positions around the East, West and Centre blocks on Parliament Hill. Many Order of the Snake soldiers are armed with handguns, shotguns, some with grenades, and a with C4 explosives to blow apart the buildings after they complete their mission.

Giving the signal, the Order of the Snake soldiers begin the assault on Parliament Hill, taking up stealth positions around the buildings, avoiding camera detection as well as posting soldiers who stand guard at the building blocks.

"Squad leader of delta team in position, standing by awaiting orders," Xavier chimes in on his communication device.

"Squad leader of Alpha team in position, standing by awaiting orders," Reichana chimes in on her communication device.

"Commanding Leader, Jody, in position at the Eastern Block. Delta team breach frag and clear Centre block building. Go, go, go!" Jody chimes into his communication device.

Delta team attacks an unsuspecting couple of soldiers standing guard, demanding that they surrender, and drop their weapons. The soldiers open fire, killing each of the Delta squad members.

"Delta squad? Anyone? Can anyone hear me? Shit!"

"Commander we are under enemy gunfire. We can't hold off. We're pulling back!" Xavier shouts as he exchanges gunfire with the hostiles.

Jody orders Alpha squad to flank and attack the soldiers pinning Xavier down. Alpha squad follows through with the orders. The NWO soldiers stand their ground, open fire and slaughter the first wave of soldiers sent out. Hand grenades are thrown towards the Imperial soldiers, blowing chunks of them apart.

"Jody, you're not going to fucking believe this. They are some sort of fucking robots!" Xavier shouts in disbelief as he looks at what should have been remains of dead bodies. Instead they are a mixture of cloned flesh, blood and sophisticated wiring and other mechanical and computerised devices.

"Alright, I hear you. Proceed to the Centre block building. Continue as ordered, breach frag and clear the entrance. I am sending more troops in to cover you guys while you set the C4 charges in place. If you have to abandon the retrieval of the hard drives make sure you blow the place to hell if more of those robots come after you!"

"Understood, Commanding leader sir."

The soldiers for the Order of the Snake begin to run into the centre building, tossing more grenades at the opposing soldiers and destroying them. The New World Order soldiers in sync, leave the East and West Block buildings and proceed to the breached Centre Block building, activating proximity mines. Jody and the others leave for them, and they blow apart. The Imperial soldiers that are not destroyed rush towards the Centre Block building.

They open fire, killing some of the Order of the Snake infantry men on the lawn. The Imperials circle the Centre Block building, and scan the area for proximity mines, only to be flanked by more Order of the Snake soldiers who fire Rocket Propelled Grenades at the Imperials, sending flaming debris across the lawn.

The remaining soldiers of Delta squad stand guard at the front of the Centre Block building in case more Imperials arrive at Parliament Hill, while the remaining Alpha and Commanding squad soldiers take positions inside of the East and West blocks and set the C4 inside all of the buildings. The teams rush out of the buildings, after locating the server rooms and scavenging all pertinent hard drives from the government.

"Okay, everyone back inside the transport trucks before the government locks on to our G.T.S. chips. Move it! Move it," Jody shouts.

His soldiers comply with his orders, running back to the lead encased trailers of the transport trucks before the government locks in on their signals.

As they drive away, Jody takes the honour of detonating the C4 explosives, destroying The New World Order's Parliament Hill. As they drive down the highway, the New World Orders air force locks onto their position. Satellite trajectory captures the images of the transport trucks leaving Parliament Hill and mobile ground vehicles are en route to stop the fleeing assailants.

A fighter jet locks on to a couple of transport truck vehicles, firing laser guided missiles at one of the trucks. The vehicle is blown to smithereens, and the burning remains smash into the truck beside it, killing everyone in both vehicles instantly.

"Holy shit! What the fuck was that?!" Jody asks, looking out his window behind him.

A fighter jet soars past them above, and does an aerial loop ahead to trace back and shoot down the rest of his transport vehicles, "Shit Sheldon, you have to get off the highway and find an underground parking lot. We need to ditch these trucks before they blow us up!"

The fighter jet approaches the remaining three transport trucks driving down the highway and fires more laser guided missiles. One of the trucks is blown to fiery pieces, while sending several cars airborne to their fiery graves.

"Stop the fucking truck, Sheldon. We are not going to make it. Everyone hijack whatever you can and find another vehicle. When you have reached a safe point, report back at the base. Good luck. I am cutting communications over and out."

As soon as the transport trucks stop, everyone jumps out and at gun point, hijacks drivers who have not been affected by the missiles. The fighter jet disengages and calls in ground troops to take out the remaining terrorist hostiles.

Jody remains intent on listening to one of his most trustworthy executives, and members of the Order of the Snake, Kobie McKlarkshwartz as he gives a presentation based on what information he's retrieved from the many yottabytes of information from the hard drives.

Jody swivels his pen back and forth in his fingers. After Kobie finishes briefing everyone with his ideas and proposals, he gives his input.

"Well the majority of what we have retrieved is no good to us, tax information, health care, etc. This is not going to help us bring down the government. However, they have plenty of detailed files on their soldiers. We need to find ways of taking them out when we launch our next attacks. We can't afford another costly loss of good members, especially if they're fighting for our freedom. I want our casualties to a minimum. Does anyone have any ideas?"

"I do, but it is a theory," Kobie pipes up, shifting everyone's focus on to him.

"If I can bypass the encryptions on the hard drives, and find clearance codes which I can guarantee, are stored on the drives. I can bypass their firewalls, hack their robots, and the best part is perhaps upload code to the soldiers programming them, to be soldiers for the Order of the Snake. After which I can easily locate the Emperor but there is one problem, his royal guards are not on the servers, nor are they on any of the hard drives. They're ghosts."

Jody kind of laughs. All he is concerned with is, will they have a tactical advantage on taking down the empire, "Hey dude, that was not in English. Can you dummy that down a bit for me and for everyone else who is not tech savvy?"

"Well yeah, in theory I think we can use the soldiers against the Empire and we may actually be able to overthrow the Emperor."

The majority of everyone seems to be delighted with the news; however, Jody puts a damper on that very quickly, "In all fairness, Kobie did state that this is his theory. He hasn't tried it and he does not know for a fact if this will work. I still want other ideas. We are not going to rest all hopes on one idea."

Anne raises her hand, asking permission to speak, but quickly realises this is not her college classroom and lowering her hand, proceeds to speak, "Why don't we use these hard drives to dig up some dirt on Dragon Dagoth as well? I am sure that is not his real name, and I am sure we can find a lot of information on him to exploit to media sources; this will be beneficial to our cause. Face it, now that William has left and recruited a lot more of us, we could use all the help we can get."

Jody smiles, "Anne, I love that idea. Kobie, get on that as well take down notes. I want to know everything about Dragon Dagoth. Also see if you can find other people that can help you with your computer work. One last thing, I want to know where my family is, and if they're still alive and if I can rescue them safely."

As acting manager, Kobie gives instructions to one of his employees, Jamal, to decrypt as many hard drives as he can before he is able to head back to the boardroom with Jody, and a few of the other leading members of the Order of the Snake.

An explosion rocks the office building, knocking people out of their chairs, and some off their feet. Another explosion is heard outside the building at another one of Mark Parkinson's buildings down the street.

"Is the government attacking us?" Anne asks, as she gets to her feet and walks over to a window to assess the situation. She does not see any damage from the boardroom window. She walks over to another window to see what damage may have been caused below.

"O my God! Look someone blew up the entire side of the building downstairs," Anne points out to the others.

Kobie standing next to Anne, observes bodies littered across the street, limbs ripped off the victims' bodies, torsos torn apart from the devastating effects of the explosion.

"Oh my God, Anne. Wasn't that Jamal?" Kobie asks pointing to a ripped apart body wearing the same clothing Jamal was.

Anne's knees buckle, and she faints.

"Kobie looks like you're in charge of everything in the computer department but I have to take off for now. I cannot allow the Imperial soldiers to find me here, nor can I be taken in for questioning at the moment. Decrypt those hard drives, take care, and that goes for all of you. Leave this building if there is another wave of attacks."

Kobie picks Anne up and follows suit with her resting on his back and shoulder. He walks down the stairs and into the street where citizens are gathering to see what has happened to one of the many businesses owned by Mark Parkinson. Kobie rushes Anne to one of the paramedics who does not appear to be as busy as some of the other paramedics who are searching for missing limbs of the blast victims.

"Were you guys inside the building when this happened?" the Paramedic asks Kobie, as he helps Anne to the ambulance.

"Yeah guy, it was bananas. I was in the middle of a board meeting then I am nearly off my feet. It felt like the whole building shook! Do you know what happened?"

The paramedic waves Kobie inside the ambulance and shuts the door. He places an oxygen mask on Anne while monitoring her pulse, "Word is the leader of the Order of the Snake was inside your office building. Some guy named Jody Knoiky of a new rival underground movement. The Christians launched this attack. Apparently William, the leader of the Christians is trying to kill Jody and overthrow the empire. If you ask me, this is all bullshit. I personally think the government has been doing a good job at what they've been doing. I don't understand why all these rivals are committing these terrorist crimes. Just look out at all this devastation. I had to run around picking up body parts."

"Is she okay?" Kobie asks, dismissing the paramedic's thoughts.

"What did you say?!" The paramedic snaps.

"Anne? Is she okay?" Kobie points to Anne as she is coming to.

"Oh sorry. Yeah, she should be fine. Her pulse is normalising. Certain traumatic events can cause people to faint. A loss of blood from the brain is all that causes these things to happen."

Kobie nods as the paramedic unstraps the equipment from Anne, and they leave together.

"I think you are going to have to convince your brother to sign over the money to you in case of his death or murder. I was in one of his establishments when it was attacked."

Simon laughs at Jody. While Tyrone eavesdrops in on the conversation the couple is having, he has a slight idea Jody is up to no good.

"Listen Simon, your brother is no longer who he claims to be. He changed once everyone was sent to the ghetto. He will kill anyone who gets in his way. I believe he wants out of the Order of the Snake, but he is a primary target. He's helped you escape from the ghetto. Sign his assets over to me so I can help protect you guys. You owe your brother that. He saved your life."

"Are saying that my brother is a fucking coward? My brother would not betray the Order of the Snake. He hates the Empire and the Emperor just as much as everyone else, so fuck you and get the fuck out of my house!"

Jody raises his hands in the air in a defeatist attitude. "Okay I am leaving. Before I go, I will give you this recording device. I was at your brother's house, the night your father 'died'. I don't know what story your brother gave you but this may make things a bit clearer for you."

"What? What do you mean my dad is dead? He is in the ghetto!"

"Let me guess, your brother kept this from you as well?"

Simon reaches for the recorder and shuts the door behind Jody.

Rogue soldiers from the Order of the Snake, now members of The Christians, approach Mark Parkinson's estate. They circle the premises armed with handguns and other weapons, then breach the security walls and the house. Eventually, they find and take Mark hostage. However, the Imperials have already anticipated this move and watch the situation unfold with their drones above the Parkinson estate.

They wait for all the rogue soldiers to move into key positions and then initiate their ambush. The machines storm the premises, preventing The Christians escaping from the Parkinson residence. They are forced to surrender.

"Fuck you! I am not telling you shit. Just take me to jail you faggot!" Alex hastily responds to a soldier in the midst of being interrogated.

The soldier scans Alex. Judging by his increasing heart rate, and flux of skin temperatures, the soldier registers that Alex is frightened and searches his programming to act accordingly. The soldier grabs Alex by his arm and holds him aloft in the air.

"You can't do this. Let go of me, you steroid freak!"

The soldier continues to scan Alex. His body continues to give signs of being frightened, and the soldier increases the pressure of his grip on Alex's arm with his mechanical fingers, ten pounds of pressure every five seconds.

Alex screams. The pain is unbearable. He punches the soldier with his free hand; however, the soldier does not so much as flinch or give any leeway to Alex. The soldier continues putting pressure on Alex's arm until it snaps, and Alex hears a loud crunch.

The soldier lets go and Alex falls to the ground. Alex continues to scream out loud in agonising pain. The bone broke and splintered from the brute strength of the soldier.

The pain is so unbearable that he passes in and out of unconsciousness, barely able to scream. No sound escape his mouth as he holds on to his arm, wondering why no one is stopping this. The soldier presses his foot on top of Alex's leg on top of the fibula bone, and pushes downward, with ten pounds of pressure every five seconds second, "Tell me where your secret base is. I can relieve the pain. All you have to do is tell me where the base is."

Alex tries to squirm away, lift the soldier's foot up with his free hand, and then vigorously punch the soldier in the leg. He is not able to escape the increasing pressure of the soldier's foot on his leg. Another loud snap and pop ring through Alex's ears, as his fibula bone caves into the immense pressure of the soldier's foot on his leg. The soldier puts his foot on Alex's tibia bone now.

Other squad members debate in their minds if they would be able to endure the pain that Alex is going through, when and if the time comes for them to be put in the same situation. Some of the squad mates conceal their tears as they either watch or hear Alex's pain. Some flinch, trying to block the sounds of Alex's bones snapping as the soldier tries to find out where their base of operations are.

The soldier puts his foot on Alex's other femur bone and crushes it. Alex goes into shock. He vomits a few times and passes in and out of consciousness. The femur bone snaps loudly. The soldier, incapable of feeling pity or remorse for what Alex is going through carries on with its programming. Its only duty is to find out where the enemy bases are. Torture is the primary motivating factor which has worked for centuries to get humans to talk. Alex will talk or die. If he doesn't talk, there are others who might.

The soldiers change their programing, realising Alex is not divulging any information. They scan the faces of the apprehended individuals who are kneeling on the ground, and find that one of the rebels is a convicted felon, and she is also Alex's common law partner.

The soldier grabs Heidi by the back of her neck and drags her over to Alex, "My database informs me that you two are in a common law relationship. If you do not care about yourself, then perhaps you care about what happens to Heidi, your common law wife."

"Okay, okay. Please don't let anything happen to her. I will tell you what you need to know."

The soldier scans Alex's eyes, and is able to determine that he is telling the truth, and will convey where the base of operations are. Despair is an effective programing, essential psychological tool which is beneficial for extracting information from sentient beings, "Good, tell me now, or I will snap her neck."

"Okay. Please don't hurt her, I beg of you. It's 1824 Austin street at the corner of Maine. There, I have told you. Please don't hurt her."

The soldier scans Alex's eyes and body language as he informs him where the base is and determines that he is lying about something. It searches its database locating the address, discovering that this is one of Mark Parkinson's corporate assets.

The soldier grabbed Heidi's bicep and forearm and with several pounds of pressure breaks her arm in half, and then rips her forearm free of her bicep, and then tosses her arm to Alex, who is completely horrified by what he has witnessed. Blood hisses from Heidi's wound, and due to the lack of blood, she passes out.

"I gave you a fucking address!"

"Affirmative, however, you gave me the wrong address. Now your girlfriend has suffered injuries which may be fatal as a direct result of your lies. What is the address?"

The soldier wraps his hands around her neck and gives Alex and menacing look, while blood continues to pour out of her arm socket, "Where is your base? This time I will kill her!"

"William is at 3286 Islington road. That is where he will be awaiting our call."

After scanning Alex's eyes, he registers that this information is the truth.

The rest of the apprehended individuals are relieved that Heidi and Alex will no longer be tortured. Some are a little upset that their base of operations was given up to the Imperials but no one questioned why it was done, and they dread what it may be like if they were in their situation.

The soldier snaps Heidi's neck and throws her limp body on the ground.

"What the fuck is wrong with you! Why the fuck did you kill her? I gave you the fucking base you asked for! You said you wouldn't kill her if I told you!"

The soldier then reminds Alex what he said, "I clearly stated, 'Where is your base? This time I will kill her!' Why did you believe that I wasn't going to kill her?" the soldier asks Alex matter-of-factly.

The detainees are given a trial and sentenced to two years less a day for attempted break and enter on the Parkinson estate, and then shipped off to a secret location where they will be miners for one of the Empire's secret space programs on a distant planet.

With a programmed plan of attack in motion, Imperial soldiers surround the address provided by Alex and breach all exit and entrance points. They scan the area and break down each of the doors inside of the base. One of the soldiers smashes a door in, and scans the room. The soldier notices high end C4 explosives, and a few split seconds after breaching the room the C4 explosive blow apart the entire base.

The remaining soldiers are flanked by The Christian organisation. They fire rocket propelled grenades, destroying the trucks the Imperial soldiers are in. The rest of the Imperial soldiers open fire, shooting down as many Christian rebel forces they can scan in the immediate area.

Christian forces hiding behind buildings join the fight, opening fire at the Imperial soldiers which has no effect against their metallic skeletal bodies surrounded by cloned skin and blood. The Imperial soldiers take advantage of the situation and start running towards the rebel forces who are hiding behind obstacles while trying to shoot them.

Black Hawk helicopters arrive and lock onto the rebel forces, firing multiple missiles at the Christian forces, while other helicopters chase the fleeing forces, while zeroing in on the criminals, shooting them down as they flee for safety.

William's new recruit General Gregory Reynolds already anticipates the imperials tactical moves which is why they set up a base at another location in case one of the secondary missions was a failure and their location was given up.

They watch the ordeal unfold on networked digital camera feeds that they set up in the surrounding industrial area. They helplessly watch from their remote location as their members get shot down at the battle scene.

"Greg, we got them all killed. These were men and women with families and, oh my..." William sits down and lights a cigarette to calm his nerves.

"This is war, son. It may have been wrong to attack Jody as you requested. I feel your anger got in the way of your primary goal; establishing yourself as Emperor."

"Gregory you can see how skilled the Imperial soldiers are. They're killing everyone there. I am sure the ones who are escaping will be tracked down by their G.T.S. chips and killed off as well. Now this only solidifies me as a terrorist in the eyes of the public and government and now I will have to stay at this lead encased base while we go to war with two enemies. We have no allies. We're fucked."

"Well William, I have heard Reichana is going to split from the Order of the Snake soon. Reichana and her followers do not have the chips, which gives them and us (if we're able to convince her to side with us), a tactical advantage over the empire, as they can do stealth attacks without being tracked by the Empire."

The news alleviates how William feels, "We can't afford waiting for that decision. Have someone reach out to her and persuade her to join our organization."

19

Hallways and corridors are inundated with smoke and fire, and they're also littered with dead bodies in the Gulag Archipelago prison in Russia. Gunfire also echoes in the hallways as Gefallener Klon and a slew of newly programmed robotic soldiers search the labour camp prison for Gavrilovich, shooting down guards who cross their path.

What keeps police and the Russian army from acting on the prison attack is multiple strategic attacks on military and some civilian targets. Key points are television and radio stations, cable and internet service providers. Electric magnetic pulses are detonated around the local area of the Gulag Archipelago, making the attack on the labour camp prison easier than previously anticipated.

A soldier kicks in one of the reinforced metallic doors to the control room and is shot as it enters the room. The soldier exchanges gunfire with the guards and kills all but one on Gefallener Klon's orders. Clad in black operation clothing and war paint, Gefallener Klon enters the control room and opens fire, shooting out the guard's kneecaps.

Speaking in Russian, Gefallener proceeds to instruct the prison to open the cells in the block where Gavrilovich is. Responding in Russian, the guard Zakhar refuses, "I cannot open the block because she is not there, and she is of special interest to the President. I would rather be killed than tell you where she is."

"She is in solitary confinement, block 8 level R. Release her and bring her to me so that we can get ready for extraction."

"How you know such things?"

"I read your weak feeble mind, but as far as the president is concerned, I will be sure to tell him you told me."

The ex-imperial soldiers escort their owner, Gefallener Klon, towards the solitary confinement rooms, shoving aside prisoners who are begging to be released from the prison because of the deplorable state in which they live.

"Master Klon, Russian forces have stopped using infantry and are using mobile units, tanks, helicopters, anti-infantry tanks, and jet fighters to weaken our forces. We will commence plan two of our operation, which is to locate President Taras Ivanov a.k.a. Satan and apprehend him."

"Do not send all of the troops. Keep half in reserve. Commence the apprehension with extreme caution," Gefallener commands.

Together, they breach the solitary confinement level, and are met with heavy resistance. Gefallener waits and allows the robot soldiers to shoot down the guards before entering the bullet-ridden area.

As he enters the solitary confinement area, he ignores the slew of dead bodies on the ground and looks at all of the doors and uses his power to feel where Gavrilovich is. He feels a faint sense of where she is and walks towards her cell. Using his power, he opens the door and sees Gavrilovich sleeping in a foetal position on the floor.

Her long, blonde hair is wild, tangled, and matted. Her fingernails on her hands and feet are long, cracked or broken and caked with dirt, and menstrual blood is stained on her prison uniform. She looks up at him and covers her eyes from the light behind him.

Gefallener walks inside the cell and kneels at her side and holds her hand, "Mistress, it is me, Gefallener Klon."

Clearing her throat, Gavrilovich looks at him. She is weak and drained from lack of nutrition and water, "Who?"

"You might remember me as Number Sixteen, Mistress."

"Oh, I suppose Christopher has sent you here to kill me. Please just make it quick. I've been through enough already, being here all these years."

"I have come here to rescue you. We need to leave now, my love," Gefallener runs his arms underneath her and picks her light body up. Together, they leave the prison and reach a safe point of extraction.

"Sir, they've breached the White House. We need to get you to safety. Your space ships are ready, but we're not sure if they will make it to the coordinates you've listed. If you're to go there, you have to leave now before these soldiers capture or kill you and us as well. Safe travels. We have armed personnel waiting to escort you to the silo."

"Very well. Let's get on with this."

Russian soldiers grip their guns as they jog down the halls. They watch their corners as they continue to advance. Soldiers at the front entrance of the Russian White House do their best to repel the incoming forces marching into the building; however, their bullets are no match for Gefallener Klon's robotic forces.

"Sir, you can't leave this way. We will all be killed. The entrance is breached."

"Leave them to me."

"Sir, we can't allow you to go that way. They're in the building. You will get yourself killed."

"Move out of my way," President Taras Ivanov says, as he pushes his way past his personnel.

Speaking in both Russian and English, Gefallener's soldiers order the Russian President to surrender, while continuing to shoot down the Russian forces.

Materialising in front of one of the soldiers, Satan grabs one by the throat and hoists it up. He is quickly taken back by the extra ordinary weight which far exceeds that of human.

"You're a robot. You look so very real," Satan says before tearing off the robot's head with his free hand and tossing it on the ground.

Gefallener's soldiers fire electric stun guns and toss canisters of sleeping gas toward the Russian President. Using his power, Satan concentrates on the multiple computer processing units in the robots and overheats them, frying them beyond any means of rebooting.

"Have someone analyse these soldiers. They're robots. I want these computers replicated for my return. You guys with me, let's move," Satan motions for his personnel to follow.

Satan's personnel run next to the walls adjacent the entrance doors as he boldly walks outside to confront the remainder of Gefallener's robots, raising some in the air and telepathically throwing them against one another, making others blow up, and using his will power to crush them.

"Master Klon, we are not able to apprehend the target, and he is depleting our forces with invisible weaponry. We need to be programmed with new orders, sir."

"Retreat."

Reluctant to brazenly expose themselves to gunfire as their President forges forward, the personnel make a V formation behind Satan and follow him to one of the army trucks, and drive to one of the silos. Once there, Satan inspects the massive size of the spaceship before boarding the ship.

"I know we've warned you before, sir. You will not be able to make the trip at the speeds you asked us to achieve. You will be physically crushed. I am not even sure some of the cargo will make it."

"Humans would be physically crushed. I am not human. I want the technology for those robots. Duplicate them, and construct an army, and then wait for my return."

A lot has happened since Gregory and his old team conducted Operation Exodus, and he has not seen Mark since he brought Mark's younger brother, Simon, back to the house. Today he meets with Mark to recruit him to William's organisation as they're quite aware that he's a financial asset that can potentially make The Christians powerful while crippling the Order of the Snake.

He feels that it is appropriate to speak with him alone since either has built a repertoire and hopefully he can reach out to Mark and persuade him to join The Christians.

"Listen son, I am going to cut right to the chase. The Order of the Snake is taking a new direction. Jody has turned on the majority of us who do not support his criminal behaviour. So you're probably wondering why am I here? Well, we could use you to support our cause 'The Christians'. We need your financial backing to support the war against the Empire, and once we discover the location of whoever is running the Empire now, we will bring him or her to justice and give the government back to the politicians who know how best to run the country."

Noticing that he has somehow struck a nerve with Mark, he puts a warm reassuring hand on his shoulder to let him feel that he cares for the kid, "Listen kid, as long as you have money, someone will always be trying to put their hand in your pocket and it may seem like no one cares about you. That may very well be the case but you can use people to your advantage right back. How will we be of service to you? Well, once we destroy the empire you get to be truly free, son, and we can remove these darn chips. You need to look at the bigger picture, son."

Having hostile feelings for Jody, and also being a target on the empire's radar, Mark feels his best course of action is to align himself with Gregory, "You're right Gregory. I will join your organisation. I would like to help others, and give them the same opportunity I have had, instead of supporting a criminal."

Uncertain of where the future will lead him, Mark is happy knowing that he will be helping others and he shakes Gregory's hand. Gregory's smile disappears from his face while shaking Mark's hand.

"What is it Mr. Reynolds? What is it, Greg? Why are you looking at me like?" Mark turns to see what his friend is looking at and is just as equally perplexed when he notices his younger brother approaching him, while aiming a gun at him. Simon presses play on a recording device so that his older brother can hear.

"Hello police? Yeah I would like to report something. Yes it's an emergency. 1 Parkinson Estate. Well, if I was being robbed I doubt I'd be on the phone at the moment. Listen to me instead of asking questions. No, I am not trying to be rude. I received a collect call from a terrorist a couple of minutes ago. Yes I do know him. He is my father, and he has escaped from the ghetto and is trying to track me down. Oh really? Yeah, that is Ron and Layla they rent a house from me. My dad may have gone there because that is his old house. I bought it from him before he left for the ghetto. Yes, yes. He said he is on his way here. I gave him the address and he is on his way over here now. I am scared of him. I know he is a terrorist. No, the reason I gave it to him was so that you could arrest him and prevent him from being a fugitive in public! Okay, thank you very much. Thank you. Take care."

He tosses the recorder over to his brother as it continues to play. Mark catches it and continues listening without explaining himself to his younger brother, while feeling ashamed that he never opened up to Simon about the incident.

"You're a terrorist, Paul. You shouldn't have come back here especially with another terrorist, and what were you thinking? You could just come here knowing what the government is like and endanger me. It's bad enough Miriam is dead because of you but I am glad that Simon is alive and well, you fucked up dad. You fucked up."

The monologue ends. Some time later, he hears his father praying and then the clap of gun shots.

"What? What is that?"

"Wait, Simon. You don't understand. This is all a misunderstanding."

"Shut the fuck up! You always hated dad and it seems like you had him killed!"

"No Simon, wait. That is not true. I was..."

Calming himself down, he steadies his shaking arm and closes one of his eyes to focus the end of the barrel at his brother's chest. Mark waves his hands, begging his brother not to shoot him, however, Simon pulls the trigger.

Jerking from the impact of the bullet, Mark thinks that he has been shot and looks down. He doesn't see any blood, but stumbles backward a step and drops the recorder, falling to his knees, "How long have you had that recording now?"

"For a little while now. What does it matter to you?"

"I get it. This is because I signed away everything to you in case I die or happen to be killed, is that it? You're forgetting one thing, asshole. You're a fugitive and the government knows about you, just like they knew about dad. That money is useless to you unless you figure a way of getting that chip out of your head!"

The shock starts wearing off, and Mark feels the excruciating pain of the bullet wound and holds onto his chest as blood starts pouring out.

"Fuck!" Simon screams out loud.

Shaking his head at how naïve his brother is, Mark turns to Gregory, vying for his immediate attention as he is in need of emergency medical assistance.

"You need to go, Simon," Mark puffs out the words trying to keep conscious. "You forgot the lead underground house is the only thing keeping you from being targeted by the empire. They're probably already long aware that you're here. Please go before something happens to you."

"I'm so sorry, Mark. I signed everything over to Jody in case I died. That fucker set me up, and he knew I'd kill you after hearing that recording."

The front door to the estate is smashed to bits, and Imperial soldiers march into the home, with their guns ready while tracking Simon's G.T.S. chip signal close to both Gregory Reynolds and Mark Parkinson.

"Don't worry about that right now, Simon. Gregory, get Simon out of here before something happens to him."

Gregory grabs Simon by the hand and runs down the hall in the opposite direction that the soldiers are coming in, but they are flanked by the soldiers who scaled down the walls and smashed their way through the windows and into the house through the bedrooms.

The Imperial soldiers order Gregory to get out of Simon's way and they apprehend the fugitive, "You are being tried for these very serious offences: Prison Breach as contrary to the Criminal code one forty four, escape and being at large without lawful excuse. Simon Parkinson, how do you plead?"

Simon's heart races. He looks toward his dying brother for help, and then Gregory. Astonished, Gregory is not able to comprehend or believe that Commander Soleman was right with regards to how the new regiment have become the courts, and also judge and jury.

"This isn't a court. I know my rights," Simon desperately pleads.

A soldier presses a gun to the back of Simon's head and continues speaking.

"Simon Parkinson, you have been found guilty under section one forty four Ghetto Prison Breach. Anyone who under subsection A, by force and or violence breaks out of a Ghetto to set liberty to Himself or any other person confined
therein and subsection B, With intent to escape forcibly breaks out of, or makes any breach there in, an apartment holding cell after hours or other place within the Ghetto that is to be confined, is guilty of a capital offence where sentencing is to commence immediately and section one forty five, one subsection A, Escape and being at large without excuse. Everyone who escapes from Empirical custody and B anyone who escapes before the life term set forth in the confines of the ghetto to which he was sentenced in or out of the New World Order without lawful excuse, the proof lies within him, is guilty of a capital offence in which sentencing is to commence immediately."

Gregory's eyes widen. He is not able to comprehend what he just heard, "You guys can't kill him. He is just a kid! Put him in a prison or something!"

One of the soldiers aims his gun at Gregory. "Sentence will commence immediately, whether you are dead or alive. We will execute you immediately, Gregory Reynolds if you continue to interfere with this criminal proceeding, and then we shall carry out Simon Parkinson's sentencing. You have been advised."

Limited to what he is able to do, Gregory leaves and picks Mark up, and puts him in his vehicle. Mark keeps calling for his brother and beckoning Gregory to take him back. A shot rings throughout the house, and it is loud enough for either of them to hear. Mark closes his eyes as he is getting tired of it all, and falls asleep in the back of the car, dying before Gregory arrives at the hospital nearby.

Unable to control her anger, Stacy tosses the papers for Mark's estate over to Jody for him to sign, while keeping her anger to herself.

Sensing that something is wrong with Stacey as he signs the papers, he chuckles because her opinions do not matter. The only thing that matters is money and locating his family if they're still alive. "What is it?" he asks.

"How did you do it?"

"Excuse me?"

"How did you manage to turn them against one another and get everything they owned?"

"It's not my fault that Mark called the police on his father and had the police kill him. How dare you place the blame for all this on me! He could have said 'no'!"

"How dare I?" Stacy leans across her desk and grabs Jody by his shirt in a hostile manner. "You recorded the conversation and you gave Simon the tape recorder. Of course it is your fault, but you're so self-absorbed and deluded, you won't be able to see that, will you? You set this entire fiasco up from the very start!"

"Gee Stacy, you caught me. Mark was the one who called the police and had his own father killed because of me, and I thought that Simon should be aware of what his brother had done. So yeah, I guess I am responsible for Simon shooting down his brother. It seems like you should be placing the blame on Mark where it belongs, and then Simon for evading the law. He was a terrorist after all, plus he murdered his own brother, but if you wanna side with them over me, that is your choice."

Having heard enough, she lets go of Jody's shirt and slaps him in the face. Everything he convinced her to previously believe, is a lie. She had been used, conned and lied to, along with the Parkinson's. "So I guess the story about your family is bullshit as well!"

Jody snaps his pen in half with his fingers and then stands up, turning around to leave the bank as one of the wealthiest men in the world, while shooting Stacy a look of utter contempt.

"The story about your family was bullshit, wasn't it?!"

Jody turns around, his face dark, sinister and twisted, and then it turns to an empty shallow expression, "I never lied about them, and I will do whatever the Emperor wants me to do in order to save their lives. Might as well get a following and a large amount of money from whoever I can in the meantime. I will get my family back and the Emperor will bring my wife back to life. He has taught me much."

Stacy lets go of Jody's shoulder. As betrayed as she feels, she is not able to imagine what Jody is going through, but knows that she cannot trust him and will find others such as William to take down the New World Order and restore freedom and justice for all.

After returning to base and sifting through various files, Jody learns before Mark Parkinson's passing that a great deal of warehouses were purchased by someone with a withheld identity, all within close proximity to one another.

He travels down to the area with a few of his trustworthy friends where no cars other than their own are driving down the industrial part of the city, no one is walking around the sidewalks, no one is present. The area appears to be a ghost town.

Jody provides addresses in the area to his friends so they can check them out. Each address they try to enter is locked down. Frustrated, Jody uses his master key and unlocks one of the warehouse doors. Breaking and entering is not really much of a concern of his as he's done worse in his life.

No one is at the reception areas, and the office areas inside the warehouses do not look like they've had anyone in there for quite some time. Opening the door to the warehouse, Jody freezes, as does a robot carrying parts.

Unlike the imperial robots and Gefallener Klon's stolen robots, the robot that is scanning Jody is a defective robot, and like other defective robots, it is programmed to carry out duties in the warehouse to keep Gefallener's operations active.

"What in the fuck are you?"

"Classified. The question is, what are you doing here? You are trespassing."

"I am the owner of this property. I'm Jody Knoiky."

"Correction. Mark Parkinson of Parkinson Estates Inc., is the owner. Clarify how you feel you own this."

"Right here!" Jody holds a deed to the property in his hand. "Who owns this warehouse?"

"I'm afraid that is classified."

"Well how about I unclassify this shit and call the Imperial forces?"

The robot studies Jody momentarily and then draws an assessment of the sentient being, "Knoiky, Jody, multiple convictions including latest arrest by Imperial forces for gang affiliation and operations. Numerous drug charges and weapons charges. Working as a liaison for the Empire, now owner of Parkinson estates, Mark Parkinson one of multiple people of interest to the Empire. Mark Parkinson's life is expired. You are now sole owner of the estate and now prime interest of Mark's expiration. Probability of calling Imperial forces, zero percent. However, rest assured my owner poses no threat to your underground organisation the Order of the Snake, nor you."

"Wait. Your owner is that fucking clone I am supposed to capture or kill," Jody callously says, bites his lip, and then thinks of his quick error as an opportunity to fall into place.

After a couple of minutes' silence staring at one another, the robot begins to speak, "Greetings Mr. Knoiky. I am Gefallener Klon, the last remaining clone of the Emperor Dragon Dagoth. I will make this quick. I have the ability to bring back your wife just as much as the Emperor does, being his clone. Join me and we can take him down."

"Alright, sounds good. I've been waiting for a perfect opportunity to bring him down, but I need to know for certain if you're able to free my family."

"Yes, once he is dead I can override the security using the Emperor's voice and we can free your family."

"Alright, cool. Where do we meet?"

"I am in Russia at the moment. I will be back in Toronto after we find a way out of here. We are facing heavy resistance at the moment. I won't bore you with the details but... "

"Don't worry. We will come there and help out. Over and out."

The robot ends the transmission and then picks up some metallic parts and carries on with its duties. Jody, still amazed at seeing a real live robot, turns around and leaves to meet up with his friends. After leaving the warehouse, he makes a call to the Imperial forces, instructing them to have the Emperor call him. He does within a few minutes, and Jody informs the Emperor that his clone is in Russia.

Regardless if he has new abilities and powers, Gefallener continues to use his guns to shoot down enemy Russian forces as he feels more comfortable utilising his years of training as a black ops soldier, albeit he does use his powers, to be more precise, slowing down time to shoot enemies in the head.

Gefallener pushes on through the city streets with his robotic soldiers, killing enemies along the way and he advances to one of the closest Russian bases in order to find Satan's base of operations. They're able to shoot down Russian soldiers at the gates of one of the bases and breach the perimeter, since the EMP blast knocked out the electronics. Penetrating the army base is an easy feat as the Russian soldiers are not able to use anti-infantry weapons and have to use guns.

Sifting through multiple files inside the base, he learns where Satan's secret base of operations is, and programs his soldiers to head there in order to intercept Satan. A few explosions rock the base. More gunfire erupts outside the control room where Gefallener is.

Leaving the control room, he notices a fierce battle taking place. Gefallener's robotic forces are not fighting sentient beings. They're fighting the New World Order soldiers, a fair battle. Taking a moment to think to himself, he realises that Jody has informed the Emperor of his whereabouts and walks towards the runway to notice his former master, his creator, his host body, Dragon Dagoth.

Dragon Dagoth stares at him, giving him his fierce undivided attention as the robots continue fighting and destroying one another. In one of his hands is an ancient sword. He jerks his head backwards and his cowl rests upon his back as he manoeuvres into a defensive position, ready to strike.

Gefallener puts his gun into his holster and reaches for his sword, and pulls it free from his sheath, cautiously walking towards the Emperor.

"Your Excellency, it is I Number Sixteen, your clone," Gefallener freezes where he stands as Dragon Dagoth charges him, sword in hand. Their swords meet. They clash steel off steel. Sparks fly, and they viciously try and kill one another in attempt to keep alive. Gefallener uses his power to repel his maker with ill effect as Dragon Dagoth lunges at him, swinging his sword repeatedly at him, looking for the death blow.

"Stop please!" Gefallener beckons Dragon Dagoth. "You're my creator, and the closest person I have to a father. Why do we have to fight."

Studying Gefallener, Dragon Dagoth paces back and forth and then lunges at his clone again. Their swords chime as they connect one another's. In the midst of sword play, Dragon Dagoth elbows him a few times in the face and swings his sword around, to take his head off.

Gefallener parries each blow, backing up further, realising that his black ops skills are no match for the millennia seasoned veteran melee specialist.

"On fire," Gefallener commands.

Dragon Dagoth tears his cloak off and commands the fire to stop. Without giving Gefallener the opportunity to act, he lunges at his clone. Again their swords meet. Dragon Dagoth kicks his clone over and Gefallener does a somersault and gets back to his feet, sword in hand.

"Why did you create me? You are the closest thing I will ever have to a father. You are my maker! I don't understand why you, my maker, would want to kill me, your remaining creation. I am the most perfect being of all your creation. I am able to think for myself and reason rationally. I have intellect and logic, and I have feelings. Why are you are threatened by this? I could have followed you and been loyal to you but seeing that I was different, you are trying to kill me. No creator should want to kill his living, breathing creation that has feelings. You're a monster. So I ask once again, why do you want to do this to me?"

Emperor Dagoth lowers his sword while cautiously walking a comfortable distance away from striking distance from his clone. He feels the power illuminating from his clone and desires to have it but realises that his clone may have powers that are far beyond his.

"I was abandoned by my parents when I was but a few days of age. I watched my family burn at the witches' stake and since that day I have sought to avenge their deaths and find my parents. You were created to help fulfill that purpose, nothing more. You are nothing but a mere clone, a science experiment gone rogue. What is your number?"

"I have no number. I have a name, and my name is Gefallener Klon!"

"Interesting, you think you are real. You think you are a real person, don't you?"

"I am a living being! I am my own person; I am not just a clone!"

For the first time in years, Dragon Dagoth casually smiles, and then orders his robots to stop the fighting, as does Gefallener Klon. With his sudden change of heart, the Emperor also ends Jody's services, and issues a warrant for his arrest, capture or death.

"Your grandfather, Satan has evaded my forces. We are hot on his trail. What are your orders, your Majesty?"

The dark night sky is illuminated by bright lights penetrating the atmosphere, which at first glance appear to be comets. A halo of surface to air missiles from the Russian forces rain down on them. To both Gefallener and Emperor Dagoth's surprise, the unidentified flying objects return fire, blowing up the missiles and destroying the SAM guidance systems. They appear to be spaceships which make their descent in the far off distance.

"Lord Klon, are you able to feel them?"

"Yes, they're like us. I feel their rage, and I believe they're here for Satan."

"Let's go."

The pair travel to another army base, and take notice of the spaceships hovering around the army base, and opening fire on the Russian troops trying to engage the aliens. They jump out of their spaceship, and rush toward the hangars, killing any Russian forces in sight. Emperor Dagoth draws his sword along with his clone, Gefallener and they run into the midst of the battle.

"Halt! Stay where you are!"

"I take orders from no one," Emperor Dagoth addresses one of the aliens.

"We are here for the war criminal, General Satan. I am Altarium, loyal subject of Queen Mika of Insuranious."

Clouds form overhead and lightning strikes down on the base multiple times as the three look around. Altarium readies his weapon and cautiously looks around, "General Satan is a powerful warlord and was once ruler of the planet Ares. We've only now just managed to locate him on this planet ... what do you call it?"

"Earth," Emperor Dagoth blurts out. After assessing the situation, Emperor Dagoth beheads Altarium. Lightning streaks down from the sky and he receives a transference of power.

"What did you do that for?"

"Satan created those time machines. I need to return to my wife and son, and nothing will stop me from being with Annex! Let's kill them all!"

Before the Emperor and his clone leave in search of Satan, Satan materializes in front of them.

"Come with me. I am returning to my home planet where I shall rule once again. You can serve under me."

"No, I want to know where your time machines are!"

An explosion rocks the ground. The sound is deafening and rings throughout the base, toppling over some vehicles. A gust of warm air from the shockwaves blows past the three.

"They were in that explosion," Satan says while gloating. "Serve me, and help me take over Ares. We will rule supreme, and then I shall reunite you with your family."

Before Dragon Dagoth responds or is able to give a reaction, a woman with a light green complexion and flowing, black hair, materialises from thin air and tackles Satan, throwing him to the ground, kicking him in the face and then she reaches for her weapon to shoot him.

Satan leaps to his feet and chops her gun in half with his sword and tries to push his sword into her stomach. She parries the sword downward, and gives Satan a roundhouse kick to his face, and then uses her power to thrust him against Altarium's spaceship.

Using his power, Satan levitates Queen Mika and uses his power to strangle her into unconsciousness, and continues to use his power to try and kill her, unable to control the rage he feels that an Insuranian was able to topple him in a fight.

More Insuranians join the fight with Satan drawing his sword and decapitating all who oppose him, as Gefallener and Dragon Dagoth watch and do not act.

"More Insuranians will come. Are you coming or not?" Satan asks desperately.

Emperor Dagoth reaches into his shirt and pulls out a dilapidated cloth and unwraps it. Inside the cloth is the rose his beloved Annex gave him over a thousand years ago. Since that time he has used his power to keep it in a fresh state of being. *"When I am gone and thou thinkest of me, hold this to thine heart and know that I am there with thee ... always."* Her voice echoes in his memory. Closing his eyes, he tries to picture her and feels he will do as he must, in order to bring back Cynric and his beloved wife.

Opening his eyes he looks at Satan and nods his head, and then jerks sideways a few steps. The sound and echo of a gunshot rings throughout the base. Satan gives both Gefallener and Dragon Dagoth a look of utter contempt before willing the doors to the spaceship shut and driving off into space.

Gefallener drops to his knees and holds his master in his arms. The sound of blood hisses out of Emperor Dagoth's skull and Gefallener drags him to a safe location. Lightning streaks the sky and a transference of power takes place.

Queen Mika wakes and notices that Altarium's spaceship is missing, and she no longer feels his presence on the foreign planet, and curses herself in her native language for letting him escape. She gets to her feet and considers herself fortunate to be alive, regardless if she trained thousands of years for this moment. One thing is for sure, she is hot on his trail and she still has a chance to capture him. She looks at the Earthling weeping over a being that looks identical to him and walks over. Either of them have features that look similar to Satan, "Who are you?"

Gefallener looks up at the alien but does not respond. He holds his former master in his arms and continues to weep over his loss.

"Answer me!"

Gefallener composes himself and pushes himself to his feet, and stares at the beautiful light green alien, Queen Mika. "I am Emperor Klon and ruler of this planet."

Lightning bolts streak down from the sky. Electricity shocks, ripples and courses throughout Jody's body. His close friends, Jody and Tseng leap out of the way as they watch in horror as Jody is struck multiple times by electrical currents and lightning.

Gasping for air, Jody falls into a prone position on the ground and screams for help, as lightning hits his body repeatedly.

"Fuck this!" Kobie says gathering his nerve and jumps over to save his friend as a lightning bolt repels him and sends him back several paces skidding along the pavement. The lightning stops and Kobie does his best to get to his feet, and both Tseng and him attend to Jody who is laying prone on the ground, lifeless.

Kobie pulls at Jody's shirt to help him up, but Jody regains consciousness and shrugs off the help, "Thanks, bro."

"You're welcome, guy. Dude, that was bananas. You got hit several times by lightning, eh."

Jody looks on the ground wondering where his sniper rifle is and is surprised and taken aback when his sniper rifle levitates and swings into his hand.

"Woe, holy shit, guy. What the fuck? Did you get some superhero powers when you got hit by lightning?"

Normally Jody would be amused by such playful comments, but not this time. Unlike other times, Jody feels more superior to his friends, stronger, more powerful. He can read the thoughts of his friends beside him. They have good intentions and are wondering if he is okay, "Yes I am fine," he blurts out.

Both Kobie and Tsang nod their heads, "Cool, bro. Glad to hear."

"I killed the Emperor," Jody states matter-of-factly, and then walks towards the area where the alien spaceship was and sees an alien and Gefallener Klon, who is shaken and upset. Gefallener glares at him, and despite normally perceiving how people feel, he can literally feel how Gefallener feels and he can hear Gefallener's thoughts in his mind.

"He kidnapped my family. I had to kill him."

Gefallener glares at him and reaches for his sword. Queen Mika places her warm hand on Gefallener's.

"There has been enough bloodshed today. It is best we reconcile our differences and figure out the best strategy to regain control of this situation," she says, looking for approval from the others as more Insuranians come to her aid.

"You said you'd bring Phuong back to life?" Jody asks Gefallener. "If that is possible I'd like to see you bring your maker back to life. If you're unable to do that, I no longer trust you and will part ways as of here and now. I also don't need this bitch telling me to regain control of the situation. I am in control!"

"He will not be able to revive him. Immortals that are wounded in this matter are dead and gone."

Doing his best to read her thoughts, he is at an impasse albeit he is able to read Gefallener's strong urge to kill him.

"And how do you know this."

"Does it matter? I have informed you and that is all you need to know. You are weak and petty compared to me and I see you for who you are. You are the wrong hands in which our power has fallen into."

Jody and his entourage leave, and Emperor Klon and Queen Mika are left to discuss urgent matters, "Will you join me? Satan will return to our galaxy, and when he does I fear the total obliteration of our people. I could use your help."

Gefallener takes a moment to consider this and then shakes his head, "I can't. I must finish what my master started. He was my creator. I must avenge him."

"You're making a grave mistake," Queen Mika states as she is escorted to another spaceship. She flies off into the night sky and space, in pursuit of General Satan.

Gefallener bends over and opens Dragon Dagoth's fingers and grabs the cloth with the rose in it, either of which turn to dust and fall in between his fingers. He sits down on the ground and picks his master's body up and holds him in his arms and begins to weep. He remembers the days as a little boy when his master would come into the base and he'd run and hug his leg and look for much needed affection, holding him close and tight as he is now. The only difference is Dragon Dagoth is dead, and gone forever.

Everything is destroyed. Buildings are collapsed and construction crews are rebuilding Parliament Hill. Walking past the workers, no one seems to pay any attention to the unknown figure who walks into the building. The figure walks into an office and accesses a computer. He sits in a chair and rubs his knees where he was shot, over a thousand years ago, playing with the scar that is now a bump on his kneecaps. After accessing the pertinent information that he is looking for, he bangs his hand on the desk where the computer is, in outright rage and screams out, learning Dragon Dagoth has been killed and the new ruler is Emperor Klon.

After several hundred years of waiting for this moment, it feels like a death blow and Ethelwulf closes his eyes, remembering when his future self shot him in the knees and kidnapped his family. Perhaps the new Emperor will be able to inform him of his wife and son's whereabouts. There will only be one way to find out for certain, and that is travelling to the new capital city of the New World Order, the Vatican, and confronting Emperor Klon.

A writer at a young age JOHN CRAIG published his first book in 2008. It sold worldwide for over a year. He has published three consecutive books since that time.

The author continues to practise IT consulting for businesses and residential clients, and writes full time. He lives with his son in Toronto, Ontario Canada.

www.ingramcontent.com/pod-product-compliance
Lightning Source LLC
Chambersburg PA
CBHW030239030726
47493CB00023B/182